M000214969

HEARTACHE AT BLACKBERRY FARM

ROSIE CLARKE

Boldw⊕d

First published in Great Britain in 2022 by Boldwood Books Ltd.

Copyright © Rosie Clarke, 2022

Cover Design by Colin Thomas

Cover Photography: Colin Thomas

Every effort has been made to obtain the necessary permissions with reference to copyright material, both illustrative and quoted. We apologise for any omissions in this respect and will be pleased to make the appropriate acknowledgements in any future edition.

A CIP catalogue record for this book is available from the British Library.

Paperback ISBN 978-1-80415-724-4

Large Print ISBN 978-1-80415-720-6

Hardback ISBN 978-1-80415-719-0

Ebook ISBN 978-1-80415-717-6

Kindle ISBN 978-1-80415-718-3

Audio CD ISBN 978-1-80415-725-1

MP3 CD ISBN 978-1-80415-722-0

Digital audio download ISBN 978-1-80415-716-9

Boldwood Books Ltd
23 Bowerdean Street
London SW6 3TN
www.boldwoodbooks.com

1

JULY 1940, BLACKBERRY FARM

Pam Talbot stood staring out of the window, a sigh escaping her lips. There was one of those early mists that sometimes crept across the low-lying fields of the Fens even in summer. The land lay at the bottom of the hill in Mepal, just a mile or so from the village of Sutton and only a few miles from the cathedral city of Ely in Cambridgeshire. It was a pleasant area, the fields opposite graced with chestnut trees and the surrounding fields with hedges that in autumn were laden with blackberries. At the moment, the fields were golden with ripening wheat or green with crops like potatoes and sugar beet.

A little frown creased Pam's brow as she turned from the window. She ought to be accustomed to misty mornings after so many years of living on Blackberry Farm as Arthur's wife, but it wasn't the dull day that was weighing so heavy on her heart. Nor was it the grey sky or the unseasonable chill in the air. It was the war with Germany that had been raging for months now that was plaguing her mind. Especially after the trauma and horrendous suffering at Dunkirk, when the British Army had been trapped on the beaches, some dying, raked by enemy fire, others wounded, hungry and unable to escape the merciless attacks. Only the bravery of British fishermen and boat owners had saved many more of them from slaughter, when, harassed by enemy planes, the navy couldn't get in close enough to take them away. Fortunately, hundreds of small boats had gone out to help and much of the stranded army had been saved – but the war was far from over.

'We should be so lucky,' Pam said to herself as she saw the headlines in her husband's copy of *The Times*. She'd been collecting the old papers, which carried terrible pictures and headlines of the recent disaster – the occupation of the Channel Islands by German troops and what was described as the first daylight bombing raid on the British mainland – to make fire-lighters, and they didn't make for happy reading as she flicked through them, making sure there was nothing Arthur wanted to keep. Her husband was a keen reader and also liked to do the crosswords, so she checked that he'd finished with them before using them to light her fires in the big black range that heated water, cooked their food and kept the house from freezing in winter.

When Pam had read about the terrible loss of life in the papers once more, she had wept again for the young men who were so valiantly giving their lives in the fierce struggle to keep the Germans at bay. The fact that two of her sons, Tom and John, were amongst those fighting made her sick with anxiety and she'd flicked away her tears, giving herself a mental shake. At the moment, the prevailing mood was fear; and she wasn't the only mother terrified for her sons and fearful of invasion and losing this war that did not seem to be going well for Britain and her Allies.

It wouldn't do to give way to her fears. She worried for her boys, but she was also very proud of them. Tom, her firstborn, was in the army, and John, her youngest boy, had recently joined the RAF and she had no idea what he was up to, because he seldom wrote to her. When he did, his letters would be bright and cheerful, telling her about the fun he was having, but never mentioning the war or the serious side to his work.

John would not want to upset her or cause her anxiety, but she worried all the same. Not that she had time on her hands to worry! Her second son, Artie, was still at home and working on the land with his father; she had two daughters, Susan and Angela, both of whom were lovely girls and gave their mother pleasure. She had great hopes for Susan's future because she wanted to train as a teacher, and Angela was only eight and not old enough to know what she wanted to do when she grew up. Tom's wife, Lizzie, a clever young woman, who owned a hairdressing salon in a small market town nearby, was living with them, to say nothing of the toddler, Tina, who often brought a smile to Pam's lips. Tina was the granddaughter of Vera Salmons and the niece of Jeanie – a friend of Lizzie's since she'd lodged with her family in London. Together with the land girls they employed, it made for a full household at breakfast time and Pam was always busy cooking, washing and cleaning.

Tina had come to them after the tragic death of her mother. Her grandmother, Vera, was a midwife and unable to take the child at present. Tina's father, Terry, was still in hospital, months after being badly injured soon after the start of the war in 1939. He'd lost a leg, but his condition wasn't helped by the death of his wife due to a fire at the flats where she and Tina had been living. It was a miracle that Tina had survived and her grandmother would have preferred to look after her herself, but with both her daughters away – Jeanie working as a land girl on Blackberry Farm, and Annie as a nurse – Vera hadn't felt able to cope with the child.

Tina had initially come to the farm for a short time – but the weeks and then months had passed and, so far, Vera hadn't asked to take her home. Pam secretly hoped she wouldn't; Tina was safer here with them.

* * *

Just then, Susan came downstairs, holding the little girl by the hand. Pam smiled, her little fit of the blues blown away by Tina's smile and the way she held her arms out to be taken up on Gan-Gan's lap and fed her breakfast.

'Are you going to study for your exams today?' Pam asked Susan, as Angela entered the kitchen and gave her mother an old-fashioned look. She'd been the baby of the family until Tina's arrival, and she might be a tiny bit jealous of the little girl.

'No, Mum,' Susan said in answer. 'I have plenty of time to study before I take my exams. I did most of my homework last night, so if you need me to look after Tina or anything...?'

'You can give Tina her breakfast if you like.' She looked fondly at her daughter. 'How are your studies going, Susan?'

'Fine, Mum,' Susan said and reached for Tina, to take her on her lap and feed her the bread-and-butter soldiers with her soft-boiled egg. Living on the farm, they got fresh eggs regularly from Pam's chickens and she made her own farm butter, but there was never enough, because they had to meet their quota for the milk board.

'What do you want for breakfast, Angela?' Pam asked. 'There's a boiled egg or jam and toast...'

'I'd like some toast with your blackberry jelly, Mum – if you have any?'

'Yes, there's a fresh pot in the pantry,' Pam told her. She hadn't had enough sugar last autumn to make as many jars of jam from the beautiful blackberries that gave the farm its name, because the papers had warned against hoarding, saying it was unfair to others. Arthur had said that some people were filling their attics with tinned goods that would become scarce and suggested she should at least buy enough to fill the pantry shelves, but she'd felt it wasn't quite right, so she'd been sensible. Now that stuff like tinned or dried fruit was less available, and meat, fat and sugar were rationed, she sometimes wished that she had. Although Arthur supplied them with eggs, milk and some game, which meant there was normally plenty of food, the luxuries were becoming harder to find, perhaps because many people had hoarded them.

However, Pam knew how to make the most of food and she'd find alternative ways of cooking her family's favourites. As long as they all came back when the war was over. The thought of either Tom or John being wounded or killed made her shiver, as though someone was walking over her grave.

As Susan fed Tina small fingers of bread and butter spread with margarine and her egg, Pam's thoughts returned to the men fighting what was clearly a hard and horrible war. She offered a silent prayer that her sons would return. Tom had his wife, Lizzie, though not yet a child to come back for; and John had a lovely girl named Faith Goodjohn, a lively eighteen-year-old, who worked as a nurse in Addenbrooke's Hospital in Cambridge and was extremely pretty. John had brought her home on a brief visit when he'd got leave soon after he'd joined the RAF. She'd seemed a sweet-natured girl, but they hadn't stayed long and it was weeks ago now. Pam wondered how Faith was getting on in her nursing training – and whether she'd had a letter from her son...

'Is there any more toast, Ma?' At the sound of her second son's voice, Pam came out of her daydream and smiled at Artie. He'd had his breakfast earlier, before he'd gone milking but had just returned and was clearly hungry again. His father entered a few seconds later and headed for his chair by the fire to pick up his paper; the headlines screaming news of the ongoing Battle of Britain in the skies.

Named for his father, Artie was the one who looked the most like Arthur – strong, hefty, with square features that made him look as if he were stern or dour. Neither her husband nor her son was as handsome as Tom's father had been – her Tommy, who had died in the first big war with Germany before they could be wed. Yet she loved them both. Arthur was a good husband, who had taken her when she was a young girl, unmarried with a new baby in arms, and Artie was a dependable son. He'd chosen to remain on the land, not because he was a coward, but because he genuinely loved farming and considered that his father would need help – help he could not get from the land girls. Good as they were, they still needed a strong man about the place at times and Artie was certainly that, Pam thought.

'I'll make you some fresh toast and another pot of tea,' she said. 'Do you want jam or an egg, Artie?'

'I'd like some dripping if you have any,' he said and smiled.

Pam nodded and went to the pantry to fetch it. She saved her dripping fat from the meat, because it was so useful in cooking and needed more than ever these days – but Artie had always loved it on toast, even as a young lad, the only one of her children who really liked it.

'Will you be home for docky,' she asked, 'or shall I pack you some food for the day?'

'I'll be hoeing down the Fen,' Artie said. 'I've got ten acres of beet to clean. It's not hard work and Jeanie will be helping me – so you'd best pack food for her too.'

'Where is Jeanie?' Pam asked, but the kitchen door opened at that moment and the land girl came in with a jug brimming with milk straight from the cow.

'You've been a long time this morning?' Pam questioned.

'It's Daisy,' Jeanie said and glanced at Arthur, who was drinking tea behind his newspaper. 'She kept kicking – I think she may have a sore teat, Mr Talbot. Do you want to take a look at her?'

Arthur put down the paper and looked across at her. 'Is it discoloured?'

'It looks a bit reddish.'

'I'll take a look,' Arthur said and got up. 'No, you sit there, Jeanie, and have your breakfast. If she needs the vet, I'll give him a call. Daisy had mastitis last year. I hope she isn't getting another bout...'

'Daisy is one of Arthur's favourites,' Pam remarked as her husband left the kitchen. 'The vet advised him to buy another cow and let her go last year, but he wouldn't. He says she still has some good years in her – and I doubt he'll let her be slaughtered if he can nurse her through it.'

'I never knew cows had problems with their teats until I came here,' Jeanie said, laughed and added, 'I never really knew what cows looked like.' She started spreading jam on her toast. 'This is really lovely, Pam.' She crunched happily. 'I like Daisy too. She is usually so placid – I hope she doesn't have to be sent for slaughter.'

'It's a fact of life,' Pam said. 'But don't look so upset, Jeanie – Arthur will save her if he can.'

'It's only a cow for goodness' sake,' Artie said. 'If she's no use for milking, it's time she went. We can't afford sentimentality, especially now.'

'Artie!' Pam shot him a look. 'Maybe that's true, but you could have some respect for Jeanie's feelings.'

'It's all right, Pam. I know he is right,' Jeanie said.

'I'm making sandwiches for your docky, Jeanie,' Pam said and gave her son a warning glare. 'Would you like cheese or Marmite?'

'Could I have a round of each please,' Jeanie smiled. 'I do like Marmite, but the cheese you make is scrumptious with vinegar and pepper.'

Pam nodded. The soft white cheese she made when she could get enough cream and milk was delicious and all her family liked it. 'A couple of each then,' she said, 'and I've got some apple pastries made with bottled fruit. I'll put one in for each of you.'

'Thanks,' Jeanie said and smiled at her. 'You spoil me!'

'You work hard,' Pam said and rustled up the sandwiches in no time.

As Jeanie scooped up her sandwiches and tucked them in her haversack, along with a bottle of tea, she was ready, still munching the toast as Artie led the way out to the farmyard. Susan and Angela following a moment later.

Pam started to clear away her table. Everyone was out at work now, apart from Angela who had gone to play with a school friend and Susan who had taken Tina out for a walk. She would be on her own until lunchtime. As she began to plan her work for the day, Pam's thoughts turned once more to the family who were not with her. Tom and John and that pretty young girl John had taken such a fancy too. Pam wondered if it would ever come to anything between John and Faith...

2

Faith Goodjohn smiled as she picked up her letter in the reception area of the nurses' accommodation. It was from John Talbot. They had been courting for nearly a year now and it made her feel better after a hard day on the wards of Addenbrooke's Hospital to read his latest letter.

Faith was in her first few months of training and, as a lowly probationer, she got all the worst jobs. Her hands were sore from scrubbing bedpans and her feet ached from hours of standing.

A sigh broke from her. When would she be allowed to look after patients? She'd thought with all the wounded soldiers and every bed occupied, so many that they were starting to set up temporary wards to accommodate them all, that she would be helping on the wards straight away, but most of her time was spent in the sluice room, attending lectures or scrubbing floors.

'You have to learn to walk before you can run,' Sister Reece had told her when she'd asked when she would be allowed to help on the wards. 'You young girls think you know everything when, in fact, you know nothing of any use when you come to us.'

Faith had felt like a scalded cat when Sister Reece had

finished, but she'd stuck her head in the air and returned to the sluice room, determined not to be beaten.

'You look as tired as I feel,' one of the other probationers, Janice, grinned at Faith when they met at the top of the stairs of the nurses' home that evening. 'We must be mad to do this. My sister, Jean, is working in Woolworths and getting paid more for selling sweets than I get!'

'Lucky her,' Faith groaned. 'I got on the wrong side of Sister Reece this morning and she's had me on the run all day.'

'Rotten bitch,' Janice said. 'Fancy going out for a drink later? I'm meeting some of the other girls – and some men, too.' She rolled her eyes at Faith. 'It's ages since I had a date. My Tony is in the navy and I haven't seen him in months.'

'You wouldn't go out with another man, Janice?'

'Tony said he didn't mind me having fun as long as I didn't sleep around,' Janice replied. 'It's only a drink, Faith – come on, loosen up a bit. If you study every night, you'll die of boredom. Besides, you're like me, only doing your bit for the war, aren't you?'

'Yes, I suppose so...' That was all it was meant to be at the start, but she'd discovered she really enjoyed nursing.

Faith hesitated and then nodded. She liked Janice Prentis and she did need a little fun. It was hard work and she'd had enough of sitting in her room every night. Of late, she'd wondered if she should give it up and go home to March, the thriving railway town in the Fens where she'd been born.

Her boyfriend, John Talbot, was away most of the time. They'd been going out for several months before he'd joined the RAF, but although he'd told her he was in love with her, they were not engaged. He thought that she was too young to think of getting married and believed it was best to wait until things settled down. John was a brilliant plasterer and had his future mapped out for him in the building trade when the war was over. However, he'd wanted to join the RAF rather than the army and had done so as soon as he could; it was what they'd both agreed but she missed him a lot.

'All right, I'll come to the pub for a while,' she agreed now. 'Give me half an hour to get ready – and I'm not stopping out late. I shall be dead on my feet tomorrow if I do.'

Janice smiled. 'I'm just going to the shop. I'll knock on your door in half an hour.'

Faith ran to her room. It was small and plain, apart from her personal things, hot and airless in these first days of August. The whole place felt a bit like a prison with all the rules and restrictions, like when they could take a bath and what time they had to be home at night and that no pets were allowed. Once inside, she flung down her bag, John's letter and her coat. She wanted a wash and a cup of tea, before changing into fresh clothes. Her hands smelled of carbolic and disinfectant. She would have to be quick if she was going out, which meant that John's letter would have to wait...

* * *

Half an hour later, Faith was wearing a pretty green dress that set off her fair hair and blue-green eyes. She had cut her hair shorter when she'd started work at the hospital, after discovering that she just didn't have time to look after it. Her lipstick was bright red and she wore a string of beads round her neck.

When she opened her door to Janice, she smiled in approval. 'Transformation,' she said and grabbed her arm. 'Gosh, you smell nice – real perfume, what luxury.'

'John bought it for me,' Faith told her. 'It's Chanel...'

'No wonder you smell gorgeous,' Janice sighed. 'Tony would

never buy me anything like that – a box of chocolates and a pair of silk stockings if I'm lucky.'

'I'm always running out of stockings,' Faith remarked wryly. 'It's just as well we have to wear those awful Lyle ones for work.'

'I'm the same,' Janice agreed. 'I wish we could wear trousers like the men do, then we wouldn't have to bother. I'm thinking of getting a pair for off duty.' The only trouble with silk stockings was that unless they were fully fashioned, they wrinkled around the ankles.

'You're brave to consider wearing trousers,' Faith said and laughed. 'I'm not sure I would dare – but it is a good idea.'

'Live dangerously,' Janice advised teasingly. 'Let's both get a pair and wear them at the same time – I dare you...'

'I'll think about it,' Faith said, squeezing her arm. 'I'm so glad we decided to go out this evening.'

'You wait until you see Slash and Rocky,' Janice said. 'They are both in the army and gorgeous – bags me Rocky. He's dreamy.'

'You can have them both,' Faith replied. 'I'm only interested in having a chat and a laugh...'

Janice raised her brows. 'You haven't seen them yet...'

Faith shook her head. She was in love with John and had no wish to date another man.

Slash and Rocky were waiting for them, as part of a group. Several nurses and men in uniform had gathered in the King's Arms for a drink and someone was playing a piano, knocking out one of the popular songs of the war. The atmosphere was warm and friendly, and after a couple of lemonade shandies, Faith was feeling relaxed, the frustration of her day melting away in the mellow buzz of friendship. Off duty, the nurses were approachable. Young women who whizzed by with hardly a glance her way during working hours, now unbent enough to smile and talk.

'Take no notice of Sister Reece,' one of the staff nurses told her. 'She is a rotten bitch. I think she's frustrated in love – or had a bitter experience in the past. She always takes it out on the probationers, but you'll be moved on in a few weeks and things will improve.'

Faith thanked her and then turned as Slash tapped her on the shoulder. He was a tall, fair-haired soldier, thin and wiry but attractive with a really nice smile.

'Do you dance?' he asked her. Several couples were dancing a kind of smooch to the music.

Faith loved to dance, but she didn't know this man well enough to be held that close. She shook her head and saw the disappointment in his face. 'Sorry, I need to be getting back,' she said. 'Another hour and they lock the door at the nurses' home. We have to be in by ten – and I don't want to get locked out.' She glanced at Janice, who was just preparing to dance with Rocky – a big hunky man with dark hair – and called out to her, 'I'm going back now before they lock the doors – are you coming?'

'No, I'll stay a bit longer,' she replied. 'You could have another half an hour if we get a lift – Rocky has a car—'

'Thanks, I'll walk,' Faith said. 'See you in the morning.'

'May I walk you home?' Slash asked her. 'I don't like to see a young girl walk home alone.'

'It isn't dark,' Faith said, because it was summer and a lovely light night. She hesitated, then, 'I have a boyfriend, but if you want to walk with me, we can talk – but nothing more.'

'Right, that's fine with me.' His face brightened. 'You're a nice girl, Faith, and I'm glad you told me about the boyfriend – is he in the army?'

'John joined the RAF a few months ago,' Faith said as they left the pub together.

'They are a brave bunch,' Slash said, nodding. 'If it were not for those young pilots, I think the invasion would be underway by now – but they are beating the Luftwaffe in the air, from what I hear.'

'John is still training, I think,' Faith said. 'He doesn't say much about his work.'

'Probably can't,' Slash said.

It was warm that evening and she could smell some kind of night-scented flower in the air. She smiled as the tall man matched his steps to hers and they strolled towards the nurses' accommodation, which was a few streets away and not far from the hospital itself. Addenbrooke's was set back in its grounds and there were cherry trees opposite, lining the street, not far from the ancient colleges and the Fitzwilliam Museum. 'John's elder brother, Tom, is in the army though. You might know him – Sergeant Gilbert? He was promoted only a few months after he joined.'

He shook his head. 'Must be a special bloke then. Me and Rocky have been in since before the start and they haven't promoted either of us.'

Faith shrugged. 'I don't know John's brother really. I've met Tom's wife and John's mother and father – but not the rest of his family. John takes me out as often as he can but hasn't had leave for a while.'

'Blooming war!' Slash nodded. 'It's messed a lot of relationships up. My sister was nearly engaged before her boyfriend went off to fight. Poor devil got killed in his first action...'

'Oh, don't,' Faith said, her heart contracting with fear. 'I don't want any of the people I know to get killed. I've got an uncle in the army too. Uncle Ralph. I didn't think he was going to join up, because Mum said he had a weak chest, but he did... I don't think they will send him overseas to fight. He's working in supplies or something.'

'Jammy,' Slash said. 'That's where the clever ones end up. They do all right – most of them are scroungers... no offence to your uncle, but that's what the chaps reckon.'

Faith shrugged. 'Uncle Ralph has plenty of money...' She felt a coolness at her nape. Once upon a time, she'd thought Uncle Ralph was wonderful, but then she'd started to feel a little unsure about him. Something in his manner had changed and she'd wondered why – but she didn't want to think about that now. Faith shrugged, changing the subject once more. 'Why don't you tell me about you and your sister?'

He smiled. 'I'd much rather hear about you – you're nursing, aren't you?'

'I'm learning,' Faith smiled. 'I was feeling a bit fed up this evening. That's why I came out.' She told him about Sister Reece and he made a face.

'We've got some of that sort in the army,' he said and stopped walking as they reached the nurses' home. 'Well, it looks as if we're here. It was nice talking to you, Faith. I'd ask you to the pictures, but we're off in the morning – maybe when we get back, whenever that is...'

'Maybe,' Faith agreed. He was pleasant and she didn't see why she shouldn't make a few friends, male as well as female. John wouldn't expect her to stay home every night.

* * *

Later, she read John's letter twice. He was really enjoying himself in the RAF, learning lots of new things and looking forward to seeing her when he got leave

I hope you're having a good time nursing. Enjoy yourself, Faith, and make the most of it. I love you, you know that, but none of us knows what is coming next. We lose chaps most days here and it makes you aware of how short life can be. If we get together after the war, I'd like us to marry – but I'm not holding you to a promise.

Have fun, my love, and think of me sometimes, that's all I ask. Not sure when I'll get leave but keep a free day for me when I do.

Love, John

Tears stung her eyes as she folded the letter. It had brought his kindness and consideration back to her. John was a lovely person and she missed him.

For a moment, she felt a sharp pang of loneliness and wished John was with her. His words had brought home the imminence of danger and she felt her throat catch with anguish. If anything happened to John, she didn't think she could bear it and she realised that he meant more to her than she'd thought he would at the start. It had sort of crept up on her without her knowing until now.

She was suddenly glad that Slash hadn't been able to take her to the cinema. Yes, there were times when she needed to have fun and she'd enjoyed their walk, but she loved John. It was just hard to bear when they didn't see each other for months, but perhaps he would get leave soon.

3

Ralph Harris yawned as he looked around the army stores at the base he'd been assigned to in Colchester. It was convenient for him, not too arduous a journey if he wished to get home, but far enough away from London and the gaze of a certain police inspector. Ralph avoided visits to London these days, hoping that the nosey policeman had forgotten him and the murder of those gangsters he'd killed. Nothing had ever been proved against Ralph in the matter of the gangland killing; he'd got away with it, but it had cost him. The nightclub he'd owned was no longer his and he'd had to lie low for a while, hence his decision to join up, even though he could have got an exemption for a weak chest.

He didn't regret killing those men who had been threatening his club; he'd done it in cold blood and made sure the gun he'd used could never be traced back to him. Although he'd come under suspicion, there were no leads back to the dead man. His sister thought he was wonderful; her husband was more reserved but had known nothing of his other life – to them and his pretty niece, Faith, he was just the generous brother and uncle he'd always been.

Faith had taken up with Tom Gilbert's half-brother, John Talbot. Ralph had met him and he seemed to be a hard-working man, more reserved than his elder brother. It didn't suit Ralph that a member of his family should have anything to do with Tom – the man he hated so much. It made his guts burn, but she was young and it probably wouldn't come to anything. He hadn't said a great deal to her about it yet, just a few veiled hints that she might be making a mistake, but as long as Talbot didn't get in his way, he was willing to let that rest for now. He had other things on his mind.

At home in March, Cambridgeshire, he was simply a respectable businessman who had done his duty and joined up. Only to that high-and-mighty bitch that Tom Gilbert had married had he shown the other side of his nature. He'd threatened Lizzie Gilbert one night, because she'd made him angry, and if he ever got the chance, both she and her husband would feel the cold steel of his revenge. Tom had ignored him at school, where he'd been the perfect head boy and Ralph had struggled to keep up at sports, and that had rankled. Tom had reported him as being unfit to play in the school teams and so Ralph had lost his chance to join in the glory of their successes. He'd felt bitter about that, and they'd become enemies as they'd grown up. Years later, Tom had humiliated him in public by knocking him down after he'd made some remarks about Lizzie, and Ralph didn't take that treatment lightly. He would pay him and his wife back one day. Somehow. When this stupid war was over and the police in London had forgotten all about him. He was just biding his time.

He savoured the power he'd discovered in himself when he'd shot those criminals in London. They were scum, feeding off the hard work of others with their protection racket He'd shot them, ridding the world of men who weren't fit to live, in his opinion. For perhaps the first time in his life, he'd felt euphoria, but then that police inspector had got a bit too interested. Yet, having experienced such power – the power to take life – had given Ralph a taste for it. He knew that having killed twice he could do it again, and when the time was right, he would take revenge on Tom Gilbert and others. Maybe even that nosey police inspector if he got in his way again.

* * *

There wasn't much in the way of profit for Ralph stuck here. If he'd been in charge of the guns and ammunition, he would have had a few outlets for those – but they were kept elsewhere, and he didn't have the keys to access them or the authority to deal with them.

Ralph had not been issued with a gun by the army. He didn't need one because he wouldn't be going to the war; his job was safe, because of his weak chest.

'We can't let you fight,' he'd been told when the army doctor had confirmed there was a shadow on Ralph's lungs and suggested that he might also have a slight heart malfunction. 'Your heart isn't going to give out on you, old chap,' the doctor had said heartily. 'But you might be a liability to your comrades if we put you in the field...'

'I can work,' Ralph had retorted, apprehensive that they were going to turn him down. In civilian life, he had been afraid that his time as a free man might be limited. By joining up, he'd hoped to escape arrest for the murder of those men. 'You must have work that it would be a waste for a fully fit soldier to do?' His persistence had impressed the doctor.

'Yes, there are always administrative jobs,' the doctor had agreed. He'd seemed to hesitate, then, 'You obviously want to do your bit, so I'm going to recommend you for light duties. You seem to me to be an intelligent chap – maybe there's a job they can find for you.'

Ralph had assumed he would be put to work in an office or taken into the Intelligence and Planning department. It would suit him to be in the know – but he'd been stuck here in the stores and it was boring.

Ralph's thoughts returned to Tom Gilbert. A scowl touched his attractive face as he thought of his rival. It was the way he still thought of Tom. At a school that prized sportsmen, he'd never been good enough. Everyone clustered around Tom, and he'd taken it all in his stride. And then he'd beaten Ralph in the local darts match the previous year and that had niggled Ralph so much that he'd let his temper show. He'd said something Tom Gilbert objected to and they'd fought, but, of course, his rival had won and made a fool of him in front of everyone.

That bastard thought himself so clever, but Ralph would bring him down as soon as he got the chance. He'd also laid claim to one of the best-looking girls in the area – one who Ralph had fancied.

He'd taken what he wanted from Lizzie, forcing her; though, for a while, that hadn't been enough and he'd wanted much more from her. He'd tried to persuade her to be his woman; if he could have taken her from Tom Gilbert it would have been sweet revenge, but she'd turned him down and that had made him even more angry.

One day he would have the opportunity to put that bastard in his place – and his snooty wife with him. A smile touched Ralph's face. They didn't know who they were dealing with; no one in his local area dreamed of what he was capable of – but Gilbert and his wife would find out. Ideally, he would kill them both, but that took planning, because he wasn't prepared to get caught...

Ralph came out of his dreams of revenge as an officer entered the stores. He saluted smartly and was rewarded with a nod of approval.

'Ah, Harris,' the officer said. 'You're the chappie in charge here?'

'Yes, Captain Whittaker. Is there a problem?'

'On the contrary, old chap. Before you took charge, there was a lot of petty pilfering going on – mainly boots. The men are forever needing new ones and a lot of boots were unaccounted for – all that has stopped.'

'I do my best, sir.'

'Yes, you do – and that's why I want you in charge of the officers' mess bar...' Captain Whittaker grinned. 'The odd pair of boots goes astray – who cares? If it's my twenty-year-old malt whisky, it's a disaster. We need someone we can trust, and I think you're the one – if you'd care for the job, of course?'

'Delighted to be asked, sir,' Ralph said promptly. At last, he was getting somewhere. There were bound to be opportunities at the mess for a clever man – and not necessarily the odd bottle of whisky.

'I'll arrange for a replacement here then.' Captain Whittaker smiled at him and walked out again.

Ralph laughed. His luck was in! Selling the odd pair of boots hadn't appealed because there wasn't enough money in it. He would find the officers' mess far more interesting. Men like Captain Whittaker got drunk when relaxing with their friends and fellow officers. They let things slip – little snippets that a man with intelligence could use for blackmail and profit. He would wait for a while... until the right moment. A chance for something that would give him what he wanted – money was no problem. Ralph needed influential friends. A chance to blend in with the right people, to escape the notice of a certain nosey police officer who suspected what he couldn't prove.

Of course, that police inspector might meet with an accident one day. If he got in Ralph's way, it could be arranged, but if it happened, Ralph needed to be in the clear. Ralph needed a free hand when the time came for him to take his revenge on Tom Gilbert and his wife and the best way to do that was to rise in the world. He was better than the manager of the stores or of the officers' mess, but with the right friends, Ralph could become what he needed to be – a gentleman above suspicion.

4

It was so long since she'd had a letter from Tom! Lizzie Gilbert had hoped she might hear something after the evacuation of Dunkirk, but months had passed since then, and so far, nothing had come. That had been such a tense time for the whole country. The realisation that most of the British Army was stranded on the beaches of France and could be captured or killed was horrifying. The evacuation had been a desperate thing because unless Britain could get her men out, the war was over and Germany had all but won.

Lizzie had wept when she saw pictures in the paper and on the *Pathé News* during a visit to the cinema; those brave men in their little fishing boats going out in their hundreds to help rescue the soldiers stranded. It was all so brave and so very British, so mad and impossible – but they'd got them back, the wounded and those able to walk. It was a miracle!

Yet since then, the Germans had stepped up their attacks on British cities: Birmingham, Cardiff, amongst others, mostly heavily industrial, and then they'd started their Blitz on London.

Lizzie worried for her friends there, but Vera had told her that, so far, her street had escaped the bombing.

Now, most of the summer had passed and it was early September. All these months apart from Tom and they'd had so little time together that her heart ached with the need for him at times. She just wished a letter would come so that she knew he was all right.

Lizzie finished cleaning the basins in her hairdressing salon in Chatteris, just a few miles from her home at Blackberry Farm, and then rinsed her hands. She was finished for the day and it was just half-past six. Because it was still late summer and the nights were light, she would cycle home rather than waiting for the next bus. Sometimes, she got a lift with her brother-in-law, if Artie had been to March or was in Chatteris on farm business. Lizzie didn't mind the cycle ride in the summer but hoped to pass her driving test one day, though they had been suspended for the duration of the war. She had a provisional licence, which she'd obtained before the new act, and hoped that meant she could drive without someone with her once she felt confident.

In another month or two, she would be living in her own house. Lizzie wasn't sure how she felt about the move. A part of her was thrilled with the house that Arthur Talbot had kindly had built for them on land near the farm. It had taken a long time to take shape – several months – but it was getting there. It wasn't always easy to get all the raw materials, because of the war, and the builder had only a few men to help him. Most – like Tom's brother, John – had gone off to war and the builder, Jack Freeman, was working almost single-handedly on much of the house.

Lizzie was looking forward to having her own home to decorate and make cosy for her and Tom, except that she enjoyed living with her mother-in-law and the rest of the family. Pam Talbot was such a warm, caring person, very different from

Lizzie's own mother. Lizzie didn't always get on with her mother, though she visited her once a fortnight at the home she shared with her friend, Mabel, in the nearby town of March.

Lizzie and her mother had lived together not far from Blackberry farm, until she'd quarrelled with Tom in March 1939 and left the area to work at a hairdressing salon in London; she'd enjoyed her time there, entering a lot of prestigious hair-styling competitions. She'd lived with Vera and her husband and two daughters, Annie and Jeanie, but she'd still loved Tom. So, when he'd asked her to marry him, she'd returned to live at his home. They'd married as soon as Tom got leave from the army.

She'd missed him terribly when they were estranged, and she still did when he was away from her. Sometimes, she lay in bed at night, wondering what he was doing and if he was well and thinking of her. All the men in the forces were in danger, but Lizzie had sensed that what her husband was doing was different. He'd joined an East Anglian regiment at the beginning but was now with an elite group that so far had no name and was secret – and she wasn't even supposed to know that much but she'd guessed what Tom couldn't tell her – and she knew it must be risky and dangerous.

Damn this war! Lizzie swore beneath her breath. Why did it have to happen? Why could things not go back to how they used to be? She just wished she knew where he was and if he was thinking of her.

* * *

Tom Gilbert stared out of the window at the creeping fog rolling in off the restless waves. Even in summer, the mist often blew in from the sea in this secret location in the salt marsh on the east coast of England, making it seem even more isolated, cut off from the world. Being part of a stealth-attack group, everything had to be hush-hush and they'd been warned never to talk of what they did to anyone but their comrades. When they went behind enemy lines, it had to be in and out quickly or they'd have no chance of success. You got used to being reserved with others, but not with your family; that was hard.

It was on mornings like this that he most missed his wife, Lizzie, his family and the Fen Land farm that was his home. Strange and ridiculous how a sea mist could cause such a feeling of loneliness.

Tom shook his head, as if to clear it of the foolish thoughts. He should write to Lizzie and to his mother, but in truth he'd had little time of late. Earlier in the year, he and his comrades had been heavily involved in the defence of Norway – mostly helping to get people out. Despite the fact that the Germans were now in control of that country, Tom knew there were still small groups of men prepared to resist. He hoped the British were not going to give up on them and would offer help. There was talk of another mission and he wondered if they were going back, secretly this time...

'Hey, Tom, you haven't forgotten the briefing in half an hour?' Shorty Linton put his head round the door and grinned at him. The tall lanky soldier so mockingly named was Tom's best friend in the army. Tom had helped to save his life when Shorty was badly wounded on their first mission, and his friend made it his business to look out for Tom, sticking to him like glue through whatever they faced, in the camp or on a mission. Shorty reckoned Tom was his lucky charm. Shorty was completely recovered now and they had spent the past few weeks training for their next mission. Rumours were flying around about where they were being sent this time, but one thing they were all certain of was that it was risky and dangerous. There had been a lot of activity, comings and goings of high-ranking officials having secret meetings. Some of the men said their little group might be swallowed up by something much bigger that was being formed, but the men hadn't been told anything officially yet.

'No, I hadn't forgotten,' Tom said and glanced at the watch his mother had given him on his twenty-fifth birthday. 'I was going to write to Lizzie and Ma too if I get time.'

'Best not,' Shorty said. 'We've been told to report half an hour early – the captain wants a private word.'

'Right! I hadn't heard—'

'The message came through just a few minutes ago. Jenks was supposed to tell you, but I thought I'd check and make sure he had.'

'Must have slipped his mind,' Tom said.

Jenks was a member of their group, what you might call a lone wolf, and handy with a knife and his fists. He was also a good shot and useful when they were in a tight spot, but Tom considered him reckless. He'd caught him sleeping when he should have been on watch on their last mission and warned him what could happen if their team leader, Sergeant Philips, had found him. Jenks had shrugged and then spat on the ground, showing that he didn't care.

Recently, since Tom had been made team leader, Jenks had been showing some resentment. Tom wasn't 100 per cent sure they could trust him and yet his skills were second to none – and perhaps for the kind of work they were expected to do, you had to accept a certain amount of attitude. The missions they undertook – and they'd been on several now, including a recent successful one to the Channel Islands to get someone important out – were precarious, apt to backfire. So far, they'd been lucky and perhaps it was that good fortune that had bonded them. Tom knew they had to trust each other, but Jenks wasn't easy to like.

Tom walked to the briefing with his friend. They talked mainly about Shorty's love life. He was courting their officer's daughter, very slowly and carefully, because he was afraid Captain Morris would forbid it if he knew. Tom grinned as he listened. Shorty was head over heels in love and the girl of his dreams was the best cook they'd ever had at base camp. Unfortunately, she hadn't been able to move to the secret location with them and the man who cooked for them here wasn't a patch on Carole Morris.

Shorty was missing both her cooking and her company, and he was worried because he hadn't had a letter since they'd been in their secret location. Mail was supposed to be passed on to them, but it didn't come regularly and Tom reassured his friend that it was probably the army's fault rather than Carole's.

He smiled as he thought of the letter he would send to Lizzie. There were no shops nearby, but he'd hidden a gift for her birthday in his parents' house and another for their wedding anniversary, if he wasn't back in time. His mother knew where they were and she would make sure Lizzie got them.

Maybe, he would be home himself. After this next mission, he was surely due some leave...

5

Pam Talbot was looking eagerly out of the kitchen window when the motorbike roared into the farmyard and a young man wearing RAF uniform hopped off the pillion seat, spoke to the driver of the bike and then turned towards the house. The bike zoomed off without so much as a nod to the house. Pam waved furiously and the young man in uniform lifted his hand in return, before breaking into a run in his eagerness to be home.

'John! It is so good to see you,' Pam cried as her youngest son burst into the kitchen, opening her arms to hug him. 'We've all missed you, love, and they are all looking forward to seeing you. Are you well? How is life in the RAF?'

John Talbot hugged his mother, lifting her from the ground and swinging her round before kissing her cheek. 'It's great, Ma,' he said and smiled at her, his handsome face alight with enthusiasm. 'I'm really glad I chose to join the Royal Air Force rather than the army. They are a great bunch of chaps, especially the ground crew...'

'What are you going to be?' she asked as he released her. 'And where's your kit?'

'I didn't bother bringing it from the station,' John said. 'I've got plenty of clothes here and I'll pick it up from the locker when I catch the train after my home leave.'

There was something about the way he turned his head that warned Pam. Instead of asking more questions, she put a plate of hot pasties, some blackberry jam tarts, rock buns and a mug of tea on the table and John reached for a pasty and began to eat it immediately.

'How did you know I would be starving?' he asked with his mouth full and she laughed at his obvious pleasure in the simple food she'd prepared. The pasty pastry was crispy and filled with minced meat, diced potatoes and carrots and tasted delicious. All her family enjoyed food like this and, with the meat rationing now, it was economical. She'd been up early to prepare it. Artie and Arthur would be back in from the fields soon and between them they would make short work of the meal.

'Because you are always hungry,' she replied. 'How long do you have with us, John?'

'Ten days,' he said. 'I've passed to be flying crew – meet Navigator John Talbot, Mrs Talbot.' His smile lit his blue eyes that were so like her own, and Pam's heart jolted as he held out his hand for her to shake. She took it and lightly dropped a kiss on the back, smiling at his delight. This son who took after her in so many ways looked even more handsome in his uniform and she'd missed him terribly these past months, but knew she couldn't show it. John was a man now and he'd become independent and stronger since he left home. He looked fit and well and the fact that he would be flying as a navigator, probably in bombers and risking his life, night after night, seemed to thrill him. The sleepless nights it gave his mother were another thing and not to be discussed or even hinted at.

'Congratulations,' she murmured with a smile. 'It's what you wanted, isn't it?'

'I'd have liked to be a pilot,' he said, 'but I was considered to be a first-class navigator, so after they explained how important the job was, I decided to settle for that – after all, I'm not going to carry on flying once the war is over, am I? I already have my future sorted.'

Pam nodded her satisfaction. John was young but so confident. He was a plasterer for a small firm of builders and before he'd joined up on reaching his eighteenth birthday, his boss had made him a junior partner – because he wanted him back when the hostilities were over. Jack Freeman valued his skills and liked him, so he'd made sure John wouldn't get lured away to another building firm by giving him shares in the business. Not that there was much profit to be made at the moment – the war had certainly put the mockers on the building trade, as it had on so many businesses. Though after the recent bombing in London, there would probably be plenty of work there and in other cities, clearing debris and making damaged buildings safe. From what Pam had seen in the papers, the damage was horrendous. She was glad none of her family lived in town. Lizzie had for a while when she'd fallen out with Tom, but, thankfully, she'd come home when they made it up and married.

'I think Jack has almost finished Lizzie's house,' Pam said as John ate another pasty. 'Would you like some more tea?' She looked round as the door opened and her husband and Artie entered.

'You're home then, John,' Arthur said and came to clap him on the shoulder. 'You look smart, lad. I hope you're not too posh to give us a hand while you're here? I know you're not keen on the farming, John, but you might give us a day with the potato harvesting if you have time?'

'I don't mind helping one day,' John said. 'Jack did say he would like me to do a bit of work on Lizzie's house for him, if I had time—'

'You're supposed to be on leave – a holiday,' Pam protested, and Artie snorted his disgust.

'Come on, Ma,' he said. 'Those fly boys do little but sit about half the time. They don't know what work is.' He gave his brother a friendly punch in the arm. 'Isn't that so, John?'

'*You* should try the training and sit the exams,' John retorted but laughed, because Artie was just joking. After the recent defence by the RAF, which Churchill had praised in a glowing speech, about how much was owed by so many to so few, no one doubted the skill and courage of the men who defended British skies. 'Anyone heard from Tom recently?'

'No. Lizzie had a letter some months ago, but none of us have heard since,' Pam said and the anxiety was in her voice even though she tried not to let it show. 'I expect he is just busy.'

'They all are,' John confirmed. 'How is Lizzie – and little Tina?' He glanced around the big kitchen. 'Where is she?'

'Susan took her out for a walk,' Pam said. 'Susan ought to be revising for her exams. She'll be assessed when she goes back to school after the holidays – and then we'll know if she is going to college or not.'

'I'm surprised she hasn't wanted to leave and apply for a volunteer group...'

'Don't you dare suggest it to her,' Pam said quickly. 'We want her to go on to college, become a teacher, have a little fun, not get married too young, or be stuck in some dead-end job.'

'Yes, she should have some fun at college before she settles down,' he agreed. 'I like my job plastering, but I'm enjoying my time in the RAF despite the war.'

Pam nodded. She could see that he was happy and that made her smile.

Arthur and Artie sat down at the table and Pam mad a fresh pot of tea. 'Where are the girls?' she asked them.

'They are still spreading muck on that field we plan to plough in readiness for the winter veg this afternoon. Cabbages and sprouts are new to me, but we've been told we need them, so I'm using that corner bit that doesn't yield much in the way of main crops,' Arthur replied. 'The new girl – Nancy – is driving Tom's tractor and Jeanie was still unloading when we brought our trailer back.' They had two tractors on the farm now; one an old one that Tom had lovingly cared for since he'd persuaded his father it was easier to repair than catching the horses that had once done all the heavy work on the land. Since he'd been forced to rely on land girls, Arthur had bought another tractor, a bit newer this time.

Pam shook her head at her son. 'Why didn't you give them a hand, Artie?'

'I offered, but Nancy refused our help, told us to get off and have our lunch. She pointed out that if we want to finish the field before it rains, we need to get on – and they can manage. Jeanie agreed, so I came back with Dad.'

Artie seemed annoyed about something. Pam wondered what had upset him. Could it be something to do with the new girl Nancy?

Although Jeanie had stayed on at the farm, seeming quite content, the girl who had come with her, Mary, had moved on some months back – she'd married a small landowner and was now helping him in the fields. Her replacement had turned out to be useless and left, announcing she was pregnant, a few weeks after she'd arrived. It had taken a while to get another girl, because Arthur had been reluctant to go through the procedure again. Pam had pointed out that Arthur and Artie couldn't manage the land alone; their one regular man was disabled and only capable of light work in the yard. Arthur had given in after a few weeks and let her apply for a replacement. Nancy had arrived two days before John's leave and, so far, appeared to be a hard worker, even though her manner wasn't as pleasant as it might be.

At that moment, the kitchen door opened and Susan walked in with Tina, followed by Lizzie, who was talking to the little girl.

'Had a good morning, love?' Pam asked Lizzie. 'Have you been busy?'

'Yes, thanks, Mum,' Lizzie said, making Pam smile. She liked it when Lizzie called her Mum. 'I've finished for the day. Rita has another customer to perm this afternoon and a couple of shampoo and sets, so she will close up for me. I made the right choice when I took her on – she is such a reliable girl and good with the customers. All the older ladies like Rita and she does most of the perms these days. I do the tinting and the young ones who want something a bit more adventurous than curls and waves.'

Lizzie's new hairdressing salon was doing very well in the neighbouring town of Chatteris, Pam reflected. She had two afternoons off each week and Rita managed alone then, but was given a whole day free on Monday. It suited them both well, as Rita liked a long weekend and Lizzie could manage that day by herself. Only a few customers wanted their hair done on Mondays, though mothers often brought their children for a cut after school, and she usually spent most of her time doing her accounts, cleaning the salon and writing letters or any other jobs she needed to catch up on.

'John, it's lovely to see you,' Lizzie cried as she spied him sitting at the table, just finishing a rock cake. 'How are you?'

'Great!' he said and got up to kiss her cheek. 'Everything all right at the salon?'

John had helped Lizzie get her salon ready, decorating and building partitions for the cubicles. He'd even found the premises for her and worked weekends to prepare it so she could open as soon as possible.

'It's fine,' she told him with a smile. 'Everyone tells me how much they like what you did, John. It has worked out really well.'

'Good. I'm glad it is doing all right – and that you're not in London now...' They both looked grave as they reflected on the carnage and destruction taking place in the capital.

'Me too,' she replied and sighed. 'But I have friends who live there.' She looked at Tina, who Pam was now feeding a jam tart. 'Vera and her family – and other friends, though Vera's family are the ones I worry about most...'

'Yes, of course you do,' Pam said, 'but we're glad you're here with us.' She glanced at John. 'Have you made arrangements to see Faith while you're on leave?'

'I thought I'd use Tom's truck and take a run over to Cambridge tomorrow afternoon. I might stay there in a bed and breakfast for a couple of nights, Mum – so I can have time with Faith.'

'Oh...' Pam smiled and hid her disappointment. She'd hoped that he would be around for a few days, but naturally he wanted to see his girlfriend while he was home. 'Yes, I'm sure Faith will be pleased to see you, love.'

'She told me she gets a couple of days off this week – but she'll be working most of the time, so I'll be back when she returns to normal duties.' He grinned wickedly. 'You'll be glad to get me out from under your feet when I've been home a few days.'

'Never!' Pam wanted to say more but didn't. John was an adult now, not her little boy, and she knew when to let go. Hiding her emotions, she turned away to serve up more warm pasties for Lizzie, Susan and Tina. The child only had a small piece of hers, before she wanted to get down and play with the cat.

'That sounds like the tractor,' Arthur said and looked at his son. 'Come on, Artie. It's time we were off. The girls are here now and they'll want their food.'

'What time shall I expect you this evening?' Pam asked as her husband and Artie prepared to leave.

'We'll be back in about four-ish for a cuppa, I expect,' he said. 'I think it is going to rain tomorrow so we'll get that field finished if we stick at it. Don't prepare a hot meal this evening, Pam. We'll have something cold – or a snack on toast when we finish at about half-seven.'

'All right,' she said, accepting that they would be busy. It was the same every year; they were out in the fields until all hours, especially once the harvest began, when it was a race to get it all in sometimes; first the corn, then the potatoes and the sugar beet, as well as mangles for stock feed. She'd known Tom to bring back a load of wheat at ten at night rather than let the rain batter it down. A little pang of regret went through her as she wished her eldest son was home, still working on the farm. 'Let's hope the weather doesn't break before you're finished.'

At the moment, the sun was warm, but even in autumn it could be really mild one day, as it was now, and pouring down with rain the next. Arthur was keen to get the new crops into the ground, which would be an extra source of income this year; the corner he was talking about quite often got left fallow and he sometimes put a few pigs or chickens there rather than crop it.

'It will keep fine today,' Arthur replied with a smile. 'But rain isn't far away – I can feel it in my bones...'

'I'll see you when I see you, then,' Pam smiled as they left, just as the two land girls entered. 'Come and have something to eat,' she said, setting down two clean plates for them. 'There are plenty of pasties and I did some jacket potatoes too – I know you like them, Nancy.'

'Yes, I do, especially when we've been working hard – is there any cheese or butter to go on top?'

'Sorry, only margarine today,' Pam said, 'but I've made a little onion gravy – if that will do?'

Nancy nodded. She had ignored the men as they left but sat down next to Lizzie. 'Your mother-in-law is the best cook ever. At my last place, the only decent thing was scrambled eggs on toast – the meat puddings were stodgy and tasted awful – but Pam knows how to make simple food tasty.'

'Yes, she does,' Lizzie answered and smiled at Pam. 'I'll have some of the gravy on my pasty, if there's enough, please.'

'Of course, there is.' Pam brought the jug to the table. 'Help yourselves.' She smiled at them, her gaze travelling round the table before resting on John. It was so good to have him home, if only for a short time. She just wished she knew where Tom was and what he was doing...

6

Faith couldn't wait for the day to end. She hadn't been able to do anything right for Sister that afternoon and the morning hadn't been much better. Asked to clean trolleys and bedpans for hours on end, she'd been feeling tired when she was suddenly called to assist a senior nurse with a bed bath for a badly injured man – not a soldier this time, but a farmer who had fallen from on top of a load of hay bales and broken his shoulder and fractured his skull. He was lucky not to have sustained serious brain injury but was now conscious. However, he was not yet allowed to get out of bed and needed bed baths. At the age of sixty-five, his recovery would be slower than in a younger man. Had it not been for the war taking all the young men, he might have been retired or doing much safer work.

As she helped turn the patient, Faith saw a scar right across his back that, although no longer red and obviously old, was still shocking.

'Where did you get that?' she asked him without thinking and then wished she hadn't, as she saw Sister was watching from across the ward, but he merely gave a wry chuckle.

'Got that one in the last war,' he told her with a wink. 'I had an argument with a bayonet. They told me I was too old this time or I'd be there now giving it to the buggers. Still, I was doing a good job till that bloody crow attacked me and I fell off the stack.'

'A crow attacked you?' Faith laughed. 'It can't have done.'

'Dive-bombed me,' he said and cackled with mirth, clearly enjoying the attention he was getting. 'I've seen them do it when there's nestlings, but it's too late in the season for that – bloomin' thing was after me sandwich.'

'Oh no.' Faith couldn't help giggling and she could tell he was enjoying himself relating the story, whether it was true or not! Unfortunately, their mirth had attracted Sister Reece's attention and Faith was severely reprimanded again before being sent back to the sluice room.

Walking back to her home when the day was finally over, she was feeling tired and a bit sorry for herself, but as she approached her destination, the sight of a parked truck made her heart leap. She'd known John was coming home but hadn't expected him to visit this evening. They had arranged that he would come when she had her two days off – but he was getting out of the truck and smiling at her and the cares of the day just fell away. He was even better looking in his uniform and her heart quickened as she ran to meet him.

'John!' she cried excitedly. 'I didn't expect you to come this evening...'

'Dad had some petrol put by for me,' he said. 'I couldn't have managed it if he hadn't – my allowance isn't sufficient for two trips.'

'Your dad is all right,' Faith replied with a smile. 'Mine was moaning the last time he and Mum came to Cambridge. He said they'd had to catch the train and walk from the station, because he couldn't waste the fuel he needs for work.'

'Dad doesn't often use his coupons,' John said. 'He saves them for us – and when Mum goes into Ely or Sutton for her shopping, she goes on the bus. Sometimes, she actually rides up to Sutton on the tractor with him when he's working in the Fen and then either walks home or gets a lift if she sees a friend going her way. Dad says everyone offers lifts these days because an empty car is unpatriotic.'

'Makes sense,' Faith agreed and hugged him. 'I must smell of carbolic and disinfectant. Do you mind waiting while I pop in and have a quick wash and change?'

'Of course, I don't,' John murmured. 'I don't mind what you do, Faith – I'm just glad to see you.'

Faith gave him another small squeeze and hurried into the nursing home. She went straight up to her room, stripped off her probationer's uniform, had a wash in the basin and put on her fresh underwear, a pretty cotton skirt and light jumper. John was leaning against the truck when she got back to him no more than twenty minutes later.

'You were quick,' he told her with a smile. 'Lizzie and Susan spend ages getting changed – and you smell gorgeous.'

'That's the perfume you bought me,' Faith told him, but he shook his head.

'It's you – your own scent. I dream about that when I'm in camp...'

'Don't be daft,' she said and blushed, but she knew what he meant. John always smelled of Imperial Leather soap and talc.

'Where shall we go?' he asked as he put his arm casually about her waist. The night was warm and it was still light. 'A walk by the river and then a drink, or are you hungry?'

'Not yet,' she said, looking up at him happily. 'Let's go for a nice walk by the river and then get some chips and a drink later.'

'Suits me,' he replied. 'We could go to a dance tomorrow

evening. I checked and there's a dinner dance on at a local hotel – if you fancy it?'

'Lovely,' she said and hugged his arm. 'But I'm happy just to do anything with you, John – a visit to the pub or a walk is fine by me.'

He nodded as he glanced down at her. 'You're as lovely as ever, Faith. Sometimes, when I think about you, I wonder if I made you up – but you're gorgeous and nice with it.'

Faith felt warmed inside. John was so good with words. When he'd first told her she was beautiful, she'd thought he was just flirting, but, as she got to know him, she'd realised that it was just his way. John said and did nice things. He was good at little surprises and she knew he bought his mother small gifts, just as he did her. After they'd been courting for a while, she'd started to think he might be the one for her and she still did.

Faith enjoyed going out with friends – both male and female – but knew that she only wanted one man to kiss her, properly... Faith became overwarm suddenly as she realised that John's arm about her waist was making her feel funny inside. She'd been a little shy before she started working at the hospital, but now, she knew that some of her uncertainty about intimacy had gone. The other nurses talked openly about making love in their free time – and some of them were in intimate relationships with the men they dated. She'd always taken it for granted that she would wait until her wedding night. It was the way she'd been brought up and her parents had told her it was the right thing to do. Faith had agreed then, but now she wasn't so certain. She thought that if John asked her, she just might... But would he think less of her if she did? Faith gave herself a little shake and a mental scold. She didn't want to be thought fast.

'Something wrong?' John asked and looked down at her.

Faith felt her cheeks flush as she met his gaze. 'No, everything is fine,' she said. 'I'm just happy to be with you like this.' She squeezed his waist.

John smiled and responded. He stopped walking and bent his head, giving her a gentle kiss. She wondered how he would react if she threw herself against him and returned his kiss with the passion she felt towards him but resisted the urge. Any upward step up in their relationship had to come from him.

To avoid her muddled thoughts, she asked, 'Had your parents heard from your brother Tom? Someone I spoke to the other day thought he might be in some sort of elite group.'

'No,' John looked at her in surprise, 'I think he's just a soldier,' he said. 'Neither Lizzie nor Mum has had a letter – but I think the post is often delayed.'

'Oh...'

They walked in silence for a while. It was a pleasant evening; the birds were singing in the trees that lined the path through the green towards the river that ran through the charming university town, and a squirrel bounded up a trunk ahead of them into the branches of a majestic oak. Cambridge was a lovely place to live, with its greens, beautiful old buildings and the river. Faith nudged John, directing his gaze towards the squirrel and he nodded and smiled but still didn't speak.

Faith frowned inwardly. Why didn't he say something about his feelings, his desire for her? Her nursing friends told her that their boyfriends were always trying to touch them or get them into bed. Why did John never say he wanted to make love to her? She might have said she wasn't ready or she might have said yes if he'd asked, but he hadn't. Why? Was it because he respected her and wanted to wait for marriage? Or perhaps he didn't feel the way she did?

Faith smothered a sigh as their walk took them towards the

Red Lion, a pub popular with men in the Forces and their girl-friends. 'I'm thirsty. Shall we go in here?'

'Why not?' John seemed lost in thought. He'd been a bit quiet since she'd mentioned his brother. Faith thought he might be worried about something, but as they entered the pub with its cosy atmosphere and the sound of laughter and music, she smiled up at him, banishing the doubts. John was just a nice man and she was going to enjoy his leave while she could.

* * *

As they walked into the pub where music was playing, John struggled to banish the feeling of anxiety that Faith's question about Tom had aroused. He couldn't tell her about what he'd guessed concerning Tom's role in the army. He believed his brother *was* in some kind of elite group, probably an advance party that went in before the main attack to sabotage the enemy's lines. He'd heard rumours about a secret force doing stuff like that – they were dropped from planes over enemy territory some-times. The group was secret and confidential obviously, but stuff leaked out and John had heard some of the missions hadn't gone too well. Tom hadn't told him anything, but it was his silence that had made John wonder and, when he'd learned about the secret missions, he'd put two and two together.

Faith was talking, introducing him to friends, and John wanted to pay attention to her – that was why he was here after all – but this gnawing in his gut was telling him something was wrong with his brother. It was ridiculous because he didn't know where Tom was or what he was doing, but he'd had this odd feeling for a couple of days now.

People were dancing. Faith wanted to dance and John held out his hand to her, drawing her close. He felt her press herself against him and his body had a natural reaction as he felt a sharp desire to make love to her. It brought his thoughts to a new focus, his fear for Tom banished as he inhaled the perfume of her hair and nuzzled against her neck. Her skin was so soft and his need was great – but his love was greater. A gentleman didn't take advantage of the woman he loved. His father had told him that long ago. John loved Faith with all his heart, but he wanted to wait until their wedding night – or at least until the war was over. There was no way John was going to risk Faith carrying a child when he wasn't around to help her and marry her. So, despite the way she was responding to his kisses and the enticing waves coming off her, he wouldn't be taking her into the park and seducing her that evening.

Faith sat on the edge of her bed and looked at herself in the mirror. She was aware that her feelings towards John had deepened and intensified over the past months. When they'd first starting courting, Faith had been too young to think of marriage or passion, but since coming to Cambridge and mixing with girls who had more sophisticated ways, she had grown up and now she knew that her feelings for him were special. He was the man she wanted to marry.

They'd had a few drinks, but John had stuck to shandies and squash like her and then they'd eaten fish and chips from newspaper on the walk home, laughing and talking. At the door of the nurses' home, John had kissed her and told her he loved her and would see her the next day, but then he'd left and she'd felt bereft, wishing they didn't have to part. She wished they could just snuggle up together in bed... but that wasn't possible for a girl like her before marriage.

Sighing, she crawled into bed. It had been a long day and she would see John in the morning. He'd found a room in a hostel and in the morning, he was going to take her to his parents' home. His mother had invited her to lunch and to stay for the night. They would have a couple of days to walk together in fields that took them far from prying eyes and perhaps then they might have the privacy that allowed them to at least talk about the intimacy of love…

Her last thought before she fell asleep was that John had been a little bit quiet after she mentioned Tom being part of an elite group, so perhaps, she shouldn't ask about his brother in future… She hoped he was safe, because it would upset John if he lost the brother he looked up to.

7

Tom felt the familiar gnawing of fear in his stomach as they prepared to land from the small boat, which they'd rowed ashore after being dropped off by the destroyer that had brought them to a spot some distance from the beach. It had delivered them at dusk and it was now well into the dark hours, perfect for the work they had to do. The fear was the kind felt by all fighting men before a battle and it would vanish like mist in the sun once they were on dry earth and the serious stuff began. It was just stage fright, he thought with a grim smile – only the stage was on a remote coastline of Norway. The Germans had invaded the country under the pretence that they were protecting the population from British invasion when the real reason was that they needed a port they could rely on not to freeze up in the winter months.

This time, Tom's group had been sent in to cause as much havoc and destruction as they could in the German-occupied country. They had received information about trains carrying ammunition and also storage depots, from Norwegian groups, still able to get information out. Although most were keeping their heads down for the moment, there were local men prepared to risk their lives to help the Allies and sabotage the invaders.

Tom's team planned to go in and blow some installations up; their job was to cause trouble for the enemy but nothing strategic was asked or expected. It wasn't going to free the occupied country, but anything that caused the enemy a problem was a help to the overall effort, or at least that was the reason they'd been given.

'We can't hope to dislodge or drive them out now,' Major Morris, recently promoted from Captain, had told them. Tom had thought he'd become more demanding since his promotion, sending them on ever more difficult missions. Like others in his group, Tom had heard rumours that a bigger, better equipped force was being prepared to be the advance for attacks in future and perhaps that was why the major was sending them on what some of the men thought a fool's errand. 'But we can keep them on their toes – stop them getting too settled...' the major had continued, sounding more and more as if he was making excuses for a reckless mission.

'Bloody idiot,' Jenks had muttered behind Tom. 'The fool is sending us on a suicide trip.'

It did sound a bit that way, Tom agreed privately, though he'd glared at Jenks and given him a lecture afterwards.

'If you want to leave the group, say so now,' he'd told the soldier. 'Just ask to be released and I'll request a replacement for you...'

Jenks had fingered his knife, a glare in his close-set eyes, 'Are you calling me a coward?' he'd demanded.

'Don't be a bloody moron,' Tom had said and gave him a hard stare. 'You should know that the only way we can hope to get out of there alive is to work together. If I can't rely on your loyalty to the team, I won't take you – but no, I don't consider you a coward.

I think you reckless but brave and reliable in a tight corner and I want you on my team – but only if you want it too.'

'Yeah...' An odd look in his eyes had puzzled Tom but then Jenks had shrugged. 'You can rely on me to do my bit. I just think it is a damned stupid idea that's all. He's trying to impress the bigwigs because he thinks this new unit will take over from him. They're calling it the SAS or SBS, so I've heard, and we'll be sucked into it, swallowed up and forgotten, as if we never existed.' Officially they didn't exist, being a secret group, though someone at the top must have authorised it – possibly Mr Churchill, who, besides being a brilliant orator, had his ruthless side, as well as a maverick streak. This mission was the kind of thing their new Prime Minister might well have got into as a young man if the need had arisen.

'It's only rumours, at the moment,' Tom had told Jenks with a frown. 'What we have to remember is that we're a secret force – or supposed to be...'

'Expendable,' Jenks had muttered sullenly. 'The major's little experiment. OK, I know. I'll keep my mouth shut and I'll do what-ever is needed – but why don't they send us somewhere we can do some good? Norway is a lost cause. They should have sent more troops before it was too late – what good is sabotage now?'

'Maybe it is just a matter of morale,' Tom had suggested. 'If it was Britain that had been invaded, wouldn't you want to make it as hard for them as you could? Blow up a few bridges and ammo depots? And wouldn't you appreciate some outside help? I reckon we're being sent in to keep the Norwegians on board and willing to resist when they can. We may not be able to beat the enemy yet – but we can prick them where it hurts.'

Jenks had shrugged, but then nodded. 'I guess so,' he'd agreed. 'The poor devils must be living under a shadow. I'd want to kill every enemy I saw in the street.'

'Knowing you, you would manage to slit a few throats,' Tom had said and laughed as he saw a gleam in the other man's eyes. 'Maybe it isn't the most important job we've done, but let's do what we can, make life difficult for them and then get out of there.'

'We'll make life difficult for them, but I've got a bad feeling about this one...' Jenks had glared at Tom. 'I don't want to pull out – what have I got waiting for me back home? I just think this is a mistake... the major hasn't thought it through enough...'

In his heart, Tom agreed. The time for action had been earlier when the Norwegians were fighting for their lives and their freedom. A lot of the men felt that the British shouldn't have evacuated when they did – they hated the fact that they'd had to get out. Perhaps that was the major's motive. He wanted revenge. Tom shook his head; it wasn't his decision.

It was time to move, time to follow orders and attempt the mission they'd been sent on. Tom pushed away his thoughts of home. It was time to fight.

* * *

As the night exploded with gunfire all around him, Tom realised they'd been betrayed. Somehow the enemy had known they were coming. He didn't blame the Norwegians; they were a great bunch and they were caught in the crossfire just as Tom's group had been. He'd seen at least three of them killed. Several of his team had been hit, including Tom. He'd taken a bullet in the arm in the first burst of fire as they attempted to blow up the ammunition dump in the railway yard. It had seemed a good idea, because if the line was severed, it would cause annoyance and halt the German advance – the more they were bogged down here the less time they had to plan invasions in the rest of Europe.

Tom believed it was the only possible reason for this attack – the faint hope of keeping the enemy on their toes here so they couldn't invade Britain.

God, it was a shambles! His arm stung like hell, though he was conscious and still in control. Thoughts jumbled and raced in his head. How could the Germans have known they were coming? It had been dark when they'd landed and they'd done everything right. His gut feeling was that someone had betrayed the partisans. Someone who wanted a quiet life – didn't want to risk the reprisals on civilians that might have come if their mission had been successful.

'We need to get out of here,' Jenks hissed in his ear and Tom nodded. They had no chance of blowing the railway bridge or the line – or anything. It was a question of saving what they could.

'Yeah, and now,' he hissed back and stood so that the others could see him as he gave the signal to move out. The explosion was a shock – the result of careless fire by the enemy – and Tom had an ironic smile on his face as the force of it blew him into the air. His group hadn't managed to cause much damage, but the enemy had done it to themselves... It was their own machine guns that had caused the dump to catch fire and explode. Damned funny really...

It was his last thought before everything went black.

* * *

Lizzie woke suddenly in the night, feeling shivery. 'Tom!' Her husband's name was on her lips. She'd dreamed that he was in trouble – in pain – and it frightened her. Getting up, she went to the window. She hadn't put her light on and drew the curtain back so that she could look out; it was still dark.

She could hear the drone of planes overhead – quite a few of them. For a moment, her heart beat faster as she wondered if they were enemy planes bound for British cities and ports. No bombs were dropped and the sound faded. Whoever they were, they were gone – on their way to heap destruction on someone. If not in this country, then they could be British planes headed for cities in Germany.

After some terrible raids on Rotterdam, the Allies had started bombing German cities in retaliation and, of course, London was suffering badly right now. The damage to homes and livelihoods was terrible. To Lizzie, it seemed such a wicked waste of life. Soldiers died in battles but killing innocent civilians on the ground seemed wrong to Lizzie, whichever side did it. She hated the idea of war altogether, especially when she had nights like this. Lizzie was missing Tom, anxious because she'd only had one brief postcard in months, and afraid that something might have happened to him.

The feeling that he was in danger or pain was receding now. It was just a bad dream. Yet she still felt cold and anxious. She wished he would write. Why hadn't he? Where was he? What was he doing?

8

Faith looked at the gold locket and chain John had given her before kissing her once more and then leaving her to return to his base. After the few days they'd spent with his family, lovely days, warm, though with occasional showers of rain, during which they'd sheltered in a barn, she'd had to return to work. John had taken her back to Cambridge and stayed at the hostel for a couple of days so that they could see each other at night.

'I love you so much,' he'd told her when they lay in the hay together and kissed. For a moment, his hand had caressed her breast over her thin dress, but then he'd given a little moan, burying his face in her neck. 'No, I won't spoil things,' he'd said. 'I want you, Faith, more than you can imagine – but I love you too much to risk it. If you fell for a child and I didn't come back...' He shook his head. 'I'd never rest easy in my grave.'

Faith had looked at him wonderingly. 'Do you love me so much?' she'd asked and he'd nodded, kissing her in a way that spoke of passion and need. Faith had longed to tell him she felt as he did, but couldn't, in case he thought her fast or cheap. When he'd first told her he wanted to marry her, Faith had laughed and said they were too young, but that was over a year ago now and her feelings had changed. Now, because of the war, John was determined to wait for her sake – and that was noble and sweet and she was lucky to be loved by him.

Smiling as she held his gift against her white throat, she knew a pang of regret, because it might be weeks or months before she saw John again.

'I'll write when I can,' he'd promised before reluctantly leaving her.

'I'll write too,' she'd whispered, holding back her tears.

Why did there have to be a war? Why couldn't they get married and be together now? Faith placed the beautiful locket back in its velvet box and put it in her wardrobe, which she locked. She knew that she would miss John even more this time.

Faith tumbled into bed and was soon asleep, but her dreams were tangled and disturbing and she woke suddenly in the dark, frightened and anxious. It was a really humid night, which was perhaps the reason for her lurid dreams. She pinched her arm to make sure she was awake and then laughed and fell into a dreamless sleep and woke when her alarm went off at six in the morning. She shut it off, groaning as she got up, preparing for another day of hard work in the sluice room.

Life went on despite her worries. Faith knew she was lucky to have been sought by John, who was as nice and genuine as he was attractive. She loved him and knew herself loved in return. One day they would marry and all this would be a memory.

John got more leave than many of the men who were in the army. He was stationed not too far away. Men serving in the army couldn't always come home on leave, but so far John had been lucky not being sent overseas.

A little shiver went through her as she thought about that eventuality. He was probably flying dangerous missions even now, but he didn't talk about them. She always thought of him as just being a few miles away, doing flying exercises or something, but if he was sent abroad somewhere, she might not see him for ages... or ever if he was killed.

No, she wouldn't think about that! It couldn't happen, not to her John. She was going to marry him one day and live happily ever after.

9

Pam got the telegram first. It was addressed to Lizzie, but the look on the delivery boy's face had told her what it must be and so, after a moment's hesitation, she opened it, giving a gasp of dismay as she sat down on a hard kitchen chair. Her legs had turned to jelly and she was shaking so much that she almost dropped the thin piece of paper.

```
Regret  Sergeant  Tom  Gilbert  missing  in
action.  Believed  dead.  Further  news  to
follow.
```

How would she tell Lizzie? Pam closed her eyes as she thought of her daughter-in-law. She would be devastated.

It couldn't be true. It just couldn't be true.

Pam stared at the brief message again. It was what she'd dreaded ever since Tom joined up – that he should be killed just as his father had been before him. Different wars but the same awful reality.

'Mum, do you know where...?' Susan's voice trailed off as she saw her mother's face. 'What's wrong?' She ran to where Pam was sitting and took the telegram from her hand. 'No! Oh, Mum... Poor Lizzie...'

The distress in her daughter's voice brought Pam out of her state of shock and the tears trickled from her eyes. She reached for Susan's hand and held it and for a moment they just looked at each other, their cheeks wet. Then Arthur walked in the back door and the spell was broken.

'It's Tom...' Pam managed and her husband strode towards her, taking her into his arms and holding her, stroking her hair as she started to sob into his chest. He held her for a while and then she moved back, wiping her cheeks with the back of her hand. 'They say he's missing, believed dead...'

Arthur was silent for a moment, then he nodded. 'If they say that, it isn't certain, love. If they knew for sure they would say killed in action.'

Pam stared at him, feeling a return of hope. 'Are you sure?'

'Yes.' Arthur went to the dresser and poured brandy into a glass. He brought it back to her. 'Drink a little for the shock – go on, love. It will do you good.'

She did as he bid her and then wiped the edge of the glass and handed it to Susan.

'Go on, Susan, take a sip,' Arthur encouraged. 'You've had a shock too.'

Susan did so and then handed the glass to him. There was still a finger of brandy. Arthur drank it down without hesitation. He looked from one to the other.

'We're not going to start mourning Tom until we're certain...' His voice almost cracked with the emotion he was holding inside. 'Now – what do we do about Lizzie? Shall I go over to Chatteris and tell her at work or wait until she comes home?'

'Wait until she comes home. There's nothing she can do and — ' Pam shook her head hopelessly. 'Nothing any of us can do—'

'Except pray,' he reminded her. 'We have to hope there is a still a chance – but if he's gone, we have to carry on. I know how hard this is for you, love. You lost his father in the first war.'

'Yes, but I was lucky you came along.' Pam nodded. She lifted her head and squared her shoulders. 'I'll put the kettle on, Arthur. No sense in grieving until we know for sure.' She had to be strong.

Nevertheless, Pam felt the heaviness on her heart as she went about the business of providing lunch for her husband and then the others as they came in from the fields. Susan had run out of the kitchen, heading noisily up the stairs to her room as her brother and the land girls entered, her tears all too near the surface, but Pam couldn't run away.

Arthur told Artie that his brother was missing, feared dead.

Jeanie looked at her and said how sorry she was. Nancy glared, because she didn't know what else to do and wasn't the sort to show emotion. Artie swore.

'Bloody fool!' he muttered. 'I told him to keep his head down. What did he have to go for?' He looked at his father, hiding his emotion behind anger. 'I told him not to go – we could have got an exemption for him. We're short-handed on the farm.'

Nancy snorted her disgust. 'We do our bit,' she muttered but subsided as Pam looked at her. 'Of course, I'm sorry if he's... but I think he was brave to go and he did his duty. If they would let me, I'd go and shoot the buggers that shot him.'

Everyone stared at Nancy. It was the longest speech any of them had heard from her.

Pam smiled sadly. 'Thank you,' she said. 'I think I would too.'

She went to the range oven and took out the big cottage pie

she'd made, putting it on the table in front of them and a dish of fresh cooked peas and runner beans.

'Thank God! I'm starving,' Nancy said and helped herself.

After a moment at the sink washing his hands, Artie came to the table and joined her. Jeanie hesitated and then did the same, but pushed her food around the plate, clearly upset. She knew what it felt like to see a brother in pain, because she'd been to the hospital to visit Terry when she'd had a few days off work and returned looking sad and pale herself, Pam thought.

Arthur drank his tea but made no attempt to eat.

Pam went to the stairs and called up to her eldest daughter. 'Susan – lunch is ready.'

'Not hungry,' Susan's reply was muffled and tear-laden.

Pam decided to leave her to it. She'd served pie to her husband and herself, but neither of them ate much of it. It was a relief when they all left, allowing Pam to get on with washing up.

Susan came down a few minutes later, bringing Tina with her. 'Where is Angela?' she asked as she settled the little girl in her high chair and cut a thick slice of bread and butter, smothering it with home-made jam, which she shared with the child.

'Staying with friends again today as there is no school,' Pam said. 'I'm glad she is – we shan't tell her, Susan. We'll have to let John know, but no need for Angela to know just yet.'

'Good.' Susan gave her a watery smile. 'Perhaps Tom is just wounded, Mum. I read in the paper that sometimes when a soldier is wounded, he is thought to have been killed and he isn't.'

'Yes, you may be right. I don't feel he is dead inside here...' Pam put a hand to her breast. 'It is strange because I did feel it when his father died.' She smiled at her daughter. 'Thank you for looking after Tina, darling.'

Squaring her shoulders once more, she poured a glass of milk for the child from the jug Arthur had brought in earlier. Tom couldn't be dead. It would be too hard to bear. Surely God wouldn't be that cruel?

* * *

When Lizzie came home from a busy day at the salon, Pam sat her down with a cup of tea and then showed her the telegram. Lizzie stared at it for several minutes in silence and then lifted her head to look at her.

'He isn't dead, Mum,' she said firmly. 'They've made a mistake. I know he's hurt. I felt it when it happened – but I also know he is still alive.'

Pam stared at her and then nodded, swallowing back a sob. 'I felt it inside when his father was killed. I believe the same, Lizzie – but when did you know he'd been hurt?'

'A couple of weeks ago, I was sleeping when I suddenly felt this sharp pain in my chest and woke up. I knew it was Tom, but then the pain went and I thought it was just a dream...'

'You didn't tell anyone?'

'No, because I might have been wrong. I didn't want to upset anyone else – but I've felt something bad had happened ever since then. I think I was waiting for this...' She glanced down at the telegram. 'I believe he is missing, Mum, but not dead.' Lizzie stood up and they embraced, holding each other tightly, both emotional and fearful but unwilling to believe that their lovely Tom could have been taken from them.

'Will you have something to eat, love?' Pam asked as they broke their embrace. 'I couldn't eat earlier – but I'll have a bit of supper if you will?'

'Yes, I'll try,' Lizzie agreed. 'Even if the worst happened, we have to go on – but I am sure it hasn't...'

'Yes, life goes on even when you don't want it to,' Pam agreed.

Her throat was tight and her chest felt compressed. Lizzie was being so brave, but whether she felt like that inside was another matter. Pam knew how much she loved Tom and ached for her, but there was nothing either of them could do but wait for news that he'd been found alive and was being cared for.

Pam blinked away her tears as she took her rabbit pie from the oven and brought it to the table. It was certain Tom was wounded and perhaps lost, but they could only pray that he would come through whatever had happened and return to them.

* * *

Later that evening, alone in the room she shared with Tom when he was home, Lizzie shed a few tears. She'd known something had happened, carrying her fear and distress inside for these past weeks, saying nothing to his mother, because she knew Pam was already worried to death. It was almost a relief to get the telegram because it said 'missing believed dead' – but his death wasn't confirmed. In war, it was possible that a man's body might never be found, but there was still hope that Tom was alive and Lizzie was determined to cling to it for all she was worth.

Tom would return to her. It couldn't end here! They were young and very much in love and they had the rest of their lives to look forward to.

'Don't be dead, Tom,' Lizzie said into her pillow. 'Please don't be dead, my darling. I love you so much. I can't lose you... I can't...'

She held the pillow close, hugging it as she fought the surge of grief and fear that swept through her. Had Tom been found and taken to hospital or was he alone somewhere and suffering? Not knowing was agony and she gave a little moan as she buried her face in the pillow. Without Tom, her life would be empty and meaningless, just a round of chores she was forced to do...

Tears flowed into the pillow until she finally fell asleep and then she dreamed of Tom and being kissed by him and her body relaxed into a deep slumber. Tom was telling her to believe...

10

Faith read her letter from John three times. He'd heard from his mother that his eldest brother, Tom, was missing in action, but he was hoping it was a mistake.

Both Mum and Lizzie think he is still alive. I've felt something was wrong for a while because it's ages since any of us had a letter, but I don't know what to believe. I hope that he isn't dead. It will devastate the family but particularly Mum and Lizzie.

Faith's eyes filled with tears. She'd liked both Pam and Lizzie and felt sorry for them. It must be awful not knowing whether someone you loved was alive or dead. If it was John, she didn't think she could be as brave as Lizzie was being, according to John's letter.

Brushing away her tears, Faith decided to have a warm bath before she went to bed. The nurses took it in turns to use the bath once a week and you could only have five inches of water; they didn't have a line painted on their bath, but all knew where it should be and seldom flouted the rules.

It had been another hard day at work, but at least she wasn't spending most of her day in the sluice room now. She'd attended lectures from Matron and senior nurses that morning, but in the afternoon, she'd been allowed to help on the wards. They were very busy with a new influx of wounded men and her scrubbing bedpan duties had been taken over by an older woman, who now did a lot of the cleaning that had been done by probationers. Every girl who had at least a little understanding of the basics of nursing had been called on to the wards as the nurses and doctors fought to save lives.

Faith was still assisting rather than tending the wounded herself, but that was more what she'd hoped for when she'd applied to become a nurse for the duration of the war. She had helped to turn and treat terrible burns cases and been complimented by the Staff Nurse she'd assisted for her steadiness and gentle manner.

'That was very good,' Staff Nurse Robins had approved when they'd finished. 'You have obviously been paying attention to the lessons you've attended.'

Faith had felt herself blushing and mumbled her thanks. Sister Reece hadn't softened her attitude, but the other nurses were kinder and she was beginning to enjoy herself. She'd actually been allowed to take patients a glass of water and one soldier who had his eyes bandaged had asked her to read a letter for him.

'Someone read it to me once,' he'd told her, 'but I'd like to hear it again – you've got a lovely soft voice...'

Faith had read him the letter. It was from his mother and it was a very loving, caring message that brought tears to her eyes. After she'd finished reading it, the soldier had thanked her. She'd had a lovely warm feeling inside and even a scolding from Sister

Reece later that day hadn't upset her much. It was good to know that she was helping young men who had suffered terrible pain and injury, even if only in a small way.

Putting her own letter away safely, Faith went to the bathroom. She was lucky enough to find it empty and enjoyed a nice soak before returning to her room refreshed and ready for bed. As she settled down for the night, her thoughts returned to John's brother. Faith was a religious girl, even though she didn't go to church every Sunday, and she said a little prayer for Tom. She prayed that he would come home safely and in one piece. Too many young men were dying or being cruelly injured for the sake of peace and their loved ones and she often prayed for them and the end of the war.

'Let Tom be all right and John keep safe...' she whispered.

John had told her that he was flying with a good crew now and enjoying it – but he hadn't told her what they were doing. Was he engaged in action against the enemy? She supposed he must be. He was a navigator now and that probably meant flying over enemy territory – most likely in bombers...

A little shudder went through Faith as she realised that now the bulk of John's training was over, he would be like all the rest of the young men in the RAF – risking his life night after night on dangerous missions.

Supposing John's plane was shot down and he was killed or simply disappeared? Faith might never know what had happened to him.

Faith bit her lip, holding back the tears. How she hated this war! She longed for it to be over so that John could be home with her once more – and she decided that when he visited again, she would suggest that they got married sooner than they'd once planned. Back then, in her quiet hometown, the future had seemed endless, lit by sunshine and full of promise but now... A little prayer left her lips. 'Be safe, darling. Be safe.'

* * *

The night was foggy. It was impossible for the pilot to see anything through the pea-souper that had suddenly come up out of nowhere once they were flying over the North Sea. The crew was relying on John to get them to their target so that they could drop their load of bombs and then run for home. Everyone hated these missions on nights like this and the navigator had a huge responsibility on his shoulders.

As John went through the checks with his pilot, he gave his whole concentration to the task in hand. The one thing he would never allow himself to think about was the damage the lethal weapons on board did to the innocent folk below. The enemy was bombing the British people, so John and his crew had to equal the score by bombing their cities. John was far happier when they were looking for factories or military targets, but tonight it was a city in northern Germany and people would be killed and maimed, their homes blasted and burned, just like what was happening back in England. It would be carnage and terrible, but the crews had been told it was necessary.

Did two wrongs make a right? John had no idea. He just followed orders. As his co-ordinates came together, he gave the pilot the information he needed and listened as the instruction to open the bomb door was given. He counted the bombs out but didn't watch as they fell to earth. He could see in his mind the destruction they would cause, feel the heat and the blast as the explosives did their deadly work.

Within moments, their load had gone. It was over and John gave the pilot the directives he needed to get them home, concentrating as they heard the flak all around the plane. The enemy must be firing blindly, because they couldn't see any more than the British crew could, but they were retaliating and that meant they might get lucky. Everyone knew that if their name was written on the bullet, it was the end.

Not this night, though. John felt the relief spread through the others as they flew out of range. They'd completed what was the third bombing raid for this crew and their luck had held. Some of the crews caught it the very first time they went on a mission like this one. You were either lucky or you weren't. It seemed they were a lucky crew thus far.

Some of the men were laughing, pleased to be on the way home, others just sat silent, reflective. You couldn't always count on getting back safely just because you'd avoided the flak, but John thought they were pretty safe on a night like this, because they weren't likely to be spotted by enemy craft.

He glanced at his instruments, correcting their path slightly. It was his job to keep them flying in the right direction, because the pilot still couldn't see a thing. Unless it was clear over England, they could easily overshoot the runaway if he didn't bring them down at the right moment.

Briefly, John's thoughts turned towards his brother. Was Tom dead? He couldn't believe it. He wouldn't believe it. Tom was his big brother, so strong and confident. He'd always looked up to him, admired him. Surely, he would come through this war even if he had been wounded?

John checked the readings again. The pilot was keeping them on course. He allowed his thoughts to wander to Faith – how sweetly she'd returned his kisses. He'd been so tempted to make love to her in the hay barn, but he'd resisted it. When he'd first mentioned marriage, she hadn't been ready, but perhaps if he asked her now, she might consider getting married sooner. John knew it wasn't fair to her, because she'd be a young widow if anything happened to him one of these nights – and the odds were that it would happen – and what kind of a life would she have then? He wanted to spend the rest of his life with her, but at the moment, life was precarious.

John cursed.

Riley, the gunner, looked at him sharply. 'Something wrong?' he asked tensely.

'Not a thing,' John replied casually. 'Just remembered I forgot to buy my mother a birthday gift...'

It wasn't his mother's birthday and he'd bought her something nice last time, but it made Riley laugh and look more relaxed.

'We'll be home in time for cocoa,' John told him and grinned. 'Don't worry, old chap, we're bang on course for bacon and eggs with fried bread.'

'Shut up,' the pilot said, 'and check that damned reading again. I should be seeing the coast by now and I can't see a damned thing in this weather.'

'It's OK, skipper,' John said. 'You'll clear the cliffs of Dover in about five minutes. Trust me, I'm on it.'

'Just keep your mind on the job until we're down.'

'He's fallen out with his wife again,' Riley leaned in to whisper.

John nodded but maintained silence. If the pilot was edgy, he was worried and he needed to be steady to bring them down safely in this stupid fog, though it looked as if it might be clearing over the land...

* * *

Faith was at work the next morning when she was told to report to Matron's office. She glanced at Sister Reece in a sudden fright. What had she done now? She couldn't think of a thing and her heart raced as she left the ward and walked towards Matron's room. Was she going to be dismissed? She'd thought she was getting on well?

Her knock brought an invitation to enter and she did so, her heart thumping as Matron continued to write in her book. Faith held her breath, but then Matron looked up and smiled at her.

'Ah, Miss Goodjohn – you've been with us six months now...' She looked at some notes in front of her. 'Yes, six months. How are you getting on – do you enjoy the work?'

'Yes, Matron. I want to learn all I can and do more to help...'

'Good, that is what I like to hear,' Matron encouraged with a smile. 'Now, the reason I sent for you – we've had a request to send more staff overseas. We cannot spare any of our trained nurses, but I've been told that you are a capable girl and would respond to more responsibility – is that right?'

'Yes, Matron,' Faith said breathlessly.

'Right – then I am moving you on to Sister Evans' ward. She is willing to give you some intensive training after hours – and then, in say three months, I shall see how you've done and if you're ready, I'll suggest sending you out to a military hospital some-where, perhaps in England, perhaps abroad.' Matron smiled at her. 'Are you prepared for that?'

Faith gulped. 'Yes, Matron, if you think I'm ready. I'll do what-ever you say to help our brave boys; they are sacrificing them-selves for us and I want to do everything I can for them.'

'Spoken like a patriot,' Matron told her. 'That is excellent... Very well, you may go. I shall speak to you again.'

Faith thanked her and left. She felt a bit as if she'd been

picked up by a whirlwind and dumped down again as she returned to the ward.

Sister Reece looked at her sharply as she entered. 'This is your last day on my ward,' she muttered. 'You are moving to the C-wards tomorrow – post-surgery. Make sure you don't let me down. I recommended you.'

'Thank you, Sister,' Faith said and felt shocked. Sister Reece was the last person she'd expected to recommend her for something like this.

* * *

John phoned that evening. One of the other nurses banged on Faith's door at the nurses' home, summoning her to the telephone in the hall.

Faith hurried downstairs to take the call. 'John,' she said, her heart jumping for joy at the unexpected pleasure. 'This is nice – how are you?'

'I'm in hospital,' he said. 'No, don't get upset. It isn't serious. We overshot the runaway last night and I ended up with a broken ankle. Stupid accident, but the plane took the worst of it. I think I'm the only one in hospital as a result.'

'Oh no! Bad luck,' she said. 'Was it the pilot's fault?'

'No one's really, just foul weather – and a bit of damage to the undercarriage we didn't count on. No need to worry.'

Faith caught her breath. What wasn't he telling her?'

'Where are you?' she asked. 'Are you near enough for me to visit on my half-day?'

'As a matter of fact, I'm in your hospital. We got redirected because of the fog and landed locally at Marshall's. It's probably the reason we miscalculated – it was a shorter runaway than we're used to and as much my fault as the pilot's.' The airport had been opened at the edge of the university city in 1938 to replace an earlier one at Fen Ditton. It had attachments to the RAF and was often used as a training base and connected to the university that taught pilots. It was useful when planes had to be redirected, though the fog had been almost as thick there as at their base.

'Oh...' Faith laughed softly. 'As long as you're not badly hurt. I'll pop in and see you in the morning when I have my break.'

'Good,' John sounded rueful. 'It might not be serious, but it hurts like hell – and it means I'm out of action for a few days.'

'At least I get to see you,' Faith replied with a little giggle. 'I've got some news for you – I've been recommended by Sister Reece, and I'll be moving to a military hospital in a few months; they are so rushed that they need help and I'm going to do an intensive course so I can be of more assistance. If I'm chosen, I might be sent abroad.'

There was silence at the other end, then, 'But if they move you to the other side of the country, I may not be able to see you as often...' John sounded disappointed, even a little annoyed.

Faith hesitated, then, 'I hadn't thought about that... but you don't know where you'll be either...' His current base at Duxford wasn't too far away, but he could be moved to another if he was needed elsewhere.

'I suppose you're right,' John admitted. 'I was just thinking... Never mind. I'll tell you when I see you.'

Faith frowned as the receiver went down his end. He had sounded a bit put out – but surely, he must see that this was what she'd joined up for? Faith wanted to be a nurse and she needed to be able to go where her services were required. She couldn't pick and choose any more than he could. He must see that...

* * *

John glared at the wall at the opposite side of the long ward. He'd been going to talk to Faith about getting married sooner. She hadn't seemed too happy where she was at Addenbrooke's and he'd thought she might be pleased to get married and forget the nursing, but now it seemed she was preparing to go off somewhere – perhaps abroad, where he wouldn't be able to visit on his leave and would be more dangerous for her.

There wasn't much point in proposing to her yet. He'd been a fool to let himself think about it. After all, they'd agreed they wouldn't marry until the war was over. John shook his head. Faith was right to put her work first and he had to accept it. His own life was precarious these days, as the small accident they'd had on landing had shown him. It only took one good hit when they were on a mission and it could be curtains for him. No, it wouldn't be fair to take Faith from the job she loved. Yet if he didn't make it through the war, he would lose so much that might have been theirs...

He glared at the nurse who unexpectedly arrived at his bed, interrupting his thoughts.

'Still can't sleep?' she asked with an understanding smile. 'Perhaps this will help – I've brought you a warm drink of cocoa and something to help you rest.' She offered a plain white mug and a small tablet.

'Thanks, nurse,' John said and took them gratefully. His mood changed and he smiled at her. She'd mentioned her name was Lucy and the way she looked at him told him she liked him. 'You are very thoughtful.'

'It's the least we can do for you,' she said. 'I admire what you're doing, Lieutenant – risking your life night after night. My brother is in the RAF, just ground crew, but he tells me a bit about how the planes come back – bits missing and sometimes having to land on one wheel...'

'That's what happened to us. We thought we'd got away with it, but we'd sustained a bit of damage to the undercarriage without realising it.'

Lucy nodded. 'Yes, I told my brother about you and he said that was probably it.' A pink flush touched her cheeks and made John wonder just what she'd told her brother. 'Josh is home on leave. He knows you by sight...'

'When can I get out of here?' John asked. 'Surely, I can still do my job?' As a navigator, he only had to sit and read dials, and he could walk to and from the plane if they let him.

'As soon as you can hobble down the ward unaided,' she said and hesitated. Then, 'Do you have a girlfriend?' she asked with an inviting smile. 'I'd be happy to help you get mobile again in my spare time... unless you have someone?'

The way she looked at him sent little tingles down his spine. It wasn't the first time John had seen that look in a girl's eyes, but he'd never taken any of them up on it, though Artie said he was a fool not to grab his chances when he could. John knew his brother had been out with a lot of girls and he thought some of them might have been up for more than a few kisses. From what Artie had told him, some of them couldn't get enough of him. Or was that just his brother bragging? John never knew for certain with Artie. He wasn't sure whether Lizzie was Tom's first love, but Artie had played the field a bit and he'd made his opinion of John's chivalry known, mocking him as a softie.

'Actually, I do have a girlfriend,' John told the nurse with a shy smile. 'She works here – a probationer nurse...'

'Ah, then she will help you,' Lucy said and looked disappointed. She walked to the door and glanced back. 'If you ever need a friend, don't forget...'

John grinned to himself as she disappeared through the open doorway. If that wasn't plain enough, he didn't know what was –

but he wasn't tempted. It was Faith he loved, Faith he wanted... even if he had to wait until they were married. But maybe they wouldn't ever be... John's little scare had made him more aware of how much he wanted to be with Faith that way. Perhaps if she was willing...

11

Marcel Waving was an art, there was no doubt about it. It wasn't Lizzie's favourite method of waving hair; she preferred to do it with her fingers and long flat clips. She found the procedure time-consuming and it sometimes made her wrist ache, twisting and turning the hot irons, but it did make lovely crisp waves and on long hair like Lizzie's customer's, it lasted for several days.

'Oh yes,' the girl said, admiring the long blonde tresses in the mirror. 'My lad is coming home this weekend and I want to look good for him. He and others like him deserve a bit of attention after all they're going through out there.'

'Yes, I am sure they do,' Lizzie agreed. She couldn't even imagine the hardships, pain and fear men fighting for their lives and freedom must experience day in and day out for months at a time. Men like that deserved the best of everything. Her Tom was one of them.

She could feel a tightness in her chest that she got whenever she let herself think about Tom. Where was he – was he still alive and why hadn't she heard from him? There had been no more news, even though summer had fled and it was autumn; the grain harvest had been gathered weeks previously and they were now lifting potatoes and ploughing some of the land for the next year. It would normally have been a time of celebration at Blackberry Farm, but at the moment, the atmosphere was tense and anxious as they all nursed their heartache.

The customer's hair was finished. She paid and chatted for a bit longer and then Lizzie's next customer arrived, so she went, promising to come back when she got the chance.

'She's got nice hair,' Mrs Brown, a regular customer, commented as Lizzie took her coat and settled her in her chair. She was in for her usual shampoo and set, finger waves and curls using a setting lotion to make it last the two weeks. 'I don't think I've seen her before – she isn't local, is she?'

'She comes from March,' Lizzie replied. 'She likes the way I do her hair so she travels to Chatteris on the bus for me to do it.'

'Well, that's nice,' the elderly lady said. 'I'm glad you opened up here, too. My hair has never been as easy to look after as it is now.'

'You have very fine hair so it is best left a little longer and waved rather than trying to keep lots of curls,' Lizzie replied, feeling pleased. It made her work so worthwhile when people showed they were happy with what she'd done.

It was a busy day at the salon and Lizzie was tired as she reached the bus stop that evening. The weather was on the turn now they were into autumn and it was cold and dark waiting, because there wasn't a shelter, and she pulled her coat collar up close to her neck, shivering. When the car drew up and a man leaned forward, opening the door invitingly, Lizzie hesitated. If it was someone she knew, she wouldn't mind a lift home, but she realised that she did know that car and there was no way she was getting into Ralph Harris's vehicle, even if she was fed up waiting for the bus. She noticed that he was wearing army uniform. Lizzie had heard he'd joined the forces, so he must be back home on leave.

'Want a ride?' he asked, smiling at her as if butter wouldn't melt in his mouth. 'You shouldn't be standing there in the cold, Lizzie. Come on, I won't hurt you – I promise.'

'Thanks for the offer, but I'll wait. My bus will be here soon.' Lizzie didn't like him and she'd sooner get cold than risk taking a lift from him. Last time she'd been in a car with him, it had almost wrecked her life! Lizzie would never trust him again.

'Still as stuck-up as always,' he said in a tone that told her he was angry at her refusal. He hadn't changed and she would never trust him. 'You might regret it one day, Lizzie Gilbert. Your old man will never do much. I'm going places. I've been promoted and I'm making influential friends. I've always had money, but I'll be powerful as well as rich. One day you'll wish you'd been nicer to me.'

'Get lost,' Lizzie said, suddenly annoyed. 'I wouldn't touch you with a bargepole. You could be the richest man in the world, Mr Harris, but you still wouldn't be half the man Tom is!'

She saw a flash of anger in his eyes, but in a moment, he had controlled it.

'Suit yourself,' he sneered and drove off without another word.

Lizzie knew that she'd made him angry, but she didn't want anything to do with him. Besides, Tom wouldn't want her to accept a lift from him. She wished Ralph wouldn't speak to her but knew that he got some perverse pleasure out it; he must do, because he knew she wouldn't go with him. She shivered for a few minutes more in the cold of the chilly evening and then the bus arrived.

Once inside, she paid her fare and settled down. The old bus rattled as it moved off and it was still a bit draughty, but she was more comfortable than she would have been in Ralph's car. Lizzie thought she'd rather walk home than get a lift with him! Even if there was no more Tom – and that thought made her gasp with pain each time it came to her – she wasn't interested in the man who had used her so shamefully. Ralph Harris wasn't the kind of man she wanted to know.

Lizzie tried to think good thoughts. Most of the time, she behaved as though a shadow wasn't hanging over her. She could manage to put her fears and grief to one side while she was working, but every now and then, it came back and caught her out. She scrubbed the tears from her eyes with the back of her hand. It wasn't fair if Tom had been killed. She didn't think she would ever find anyone else – didn't want to – but the idea of being alone for the rest of her life was too awful to face so she shut it away. If she didn't let herself believe that Tom was dead, he was still alive – and if he was alive, he would come back to her.

'Tom, I love you,' she whispered. 'Tom, I need you – please come back to me. Please...'

He was alive somewhere; she had to believe that, because the alternative was too painful to accept. Somewhere, Tom was still breathing, perhaps thinking of her. Her heart called to him, willing him to live and to come home to her and his family.

* * *

Tom groaned through his fever. The pain was unbearable. He didn't want to come back to the light because it was too hard. He just wanted to lie there, to drift back into that state of hovering between life and death, to let go and slip away so that it stopped hurting...

'Tom, come back to me... I love you...' The voice penetrated his subconscious, seeming to come from far away, reaching him through the fog of pain.

Something was tugging at him, refusing to let him go. Tom begged it to let go, but it wouldn't. It kept nagging at him, holding him, refusing to let go when all he wanted was peace.

'Bugger you, Tom Gilbert!' a different and very loud voice pierced his drugged dreams. 'I refuse to let you die. Come on, I need you – you're my only friend. Damn you! You can't just let go. You wouldn't let me—'

Tom's eyes flickered. His lids were heavy and seemed to be stuck down, but as the insistent voice went on and on, he found the strength to open them and saw his friend bending over him.

'Damn you, Shorty,' Tom muttered as the light hurt his eyes and made him flinch. 'Sod off...'

'Nurse!' Shorty's voice was elated. 'He just spoke to me... He swore at me...'

Tom's eyes closed again. The light hurt them. He hurt all over. Something had exploded and he'd been blown off his feet... the raid on the explosives dump had gone wrong at the railway head. As the memory of chaos, the screams of wounded and dying men returned, he moaned aloud. He should be dead – he'd led them into that deathtrap – his men and the partisans – and he knew that some of the team were dead. Why wasn't he?

'Lizzie...' he murmured with dry lips. 'Water...'

'I've sent a telegram to Lizzie,' Shorty told him. 'As soon as we were rescued, I told them to let your family know, but I'm not sure they understood me – they were foreign.'

'It is time you left,' a woman's voice interjected and then Tom felt a gentle arm under his head lifting him and a glass of cool water touched his lips. He was allowed just a sip before it was removed, but it felt good.

'Where am I?' Tom asked. 'Am I home?'

'No, you're on a hospital ship heading back to England,' the soft voice told him. 'And very lucky to be alive. You were both more dead than alive when you were fished out of the sea, Sergeant Gilbert. Your friend got you as far as the sea and into the dingy after your mission was aborted, but he was injured, too, and you were just drifting at the mercy of the wind when you were spotted off the coast of Norway by that fishing boat.'

'Don't remember,' Tom muttered. 'Water... please... more water.'

The glass was held to his lips again and he gulped. It felt cool and soothing, unlike his tortured thoughts. He didn't remember anything – except that the enemy had been waiting. Somehow, they'd been spotted – or had they been betrayed? – so that the element of surprise had been lost and they had walked into a hail of fire. That was when most of the local group were killed. Then something had exploded just in front of him, tossing him several feet. Tom recalled shots, screams, but saw nothing after that blinding light. He was aware that his vision was not quite as it should be. Shorty's face had been fuzzy, but he'd known him by his voice. He couldn't see the nurse's face properly.

'Am I blind?' he asked. 'I can't see your face clearly.'

'We've had bandages over your eyes for a couple of weeks, but they weren't badly burned, only seared by the heat of the explosion,' she reassured him. 'The doctors were pleased when we took them off this morning. Your sight will come back in time, Sergeant. You just need to be patient...'

'I hurt all over – what else happened to me?' If there was a note of panic in Tom's voice, he couldn't help it. 'Tell me, please – what is wrong with me?'

'You're lucky to be alive...' the nurse soothed. 'You did receive several injuries – but nothing that should stop you living normally once you're healed. You have a lot of nasty cuts and a few broken bones, but that's all. You have a good friend and he got you out of there. I told you – you were lucky.' He felt a firm hand on his arm, pressing him back against the pillows, because he'd half risen in his moment of panic. 'Just rest now and Doctor will talk to you later.'

Tom relaxed back against the pillows, his natural calm taking over. There was no use in panicking even if the worst had happened. He couldn't feel his toes, but perhaps that was because he had a heavy plaster cast on his left foot... He was alive and on a ship that was taking him home. He would be able to see Lizzie again and as the tears came, he thanked God for sparing his life. He could so easily have been dead and buried in a foreign land – Lizzie probably thought he was and had been grieving all this time.

12

Pam was waiting at the kitchen door as Lizzie approached the house, just two nights after she'd turned down the offer of a lift from Ralph Harris. She was waving something at her and her face told Lizzie it was good news even before she heard the words.

'He is alive, Lizzie. Wounded but alive! It came just a few minutes ago – sent by a friend, I think—'

Lizzie snatched the telegram from her, tears bursting out of her in relief. She'd been holding it all inside and now it just tumbled out of her as she wept. Pam took her in her arms and hugged her.

'It's all right, love,' Pam said against her hair. 'You've been such a brave girl, carrying on as if nothing had happened, but I knew it was hard for you.'

'I didn't want to believe he'd gone. I didn't tell anyone else about the other telegram. Sometimes, I felt he was alive, Mum, but sometimes I...' She shook her head as Pam smiled at her.

'I know. It was the same for me. I didn't want to believe he was gone, Lizzie, but now and then I feared it – and it tore the heart out of me...'

'We're idiots,' Lizzie said and pulled away from her mother-in-law's embrace with a choked laugh. 'We should've have known they couldn't kill Tom just like that.'

'What I can't understand,' Arthur said as they went into the kitchen and he witnessed their mingled laughter and tears. 'Why have they been all these weeks before they let us know – and that telegram came from a friend. Yes, it came through official channels, but it was signed by that mate of his – Shorty Linton. Tom told us once – he's a great lanky bloke...'

'I know,' Lizzie giggled, scrubbing away her tears with the handkerchief Pam had just given her. 'Tom told me how the men liked to tease each other. They give some of them terrible nicknames – Basher Bloggs and things like that.' Tom had told her they all had nicknames that stuck and that his was unrepeatable. She'd tried to get it out of him, but he wouldn't tell her, but she'd teased him and, in the end, he'd said it was Basher Bloggs, but she didn't believe him; it was more likely to be something rude. 'The telegram didn't say much about his wounds...' She bit her lip because it hurt to think of her Tom injured. 'At least we'll get him home, Mum...'

'Yes, he's coming home,' Pam replied and they smiled at each other.

Lizzie crossed her fingers behind her back. Tom was wounded. She couldn't know how badly and she'd seen men with wounds once or twice in London when she'd popped there to visit Vera. As yet, she hadn't seen any local men walking about with facial scars or empty sleeves, though she knew of a couple of deaths in Chatteris where she worked. Every town and village had someone wounded or killed. This war left no one untouched for long.

* * *

Lizzie thought about Faith. She was only a probationer nurse for now, but she must see a lot of badly wounded men, because the hospitals were full of them. It might be nice to take the train from Sutton, the village up the road from them, on her afternoon off, and visit John's girl. She would ring her this evening and make the arrangement – and on Sunday she would go up to London and visit Vera. It was a few months since she'd seen her, though they wrote and telephoned regularly. Lizzie was meticulous about giving her friend news concerning her daughter, Jeanie, and her granddaughter, Tina.

It was strange how the two families had come together. These days, Lizzie considered the Salmons family as close as her own folk and she knew Pam was very fond of them too. She'd told Vera to come and stay as often as she liked, though she didn't get much time to. Soldiers came home on leave from time to time and babies got born, keeping Vera busy.

'I know Jeanie and Tina are fine with you,' Vera had said last time Lizzie had rung her. 'I do want to visit – but Terry is back in hospital. They sent him home too soon and his leg suppurated where they'd done the amputation, so they took him back and did another small operation. I've been told it will heal now, but he is so depressed that I fear for his sanity, Lizzie. I'm not sure he will ever get over his wife's death – though I think she might have left him if she had lived—' A little sob had escaped Vera then. 'I heard her say she couldn't bear being married to a cripple – now how could she say that if she loved him?'

Lizzie had sympathised with Vera. She had her hands full looking after her husband, visiting her son when she could and holding down an important job. Her eldest daughter, Annie, was still away nursing and seldom wrote, which made Vera uneasy for her. Jeanie rang her mother at least once a week and sent her funny postcards, but it seemed that Annie was too wrapped up in her work to write often.

Jeanie and Lizzie had become good friends. Lizzie had always liked her, but these days they could have been sisters and spent a lot of their free time doing things together. For a while, Jeanie had had a regular boyfriend, but after he was sent overseas, she had been happy going out with other girls in a group. Sometimes she and Lizzie went into Ely or Cambridge together on the bus and they'd been to a church social over in March one Saturday night; they'd gone to the fair in Ely together and to the midsummer fair in Cambridge, though neither were the same as before the war.

Lizzie had asked her once if she was serious about Ken, the young man she'd gone out with for a while, but Jeanie had shaken her head.

'I liked him, but we were just friends,' she'd told Lizzie with a smile. 'I'm a bit young to settle down – and things aren't easy, at the moment. If you promise to be true and then you meet someone else while they're away, it seems mean to let them down.'

Lizzie had smiled and nodded, though she wasn't sure if Jeanie had told her the whole truth. She knew that Lizzie kept an eye on her and would have spoken out if she'd done something foolish, but she seemed to know what she wanted. Recently, she'd been out to the cinema in Ely with Nancy a couple of times. They appeared to work well together, though Nancy could be moody and a bit taciturn. Lizzie wondered if she'd been let down badly, but she hadn't asked, because she didn't know her well enough.

Lizzie's thoughts turned Faith once again. John's girl must get a bit lonely, away from her family. Since they might one day be sisters-in-law, it would be nice to keep in touch with her more.

* * *

'If you make it next week, I have three days off and can meet you for tea,' Faith told Lizzie when she rang. 'I'd love to see you – and I'm so pleased Tom is alive. I'll tell John when I see him. He's fine, Lizzie. Tell his mum that he is absolutely fine. His ankle is still a bit sore, but they took the plaster off and he walks without a stick – bit of a limp, but that will go as the ankle strengthens. He's just impatient to be out of hospital and back to work.'

'Pam still worries about him,' Lizzie replied. 'I know he's a grown man and able to take care of himself – but he's her youngest son, Faith. She didn't say much when you rang to tell us he'd had a bit of an accident but was recovering in hospital...' There was a pause then, 'She still doesn't know his plane overshot the landing. She thinks it was an injury in training – like you wanted her to.'

'John asked me to tell a white lie,' Faith reminded her. 'It wasn't my idea, Lizzie. He said his mother would worry if she knew and that she was worried enough about Tom.'

Lizzie took a deep breath. 'We're just relieved he is alive, Faith. So, I'll come over on the train next Thursday and we'll have tea at the Copper Kettle, my treat. I know you nurses don't get much money.' The café wasn't that far from where Faith worked and lived and a lot of the nurses popped in for cakes and tea when they could afford it. The café was often frequented by university students, though their ranks were much depleted these days as so many had joined the armed forces.

'Dad makes sure I'm all right,' Faith said. 'They came over last week and brought me some nice biscuits and cakes Mum had made for me – and Dad gave me ten pounds.'

'Gosh, that was a good present,' Lizzie said. It often took her half a week to earn that much at the salon and by the time she'd paid wages, rent and electric, most weeks she didn't keep much more.

'Yes, I know. I told him ten pounds was too much but he insisted...' Faith sighed. 'I'm lucky. I think I am going to buy myself a new costume with a fur collar at Rose's Fashion Centre.'

'Oh, I love it there,' Lizzie agreed. 'I saw a lovely costume when I was there last month, but it was seven pounds and ten shillings and I couldn't afford it – but I might treat myself at Christmas.'

'Don't talk about that yet,' Faith groaned. 'There's another couple of months.' It was November and, after some milder weather at the beginning of the month, autumn had set in with a vengeance that very morning. 'Mum was asking if I'll get time off and I couldn't tell her – they haven't notified us yet. Besides, it's a long way to go just for a couple of nights...'

'Not that far on the train,' Lizzie chided. 'March has a really good train service. You're lucky. I have to catch the train in Sutton and they aren't as frequent as yours. Don't you want Christmas at home with your parents?'

'Not if I can see John here,' Faith laughed ruefully. 'It's hard juggling my free time, Lizzie. Mum was asking if I'd get time off for Christmas; she thinks I should go home every chance I get – but if I did, I'd never see John.'

Lizzie agreed and they chatted a bit longer, promising to meet the next week at the popular café in Cambridge.

13

Faith smiled as she went back to her room. It had been a surprise when she discovered that it was Lizzie waiting for her on the end of the phone; she'd assumed it would be her mother when she was told a woman wanted to speak to her

Life was getting better for Faith. She was beginning to feel more confident at work on the wards and now took temperatures easily and helped to change dressings and bathe patients who had to be carefully turned and patted dry after their wash, because they were too ill to get up and go to the bathroom. It was interesting and fulfilling work and she enjoyed talking to the patients who were recovering. As yet, she hadn't been told if or when she was being sent to the military hospital, but Sister Evans was pleased with her.

Working with the efficient but pleasant-mannered Sister Evans was so much better than being lectured all the time by Sister Reece. She took the time to explain in detail and Faith found it easy to follow her instructions – perhaps because she was no longer so nervous. Now she was doing what she'd wanted to do when she began at the hospital and enjoying it. She'd even administered a diabetic patient's insulin and taken blood from another. It was proper nursing and she loved it.

John was now out of hospital and kept asking her when she was being moved every time they spoke on the phone or met on her free afternoons when he also had leave. The men in the RAF were luckier than those in the army, because they were more often stationed in England and, although they risked their lives constantly in the air, had more time to visit friends and family than men sent to overseas bases.

The last time John had been with Faith, he'd held her very close and kissed her passionately several times. 'I want you so much,' he'd whispered against her ear. 'I wish we could marry sooner, Faith, but I know it isn't fair to you...'

'I don't think I'm allowed to get married yet... not if I want to keep on nursing,' Faith had told him. 'But we might...' Her courage had failed her as he'd looked down at her. She wanted to make love with him so much, but she was scared of the consequences if she fell for a baby. It was so frustrating when you were young, full of life and so much in love that you burned to be together in every way.

John had nodded, clearly understanding her natural reserve. 'We could, but we'd have to be careful,' he'd said and kissed her again. 'If you're sure, Faith – we might go somewhere for a couple of nights next time I get leave...'

It was a big jump forward. Faith's breath had caught in her throat but she let it expel gently. 'I think I should like that,' she'd said shyly. 'If you would...'

John's kiss had answered that one and she'd clung to him, hiding her face in his chest. She loved him so very much and longed to make love with him but was still a bit scared – Faith was torn by her need to be one with John and her nursing. She was at last getting on, achieving some of what she'd hoped for, and she wouldn't like to leave in disgrace – let alone what her mother would say. Her father would just look sad and disappointed and that might be worse than her mother's tears and recriminations.

Faith's stomach churned each time she thought about it and yet she wanted it to happen. John's brush with near-death had made her realise what she could lose if they never made love and he was killed. In these war-torn days, the fear that a loved one would never return was ever-present. Poor Lizzie had had to live with the idea that Tom might be dead and even now she had no idea how badly injured he was...

* * *

'Rocky and Slash are back on leave,' Janice told Faith when they met in the hospital that morning. 'I met them at the pub last evening – Slash asked about you, Faith, wanted to know if you were free to go to the pictures with him this evening?'

'I'm courting,' Faith said, though a little smile touched her mouth, because she'd liked the soldier when he'd walked her home earlier that year.

'I'll tell him,' Janice promised. 'He will be disappointed. I think he is quite keen on you, Faith.'

'He's nice and I like him, too,' Faith said, 'but I can't go out with him. I love John. We're going to get married one day.'

Janice shrugged. 'I think you should have fun. My boyfriend hasn't written to me in ages. I know he was home because I saw his mother. You can't trust any of them, Faith. Why should you be faithful – none of them are.'

Janice was hiding her tears. Faith felt sorry for her, but it didn't change her mind. Yes, she would have liked to go to the pictures with the good-looking soldier, but John wouldn't like it – and she did love him so very much, she really did. It was just boring spending most of her nights at home. Janice was always meeting men and having fun. Perhaps that was why her regular boyfriend hadn't bothered to contact her on his leave, Faith thought, but didn't say it aloud.

'We could go another night – to the pictures. You and me,' she said hopefully, but Janice laughed.

'I've got a lot of young men waiting to take me out,' she replied. 'I'm not sure when I can fit you in…'

Faith nodded and laughed, but felt a bit let down. She ought to make more friends and then she wouldn't spend as much time alone. It would be nice to meet Lizzie when she came over, but Lizzie was going to see friends in London this weekend. Faith was missing her family and friends at home and decided she would try to visit her parents as soon as she could. However, as she began work on the ward, her feeling of loneliness soon evaporated and she felt the inner satisfaction that nursing gave her.

Faith was surprised to see her uncle waiting for her when she left the hospital that evening. He was in his car and wearing a smart new uniform with three stripes on the arm and smiling at her in the way she remembered from her childhood so that she warmed to him.

'This is a nice surprise, Uncle Ralph,' she said as he leaned across and opened the car door for her. 'There's nothing wrong at home, is there?'

'Not as far as I know,' he replied. 'I've been given a few days leave, so I thought I would drive over and see how you were getting on.' His eyes studied her for a moment. 'You look tired. 'I hope they are not working you too hard...'

'The work is hard,' Faith said, 'but I enjoy it. The patients are so grateful for anything we do for them that it is a pleasure to do our job.'

Ralph nodded and a calculating expression entered his eyes, making her retreat mentally. She wondered what he was thinking, but then he was smiling at her again.

'How is that boyfriend of yours?'

'John had a bit of an accident and was in hospital with a broken ankle,' she said. 'He's better now and back at his base camp.'

Ralph nodded and again the look in his eyes made her uncomfortable. 'What about his elder brother?'

'You mean Tom Gilbert?' Faith was wary. Lizzie had mentioned that Tom didn't get on with her uncle when she was at the farm, just casually, but something had warned Faith that it was a serious quarrel. 'I think he may have been wounded, but I really don't know anything.' Faith thought that she wouldn't have told him even if she'd known all the details. 'Where are we going? This isn't the way to the nurses' home...'

'I thought I'd take you home for the evening. Your mother is cooking dinner and wants to see you.'

Faith hesitated. She didn't much like the way he'd just taken it for granted that she had nothing else to do, but it would be nice to go home for a short visit and a ride in a comfortable car would take half the time it needed to get on and off trains and then walk from the station.

'That's nice,' she said, settling back in her seat. 'I probably smell of carbolic, but I have clothes at home I can change into.' She looked at him as he concentrated on his driving. He was an attractive man and she'd always liked him as a child and a young girl, but in the past few months, she'd sensed a change in him and she wasn't sure she really liked or trusted him now. 'What are you doing now, Uncle Ralph? You joined up and Mum was most upset because she says you're not fit enough.'

'I'm only on light duties,' he told her with what she could only think of as a smirk on his face. 'I work in the officers' mess serving drinks. It is hardly work at all and I pick up a few tips – money as well as other things...' Again, the smirk that made him look like the Cheshire cat that had found the cream. 'Useful bits and pieces of knowledge. For instance, I've discovered how to get extra petrol coupons, which is why I was able to drive here today.'

Faith felt a cold shiver at her neck. Just why was her uncle looking so pleased with himself? Everyone knew there were petrol coupons to be had on the black market, but most people resisted the temptation out of patriotic duty. It had to be more than a few petrol coupons. She almost asked him what his other perks were but then decided against it. If he was doing something illegal, she didn't want to know...

* * *

'I don't know where you got that lovely joint of pork,' Faith's mother said as she kissed her brother's cheek, 'but it was certainly delicious with the apple sauce you brought.'

'And that was a seriously good wine,' Faith's father joined in. 'You must have good contacts, Ralph. I can't buy anything decent these days. I suppose it came from the black market?' He frowned, not quite approving, though he'd enjoyed the good wine.

'No, it didn't, as a matter of fact,' Ralph told him. 'The joint was a gift from a grateful officer whose wife is still running his farm – and the wine came from the officers' cellar. They have more than enough and will never miss it...'

'Do they know you help yourself?' Faith's father asked.

'Naturally,' Ralph replied. 'I wouldn't risk my job or a spell in the cooler for a bottle of wine. I was told I could take a couple of bottles – providing I didn't take the really good stuff. What we had is just their everyday wine.'

'They must have been kept in a good cellar before the war?'

'I imagine they bought all they could,' Ralph told him. 'I have some put by myself and I shall sell it at a considerable profit when I'm ready.'

'Got your finger on the pulse still,' Faith's mother said admiringly.

Faith looked at her father. He was trying to hide it, but she could sense his disgust and his dislike. She knew he would bite back the criticism he would like to make for her mother's sake, but it confirmed what she had sensed for a while. Uncle Ralph had been a bit of a chancer all his life – but she'd always seen him through rose-coloured glasses and thought his little fiddles amusing – now she was older, she saw things differently. Some people were making money from this war, profiting from the hardships and shortages – and she wouldn't mind betting her uncle was one of them.

He looked at her as they were driving back to Cambridge. 'You are very quiet, Faith. Something on your mind?'

'Did they really give you the wine?' she asked. 'Or did you just take it?'

'I was given it – for favours rendered,' he said. 'Don't you trust me, Faith?'

'I'm not sure,' she said honestly. 'Even that pork joint wasn't quite legal, was it? We shouldn't take advantage just because we can...'

'Don't go high and mighty on me,' her uncle warned. 'I'm a good friend, Faith – but I make a bad enemy. I shouldn't like us to be enemies.'

'I'm not your enemy,' she said. 'I just think it isn't fair to take advantage. The officer who gave you that pork – well, he was breaking the law. Just because he has a farm doesn't mean he can kill his own pigs and eat them or give the meat to friends.'

'They all do it on the quiet,' Ralph told her. 'Be realistic, Faith. In this world, you get what you go out and grab for yourself. Stand in line and you'll get trampled in the rush, by those who don't abide by the rules.'

'I suppose so,' she agreed, but let the discussion lapse. Just because others did it, that didn't make it right.

* * *

Ralph frowned as he dropped Faith outside her hostel just a few minutes before she would have been locked out for the night. 'Don't think too badly of me,' he said with one of his charming smiles. 'I only wanted to help...'

She nodded and thanked him and ran in before the door was locked, but she didn't turn round and wave at him before disappearing inside. She would always have done that before. Ralph felt a surge of anger. Was it John Talbot telling tales that had turned his niece against him? If he knew for sure, he'd make the young man sorry...

Driving away into the night, Ralph dwelled on the injustice of life. Faith thought him wrong to make the most of his situation, but why shouldn't he help himself when it was so easy to beat the system? The wine cellar belonged to one of the senior officers, who also happened to be a lord. He had openly admitted that he'd bought cases of fine wines before the conflict started so that he wouldn't go short during the war.

'God knows how many bottles I have,' he'd boasted when drunk in the mess one night. 'Damned good brandy this, though I say it myself. Know how much I've got of that – but the wine is another matter...'

Ralph had ignored the expensive brandy. It was too traceable and if the officer knew how much there should be, he would cause trouble if any of it went astray. Personally, Ralph preferred whisky anyway or a nice table wine. He'd got cases of the stuff stored away at his home in March, but he was waiting to sell when the shortages really began to bite. A bottle of the Major's wine was easy to obtain and very drinkable. Not that he often drank alone; he'd liberated that bottle to impress his sister – but clearly her husband and daughter didn't think the same way as she did.

Ralph had always tolerated his brother-in-law and he'd been fond of Faith, but if she'd turned against him, so be it. He'd never needed anyone. Whether he could ever truly love was debatable, though he was fond of his sister. He liked doing nice things for her and at least she'd appreciated the gesture.

Ralph had been trading on the black market for a while now, buying things for his officers and being given extras as rewards. The pork genuinely was a gift from a grateful officer.

So far, Ralph hadn't picked up any information that might be profitable in the mess, but he was certain it would happen – something he could use as blackmail when the time was right.

At least he was safe from the law. No one had come sniffing round or asking awkward questions and Ralph had begun to think that he'd got away with his crimes. If it was a crime to kill men who deserved to die... those slimy crooks had it coming. Just the way that bloody hero Tom Gilbert had it coming one day!

Trust him to be wounded but get out alive... the smarmy so-and-so! If he fell down a sewer, he'd come up smelling of roses.

Ralph scowled as his thoughts festered, dwelling on old scores. He might have to wait years for his chance, but he'd made up his mind. If Tom didn't get his comeuppance during the war, Ralph would make sure he didn't live long enough to celebrate his good fortune...

14

'How are you, Lizzie?' Vera asked when Lizzie visited that Sunday.

Evidence of the bombing had been everywhere as she took a bus from Liverpool Street Station, sending little tingles down Lizzie's spine. Holes in the middle of the road, broken glass and buildings with black scars from fires, as well as piles of rubble where the houses had been obliterated. Sandbags were piled up against windows to try to stop glass splintering and injuring people and there was a pall of smoke over some areas. She felt shocked and stunned. It was one thing to read about the Blitz safe in the country, another to see it with her own eyes, which filled with tears. She'd been so relieved to see Vera's house still standing, overwhelmed with emotion when she opened the door. Vera gave a whoop of delight.

'Give us a hug, Lizzie love. It's so good to see you.'

Lizzie put her arms around her tightly. For a few moments, they just held each other, finding comfort in the embrace.

'I'm really glad to see you.'

'Me too,' Lizzie told her. 'I've been worried about you here since all this started. Talking on the phone is all right, but it isn't like actually seeing each other...'

'I know. Come and have a cup of tea and we can talk.' Vera led the way inside. 'How are you – and Tina?'

'She is fine. I would have brought her but didn't think it was a good idea, at the moment.' Vera nodded her agreement. 'Your family – and Annie?'

'Annie is doing well and my husband is busy, harassed but as fit as a fiddle. I only wish Terry would improve. I can't get to see him as often as I'd like in that military hospital.' She sighed. 'Have you heard anything more about Tom?'

Lizzie shook her head. 'Not since they said he was alive. I haven't been told I can visit...'

'I know you were glad to get that news – but you must be worried about him?'

'I am,' Lizzie said. 'Of course, I am, Vera, but I was just so relieved that he wasn't dead. The first telegram said, "Missing believed dead"... it was awful not knowing.' Lizzie had suffered while Tom was missing, sometimes resenting the war that had taken him away, but seeing the destruction in the capital, she understood that this was what Tom and others like him were fighting for. It was only their sacrifice and that of the airmen who daily risked their lives that was stopping the enemy from walking in and taking over all their lives.

'I don't think they should put that sort of thing in a telegram,' Vera said, shaking her head. 'Why don't they just put missing and leave it at that unless they know for certain?'

Lizzie frowned, because she didn't know why they did it either. 'Someone in Sutton Village had a telegram like that and then a letter came a few weeks later to say he was confirmed dead.' A little shudder went through Lizzie. 'I suppose in the chaos of a battle it isn't always easy to know for certain.' She hesitated for a moment, then, 'Terry is no better, then? The last thing you told me was that he was being sent to a convalescent home somewhere to be fitted with his new leg and get used to it before he came home?' Terry's first home visit hadn't gone well, so this time they were making sure he was ready before sending him back.

'Yes,' Vera replied, looking sad. 'I think he's had it fitted and he's getting on with it all right – bit sore at times – but it isn't his leg I'm worried about, Lizzie. He still won't talk about his wife or Tina. I've asked him if he wants to see his daughter, but he says no and refuses to talk about it. I don't think he wants to come home.'

'Surely, they will refurbish his flat for him?' Lizzie said, puzzled. 'I know it was pretty badly burned when the gas explosion happened but repairable?'

'It has been done ages, but he won't go back there – says it is a deathtrap.' Vera shook her head. 'I can't say it's a mistake, Lizzie. He would always be haunted by what happened to Ellie. I've asked him if he wants to give it up and save paying the rent, but he wouldn't answer me.'

Terry's wife had died after there was a gas explosion and fire spread through the block of flats they'd been living in. The little girl – Tina – had miraculously survived, but it seemed that Terry still couldn't face up to what he'd lost.

'You can't blame him,' Lizzie said to Vera. 'He was badly wounded fighting soon after he joined up. After losing a leg while serving his country and then his wife dying in that terrible incident – well, he must be devastated.'

'Yes, and I feel sympathy for him,' Vera replied. 'He is my only son and I love him, but what about that little girl? She is being brought up by your family when she ought to be here with her own. He has a duty to her, Lizzie, and he has to accept it. We can't rely on your mother-in-law's kindness forever and, if I am going to look after her full-time, then Terry needs to be around to help. His father says there is still a job for him where he works. Terry won't be able to do all he could before the war, but even if he is in the office, he can still help with bits and pieces, he can earn money and provide for his family. He must understand that he has a daughter and needs to be responsible for her.'

'He used to work on the roof, didn't he?'

'He is a trained carpenter,' Vera said and sighed. 'He could still do a bit of that, though perhaps not everything – no heavy lifting or going up ladders.' She wiped a stray tear from her cheek. 'I don't know what he will do, Lizzie, if I'm honest. I'm worried that in his present state he will stick in that place and never leave it...'

'Surely, they will send him home?'

The hospitals and convalescent homes were overflowing with patients and, once Terry was fully mobile and able to cope, they were sure to discharge him, but that didn't mean he would be able to face up to his life.

'They probably will quite soon,' Vera said, 'but if he's too down, not right in his mind, he won't cope. I've tried talking to him, but he refuses to listen, to me or his father.'

Lizzie looked at her in silence for a moment. 'If he came to visit us at the farm, it might help. In London, he is bound to be reminded of all he lost – but in the country, he might feel more relaxed. He could get to know Tina gradually and there are always small jobs that need doing, light work that he could probably handle – mending fences, feeding the stock, milking – he might even manage the tractor once he gets used to his false leg... Just different surroundings for a time?'

'He might,' Vera agreed. 'If he would, the fresh air would do him a power of good, but I doubt he would come...'

* * *

The rest of Lizzie's visit seemed to fly by. She only managed a few hours before she had to catch her train back home. Vera hadn't talked much about her daughters, though she'd mentioned Annie was keen on a doctor at her new hospital.

'She's passed all her exams,' she'd told Lizzie. 'Now, she says she wants to be sent abroad to help nurse the wounded sooner. Annie has strong feelings about it. She thinks that more ought to be done when the men are first injured, so she has put in for a transfer to the front line, where she believes she can do more for them.'

'She is a brave girl,' Lizzie said. Nurses could get caught in crossfire when there was an attack and some had died.

'She knows it is dangerous but still wants to go,' Vera replied. 'I'd rather she didn't – but you can't control your children's lives...' A tear slid down her cheek as she hugged Lizzie goodbye. 'It was good to see you – you know I think of you as family.'

Lizzie smiled and hugged her back. Vera was her friend, but she did mother her if she got the chance and sometimes Lizzie thought she cared for her more than her own mother ever had. Lizzie's visits to her mother in March, where she lived with her friend, Mabel, were not always a success. If Maud Jackson was in a bad mood, she tended to take it out on her daughter, which was why Lizzie didn't visit every week, just once a fortnight. 'It was my lucky day when I came looking for a room here,' she told Vera as they parted at the front door that evening. 'You know you're always welcome to visit us – and to see Tina whenever you like.'

'Yes, I know, but I don't get much time.' Vera sighed. 'I feel guilty leaving her with you, Lizzie, but I know she's happy and Terry won't talk about her...'

'No need to feel guilty,' Lizzie replied. 'She has got her Auntie

Jeanie – who spoils her all the time – and perhaps Terry will come to realise that he does care about his daughter in time. Besides, everyone loves her. Susan and Angela play with her whenever they get the chance. We shall miss her when you do fetch her home.'

'One day,' Vera said wistfully and kissed Lizzie's cheek. 'Get off now, love, or you will miss your train – and there might be a raid again tonight. You don't want to get caught in it; you could be stuck in London for hours.'

Lizzie was thoughtful as she walked to the bus stop that would take her to the train station. Vera was missing so much time with her granddaughter, missing her sweet little ways and the look in her wide eyes when she learned to do something new. Tina enjoyed her life on the farm, petting kittens, calves and the pigs whenever she got a chance, and she liked nothing more than being allowed to wear her little wellingtons to go splashing through mud. If permitted, she would happily sit in the mud and make pies, smearing it over her face, hands and the dungarees that covered her proper clothes. She was, in fact, a little darling and the family would miss her if she went back to London, to her home. But for the moment, the threat of more air raids made London dangerous and so perhaps the child was better off with them for now. Yet there was a danger she would forget her own family if she never saw them.

It was sad that Terry wouldn't see his own child. Lizzie wondered if it might be a good idea to ask him to visit. It wouldn't be long now before the house Arthur was having built for Tom and Lizzie was ready and then she would move in there. That would leave her room empty at the farm and Terry could stay for a while, get to know his child in the peace and quiet of the country – in the place where Tina was happy. Perhaps more importantly, in a place where there were no memories to disturb him. He might then begin to recover from the grief of losing his wife – and, of course, his leg.

Lizzie couldn't begin to imagine what he must be going through. She'd suffered enough when Tom had been missing, but she'd had all her family and friends and her work. Terry was stuck in a convalescent hospital with little to look forward to. He must be concerned about his future. The building trade would be hard for him and he really needed to train for something less physical – though she didn't know what he would be comfortable doing.

It was sad. Lizzie sighed. She didn't yet know the extent of Tom's injuries. It wouldn't matter to her personally if he was scarred or maimed. She would just have to help Tom adjust to whatever life held in the future...

Shaking her head, she pushed the morbid thoughts away. Tom was alive and that was all that mattered to her.

'You must be terribly worried about him?' Faith said when they sat drinking coffee in the Copper Kettle café the afternoon that Lizzie got over for a visit the following week. 'I felt bad enough when John was hurt, but he was lucky. It could have been a lot worse.'

'Pam still doesn't know the truth about the accident,' Lizzie said. 'She's been so upset over Tom that I haven't mentioned it.'

'Well, he didn't want her to know,' Faith replied with a shrug. 'After all, he's over it now and back to work.'

Lizzie nodded and ate a forkful of the meltingly good coffee and walnut cake. 'This is delicious. If they made it with margarine, you can't taste it. You're lucky to have a place like this on your doorstep, Faith.'

'Yes, I know. A lot of the college students come here and so do the nurses.' Faith smiled. 'Cambridge is a nice place to work. I shall miss it when they transfer me.'

'Have you been told when you're going or where?' Lizzie asked.

'Next month,' Faith said. 'I was quite looking forward to having Christmas with John. We'd talked about what we might do if we both got leave – but it isn't likely to happen now. I'll be too far away to come home unless I get several days off work – and he might not get a long enough leave to visit March or the farm.' She sighed. 'It's going to mean a lot of travelling when we do meet – and it may be months before we get the chance...'

'Rotten luck,' Lizzie said. 'I suppose you couldn't ask to stay here?'

'It's a sort of honour to be picked,' Faith said. 'Matron told me I had the makings of a good nurse – so, no, I don't want to refuse the chance to go where I'm needed, Lizzie. I just want to do my bit for the war effort.' She fiddled with her napkin. 'It might be better in a way; it gets a bit intense sometimes. You know, not being really together...' Faith blushed, but Lizzie just nodded her understanding and she relaxed. It was the same for most young courting couples she supposed.

'I suppose your parents wouldn't want you to marry until you're a bit older?' Lizzie questioned.

'It would mean giving up the nursing...' Faith frowned. 'I want to be with John and yet I want to nurse, to do what I can to help – does that sound selfish to you?'

'No, it doesn't. I felt the same about coming back this way when I had a glamorous job in London. Of course, I had my salon to open and I'm too busy now to think about it – but it was exciting in London and sometimes I feel a pang of regret, but not often. Not when Tom is home... just when I'm a bit down, I suppose.' She smiled. 'It was fun and I had friends there – but it isn't really a regret. I am happy as I am. You can't have everything, Faith. You're still young, a lot younger than I was when I started courting Tom. Marriage is a forever thing. Perhaps it is better if you just enjoy life for a while and then you'll be ready to settle down after the war...'

'Yes. I know you're right. We'd agreed all that before John joined the RAF and then I came here – but...' She shook her head and sighed. 'It's just hard sometimes...'

'You mean when the kissing gets intense and you both want more but also don't?' Lizzie laughed. 'I do remember that – but Tom never went too far. I wasn't sure he even wanted to marry me for a long time. I suppose that's part of the reason why I went away for a while, though there were other reasons. They say absence makes the heart grow fonder. You'll work it out when you're ready, Faith.'

'Yes, I know.' She laughed and changed the subject. 'I do like that jumper you're wearing, Lizzie – did you make it?'

'I did some of the knitting. Pam helped me and she sewed it together. It's lovely and warm.' Lizzie smiled. 'Before you go off to your new posting, you should come and see us. I know Pam would love that.'

Pam had sent some home-made cakes and biscuits over for Faith because she thought perhaps she didn't get enough to eat at the nurses' home. The food at the Copper Kettle was brilliant, but Faith wouldn't be able to afford to eat out often on the wage she received as a probationer, although she would soon be through that stage and her work, life and finances would all improve.

'How did you get on with the exams you took the other day?' Lizzie asked.

'All right, I think,' Faith told her with a smile. 'I haven't had the results yet, but I found the questions easy enough and I know the practical went well – so, yes, I think I am getting on well.'

'That's good. It will be nice having a nurse in the family,' Lizzie said, eyes twinkling. 'You can patch us all up when we come in from the farm with cuts and bruises.'

'I'm not sure what I'll do after the war,' Faith responded. 'I shan't work in a hospital, but I might do district nursing. If I can get a job...'

'Surely they will give you one,' Lizzie replied. 'I think some hospitals are relaxing the rules for nurses who want to marry. Why waste all that training?'

'It makes more sense. I suppose it is to discourage young nurses from wasting their training – make them think twice before getting married and having a family.'

'Probably, but it isn't fair or right. Nursing should be like teaching – a job you can go back to when your family are grown.'

'Will you keep working when you have children?' Faith asked.

'Yes, of course,' Lizzie told her. 'We want a big family – but I'll keep the salon and employ girls and then I'll do part-time when the children are grown up... At least, that is the idea.' She sighed. 'To be honest, Faith, at the moment, all I want is to see Tom again.'

'Yes, I know.' Faith looked at her in sympathy. 'Being in love is wonderful, but it hurts too much sometimes.'

'Unfortunately, it does,' Lizzie agreed and looked thoughtful. 'I think Jeanie might be in love, though she says she doesn't have a boyfriend, but I've seen her drifting off at times and I'm certain there is a man somewhere.'

'Jeanie – that's your friend Vera's daughter who works for John's father, isn't it?'

'Yes, that's her,' Lizzie said. 'She's a lovely girl, but she's been a bit quiet recently. I'm not really sure why – unless she is worried about her family – or has a fancy man, though as she hardly ever goes anywhere on her own. I am not sure...' She chuckled. 'Oh, what tangled lives we do lead! Why can't everything be happy and the sun shine all day long?'

Faith laughed. 'Because this is real life, Lizzie, and it has a habit of biting you back.'

15

Jeanie finished mucking out the cowsheds and barrowed the last of it to the heap in the corner of the yard. It had grown considerably since they'd brought the cows into the sheds for the colder months but would soon be spread over the ploughed fields once it stopped raining, which it had seemed to do forever recently. It had stopped this morning, however, so the others were making the most of the break in the weather. Nancy and Artie had fetched a load earlier and she could just see them in the bottom field. They were standing there and appeared to be talking angrily, and as Jeanie watched, she saw Nancy slap Artie round the face.

Jeanie tucked back a wisp of her red hair and frowned. What would make Nancy do that to her boss's eldest son? It could only be that Artie had been coming on to her a little bit too much. Jeanie had seen the way he'd tried to flirt with the older girl and smiled inwardly at Nancy's rebuffs. She could have told him he wouldn't get anywhere with her, but if she'd spoken of what she suspected, the Talbots might have asked Nancy to leave. She thought they might disapprove so had kept her mouth shut.

Jeanie was fairly sure that Nancy was one of those women who preferred her own kind to men. She didn't know much about relationships between two women, but she knew that it happened.

Once or twice when she'd stripped off in the attic bedroom they shared, Jeanie had seen Nancy staring at her breasts and it made her uncomfortable when Nancy stared like that. She'd never felt that way with other woman and there were other things, odd remarks Nancy had made when they were working together that made her suspect that the older girl didn't like men – and she did like looking at women. Jeanie had ignored her remarks and nothing else had happened, but she was pretty sure she was right. If she'd given Nancy the slightest encouragement, she would have come on to her more, but she hadn't and wouldn't.

Since she'd been living on the farm and working manually, at nineteen years of age, Jeanie's figure had suddenly developed far more. She now had what was described as an hourglass shape, though she did her best to hide it under the loose slacks and jumpers that she wore for work. Jeanie seldom got dressed up these days, except when she went to church on a Sunday morning. Artie never saw her then, because he was always milking on her mornings off – and he didn't finish until after she got back and joined him in the sheds, once more dressed in her baggy clothes.

Jeanie didn't want Artie to pay her attention because she was afraid that if he did, she might fall for him and then her heart would be broken. He had such a wonderful smile, but she'd been at the farm long enough to know that Artie played the field with a lot of girls. She'd heard him teasing John and boasting of his own prowess, and though she thought a lot of it was just men's talk and foolish bragging, one thing Jeanie wasn't prepared to be was another notch on Artie Talbot's bedpost. She liked him a lot, laughed at his jokes and took his teasing with good humour, but she wasn't going to sleep with him and then be thrown over when the next girl came along.

Not that Artie had shown the least interest in dating her. She knew he'd asked Nancy to a dance and to the pictures; both invitations had been turned down with a scowl. Artie seemed to be fascinated with Nancy, perhaps because he imagined she was playing hard to get, when, in reality, she just wasn't interested.

Sighing, Jeanie took her empty barrow back to its place next to the cowsheds. She was finished here and it was time to return to the farmhouse for tea. It was getting dark now, even though the clocks had not gone back this year at the end of summer, and she had to pick her way carefully through the mud and bricks of the yard. They were going to put the clocks forward again in the spring and they would be two hours ahead of GMT then, because all the daylight possible was needed to help during the blackout. No lights were showing from the house, because of the risk of attack from enemy planes, and once inside the porch, she had to shut the outer door before she could enter the bright warm kitchen.

The war had seemed to drag on this year with very little going right for the Allies as the battle raged for the Atlantic in mid-ocean, and in the skies brave young men duelled to protect the lives of their countryfolk; and London suffered heavy bombing raids. Jeanie tried not to read the frightening headlines or listen to dire news reports on the radio of heavy bombing in cities all over the country, because it made her sick with worry for people she knew and loved: her family in London, her sister and her brother languishing in hospital, and everyone else too. She sometimes felt guilty because she was so much safer on the farm than those who worked in the factories and dockyards. However, Artie talked about it sometimes when they were working and she listened to him – perhaps because she liked the sound of his voice.

* * *

Pam greeted Jeanie with a smile of welcome as she went in. She was such a lovely person and Jeanie appreciated how lucky she'd been to get a place here. She'd heard from Nancy that it wasn't the same on every farm. Here, they were treated as part of the family and given the same food; that didn't always happen, according to the older girl. She'd told Jeanie that at her last place the farmer had tried to seduce her in the hay barn and when she held him off with a pitchfork, she'd had nothing but bread and dripping for a week. Jeanie didn't know whether to believe her or not.

'There's a letter for you on the shelf,' Pam told her as she went to the sink to wash her hands. 'I think it is your sister's writing...'

'A letter from Annie?' Jeanie's smile lit up her pretty face. 'Oh, that's lovely. She doesn't often have time to write. Mum was complaining about it the last time I rang her.'

'Well, now you can read your letter and then tell your mum what she says when you ring her this evening.'

'It's ever so good of you to let me ring Mum when I like,' Jeanie said. 'You're very kind to us, Pam.'

'You're a good girl and a hard worker,' Pam replied. 'Arthur hopes you'll settle in the country and stay on after the war. I told him you'll settle where your heart is.' Pam smiled at her. 'Have you heard from that lad you went out with for a while?'

'No – we weren't serious,' Jeanie said. 'I liked him but—' She stopped speaking as Artie came into the room. He looked so chastened that Jeanie forgot she was keeping a distance and smiled at him. Her smile was unconsciously warm and inviting. 'Have you finished spreading the field, Artie?' she asked. 'Where is Nancy?'

'Putting the tractor away,' he said and his hand went instinctively to the red mark on his cheek. Jeanie giggled as she remembered what she'd seen and his eyes narrowed. 'Something funny?' he demanded with a glare.

'Just my letter from Annie,' Jeanie replied, though she hadn't opened it yet and it was in her pocket. She saw Pam look at her enquiringly but shook her head. It wasn't Jeanie's place to tell tales. If Artie had been forcefully rejected by Nancy, that was his affair, not hers.

'Come and sit down the pair of you and eat your tea,' Pam said. 'Are you going out this evening, Artie?'

'I might,' he said. 'There's a dance on at the village hall in Sutton.'

'That's nice,' Pam said innocently. Then, in the same breath, 'Why don't you ask Jeanie if she will go with you? It's ages since she went anywhere, and she works as hard as any of you.'

Jeanie's startled gaze flew to Pam's face, but she was intent on slicing a crusty loaf and didn't look at either of them.

Artie glanced at Jeanie. 'Do you want to come?' he asked. 'It's not bad – more girls than men, of course, but I'll dance with you a couple of times.'

It was on the tip of Jeanie's tongue to refuse, but before she could say anything, Pam accepted for her.

'Of course, she will – and you will dance with her several times, Artie,' Pam said and gave him a straight look.

For a moment, there was defiance in his eyes, but then it disappeared. 'Naturally, I'll dance with her if I take her,' Artie said. He looked at Jeanie. 'It starts in an hour, so you'd better use the bathroom first.'

Jeanie picked up the warm cheese on toast Pam had given her

and started for the stairs. She munched as she went, frantically wondering what to wear. Meeting Susan on the stairs, she paused and told her where she was going.

'Why don't you come with us?' she asked.

'And cramp my brother's style? He'd have my guts for garters,' Susan said and giggled. 'I've got homework anyway – but you can borrow my red dress if you like?'

'That lovely new one you bought for your cousin's wedding in the summer?' Jeanie looked at her in gratitude. 'It might fit me...'

'I am sure it will. We're about the same size,' Susan said. 'Besides, I've only seen you in skirts and jumpers or what you're wearing now – I don't think you've got a pretty dress, have you?'

'Not one that fits me now,' Jeanie admitted. 'I was a bit plumper when I came, and those I have need alterations.'

'We could do them together another evening,' Susan suggested. 'Lizzie, Mum and me – we're all good with the needle and we'll help. You could get a length of material off the market in Ely and make a new one.'

'I might do that for Christmas,' Jeanie agreed. 'Thanks for lending me your dress, Susan. It's kind of you.'

'It's all right.' Susan shrugged. 'I like having you here – and I love Tina. You're both family to me now, Jeanie.'

Jeanie felt warmed as she ran upstairs to have the quickest bath in history and change into the red dress that Susan brought along the hall for her. It fitted perfectly and suited her even more than it did its rightful owner.

Annie's letter lay forgotten in her pocket as she tripped happily down the stairs to join Artie, who had washed at the kitchen sink and was now dressed in his best blazer and slacks. He looked smart and handsome and Jeanie's heart did a flip.

He nodded at her and a gleam in his eyes told her he'd noticed how the dress emphasised her figure. Artie usually treated her as another sister, but, perhaps for the first time, he'd seen her for the woman she had become.

'Nice dress,' he said. 'Come on. I don't want to be late. There will be a queue at the bar.'

Jeanie bit her lip. So much for him appreciating her looks. He was more interested in drinking with his mates than dancing with her!

As they went out to the car Mr Talbot allowed his son to use, Jeanie recalled the letter from Annie and wondered what had made her sister write to her. She would read it when she got home, but for the moment, she was just going to enjoy herself.

* * *

Annie was packing her suitcase that evening. It was all she had left to do before leaving for the Front. She'd been told that day that she was being sent overseas and that she would need light clothes.

'Your uniforms will, of course, be provided, Nurse Salmons,' the sister in charge of her ward told her. 'Don't forget that you may want your own clothes for when you have some free time – however little that may be.' She'd smiled brightly. 'You are a brave girl to volunteer for duty at the Front and I applaud you. Someone has to go and the girls who volunteer risk many things – illness and death are not beyond possibility. You do realise that you will be battling very unpleasant fevers out there, as well as tending wounds that will probably be worse than anything you've seen here. You may well contract one yourself.'

'Yes, Sister Marsh,' Annie had said seriously. 'I do understand and I still want to go.'

'There are six of you and Doctor Endersby. I believe you have worked with him several times over the last few months?'

'Yes, Sister Marsh.' Annie had hoped she wasn't blushing. The eminent doctor wouldn't have noticed her, but she'd watched him from afar since her days as a probationer. When she'd been sent to the military hospital, he'd been one of the doctors who split their time between his former hospital and the military establishment Annie had been working in. She'd been in the operating theatre with him several times and her admiration for his work had built to a kind of hero worship. Now she would be working with him in the field hospitals, where his skill would be invaluable. 'It is wonderful that he has chosen to go out there, too.'

'We shall certainly miss him here, but he believes he can make a difference out there, so we have to accept the loss. Go along then, nurse – and good luck.'

Annie had been given the day off. She'd spent it shopping for the kind of clothes she would need in a hot climate and writing letters to her mother and her brother. She'd recently written to her sister, so she would just send Jeanie a short note to tell her she was being sent abroad, but she wanted to write longer letters to her parents and to her brother, Terry.

Annie knew that her brother was suffering terribly, not just physical pain but of the heart. His grief for his wife was hindering his recovery. She'd put off writing to him for a long time because she wasn't sure what to say – but now she had to write. It was possible that she might not return and she had something to say to him – something that he might not like but needed to know.

Ellie had been cheating on him. Annie had seen her with another man twice when she was on her way home from work. They'd been laughing and they hadn't seen her – but she'd seen them stop and kiss. Terry ought to know that, even if it made him angry. Perhaps then he could begin to forget the woman he had lost – but he might never forgive Annie for telling him and it would be a hard letter to write. Yet she knew she must do it. She had waited for him to recover from his debilitating wounds, but now might be her last chance.

So, she'd written the unforgivable words. Annie wished her mother was closer so that she could ask her if it was the right thing to do, but she was in London and Annie hadn't been given leave. It didn't seem right to make such accusations on the phone either. She had had to write her letters and pray that she was doing the best thing.

'I just want you to be happy, Terry,' she whispered as she went out and posted her letter. Perhaps if he knew the truth about Ellie, he would cease mourning her and begin to live again.

Annie thought about her sister Jeanie too. She thought she was happy living on the farm and at least she was with friends. Annie sometimes missed the companionship she'd shared with her family and with Lizzie in London – but what she was doing was important. It had always been her wish to be a nurse and she was dedicated to it – as dedicated as the doctor she admired from afar. She was happy that they would be working together and helping the men who really needed it.

* * *

Jeanie lay in bed later that night and thought about the dance. It had been fun. All the local men had wanted to dance with her, including three in uniform who were home on leave. Artie had only managed three dances with her and she'd seen him frowning as he watched the men line up to ask her to be their partner.

'Mum told me to look after you,' he'd said when they did dance. 'You want to be careful of that Ernie Fawks. He's a flirt – he'll have your knickers off before you know where you are if you go outside with him.'

'But I shan't,' Jeanie had said and gave him her brightest smile. Ernie Fawks was a nice, shy man – so could Artie be a bit jealous? She hoped so because it would do him good. 'I know you want to dance with other girls, Artie, so I'll dance with anyone that asks – but I'm not easy and I shan't go outside with any of them.'

'Even me?' Artie had said and grinned wickedly.

'Especially you!' she had retorted. 'I'm not going to be another notch on your bedpost, Artie Talbot!'

'I wouldn't do that to you, Jeanie,' Artie had said. 'You're family – almost like my sister.'

'But I'm not your sister, am I?' Jeanie had given him a naughty smile and went off to dance with her next partner, leaving Artie glaring after her. She hadn't told him yet, but Ernie Fawks had said the same thing about him. They had a bit of rivalry going on and were probably vying to see who could get the most girls or something. Both were in their twenty-first year and would have been serving in the army if they hadn't been needed for land work.

She'd laughed a lot as she had danced with Wally Fitch, who was a year or two older. He was in the navy and a big handsome man, taller than Artie and broader too. He had a good sense of humour and she'd liked him.

Jeanie was attracted to Artie and felt it could easily be more if given a chance, but she knew he was only interested in her that evening because other men were. If she let herself like him too much, she would get hurt.

No, she had to give Artie a little of his own medicine. Make him realise he couldn't just snap his fingers and have her come running like all his other girls.

Jeanie sighed as she read Annie's letter. She was hoping to be sent abroad soon. She enjoyed her work – and she was still in awe of the same doctor. Jeanie thought her sister was in love with him but wouldn't admit it, even to herself.

Jeanie put the letter away and turned over, burying her face in the pillows. She'd enjoyed her evening but knew she would have to be on her guard with Artie in future. She could easily get to like him too much and he was such a flirt!

16

The pain was easier to bear now, but the memories had become clearer, haunting him with his failure. His first real test as team leader and he'd led the men into a trap. Tom knew that several of them had been killed. If his friend hadn't acted swiftly, applying a tourniquet to his wound, he might have died too. Shorty had got him away, but from what he'd seen and what Tom remembered, they were possibly the only two to survive a mission that had probably been doomed from the start. Shorty didn't know what had happened to Jenks and Tom recalled that he'd been reluctant to go that time. Maybe he'd sensed the disaster. It was a bitter pill to swallow and Tom had plenty of time to dwell on it.

It had been bad enough on the hospital ship coming back, but at least he'd had Shorty's company. He'd thanked him for saving his life, but his friend had just grinned. When they'd reached the shores of Britain, Shorty had to leave to report back to base. Their commanding officer would need to know what had happened, why the mission had failed, and Shorty would have to face a stern debriefing. God knows what Captain Morris would have to say. Tom had let him and everyone else down and he was ashamed.

The memory of the chaos that had ensued after they walked into the ambush and the realisation that he'd led his men – men that were relying on him – into a trap was heavy on his conscience.

'How are you this morning, Sergeant?' the nurse's voice and sweet smile broke into his tortured thoughts and he looked up at her.

'Better, I think,' he replied. 'When do I get out of here, nurse?'

'When you've healed enough to walk,' she told him. 'Why the hurry? You deserve a nice rest, Sergeant Gilbert. I think you men are so brave. If it was me, I'd be glad to stay in a nice comfortable bed for as long as I could – but you are all itching to get back out there before you're ready.'

'We have a job to do and it isn't done yet,' Tom told her. 'It isn't that I don't appreciate what you've done for me. I just feel wrong lying around all day now that the pain is easing.'

The worst of his injuries had been a deep cut on his left leg where a piece of flying shrapnel had cut it to the bone. It had bled a great deal and might have done for him if Shorty hadn't acted swiftly. He knew he was lucky to be here.

'How about I help you walk for a while?' the nurse offered. 'You need to exercise that leg, to keep it from getting stiff – and stop you losing muscle. The wound to your arm healed well, as did the head injury, but your leg is taking longer. Once you can walk out to the corridor and then down to the day room unaided, I think Doctor will let you go home. I believe you will still need to rest for a while, but at least you won't be stuck in hospital.'

'Great!' Tom's spirits lifted. 'If he could just get home to Lizzie and the farm, he might be able to stop the bad dreams haunting him day and night...

* * *

Tom was in the military hospital in Portsmouth, in the day room when a nurse he didn't know wheeled a patient in; the poor devil had lost a leg and bore a few other scars. Tom's own facial scarring was minimal and the temporary blindness had gone completely now. He'd had blurry sight for a while as he recovered, but it was more or less back to normal. The doctors had been pleased about that. Tom was relieved. He thought it was one of the worst things that could happen, to lose your sight. Blindness robbed you of so much that was good.

'Hi,' he said as the nurse left the wounded soldier and returned to her duties. 'Fancy a game of something? They provide us with cards, snakes and ladders, dominoes and puzzles or books – there's the pool table over there, if you play?'

'I don't,' the soldier replied, hesitated, then, 'I'm Terry Salmons. You're Tom Gilbert, aren't you? I think I've seen you before – not here, in London just before the war?'

'Yes, I am, but I'm sorry. I don't remember,' Tom said. 'Did we meet in the army?'

'No, we haven't met. My mother showed me a photo of you and Lizzie Jackson. And I saw you leaving my parents' house once, I think.'

'Ah, that's it then. You're Vera's son. Lizzie often speaks of your family,' Tom said and nodded. It was a coincidence and yet it wasn't that much of a surprise they should meet one day; they were both in the army and this was a military hospital. 'Sorry about what happened to you. You've had a bad time. Must have been rough out there?'

'It was a shambles,' Terry said. 'We had to retreat. They were too bloody strong for us – and we kept running out of things. I reckon the enemy have got more money than us and were better prepared.'

'I think you may be right,' Tom agreed. 'Are you getting on all right now?' He didn't particularly want to talk about the war because he couldn't tell anyone about his activities; they were supposed to be secret, though he sometime wondered how much leaked out. Some of the nurses and doctors seemed to know what he did, though perhaps they just thought they did.

'Bloody leg hurts as though it was still there. I've got a false one, but it takes a while to get used to it, so I use the chair some of the time,' Terry Salmons muttered and Tom nodded. He'd heard other amputee patients say the same thing. 'Have you got a cigarette?'

'Yes.' Tom took the packet from his dressing gown pocket and offered it. 'Your sister is getting on well on the farm. Lizzie often tells me how much Jeanie enjoys her job. She tells me about your lovely little girl, too. You're lucky to have her. Lizzie and I want children one day.' He lit a match and Terry drew on his cigarette inhaling deeply.

'Thanks for this...' He looked at the cigarette. 'They wouldn't let me have one on the ward – said it upset the patients with lung problems. Some of them cough all night... Bloody war...'

'Yes, bugger, isn't it? I've just heard that I may be going home in a few days,' Tom remarked. 'If you want somewhere to relax for a while, come and stay with us. Mum would put you up and so could we – our house is just about finished. The wheelchair would be fine in the house and the yard, but you'll need to use your crutches to get about on the land until you find it easier with the false one. It's up to you. You would be able to see your sister and your daughter. It's not the Ritz, but we make people welcome.'

Terry stared at him in silence for a few seconds and then inclined his head. 'Why not?' he said at last. 'Thanks, Tom. Yes, I might come for a few days before I go back to London. I'm not looking forward to that much...'

'I know what you mean. Lizzie told me that you'd lost your wife...' Tom looked awkwardly at him. 'It must be hard for you. You've had a bad deal, mate. Words don't help much I know, but if there is anything in the practical sense I can do?'

'I'll give you a game of cards,' Terry said, clearly not wanting to speak of his loss. 'Do you play gin rummy – or whist?'

'Either.' Tom grinned at him. 'I don't have any money on me – but we'll play for pennies and IOUs if you like?'

'Why not?' For the first time, Terry really smiled with his eyes. 'I play a mean hand of gin rummy...'

17

Back in the ward later that afternoon, Terry reflected on the strangeness of life. He'd received a letter from Lizzie Gilbert only that morning and it had annoyed him. Who the hell did she think she was? Telling him he could come and stay if he would like to see his daughter, telling him how sweet and pretty she was – just like the wife he'd lost... He would have ignored the invitation, but meeting Tom had changed his mind. He wasn't sure why – but, when he thought about it, the reason he'd been so angry wasn't really Lizzie's letter. It was the other letter – the one from his sister.

According to Annie's letter, he'd been in danger of losing Ellie to another man before the accident that killed her. Terry wasn't sure which hurt the most – and he was furious with his sister. What did she think she was doing making up lies about Ellie? They had to be lies, surely? Ellie would never have done that to him – would she?

He groaned as he felt the pain in his missing leg wash over him. Why did it still hurt when they'd amputated it months ago? The stump was continually sore and wearing the prosthetic leg hurt him like hell. The nurses and doctors kept nagging him to try wearing it, but what did they know? They couldn't feel his pain or his grief. How could they understand the hopelessness inside him? His world was in ruins. His mother kept saying he had to think of his daughter, but every time he did, the grief over Ellie came rushing back. Terry had been given a double blow and he didn't know if he could live with his loss.

It wasn't supposed to be like this! He'd volunteered because he'd thought it was his duty. Every able-bodied man in the country had to fight if they were to defeat an enemy that seemed to have more of everything than his army did. More weapons, more men, more ammunition. They'd run short of ammunition the day Terry had been hit by a sniper's bullets. He'd been sent to fetch more and a machine gun had cut him down. He'd been lucky to survive it, so they said, but Terry didn't feel lucky. He wished he was dead like Ellie, then he wouldn't feel anything.

Damn the war that had taken his leg! Yet it wasn't the war that had killed his wife. It was a faulty gas cooker that someone had neglected to report. He moaned aloud and a nurse came to the bed, looking at him anxiously.

'Are you in a lot of pain, Private Salmons?' she inquired gently.

He hesitated, then shook his head. The physical pain wasn't always there now, it just came in waves and then went. It was the grief of losing the woman he loved and yet... Terry closed his eyes as he vaguely recalled her running out of the hospital ward after giving a cry of horror. Perhaps he'd already lost her before the gas explosion. Perhaps it was his injury that had made her look for another man. Tears stung behind his eyes, but he blinked them away. He was going to fight the physical pain and he would fight his grief too.

'Not too bad, nurse,' he admitted. 'I was just thinking...'

She looked at him with sympathy. 'Would you like to go out in the gardens for a while? I could take you even if it is cold. The fresh air might do you good?'

Terry hesitated and then looked at her. 'Are my scars disgusting, nurse? You don't seem to notice them – but perhaps you're used to seeing them?'

'What nonsense is this? You've got a deep scar here, as you know...' She touched her right cheek and then her forehead. 'But they are nothing like some of the men have – it's just the leg that is causing concern. I think the doctors may operate yet again to try to make it more comfortable so you can walk – better than being in a wheelchair all the time, isn't it?'

'I suppose so...' He sighed. 'We haven't spoken before – what is your name please?'

'I am Christine – or Chris, that's what my friends call me.'

'Thanks. I'm Terry.' He managed a smile. 'I think I should like to go for a walk –well, you walking and me in the chair. If you can spare the time.'

'Yes, I can,' she told him. 'That's why I'm here, Terry. I'll take you for a walk and then it will be time for supper.'

Perhaps the best way to start finding his way back to a life he could bear was by accepting the invitation to stay at Blackberry Farm with Tom and his family. Terry wasn't sure how he felt about seeing his daughter, but he would *try* to care about her, though, at the moment, he could barely recall what she looked like.

18

'I can't believe this is the last time I'll get to see you without having to travel miles on the train,' John groaned as he held Faith close that afternoon in the park. 'I was lucky to get this time off – I'm going to miss you like hell, Faith.'

'I'll miss you too,' she admitted and reached up to kiss him, blushing as she saw a passer-by giving them a disapproving look. 'I wish we could go somewhere private, but there just isn't anywhere...'

John hesitated, then, 'There is if you really want to go...'

'What do you mean?' Faith stared at him in surprise. They usually bought tickets for the cinema for a kiss and cuddle in the back seats, but they'd wanted to talk so had headed for the park instead and found a seat on a bench. John's ankle had recovered from his accident, but it still ached a bit if he walked any distance. Had he been in the army instead of the air force, it might have hampered him.

'A friend of mine has a house in Cambridge. He lent me his key...'

'He lives there?'

'No...' John made a wry face. 'He let it out to a mate when he joined the RAF – but then his friend was called up too and now they both use it when they get leave. He says no one is using it this weekend. We should be alone there, Faith...'

Her spine tingled as he looked deep into her eyes and she felt a frisson of something delicious down her spine. Suddenly, all her fears and doubts vanished and she knew what she wanted. 'Why are we wasting time here then?' she asked and stood up, offering her hand. 'I want to be with you, John. We have to be careful because I need to go on with my nursing, but—'

He nodded. 'I know and we will be careful, Faith. I don't want you to get into trouble. I love you too much – but if it did happen, you know I'd marry you, don't you?'

'Of course I do – but...' She sighed, looking up at him earnestly, 'Don't let's spoil it worrying. We might not have a chance like this for months... even years...'

* * *

The house was a small, terraced building, tucked away from the centre of the university town. It was situated in a street at the back of the busy Mill Road and there were a lot of similar properties in the area, many of them let to students in normal times, but these were not normal times. In the middle of a war, this ancient seat of learning had seen its advanced students disappear into the armed forces as the men – and young women too – joined either the fighting force of their choice or the women's equivalent. Young women were driving the ambulances, staff cars and working in vehicle maintenance, as well as lots of administrative jobs, leaving the men to swell the numbers fighting for their country overseas.

Inside, the house was rather dull with what looked like worn second-hand furniture and had a bit of a musty smell from being shut up a lot of the time. Sometimes no one lived in it for months and it needed some furniture polish to make it smell lived in and fresher.

John looked round with a rueful grimace. 'Sorry, Faith. I thought it would be better than this... If I'd known, I'd have spruced it up with some flowers or something.' His hand reached for hers. 'Would you rather we went to a hotel somewhere?'

'No – that's a bit furtive, isn't it? Having to pretend to be married.' She smiled at him, curling her fingers through his. 'I'm not bothered about the furniture, John. I came here to be with you. Let's explore upstairs.'

The bedrooms were nicer than the sitting room. The bedcovers looked bright and fresh and one room actually smelled of something that might have been lavender. Faith thought this room looked as if it had been furnished for a girl and she felt more at home in it and sat down on the bed.

'We can sleep here,' she said and smiled at him. 'Is the wardrobe empty?'

John opened the door, revealing a row of satin hangers but no clothes. It was clear where the pleasant smell came from; the hangers were perfumed with lavender and Faith was sure a woman must stay here sometimes.

She put her suitcase on the bed and unpacked, using the scented wardrobe. John had his kitbag and he took out his sponge bag and a clean shirt.

'We'll go out for dinner,' he said, 'and then come back. We can stay for a couple of nights – if you still want to...'

'Yes, I do,' Faith said and turned, going into his arms and kissing him. 'I've thought about this quite a bit, John. Before I left home, I wasn't ready, but I've grown up a lot since I've been nursing and I want us to have this time together.' It might be the only time they would ever have like this and Faith didn't want to waste her chance. 'I do love you very much, John.'

'It isn't what I'd planned for our honeymoon...'

'We'll still have that and the wedding our parents will expect,' Faith said. 'All that stuff is really for family and friends, isn't it? Being together is what counts for us – don't you think?'

'Oh, Faith, I do love you so much, but you know that...' John's arms closed about her and he nuzzled her neck.

After that, it all happened naturally. First, they were kissing with a deep hunger that had been building up for months. They'd held it inside out of respect for each other and their families, but now it came flowing out and what happened next just happened. Neither of them could have stopped it. Kissing became touching and stroking and then they were stripping off their clothes, laughing as buttons went flying in their sudden haste, and then they were lying on the bed, which smelled of the same lavender perfume, the sheets laundered and clean.

John's caresses drove all the remaining doubts from Faith's mind and she gave herself to him without reserve, crying out in pleasure as their love moved swiftly to a crescendo. Too soon for either of them, but neither was experienced and they laughed as John kissed her and promised better things to come.

'Sorry,' he said. 'You may not believe this – but it was the first time for me too...'

'I'm glad,' she said and hugged him. 'We'll learn together, dearest John, and it will be fun.'

After that, they just held each other for a while and then, when they were ready and got up, John discovered how to make the geyser in the bathroom work while Faith made a pot of tea. When the water was hot, they had a bath together, ignoring the water rationing for once and laughing and touching, splashing a lot of water on the lino as they experimented and discovered new ways of making love and pleasing each other. It was all so new and exciting that their surroundings were no longer important. Had it been a palace, they couldn't have been happier than they were that afternoon.

The water was nearly cold by the time they got out, but everything seemed fun. They were so joyous together, so right for each other and so much in love that it was all fresh, enticing and wonderful. Faith couldn't stop laughing and John looked like the cat that had got the cream. She told him so and he tickled her until she begged for mercy. When they were eventually ready, towelled dry, dressed and satiated, they locked the house and went out for a meal in a nice intimate restaurant back in the centre of town.

It was so good to be young and in love. They were more together now than they'd ever been and Faith didn't regret her decision for one second. She'd thought it would be good, but it was better than she could have imagined. They were so in tune in everything they did, laughing freely now that all the barriers were down. As they ate food that had never tasted better, though it was basic fare that was all that was available these days and not particularly well cooked, they held hands and watched other young couples. Several of them were in uniforms and not just the men, the girls too were clearly in the WRACS or the WRENS.

After their meal, they walked back to their temporary abode. John saw a flower shop on the way and purchased a big bunch of huge dark crimson chrysanthemums, Christmas flowers, Faith thought.

'They'll cheer the place up a bit,' he told her and smiled.

'They are beautiful, thank you.'

'You're beautiful,' John said and bent his head to kiss her softly. 'I love you more than I know how to tell you, Faith. I want to spend the rest of my life with you.'

'I feel the same,' she said and hugged his arm. 'It's all right, John. We've got years and years to do all the things you wanted to do... but if...' She reached up on tiptoe and kissed him. 'If anything should happen to either of us, we've had this time and I'm glad...'

'Yes, me too,' he said. 'Come on, let's not waste a moment of it...'

* * *

And they didn't, packing as much as they could into the next two days, which was all they would have together until they both got a long enough leave to make it possible to meet again.

John had been given more leave than Faith and he saw her off on her train, promising to write once she sent him her address and to visit as soon as he could. He held her pressed tight against him until the last minute and then reluctantly let her board her train.

'Take care of yourself, my darling,' he whispered against her ear. 'I wish we didn't have to part ever again...'

'So do I,' Faith replied huskily and her eyes filled with tears, but she broke away from him and got on the train quickly. Even if she gave up her job so that they could marry, it would just mean waiting at home for him to return for a few hours. It was hard leaving him. Harder than it had been before they'd spent those perfect days together, because she hadn't known how good it could feel to lie next to someone in bed and feel their warmth. Their lovemaking had just got sweeter and sweeter and she knew she would miss it – miss the smell of him, the laughter and the loving. She was a passionate young woman, something she hadn't acknowledged until now, and the physical side of love was important to her.

As the train taking her towards her destination in Portsmouth left the station far behind and she could no longer see John waving at her, Faith settled down to think about her life. She had no doubt that John Talbot was the right man for her and she did wish they could still be together, but while there was a war on, they were both needed in their various ways.

Faith knew that her work was important. John was fighting for the right to live in peace and she was providing a very necessary service by helping to nurse men like him, brave men who had been wounded and were suffering from terrible injuries. If she'd got married and given up her job, she would have felt she was letting down the people that needed her – besides, it wouldn't really be much different. They would still have had to part.

No, this was best, she decided, even though her parents would be shocked if they knew. Faith crossed her fingers. She prayed nothing unwanted would come from her few days of love. A baby wasn't on the cards for her yet – and her mother would hit the roof if it happened. John had tried to be careful, but she knew it might have happened. Faith just had to hope it didn't ruin her plans...

* * *

John still had a couple of days left of his leave. He could have gone down to Portsmouth with Faith, but she'd said it was best not as she had to report for duty and would be sleeping in the nurses' home, so he'd decided to go home to his parents.

His mother was delighted. She was preparing for Christmas and the big kitchen smelled of cooking as the puddings were steamed; not as rich in fruit this year, she'd added more brandy from Arthur's store. He hadn't hesitated to stock up and had several cases of wine and spirits bought before the start of the war up in the loft. Pam had discovered recently that he'd bought some tinned fruit and salmon, too, without telling her.

'Well, I thought they might come in handy,' he'd said as he handed her a big tin of peaches. 'You'll want something nice when the boys come home on leave.'

Arthur was right, of course, and she couldn't be cross with him. Besides, he wasn't the only one. Pam knew that several of her friends had done the same. One admitted that they had enough tinned food to last for three years in their attic.

The puddings Pam had made would be stored on the big pantry shelves, along with the hams from the pig they'd killed – one that Arthur hadn't declared to the ministry – but a nice leg of pork was eaten for dinner that day in honour of John's visit. Pam had rolled her eyes at Arthur when he'd brought the butchered pig home for her to cook and salt, but he'd shrugged his shoulders.

'I know I'd get into trouble if they caught me,' he told her when they sat down to a lovely roast for lunch. 'But we've got to have a few perks now and then, love. I'll give a few bits to friends I know I can trust. It isn't just for us...'

Pam shook her head at him. 'As long as you don't sell any of it – that butcher who was caught selling under the counter meat off ration went to prison.'

'Dad didn't do it for profit, he did it for us,' John said and smiled as she nodded. 'I shan't say no to a lovely roast pork dinner – and you've spoiled me with Christmas pudding, Mum.'

'You might not be here for Christmas,' she said. 'You could be on duty – or visiting Faith. Did she get off all right, love?'

'Yes, I saw her off on the train,' John replied carefully and hoped his mother wouldn't ask too many questions. She didn't, but his brother Artie had a lot more to say when they were alone on the way to the pub that evening.

'Had a good time with your girl, did you?' Artie asked with a sly look.

'Yes, thanks. We made the most of our leave – went to the pictures, dancing and dinner...'

'I'll bet that's not all you did either...' Artie jested. 'Made a man of you, has she?'

John squirmed inside. He didn't like the tone of his brother's questions and decided to lie. 'We're waiting for marriage,' he told Artie, to protect Faith's reputation as much as anything. 'I love her and respect her.' And he wasn't going to discuss his love life with his brother anyway.

'Pull the other one,' Artie taunted. 'I can see the difference in you, lad. About time too, if you ask me. I thought I might have to introduce you to a few of the right sort of girls – but you fly boys know how to go on. If it wasn't Faith, it was someone else, right?'

'Mind your own business,' John said. 'I don't spread it around the way you do... and Mum wouldn't like it if she knew the way you carry on...'

'I take what I can get,' Artie told him. 'If they're easy, why not? I don't want to get married for a few years, but that doesn't stop me having a bit of fun.'

'What if something happens?' John asked. 'Are you going to marry the girl?'

'Which one?' Artie said and grinned. 'I play the field, little brother. I don't have a regular girl – haven't found one I like enough.'

'I thought you liked Janet Baker?' Artie had taken a friend's daughter to a dance the previous year.

'I do – but she's only a kid,' Artie said. 'All wrapped up in her ambition to be someone. I take her out occasionally, that's all. Besides, she's the marrying kind and I don't want to get married for years. Once you have kids, it's the finish – all downhill after that – just work and the same old faces until you're dead.'

'I want the same face beside me in bed every morning when I wake up,' John said and the look on his face might have given away more than he intended. 'I know that I'll be happy to marry when the time is right.'

'Lucky you...' Artie sounded wistful rather than mocking now. Something flickered in his eyes and John wondered if perhaps there might be someone Artie liked a lot but perhaps couldn't have. 'You've always known what you wanted... building rather than the farm. I never got the choice. Dad expected me to work with him, so I did, but I need a bit of fun – some time to enjoy life away from the land. Maybe one day I'll meet a girl who will make me feel the way yours does and I'll be ready to settle down.'

Artie lapsed into silence and John was thoughtful. He'd taken it for granted that Artie enjoyed his work. Why hadn't he gone off to the army and let Tom stay home if he didn't? Tom loved the land. He loved Lizzie. Yes, he'd volunteered for the army, but he'd given Artie the choice. A spell in the forces might have been just what Artie needed to break the monotony of his life by the sound of it.

John's thoughts moved to his eldest brother. Tom had been badly wounded in action. John must ask Lizzie how Tom was getting on when he got the chance; she'd smiled at him, but they hadn't talked privately and John wanted to give her a message for his brother when he got home. Just that he was glad he was OK and that he cared.

19

'So, they're releasing us both this weekend,' Tom said when he met Terry in the day room a week or so after their first meeting. Terry was using his crutches instead of a wheelchair and seemed to be getting on well with them. 'Just a few more days and we can leave this place. I'm getting a lift home in a car – come with me if you like? I know Ma will be pleased to meet you and you'll get to see your sister and the little girl. Lizzie says she's a proper darling...'

'Yes, I'd like to come, if you're sure it's no trouble,' Terry agreed. 'Your mother must be run off her feet with half my family there as well as her own?'

'Ma loves it,' Tom said and laughed. 'She cooks enough to feed the forces and there's always room for another at her table. We're lucky with the farm, always some game to be shot and cooked when the meat ration runs out. I pity the poor devils in town if all they get is their rations.'

'Mum says it is the fresh eggs she misses most, but it must be hard for all civilians, at the moment,' Terry agreed. 'I expect you keep chickens, probably ducks too?'

'Yes, the eggs are Ma's, to sell or use as she chooses – and she loves the bantams Dad bought her before the war; they give her lots of eggs, so she tells me.' He smiled. 'Dad might have bought a few geese just before the war – probably got one or two more than he declared.'

'I wouldn't mind betting most farmers do that.' Terry nodded and grinned. 'You sound as if you've got a lovely family, Tom. I can't complain about mine either but—' He sighed deeply. 'I just don't feel like going home yet. I can't face the idea that Ellie isn't around, and it will be so much harder in London than in a different location.'

'I can't even imagine what I'd feel like if I lost Lizzie now,' Tom said. 'It was hard enough when we split up for a while – but if I knew I could never see her again...' He looked at Terry with sympathy. It was traumatic to lose a limb, but to lose your wife while you were lying in hospital, unable even to attend the funeral, was devastating. 'What you need, mate, is some good country air.'

'Yes, I'm looking forward to it. I've hardly ever been to the country, always been a town boy – but I think I'll enjoy the change.'

Tom thought about his home. He'd never wanted to do anything but work on the farm. There was something about getting up at first light and looking out over the land you worked, watching the mist lift and the sunlight break through, a feeling of belonging, of being where he wanted to be. He'd never felt it anywhere else. The men he'd fought with were mates and Shorty was a true friend, but for Tom, home was best. He wanted to get on and he'd got plans for after the war, but he could never see himself preferring to live in town. Maybe Terry would hate being in the country, but if he did, it might make him realise that he wanted to go home...

* * *

Lizzie opened her greetings telegram at breakfast that Tuesday morning in early December and gave a little cry of joy. 'Tom's coming home this weekend,' she told Pam. 'He has to have his wounds dressed, but he thinks a nurse will come out and do that... Oh, he says he is bringing Terry Salmons with him for a visit.'

'Tina's father?' Susan looked at Lizzie with interest. 'That's good. I wondered why he had never come and now he is. Do you think she will remember him?'

'I doubt it,' Pam said. 'She was tiny when he went off to war and it must be more than a year since she has seen him. He won't recognise her either. She has grown a lot.' The child was growing in confidence as well as inches and spent a lot of her time in the farmyard, following whoever was about and stamping in every muddy pool she could.

'Where will Terry sleep?' Lizzie asked. 'My house isn't furnished yet. The things I ordered arrive next week...'

It wasn't easy to buy furniture these days, but Lizzie had managed to order a few bits and pieces for the downstairs but, as yet, she hadn't been able to get a bed.

'You can take Tom's bed to your house,' Pam said. 'Artie will move it for you, Lizzie – and we'll put a single in Tom's old room. I can give him Jeanie's bed and she can have the camp bed we kept spare. She won't mind as it's for her brother.'

'I've been promised a bed sometime next month,' Lizzie said. 'Well, the brass and iron headboard and the sprung bedstead are coming from Mrs Stephens down the road. I went in and did her hair for her the other evening, and she said I could have them because she doesn't need as many since her children left home.

So, I can put them in one of my spare bedrooms – but I can't get the mattress for a few weeks.'

Pam shook her head over it. Lizzie had told her before how difficult it was to buy what she needed for the new house. Even before the war, a lot of newly-wed couples were given furniture from their parents' or a relative's home to help out, but Lizzie's mother had got rid of her surplus stuff when she moved to March and she hadn't offered her anything for her new home. Lizzie had a few things that she'd managed to put by, but it was bottom-drawer stuff: linens, glass and porcelain, not furniture.

'You should ask Arthur if he has anything in the barn down the Fen,' Pam suggested. 'He won't have mattresses, but he kept some of his uncle's furniture when his house was sold years ago. Henry Talbot had some bits, too, I seem to recall. We'd got our own things so we didn't keep much – except for that pad-foot table in the sitting room. I think a lot of it was antique...'

Lizzie looked at her doubtfully. She wasn't keen on the idea of old furniture in her nice new house. The offer of the brass and iron bed-ends had only been accepted because she was having difficulty in buying new furniture. She wanted nice dark mahogany wardrobes and matching dressing tables that she could polish until they shone but wasn't sure when she would be able to buy something she liked. The utility furniture was all that was available now and it wasn't as attractive as stuff she'd seen prior to the war, but Lizzie hadn't had much choice. It was no use complaining. With a war on, there was nothing else she could do but buy what she was offered, so the brass and iron set had appealed. She would change them one day, but for now, they would come in handy. Perhaps a few pieces from Arthur's barn would help to fill up her empty rooms, so she would ask him if she could borrow a few things until she got her own. If there was anything that appealed...

Lizzie sighed as she thought about all the things that were now either on ration or in short supply. It wasn't always easy to get what she needed for the shop either and she'd had to find new suppliers to buy some of the lotions she needed.

* * *

When she came in from the milking, Jeanie was surprised and pleased that Terry was coming to visit and readily agreed that she didn't mind sleeping on a camp bed for a while.

'I never thought he would come. Mum said he didn't want to see Tina,' Jeanie said and smiled happily. 'She will be relieved that he changed his mind, I know.'

'Yes, you must ring and tell her,' Pam replied, nodding. 'I don't think we could put her up too just now, but she is welcome to visit for the day.'

'Are you still on for the cinema on Friday night?' Jeanie asked Lizzie. 'We've been offered a lift in and back.'

'Yes, I'll come,' Lizzie agreed. 'I haven't been for a while and there isn't much I can do in the house yet. Who is taking us in and fetching us?'

'Roy Hadder,' Jeanie replied with a smile. 'I went out with his brother last year a few times. When Ken joined up, Roy said he would take me into Ely if I wanted to go. He's older than Ken, but he's all right, doesn't try to take liberties or anything.' Roy worked his own land and had an exemption from duties in the armed forces, because of his flat feet. He'd recently joined a group of men who called themselves the Civil Defence Forces and drilled in the fields, though they didn't have uniforms or official weapons. However, all were farmers and had their own rifles or shotguns. They were used mainly for killing game, rabbits, hares and pheasants or partridges, but would kill an enemy just as easily – or more likely give him reason to surrender if he bailed out of a burning plane shot down by the RAF.

'Do you still write to Ken?' Lizzie asked her.

'Yes, now and then,' Jeanie replied. 'It was never serious between us, Lizzie. We just went out for fun. I haven't met anyone I'd like to marry yet... At least I don't think so...' A faraway look came into her eyes then, but she didn't say anything more and Lizzie knew she didn't go out often enough to be courting. Here in the village, she didn't meet many young men, because most were away fighting.

'You're too young to think of settling down yet,' Lizzie told her with a smile. 'Not quite nineteen. You should have lots of friends, Jeanie, and then you'll know when you find the right one.'

'That is what Mum says.' Jeanie laughed and the slightly wistful look had gone. 'Nancy says they're all the same – a waste of time – but they aren't, are they?'

'Not in my opinion,' Lizzie said. 'Where is Nancy this morning?'

'She was up early and caught the bus into Cambridge,' Jeanie said. 'She wants to go Christmas shopping and it's her day off...'

'I offered her a lift into Ely. She could have caught the train there,' Artie said coming in and sitting at the breakfast table. 'Saved all that time going round the villages, but she refused.'

'Nancy goes her own way,' Pam said. 'You need to look sharpish, Lizzie, or you'll miss your bus to Chatteris.'

'I'm not going into work today,' Lizzie told her. 'I want to visit the market in Ely. Sometimes you can pick up a few nice bits and pieces there. I might see something for the house. Why don't you come with me, Mum? You might find something you want for Christmas too.'

Pam smiled at her daughter-in-law but shook her head. 'No time today, love, but you can buy me some dried fruit if you see any. Look out for anything that's going and bring it, whatever it is...' Foodstuffs came into the shops unexpectedly and vanished again within hours as people bought whatever was available.

'That's an open order,' Lizzie laughed, but knew what Pam meant. 'I'll see if I can buy some knicker elastic. I've tried twice, but there wasn't any in stock – and I'd like to renew mine in my favourite silk ones. The material is still good, but the elastic is failing...'

'I know what you mean,' Pam said ruefully. 'I had to pin the ones I wore yesterday because they threatened to fall down!' Everyone laughed and grinned at each other. It was a little-known hazard of war but an awkward one at times.

'Nancy wanted to buy a new hat,' Jeanie said getting up. 'She says it is the one thing you can still buy plenty of – but what's the point of a new hat if you can't buy a new dress or coat to go with it?' She saw Pam's quizzical look. 'I meant a stylish one. There's nothing nice in the shops now.'

'At least they will keep you warm,' Pam answered. 'I've got a nice coat with a fur collar you can have if you want it, Jeanie – one I had when I was about your age. It is still as good as new because I only wore it for best. You're welcome to it if you'd like it?'

'Well...' Jeanie hesitated. 'I might be able to remodel it – if you don't mind?'

'I don't mind what you do with it, love. I'll fetch it down for you when you come in at docky time.'

'Thanks.' Jeanie sent her a brilliant smile. 'You're really kind to me, Pam.'

Lizzie looked at Pam as the younger girl went out. 'Did you keep all your things?' she asked. 'Mum kept most of hers for years, but she threw a lot out when she moved, said she would never need them – but some of the material was good. We all have to make do and mend these days, don't we?'

'Unfortunately, yes,' Pam agreed. 'I kept all my best things, Lizzie. I've got a few nice dresses that I used to wear when Arthur took me to a dinner dance at the farmers' club. Well, we actually went to a lovely hotel in Cambridge, but it was a club affair...'

'Surely you don't want to part with them?'

'Oh, I don't mind sharing them out amongst you all,' Pam told her with a smile. 'I couldn't get into them now, but you young girls can make them over for yourselves.'

'Susan might like them...' Lizzie said hesitantly.

'She can have her pick too. I'll get them all out this evening and see what you think, Lizzie. I know there is a black velvet dress I believe would suit you.'

Lizzie nodded. With her red hair, she could wear black and the dress sounded lovely. It might be fun to make over some of Pam's old dresses; they could all do it together in the evenings. The winter nights were long and dark in the country, made worse by the blackout, of course, and there wasn't a great deal to do once the ironing was finished. Sometimes there was a programme on the wireless, but a lot of the time it didn't interest her. Lizzie often spent her evenings doing the other women's hair or knitting, mostly little things for Tina, but it might be fun trying on the clothes and helping each other to pin them up or cut them down to size...

She smiled as she got ready to leave for her shopping trip to Ely, collecting a list of what was needed from Pam – should she see anything available. Tom would be home for Christmas, and she was determined to make it as special as possible, finding little gifts and something nice to eat if she could, though just having him there was all that truly mattered. They would be together again, able to hold each other and she knew that was all either of them needed.

20

'Did you enjoy your visit to the cinema with Lizzie?' Artie asked Jeanie on the Saturday morning after their trip into Ely. 'I'd have taken you and fetched you, if you'd asked. You didn't need to trouble Roy Hadder.'

'Oh, he didn't mind,' Jeanie said innocently. 'He was going in anyway and he told me he visits twice a week. I can go in for the ride any time. I think he sits with his grandmother – talks to her and buys her fish and chips. She is nearly ninety, so he said...'

Artie stared at her moodily. 'Next, he'll be asking you to go somewhere with him – the pub or a dance...'

Jeanie paused in her task of milking, giving him a butter-wouldn't-melt look. 'So what?' she asked and avoided the cow's kick as she stood up to empty her bucket into the churn. 'He's told me he has tickets for a dinner dance in Cambridge next week – do you think I should go?'

'That's the county do for young farmers,' Artie growled. 'I've got a couple of tickets too. I was thinking of asking if you wanted to go...'

'Did Pam tell you to ask me?' Jeanie said and received another glare.

'I don't always do what my mother asks me to do,' Artie replied. 'I'm asking you if you'll come as my partner...'

Jeanie hesitated and then smiled. 'Yes, thanks, I'd like to – if you're sure you want to take me?'

'I wouldn't ask if I wasn't,' he muttered and then saw the laughter in her face. 'You are a minx, Jeanie Salmons. I should put you over my knee and give you a spanking.'

'You'd get a kick in the shins if you tried. I bite too,' she retorted. 'But you're not too bad a dancer, so I'd be pleased to go with you.'

His eyes narrowed. 'I bet Hadder didn't ask you at all,' he challenged. 'I thought he'd got a regular girl.'

'Has he?' Jeanie asked. 'Perhaps he'll take her then...' She threw him a wicked smile that would leave him guessing.

Her share of the milking done, Jeanie went off singing to herself as she ran up to the farmhouse kitchen. She was giggling inside. Roy Hadder had told her he'd got a couple of tickets, but he'd stopped short of asking her. She didn't think he was courting steady, but he was probably too shy to ask her to the dance. She'd known Artie had purchased some tickets, because Pam had told her he went to the dinner dance every year.

'You sound happy,' Pam said as she entered the kitchen, still singing one of the popular songs of the war. 'What are you up to?'

'Nothing much,' Jeanie said and smiled. 'Can I borrow your sewing machine again, Pam? I want to make a new dress.'

'Of course you can, and I'll help,' Pam offered instantly. 'Have you bought some material – or would you like to alter one of the dresses I showed you?'

'That black satin and lace one,' Jeanie said tentatively. 'If you really don't mind? Lizzie suggested what we could do with it, to make it suitable for me – and she thinks I can wear black.'

'With your hair and that complexion, you can wear almost anything,' Pam agreed. 'Come on, tell me – I know you're up to something...'

'Artie asked me to the young farmers dinner dance,' Jeanie said. 'I want something that will knock his socks off.'

Pam laughed, as Jeanie had known she would. 'Are you planning to seduce my son – or teach him a lesson? It is time someone did... All the girls he's taken out and none of them have touched his heart.'

'Has he got one?' Jeanie asked her with a wicked look and Pam smiled.

'I imagine that when Artie finally falls, he will fall hard,' Pam replied thoughtfully. 'I think you like him, Jeanie. You won't be too hard on him, will you?'

'I don't want to break his heart, just make him realise he can't break mine,' Jeanie said and turned as she finished washing her hands at the deep sink. 'I like him but—' She broke off as the kitchen door opened and Artie entered. He hadn't heard anything because he was too busy talking to his father.

* * *

Artie had finished his chores for the day. He was going into March to do some Christmas shopping for himself and for Pam, who had given him a list of things she wanted. Jeanie would clean out the cowsheds after breakfast and then she would be finished, too, for a few hours. In the early evening, she would feed the cattle in the barns and milk again, and Nancy would help. The animals needed attention every day, even at Christmas, but for now there wasn't as much work to do on the land.

Most of it had been ploughed and prepared; where winter sowing of crops was needed, the land girls had helped get them in and now it was more a question of maintenance. Artie had been hedging and ditch-clearing all week. The fields were divided by deep ditches and there were more at the side of the road that led up to the farm and all the way to Sutton. That land, though, was off limits because of the new airfield – it belonged to the Air Ministry now and the road was officially closed for the duration.

Many acres of land farmed by the Talbots and other local men had been put off limits for the local population. The airport would serve military planes and was therefore dangerous for the general public. Arthur Talbot had complained that some of his best land had been taken over, but, like the other farmers, he could do nothing but accept that it was needed. He'd managed to buy other land, some of it arable, and he hired some grassland on the washes, where the animals were kept to graze during the spring, summer and autumn. In winter, they were either sent to market, in the case of the bullocks, or brought inside if they were valuable milking cows.

Artie and Arthur were discussing the potato crop, the last of which had been lifted the previous week and was now stored in clamps with straw over the heaps to protect it from the frost. Arthur had shown a sample to a government-approved merchant that Friday and he'd been offered a price that was fair, but they'd received a higher offer from a fish and chip shop in Chatteris. They were discussing whether to sell a few bags on the quiet to the shop owner.

'Is it worth it, Dad?' Artie asked him. 'So, you'll get five shillings extra a ton – but if the ministry discover you've sold them under the counter, you'll be fined more than that...'

'You risk more than a fine,' Pam remarked. 'It's OK to hold a couple of bags back for our use, but I'm not sure it is wise to sell to that shop.'

'I've known Charlie for years,' her husband said. 'He won't say where he got them – besides, who will know? He's allowed to buy his quota, no one will guess he's had a few extra bags from me.'

Jeanie listened. They trusted her, thought of her as family, and she would never tell anyone their little secrets, but others might. Jeanie knew that Nancy didn't approve of black-market trading and it might be an idea to warn Pam of her views.

Her husband was always looking for an extra profit where he could get it and there was no crime in selling a few bags to a local chip shop in peace time, but in war there were rules about where and to whom you could sell your produce – and maybe the merchants were using that to keep the price down. But Artie was right, it was hardly worth the risk.

'It's not as if I'm selling him a bullock,' Arthur replied. 'If I'm asked, I'll say they came from my garden. No one says you can't give your own potatoes to a friend.'

Everyone was exhorted to grow their own vegetables if they could and there were no regulations about what you managed to produce from your own garden; many people also kept a couple of hens for their eggs. There were lots of little fiddles going on everywhere and, providing Arthur didn't do it too often, he would probably get away with it. The ones the authorities were after were the regular black marketeers who made a fortune from selling stuff that was either stolen or illegally hidden from the food ministry. Besides, Jeanie thought, Arthur Talbot was a law unto himself and you could talk until you were blue in the face and he would still do it if he'd made up his mind.

Nancy came in then and the conversation turned to more general subjects. Maybe they didn't need Jeanie to warn them to be careful after all. 'You'll be going home for Christmas, Nancy,'

Pam said. 'Jeanie will have her time off in the New Year – is that all right with you?'

Nancy shrugged. 'I don't much care,' she admitted. 'My parents don't celebrate much in normal times – they won't be having roast dinners and Christmas puddings. We'll get a meat pie if we're lucky...' She gave Artie a resentful glance as he looked at her. 'Your family doesn't know how lucky they are, Pam.'

Pam seemed stunned for a moment, then, 'You can stay here for Christmas if you want, Nancy? We thought you would like to go home.'

Jeanie was shocked. She'd known Nancy didn't have as good a home as she did, but it was the first time she'd really spoken out about it.

Nancy gave a mocking laugh. 'I have a room with a bed and a chest to put my things in, and it's always freezing. Pa is an invalid and he drinks all the time – and Ma is always working or crying. The reason I became a land girl was because I could be sure of gettin' away.'

'Then stay with us. You'll be very welcome...'

Nancy shrugged. 'I'll go for one day,' she said. 'I bought them presents – my sister too. She doesn't get much, stuck at home helping Ma. If she gets the chance, she will be off too...' Her gaze rested on Jeanie. 'I'll be back on Boxing Day if you want to go home?'

'Thanks. I might pop up to London for a couple of days if that is all right?' Jeanie looked at Pam, who nodded.

Nancy looked at Pam too. 'That coat you said one of us could have – would it be all right if I took it for Ma? She hasn't had one in years... If no one else wants it?'

Pam hesitated and glanced at Jeanie. She inclined her head. She'd liked the coat, but she'd asked for the special black dress. It was only fair that Nancy should have the coat for her mother.

'Yes, of course, you can,' Pam told her. 'I offered the clothes to you girls because I know how hard it is to buy decent stuff now. If the coat is of use to your mother, Nancy, she is welcome. It hasn't fitted me for years.'

'Thanks.' Nancy's cheeks were pink. 'I bought her a new jumper, but I couldn't afford a coat. She really needs it – and it is better than she has ever had in her life.'

'Then take it,' Pam said and smiled. 'I am lucky that I bought a nice one a few months before the war. I don't need the things I showed you girls. Jeanie is having the black lace dress and Lizzie the velvet, but if there is anything else you wanted, Nancy, feel free to say.'

'No. It was just the coat for Ma,' Nancy said. 'Thanks, Pam. I'll give you a hand with the ironing if you want...'

'Done,' Pam said and laughed. 'I never refuse an offer like that.'

The slight tension was broken and everyone tucked into the breakfast Pam had prepared, before going their separate ways.

Jeanie wondered about Nancy. Was her terrible home life the reason she'd turned against men – or was it something else?

* * *

Jeanie finished her chores and returned to the house in the middle of the morning. Pam had fetched her sewing machine out and the dress was ready, waiting for Jeanie to try on. It would need taking in a bit and Lizzie had suggested that she make the sleeves shorter and lower the neckline.

They spent the next half an hour cutting and then Pam got on with cooking dinner while Jeanie sewed the new hems. She pressed it and took it upstairs to try on. It fitted her beautifully and when Pam saw her in it a few minutes later, she nodded her approval.

'It does look good and up-to-date with the latest fashions now,' she remarked. 'I'm glad you chose it, Jeanie. Did you want the coat too?'

'It was nice, but Nancy's need was greater,' Jeanie said. 'I've got the dress, Pam. I'm very satisfied, thank you.'

'Well, that just proves you're a nice girl,' Pam said and chuckled. 'I hope Artie appreciates the dress when he sees you in it – you'd better take if off before he gets back. We want it to be a surprise when he takes you to the dance.'

* * *

Artie was thoughtful as he did his shopping in March. It was an important railway terminal and a busy little town with a fair number of shops, and he liked to visit now and then. He would call in for a drink at the Royal Arms when he'd finished his chores.

After an hour or so searching, he was able to get about half of what his mother had wanted, but his own shopping went better, because he'd decided to buy jewellery for his family. There was a nice, old-fashioned jewellers in the main street that sold both second-hand and new jewellery and it still seemed to have plenty of stock on its shelves. He found a pretty silver bangle for his sister-in-law. A pair of shiny gold filigree earrings would be just right for his mother, and a tiepin with a garnet inset for his father – though he'd probably never wear it. For Tom and John, he bought cufflinks, and for his sisters, intricate silver charms to wear on a bracelet. Susan already had her bracelet, and he knew his mother had bought a small one for Angela's Christmas present.

Artie was about to leave the jeweller's when he remembered Jeanie and Nancy and frowned. He supposed he'd better buy them both something, but what? Nancy didn't strike him as being fond of trinkets – and Jeanie... well, he would have to be careful what he gave her.

After some deliberation, he bought a small silver locket on a chain for Jeanie and then left the shop. He would buy some perfumed soap for Nancy. He'd seen a presentation box in Woolworths and that would be as good a gift as any for a girl who had shown him nothing but contempt. She would more than likely refuse it anyway.

After he'd done his shopping, Artie went to the pub and had a drink. He met a couple of friends he'd known at school and one of them was talking about a gift he'd bought for his girlfriend.

'I bought her a gold locket and chain,' he told Artie. 'It's a big oval one with a heavy chain. Cost me a small fortune – but she's worth it...' He laughed. 'Besides, if I'd given her anything less, she would think I was a miser.'

Artie nodded. He was thoughtful as he left the pub. How did he really feel about Jeanie? It struck him that perhaps the silver locket was a bit mean and maybe he should have got a gold one...

Realising that he didn't want Jeanie to think him tight, he decided to go back and change the locket for a better one. However, when he got there, the shop was shut and he felt annoyed. It was too far for him to come back just for the locket and he wouldn't be able to spare the time before Christmas.

Cursing himself for a fool, he turned away. He would try to get into Ely and buy something more suitable there...

A smile touched his face as he recalled the little exchange in the cowsheds. Jeanie was worth an extra trip into Ely and he could always give the locket to Susan as well as her charm.

Artie wasn't certain what his feelings for Jeanie meant, nor if she had any for him. He'd been out with a lot of girls, some of them a little on the wild side and others decent girls who had looked for marriage, but none of them had lasted more than a few weeks, before he was bored. He just didn't fancy being married to any of them. He wasn't sure he would ever want to be married – but he liked taking Jeanie out and he'd discovered that he needed to protect her from men who might hurt her.

Shaking his head, Artie wondered at his own thoughts. Surely, he wasn't getting serious? Nah, it was just that he liked the girl, she made him laugh – and he definitely didn't want her to think him mean...

21

Faith wondered for a while if she would be unlucky enough to have fallen for a baby, despite John's efforts to keep her safe, which she wasn't sure had worked every time. However, her monthlies came, though lighter than normal, and she was able to relax again and forget that particular worry.

There were plenty more to replace it. The military hospital she'd been sent to in Portsmouth was overflowing with wounded men and Faith was kept on her toes all day long. The hours were extensive, sometimes much longer than her normal duty at Addenbrooke's. She'd thought they were busy there and they were, but not like here at the hospital she was on loan to. Volunteers like Faith could be sent wherever they were needed, and she'd wondered if she might end up overseas, but instead she was lodged in the busy port.

'It sounds as if you're a library book,' Faith's mother had complained when she'd told her about the transfer. 'On loan – as if you're a piece of property! I don't see why they have to send you all that way down there.'

'It's where I'm needed, Mum,' Faith had told her. 'I know it means I can't get home as often as I could – John doesn't like it either, but it's what I went into nursing for.'

And it was exactly what she'd wanted. Here in Portsmouth, she was doing the work of a professional nurse, exactly as if she'd completed her training. Taking temperatures, injecting medicines prescribed by the busy doctors, and changing dressings, as well as giving bed baths were now all a part of her day. She was on her feet throughout the day and night at times and would collapse into her bed when she finally got there, sleeping like a log until her alarm shrilled at her in time for her to eat, wash and dress and go back on the wards. Faith loved it. She'd had hardly any free time and when she did, she just went to bed and slept. It was an important naval base, so there were a lot of men in uniform walking around: navy, army and air force – all the various uniforms – were glimpsed as she travelled to and from her lodgings.

She'd only gone into nursing because of the war. Had it not happened, she would probably have remained at home, helped her parents in whatever way she could, and then got married. Being here in this hectic environment had changed her perspective and given her a new feeling of confidence. She considered whether she could stay in nursing after the war was over.

She wanted to marry John, of course she did, and they would have a family in time – but she might be able to keep her job. Even if she couldn't work in a hospital, because of the travelling she would need to do, she might work as a district nurse. They were necessary too and in peacetime the hospital wouldn't be quite the same.

Faith thought it was the young men's cheerful attitude despite their horrendous injuries that made her work so fulfilling. Even those who were terribly wounded usually managed a smile or a quip when a pretty nurse attended them. There were times when they cried, too, for torn lives and lost hopes, often under cover of darkness, but most tried to joke and laugh, even if they felt otherwise inside. She was one of the prettiest and she got a lot of wolf whistles, especially from the men who were getting better and beginning to be able to move about, either on their own two feet or in a wheelchair.

All the nurses accepted the jests and the whistles in good part. There was a silent agreement that it was necessary to keep up the morale of the men who were terribly maimed and injured. Some of them were never going to live a normal life again, and all had known fear and pain – more than they could have expected in their lifetime. Their silent bravery was masked by their cheeky remarks and none of them got a rude reply from a nursing team that was filled with admiration for what they'd done – and in many cases might be asked to do again when they'd recovered.

* * *

Faith had been working at the hospital only a matter of days when she met someone who introduced herself as Annie Salmons.

'I think we have a mutual friend – or friends,' Annie told Faith. 'Someone said you're engaged to John Talbot from Mepal in Cambridgeshire – is that right?'

'We are sort of engaged, though not officially yet. My parents don't know, but we've talked about marriage,' Faith agreed. Being engaged to be married might be frowned on, but it wasn't forbidden. Faith knew of at least three nurses who were. They wore their rings on a chain beneath their uniforms. She thought one of them was actually married. If anyone guessed the truth, then nothing had been said, perhaps because they were short of nurses. 'Do you know the Talbot family?'

'Not really – but I know Lizzie Gilbert and my sister, Jeanie, is a land girl... She works with them.'

'Yes, I met Jeanie briefly when I visited the farm,' Faith said and smiled. 'Lizzie talked about you – she said we might meet one day. I thought you had volunteered for overseas duty?'

'I have,' Annie agreed. 'I'm off in the morning. We were going last month, but our transport got attacked and it was badly damaged, so it was put back. We're definitely off tomorrow, though, because the ship docked this morning and we've been told to report first thing. It was the reason I introduced myself. I might not get another chance...'

'I think you're very brave to volunteer,' Faith said.

'Someone has to do it,' Annie told her. 'They protect us as much as they can, of course, but I want to go. The nurses and doctors in the field are needed to save lives. We don't lose too many patients here, but if it were not for the doctors and nurses out there, many more would die before they were treated.'

'Yes, I'm sure that's right,' Faith replied. 'I still think you're brave to volunteer, though, Annie.'

She shrugged her shoulders, giving a wry smile. 'I'm doing what I enjoy.'

'Yes, I enjoy nursing too,' Faith replied. 'It's hard work but rewarding.'

'Yes...' Annie nodded at her. 'A group of us are going out for a drink tonight – would you like to come?'

'Yes, please,' Faith agreed instantly. She never turned an invitation down if she had time off, though this would be the first since she'd arrived in Portsmouth. 'I'd love to if I can – but if I get extra duty, you'll understand?'

'Yes, of course. We're meeting here and there's a car coming for us at eight this evening. Be outside the main entrance if you can make it.'

They smiled and parted ways. Faith looked forward to the outing, but as the time approached, she knew she wouldn't be able to go. A fleet of ambulances started to arrive and she was told a hospital ship had docked; they would all be kept on the ward as a new influx of wounded was admitted. She thought that Annie Salmons and her friends would probably be working through the night too. It was what they all did when they were needed.

The pressure of work was relentless that day and the next. Faith was given a brief note by someone; it was from Annie, saying that she was sorry they hadn't been able to meet up and asking Faith to give her love to the family at Blackberry Farm when she saw them.

Faith made a mental note to mention Annie's wishes in her next letter to John's mother. She wrote to Pam once in a while, and to Lizzie once a week. She also wrote to her parents every week. Since starting her nursing, Faith had tried to write something to John every night, though she couldn't always send the letter for a while. He wrote when he was able, and he'd phoned a couple of times at night since she'd arrived at her new posting. Faith hadn't been there when he'd tried to reach her and she'd apologised for that in her letters, explaining how busy they were.

I wish I'd been there when you rang.

Faith wrote that night.

We were on the ward until gone midnight and I was due back on at ten the next morning. I think of you often and miss you. I am hoping to get a long leave after Christmas. I haven't been given leave over the holidays, John. Some of the nurses have been working for months with only short periods of time off and so they asked if I would be prepared to fill in while a few of them went home. I couldn't say no – but I should get a week off in January. I'll let you know the exact dates and perhaps you can arrange some leave too?

Faith sighed as she sent her letter. She'd already telephoned her parents and told them she wouldn't get home, and her mother had been upset.

'Do you really have to work all the time, Faith?' she'd asked. 'I mean, I know things are difficult, but surely you must get leave?'

'Not yet,' Faith had told her.

She wanted to spend her leave with John if she could, but if he couldn't make a whole week, she would pop home and see her parents.

John didn't reply for a week. His letter was brief. He too was working most of the time and he wasn't sure he could get a whole week off, but if she let him know in time, he would try.

We might go away somewhere for a couple of days...

He'd suggested in his letter, and she smiled. The brief time they'd had together was a precious memory and Faith was looking forward to spending more time with the man she loved.

Since coming to Portsmouth, Faith had met a lot of young men. Many of them were wounded but recovering and she'd been asked out on dates more times than she could count, but she always said no. Her free time was limited and she used it mainly to rest. There were plenty of men on shore leave from their ships and she met them when she went for a drink in the canteen in the evenings with other nurses, before going back to her lodgings. The sailors were relentless in their pursuit of the young women from the hospital, but Faith was steadfast in her refusals. She would go to the pub, the cinema or a dance in a group on the rare occasions she got the chance, but she didn't go out on dates with a young man, ever. She didn't want to.

In her heart and her mind, she was married to John and she loved him. She thought there would never be anyone else for her. He was constantly in her thoughts and she spent most of her free time wondering where he was and if he was safe…

* * *

John heard the siren and ran for the nearest plane. They had to get the craft off the ground, because left where they stood, they were sitting ducks when an air raid happened, and the enemy planes would wreak havoc in a short time. Three of them got there at the same time: the pilot, the gunner and John.

'We'll take her up and do what we can,' Mike, the pilot, said.

John and Pete, the rear gunner, scrambled on board after him and the plane taxied down the runaway and took off. Fighter planes were making a dash for the freedom of the air, where they stood a chance. Already, the first enemy bombers were overhead, and an explosion sent flames soaring as John's plane cleared the runway and swept up into the grey murk of a winter's sky.

'Bandits ahead,' warned the pilot.

John took the co-pilot's seat and fired the guns at an enemy craft. He hit it and saw a flare as it exploded mid-air and then they were soaring into the sky, getting out of danger, the rear gunner firing like mad at a pursuing bandit.

'Did most of our chaps get away?' Mike asked John as he plotted a course for them to the nearest safe base.

'I think they got a couple of fighter planes on the ground,' John said and Mike swore.

'If we can get this baby up with half a crew, they should have got theirs off,' he muttered.

John nodded but knew that it was only fortune – good or ill – that had seen the bomber craft standing on the runway. It was being refilled for the mission that was planned for an hour's time and would normally have been hidden in a hanger. However, there in the open, it was vulnerable. The mission for that evening would have to be aborted or transferred to another squadron.

John's thoughts were interrupted as the bandit – their term for enemy planes – came out of the blue, firing at them with all guns blazing. John heard Mike grunt and saw him slump forward and knew the enemy had found his target.

'Can you take over?' Mike asked faintly. 'I've been hit and I may pass out—'

'Yes,' John said confidently. Even though he'd been picked as a navigator, he'd continued to take flying lessons whenever he could and knew that he was capable of doing it. 'Don't worry. Hang on in there, Mike. I'll get us back safely on the ground.'

Pete called out something from the back and there was a burst of firing, then a gleeful shout. 'Got the bastard!'

'Come and see if you can do anything for Mike,' John instructed and the gunner came up through the plane and leaned over their unconscious pilot, feeling for a pulse.

'He's still alive,' he muttered. 'Bleeding like hell from a hit in the shoulder, I think... and his arm... Oh God...' There was the sound of retching as Pete was sick. 'His arm is hanging by a thread...'

'Do what you can to stop the bleeding. You need a tourni-quet,' John said through gritted teeth. He wanted to do it himself, but he had to fly the plane and navigate. 'Pull yourself together. I'll talk you through it. You can still save his life.'

'If the poor bugger wants to live like this,' Pete muttered, but he did as John instructed, following every word to the letter. 'It's

OK, I've done it...' He sounded muffled, as if he was still struggling to keep the contents of his stomach down.

'Get back to the guns in case we get attacked again,' John said tersely. He felt sick himself. They'd saved the plane, but at what cost? Mike would probably never fly again – that was if he lived through the night...

They weren't far from their objective now. John decided it was safe enough to break radio silence. He needed an ambulance waiting when they landed, or Mike didn't stand a chance...

* * *

John phoned Faith. For once, she was there and he drew a sigh of relief. She sounded so like herself, confident and happy and it was a breath of fresh air.

'John – are you all right?' she asked. 'You don't usually ring at this late hour. I've just got back from my shift and it's the middle of the night.'

'Something came up,' he said. 'I should have been on a mission tonight, but I'm not... One of my crew was hit during a raid.' John took a moment to compose himself. 'He may not make it, Faith. He has a wife and two small children...'

'I'm so sorry,' Faith said, and her breath caught as if she was close to tears. 'Was he a good friend?'

'Yes...' John knew he sounded terse. 'When you fly with someone all the time... It means we need a new pilot. Mike won't be flying again for a long time, if ever.'

'That's rotten luck...' Faith hesitated, then, 'Were you in danger too?'

'For a while,' he said. 'Look, they've given me three days off to get over it – can you get a little time off if I come down?'

'Yes,' she said without hesitation. 'I'll get one of the girls to swap with me. It may only be a few hours, but we can be together for a while.'

'I'm going to borrow a car and come,' he said. 'I'll see you about three tomorrow afternoon. Where shall we meet?'

'Outside the main gates of the hospital,' Faith said. 'I'm sorry about your friend, but I'm glad you're all right. I love you, John.'

'I love you too – more than I know how to say...' John replaced the receiver. He was welling up inside and it didn't do to let yourself get too emotional. Men were killed all the time and you had to take it on the chin and keep going. He'd been commended for bringing the plane in and for giving his pilot a chance. They'd said he deserved some leave – because when he returned to his base, the aborted mission would be on again.

It was a risky mission, one they all knew they might not come back from, and John wanted to see Faith before then. He knew he'd used up a big slice of luck and although everyone wanted to fly with him, because he was known as a lucky so-and-so, his luck surely wouldn't last forever...

22

'Tom...' Lizzie ran to greet him as he got out of the car that Sunday morning. His visit was a week overdue because he'd been unwell and the hospital had kept him in a little longer. He was walking with a stick, but as she approached, he let it drop and opened his arms to receive her. They hugged and then kissed passionately, the ache of separation making it feel so wonderful to just hold one another. 'How are you, my darling? We've been so anxious about you. We expected you a few days ago...'

'I had a bit of a fever, so they delayed my release. You did get my message?'

'Yes, but it didn't tell us much.'

'I wasn't sure when they would let us come.'

'Oh, Tom,' Lizzie said. 'We were all worried about you.'

'I'm all right now,' Tom told her. 'It was a bit rough for a while.' He smiled at the man leaning on his crutches just behind them. 'I've brought Terry to stay, for as long as he wants – I think you know him, Lizzie?'

She smiled at the young soldier. 'Yes, of course, I do. Sorry, Terry, if I neglected to say hello. I was just so happy to see Tom.'

'Of course, you were,' Terry answered, smiling, but his eyes went to the young woman who was leading a tiny girl by the hand. 'Tina...? My you've grown...'

The little girl clung uncertainly to Susan's hand, looking up at him with big inquiring eyes before burying her face against Susan's leg.

'She's a bit shy because she hasn't seen you for a while,' Susan told him and bent to lift her up. She whispered something in the child's ear, and Tina lifted her head to look at her father.

'Dadda,' she said and held out her arms to him.

He balanced himself with one crutch and took her hand in his, placing it against his face, and tears were in his eyes.

'Dadda can't carry you,' Susan told her. 'Let's go into the house and sit down and then he can have you on his lap.'

She led the way, still carrying Tina in her arms, and Terry followed, using his crutches, stepping carefully though the yard had well-beaten tracks of old bricks and slabs set into the earth as a path to the house. Although he was wearing his new leg, he still needed the support of the crutches, and the concentration was there for all to see as he negotiated his way to the open door.

Lizzie and Tom waited while they disappeared inside the kitchen, holding each other and talking softly, laughing in pleasure at being together.

'He's had a rough time,' Tom told Lizzie, his arm about her waist. 'He can't seem to get the hang of the false leg yet – I think it makes his stump sore still. Poor devil. First, he loses his leg and nearly dies, then, when he's recovering from that, he loses his wife.'

'Yes, it was rotten luck for him, Ellie dying like that – though...' Lizzie lowered her voice as if Terry might hear, despite being in the house. 'Vera said Ellie was planning on leaving him, because of what had happened.'

'She wouldn't have done that? Surely, she couldn't if she loved him?'

'Vera thought she might not be able to help herself. Apparently, she took one look at him in the hospital bed and ran... She told Vera she couldn't bear to be near him like that, only she didn't use those words.'

'Poor devil. He lost all round, didn't he? Good thing he doesn't know what she did or said...'

'She couldn't have really loved him,' Lizzie said. 'I wouldn't react like that, Tom. I'd want you back alive no matter what...' Her throat caught with emotion. 'You just remember that and always come back to me, do you hear?'

'I'm not sure they'll want me to return to active service,' Tom said and his eyes were dark with memories he didn't relish. 'You need to be fully fit and I've got this limp. It may go, but it may stay with me for life, so the doctor says.' He drew a long breath. 'I could get stuck in the stores or, if I'm lucky, training others. I haven't been discharged medically yet anyway, so it won't be for a while.'

'You wouldn't like being stuck inside much,' Lizzie said, her eyes on his face. 'I'd be relieved, but I know it isn't you, Tom.'

'Well, I'm on sick leave for the moment, same as Terry. His active service is over. I'm not sure if they will discharge him or put him on light duties. I suppose we can do jobs that men who are completely fit are wasted on. We need all the men we can get to fight.'

'Perhaps they will let you go back when you've had a rest and are properly well again,' Lizzie told him encouragingly, though in her heart she hoped they wouldn't. Ideally, the army would discharge him and he could stay on the farm, but she doubted they would be that lucky. As Tom said, the fit and able men were needed to fight this awful war that showed no sign of ending, so he would be transferred to light duties, perhaps in a camp in England. Even that wasn't completely safe, with air raids happening all the time. If the enemy didn't bomb cities, they concentrated on military camps and factories, so no one could truly be safe until the conflict was over and that didn't look like happening for a while.

'I'm not going to worry about it,' Tom said and smiled down at her. 'I'm home with you and the family – and for as long as they let me, I'll enjoy that and make myself useful.'

'We'd better go up to the house,' Lizzie said, pressing close as they walked to the back door arm-in-arm. 'Your mum will be waiting anxiously to see you.'

Pam was at the kitchen table, pouring tea into big cups and dispensing her pound cake, made with rice and a drop of almond essence she had in the cupboard. Lizzie knew it tasted delicious and Terry was already eating a slice, sharing it with the little girl on his lap. Susan was sitting at the table watching them. She looked up as Lizzie and Tom entered.

'Good to see you home,' Susan told her brother. 'You look just the same…'

'Thanks, Susan,' he replied. 'You look very nice – new outfit?'

'Yes, I made it myself out of some of Mum's old things from the attic,' she told him with a little grin of triumph. 'Lizzie, Jeanie and I are getting quite clever. We made Mum a new dress out of an old one, too, didn't we?' She looked at her mother for confirmation.

'You did and it looks better than the original when it was new,' Pam confirmed. Her gaze rested on Tom and she smiled. 'Good to have you home, son.'

'Good to be here.' Tom walked round the table and hugged her. His limp was noticeable but didn't seem to distress him. If he was feeling any pain, he didn't show it.

Lizzie's heart caught as she realised how badly he had been hurt and how lucky they were to get him back.

* * *

'I'm not going into the shop tomorrow,' Lizzie told him when they were alone in the bedroom of their new house later. Tom had eaten a good meal at his mother's table, but then said he needed to rest for a while. 'I'll be here all day to look after you if you fancy a day in bed?'

'I might with you in it,' Tom said and gave her a look that made her giggle. 'I don't need to stay in bed, Lizzie. It's just that the journey took it out of me a bit. I'll be fine in a couple of hours.'

Lizzie lay beside him on the bed until he slept and then went down to the kitchen. It was all spick and span, because she'd spent ages cleaning and unpacking in the evenings the past few days so they could move in. She had a pine table and chairs, a Welsh dresser with all her crockery and a deep butler's sink with draining boards each side and chests of drawers to fill in the gaps. Arthur had stored much of the furniture in the barn, and he'd given it to her, but her living room had only a couple of occasional tables and one chair with a wooden back and arms that Arthur had thought she might like.

'It's old, Lizzie,' he'd told her. 'There's a lot more under tarpaulin, but I just brought what I could see that I thought you might like?'

'The pine table is useful, thank you, and I love the oak dresser and the chests of drawers fit just right,' Lizzie had said. 'The table is similar to Pam's, and I shall keep it if I may – and the elbow chair is nice, too. Do you think it was part of a set?'

'I can't recall all the stuff I brought from my uncle's house,' Arthur had told her. 'I don't think this came from a set. I seem to remember seeing it at Uncle Dick's desk. He had a huge mahogany partner's desk. That must be under the tarpaulin, but I don't think you would want it; it's too large.'

'I've ordered most of our stuff,' Lizzie had said, smiling. 'I think the suite comes first and then the dining room furniture – but we can use the kitchen most of the time until then.'

'You need a nice chair by the range – I think there is a wooden rocking chair that looks comfortable. Artie can help me get it down another day...'

The rocking chair hadn't arrived yet, but the pine chairs were comfortable. They could eat breakfast and a bit of supper in their own kitchen, but Pam would expect them to lunch and tea. She'd made a point of it before they went to their new home for Tom to have a rest.

* * *

Tom wanted a good look round the house when he got up and they enjoyed planning what they needed to buy, as and when they could, and hugging each other as the pleasure of being together in their own home began to seem real.

'It's a dream come true,' Tom told her as he kissed her and held her close. 'This is where we'll spend the first few years of our married life, Lizzie – where our children will be born.'

Lizzie smiled up at him. 'I'm so glad you like it all – the colours. I wasn't sure, but I know you like blue and yellow...'

'What you've been able to do is great,' Tom assured her. 'It is just a house for now, Lizzie, but we'll make it our home. One day I might get us something bigger and better – perhaps on our own land, but we're lucky to have this. It was good of Arthur to have it built for us.'

'Yes, we have been lucky,' Lizzie said and kissed him. 'I'm just so glad you are back, Tom.' A little shiver went through her as she recalled the fear she'd felt when the telegram came.

'I had something to come back for,' he murmured and kissed her again. 'I was lucky a friend got me out of a difficult situation...' Tom hesitated, then, 'Things didn't go as we'd hoped and several of my group were killed – men who were under my command. I feel responsible for them, Lizzie.'

'Yes, of course you would,' she said. 'I am so sorry those men were killed, and I understand why it hurts you – but you can't let it destroy you. You didn't start this war and you go where you are sent. I don't think you did anything stupid or wrong – did you?'

Tom looked at her for a long moment and then he inclined his head. 'You're right, Lizzie. I feel guilty that I am alive, and they aren't and that I was the group leader, but... I think we were betrayed... and that's all I can tell you.'

'Then it wasn't your fault,' she said and put her arms around him. 'I know it hurts you, Tom, but don't blame yourself. I know you and you sometimes brood too much.'

'Right again,' he said. 'Let's go and see what Mum has for tea.'

* * *

Arthur had been out checking the cows when Tom arrived, but he was enjoying a mug of tea and a slice of cake with his wife when they got back and he smiled at them. Artie, Nancy and Jeanie were all out. The two girls had gone to a pre-Christmas lunch with some other land girls, tactfully making themselves scarce for the day so that the family could be alone. No one had any idea where Artie was, but he turned up at a quarter past four with a Christmas tree and the evening was given to decorating it.

'I thought I'd try to make it as normal as possible,' he told his mother with a grin of triumph before turning to Tom. 'It's good to see you back. How are you feeling?'

'Much better now,' Tom told him. 'It's good to be home.'

Jeanie and Nancy returned as the tree was being trimmed and while Nancy went upstairs to change out of her best slacks into something more suitable for the evening milking shift, Jeanie embraced her brother, Terry.

'Sorry I wasn't here when you arrived – but there was a big luncheon for us land girls in Ely. Thought it might be better for Tom and you to have a bit of space when you got here.'

Terry nodded. 'Yes, gave us a chance to settle in. It was good of you to give up your bed for me, Jeanie.'

'I'm all right with the camp bed,' she said and gave him a hug, which he allowed but didn't return. 'I'm sorry for everything – you being wounded and Ellie...'

Terry frowned at her. 'We'll talk privately later,' he told her.

Lizzie, who had been watching their meeting, turned away. They needed their privacy. She went to help Pam dish up their supper, which was a big vegetable and potato pie to go with some of the cold pork left over from lunch. The top was crusty and golden and it all smelled delicious.

Arthur raised his beer glass. 'To our heroes – Tom and Terry,' he said with a smile of welcome. 'We're glad to see you both here, and you are welcome in our home, Terry.'

Terry thanked them. He looked a bit uncomfortable but relaxed as he tucked into the appetising food. 'This is so much better than we get in the army,' he told Pam and took a sip of the beer. 'You're a wonderful cook, Mrs Talbot.'

'I do my best with what we're allowed – and a bit extra sometimes.' She looked at her husband and smiled. 'We're a family here – so I'll toast John, too. I don't know where he is, but I pray he is safe.'

'He must be all right, Mum,' Susan said and told Angela to stop fidgeting. 'Help me feed Tina,' she instructed her sister, who had eaten her small plateful. Angela preferred to have bread and jam, but her family made her eat proper food too.

'Are there any jam tarts?' Angela asked her mother, ignoring Susan's request.

Lizzie, who was sitting next to her, whispered in her ear and she giggled and smiled. 'I'll get them for you in a minute,' Lizzie promised aloud, and Pam looked at her sharply.

'You spoil her, Lizzie. Between them, Angela and Tina have all your sweet ration.'

'She can have mine,' Tom said and smiled at his sister. 'Angela has a sweet tooth, and I haven't.'

'No, you always preferred a bit of cake or something savoury to sweets,' Pam said, looking at him fondly.

Lizzie smiled. It was lovely to see the family together. John wasn't with them, but everyone else was and Jeanie and Terry fit in perfectly. Nancy had gone to the cowsheds, saying she didn't want any supper and would have a piece of toast later if she was hungry. Jeanie only wanted a small plate as she'd had a good lunch out, but she'd wanted to be there at the table with all her friends and family.

As Terry began to join in the banter occasionally, Lizzie felt really happy. Tom was home and for her that was everything, but it was nice to see Vera's son relaxing a little. Even in the middle of war, with all the restrictions and shortages, life could sometimes be very good.

* * *

That night, when they'd wished their friends sweet dreams and strolled the short distance to their new home, Lizzie was conscious of her good fortune. It could all have been so different and she felt blessed. Later, when they were in bed and had made love twice – once with feverish passion and then slowly, sweetly, she felt a new contentment, something she had never felt before.

As Tom lay beside her gently snoring, Lizzie felt certain that they would have a long and wonderful life together. If she was lucky, Tom wouldn't have to fight again, and even if he did, she had this odd sensation, this certainty, that he would come through.

She smiled and nestled up to him in the darkness and then fell into a deep sleep, peaceful and able to rest for the first time in months. When they woke, it was past ten in the morning and neither of them were in a hurry to get up...

23

John returned the car he'd borrowed for his trip to Portsmouth. It had taken several weeks' worth of petrol coupons that he'd borrowed or bought from friends and he knew he couldn't do it again. Next time he went down, it would need to be on the train, but as that was likely to be a long way off, he put the problem from his mind, irritated a little that Faith had agreed to be moved when she knew it would make it so much more difficult to meet.

Why couldn't she have been content to stay in Cambridge? It had been easy for them to get together there and she'd been well on the way to earning her nursing belt. Surely, it was as satisfying to nurse near her home as it was to go all that way?

For the first time ever, he was a little annoyed with her. Half his leave had been wasted getting there and back, so they'd hardly had any time together. They'd managed a meal out and a long walk by the sea, which was bracing, even though they'd found a sheltered spot where they could sit and cuddle up. John had taken a room for himself and his 'wife' at a small hotel. The beds were clean, but it wasn't very special and there had been a smell of stale cabbage when he'd opened a window. Their lovemaking had been good, but the magic of that first time was missing, and he thought it was due to the poky little room and the stares of the night porter who looked as if he knew they weren't man and wife. It had made the whole thing feel a bit sordid and seedy and he thought Faith felt it too and was disappointed.

John had wanted to leave the moment he'd seen the room, but it was their only chance to be together intimately. It was nearly Christmas and, although the shops were not lit up as usual, there should have been an air of festivity. He'd taken Faith's present with him. It was an engagement ring, a three-stone diamond and ruby, and she'd said it was beautiful when he'd put it on her finger, but somehow it hadn't been romantic the way he'd wanted for her.

'I'm sorry, Faith,' he'd told her when they parted the next day after lunch, because she'd only been able to get one night off, as she wasn't due for a longer leave until the next month. He'd had to leave to get back to base in time to report for duty the next day. 'It wasn't as I wanted things to be for us.'

'It was fine,' she'd answered brightly. 'Thank you for my lovely ring, John.'

She'd looked miserable as he'd waved to her and driven away and it had wrenched at his heart to leave her standing there alone. He cursed himself for being a fool. He should have found somewhere better to stay, but in his heart, he knew that wouldn't have helped much. This furtive liaison wasn't him and he didn't want it for Faith. He would phone and ask her if she wanted get married the next time they both got leave. And, if she agreed, he would make sure he found time to go over to her home in March and speak to her father, and ask for his permission first. If she wanted to continue nursing, they could keep it a secret. He felt now it was what they should have done before Christmas.

Yet *would* Faith agree? If it meant she might have to give up her nursing, would she be willing to be his wife? Had she continued to work in Cambridge, John might have found a little cottage they could both use whenever they chose. He had some savings. Not enough to buy a house, but he could rent one and afford to furnish it. If they married, his father would help him to buy a house.

Somehow, his mood of disappointment turned to annoyance with the girl he loved. Why couldn't Faith be like other girls? John knew that a lot of girls would have been eager to get married after they'd been courting for a year or so. Yes, they were both still young, but if they were in love, marriage was best. Perhaps Faith didn't love him... The thought sent cold shivers down his back. John couldn't imagine life without Faith now. He just wanted to make things wonderful for her but... if she preferred to keep working, there wasn't much he could do to persuade her.

* * *

'You look as if the world just fell around your ears,' one of his crew said as he walked into the mess room at his base that afternoon. 'Did your lady friend ditch you?'

'No – and she is my fiancée, not my lady friend,' John said and then regretted it as he saw the gleam in the other man's eyes. Roger was the bomb aimer and a bit of a bully at times. He liked to mock the other men and now he knew John was engaged, he would never leave it alone.

'Oh my! Touchy, aren't we?'

'Shut it!' John muttered.

'Do as he says, and shut it,' another man said. John looked at him. He was new and the wings badge sewn to his uniform sleeve showed that he was a pilot. He offered his hand to John. 'You must be Talbot, my navigator. I am Dave Carson and I understand you made a fine job of getting your last pilot back when he was badly shot up... Welcome to my team.'

'Good to meet you, sir.' John shook hands with him. 'Pleased we've got a replacement so soon.' He glanced back at Roger. 'Have you heard how Mike is?'

'They say he will make it – but he won't fly again,' Roger said and shrugged. 'Poor bugger would rather have died; they took his arm off—' He swallowed the whisky down and shouted for another.

'You'd better lay off that stuff,' Dave Carson warned him. 'We have a mission at eighteen hundred hours. I don't want you drunk, lieutenant.'

'Take more than a couple of these to make me incapable,' Roger said, but the look in his new captain's eyes silenced him and he shook his head at the waiter who brought the whisky. 'Put it back and I'll have it later.'

'Good,' Dave nodded. 'You all need to be on your toes this evening. We shall need accuracy if we are to succeed. I've been briefed on where we are going. It's an important factory – making some kind of weapons and well-protected, both by guns and its concrete walls.'

'In Germany?' John asked and received a nod in return.

'Not far from Munich,' Dave replied. 'I'll show you the aerial photos in the briefing room. You'll need to get us in and out by the shortest routes, John, because once we've made our attack, they will be after us like hornets.'

John nodded, his thoughts of Faith and the slight irritation he'd felt at wasting much of his leave travelling faded away. He would write and ask her to marry him when they got back. Surely, she would say 'yes'? She must feel as he did or she wouldn't have responded to his lovemaking – and that bit of it had been good, even if the rest of it hadn't been quite as he would have liked.

'Pay attention, John,' Dave reprimanded him. 'I just asked you if you had flown over Munich before?'

'Sorry. Yes, I have,' John replied. 'How many of us are going, do you know? Is it a big raid?'

'They are sending six bombers and a squadron of fighter planes,' Dave said. 'Apparently, the factory is important, and they want to make sure we destroy it.'

John nodded, thoughtful. He preferred it when they went for the factories rather than the cities, but if it was essential it would be well-defended, which meant it was going to make their mission more difficult and dangerous. So far, luck had been with them, but he was well aware that each mission could be his last and his thoughts returned to Faith. Had he told her how much he loved her? He'd given her that ring, but did she know how he longed for her to be his wife?

* * *

Faith was conscious of a feeling of regret. John's visit had been so fleeting and the hotel had been a bit disappointing. It hadn't mattered that much to Faith, even though it wasn't as nice as having a house to themselves, as they had in Cambridge, but she knew John hadn't liked it.

She smiled as she thought of the lovely ring, he'd given her. It was beautiful, ruby and diamond, and she'd admired one like it in a jeweller's shop in March once when they'd been walking home after a trip to the cinema. It might even be the same one, because it would be just like John to go back and buy it the next day.

Faith realised that she missed him more than she'd expected to when she'd agreed to the move. It had been nice to be picked out for a special posting and she'd gone along with it happily, but

John's visit had been so brief because of the need to get back on time. They would have had longer together if she'd still been in Cambridge.

John had travelled for hours and hours just to spend the night with her. It wasn't fair on him and she knew it couldn't happen often. The time was coming when she would have to make a decision – either she asked for a posting nearer home or she just gave it up and got married.

24

Faith was working that morning, a week after John's visit, when a nurse came to see her and told her that she was wanted in Matron's office. Feeling startled and wondering what she'd done wrong, Faith wiped her hands and handed over her task of bathing a wounded sailor to another young nurse, before following the nurse who had summoned her. She hesitated outside the door of Matron's office but was told to go straight in. When she did so, she saw that a man was already there and, when he turned, she gasped, because it was John's brother, Tom. He looked so serious and grim that Faith recoiled and for a moment, it felt as if her heart had stopped beating.

'Ah, Nurse Goodjohn,' Matron said. 'I am afraid your visitor has brought bad news—'

'John...' she breathed and swayed. Tom reached out and caught her, holding her and helping her to sit in a chair Matron provided. She looked up at him, an agonised appeal in her eyes. 'Is he dead?'

'His plane was shot down over Germany,' Tom told her, and she saw that he looked drained and exhausted himself. 'We heard the day before yesterday and we decided that one of the family should come down and tell you, Faith. Artie drove me, because I'm not up to a long drive on my own yet – but he felt I should be the one to tell you. The telegram didn't say whether John got out or not – but one of his friends from the base rang us yesterday and told us that he saw two parachutes land safely before the crash. Anyone still in the plane would have perished on impact...'

Faith bent over double as the pain seared through her. She covered her face with her hands, giving a choked mewl of grief as she saw the flash on impact and felt the heat as the plane was convulsed in flames. No one could have lived through that – and there were several men on board the bombers that John flew in.

'Two got down safely?' she asked, praying he would be one of them.

'An eyewitness saw two chutes float down. That doesn't mean those men are still alive, Faith,' Tom said grimly. 'It was over Germany, so the likelihood that they could get home is slim. If they weren't shot on the way down...' Tom drew a deep breath. 'The best we can hope for is that he got picked up and taken to a prisoner of war camp.'

Faith raised her head and looked at him, but her eyes were misty with tears. 'You don't give much for his chances, do you?'

'I am sorry, Faith, I don't,' he said. 'I know how much this must hurt and distress you – but I don't want to give you false hope. Mum says that he is still alive. She says she feels it in her heart – but she always had a special feeling for John, and I doubt she will ever stop hoping he'll come back.'

Faith nodded. She couldn't speak because her throat was constricted with grief. Tom clearly didn't think his brother had much chance of survival – and she could see the scars of battle on his face and the knowledge of hurt and pain was in his eyes. Tom Gilbert had been there and seen men die and Faith's heart sank.

John's mother would cling to hope, but she had none. John had gone and she was devastated.

'You are excused duty for a week, Nurse Goodjohn,' Matron said now. 'Mr Gilbert could take you home if you wish to be with your family?'

'May I have today off and return to work tomorrow?' she asked, raising her head. 'Thank you for coming to tell me, Mr Gilbert, but I don't want to go home. If I do, I'll just upset my family. I'd rather carry on with my work, helping others...'

Matron looked at her for a moment and then inclined her head. 'Spoken like a true nurse,' she said. 'You may, of course, return tomorrow – if you feel up to it.'

Faith thanked her, was dismissed and left.

Tom Gilbert followed her and took her arm. She turned her head to look at him. 'Are you certain, Faith? You could come and stay with Lizzie and me if you wanted...'

'Thank you. I'd like to visit one day but not yet,' she told him. 'If I give in, I shall cry and I'm not sure I could stop.'

'Just remember we are your family,' Tom told her. 'We care about you, Faith, whatever happens in the future. Even if John is gone, you are still the girl he loved and wanted to marry...'

'Thank you.' His sincerity almost broke her. It was the reason she couldn't go home, because her mother and father would treat her like fine porcelain and their concern would weaken her. 'I loved John – perhaps more than he or I realised. I wish...' Faith shook her head. Wishes would not bring him back or put his wedding ring on her finger. 'I am sorry; if John is gone, you've lost a brother and I know how much this must upset Pam...' Tears trickled down her cheek, but she brushed them away.

'Ma is refusing to cry, says she knows he is alive – and perhaps she is right,' Tom said awkwardly. 'I am sorry if I sounded too negative...'

Faith looked into his face. 'You are exhausted,' she said, the nurse in her coming to the fore. 'Shall we go and have a drink of tea or something? I think this trip was too much for you.'

'I've been ill for a while,' Tom agreed with a wry smile. 'I am better than I was, and I wanted to come. It would have been too cruel just to telephone.'

'Thank you. It was kind, but now I think we'd better go to a little café I know and sit down before you fall down.' Faith was back in nursing mode, her grief held down tight inside her. Later, when she was alone, she would let it come out, but for the moment, she felt concern for John's brother, who looked as if he ought to be in bed rather than here in a busy port bringing her bad news.

25

'You look terrible,' Pam told her eldest son as he entered the kitchen, closely followed by Artie. 'It was too much for you. You should have let Artie go on his own.'

'I owed it to John to go,' Tom said but sank down into his father's armchair by the range. 'I am pretty tired, Mum. I'll go home and have a rest soon, but I wanted to tell you about Faith... She was very brave.'

'If you ask me, she didn't care much about John,' Artie said and sounded angry. 'She refused Tom's offer to bring her home and she's going back to work – probably already there.' He glanced at his watch. 'We drove for hours and wasted all those petrol coupons just for a girl who cares more about her nursing than John.' He sounded so bitter than Pam shook her head at him.

'I know this news has hit us all hard,' she said. 'Your father as much as anyone – but he is back at work, because he couldn't just sit here and do nothing. I expect Faith feels the same. I carry on as usual, Artie, but that doesn't stop me hurting inside.'

Artie looked down. 'I know you do – bloody war,' he muttered in a choked voice, and she saw tears in his eyes. Artie seldom showed his emotions, but this had really got to him. When John was home, Artie often mocked him, but it was clear that he was feeling the grief now.

'John was doing his duty and what he wanted,' Pam said firmly. 'Besides, we don't know for sure that he is gone. My hope is that he will turn up in a prisoner of war camp somewhere and come back to us when the war is over.'

'I don't envy him if he is a prisoner,' Artie said fiercely. 'Bloody Jerries. I should like to kill the lot of them.'

'If you are thinking of joining up out of revenge, you can stop right there,' Pam said sternly. 'We were lucky to get Tom back and we may have lost John, though I still feel he is alive – but you are needed here. Do you want to kill your father?'

Artie mumbled something that might have been an apology. She knew he was feeling guilty that he was safe at home on the farm while his young brother was either dead or had been captured.

Pam's gaze moved to her eldest son. Tom had fallen asleep in his chair, his tea untouched on the occasional table beside him. She was pleased because she would rather he rested here, under her watchful eye. He could go home when Lizzie got back from work.

Lizzie had hesitated about going in and would be home on the earlier bus this evening. Tom should never have gone all that way. He hadn't got his strength back yet, but he'd insisted on doing it and in a way she was glad. Faith was a nice girl and she deserved to hear it from someone she knew. She'd only met Tom once, of course, but he was Lizzie's husband and Pam knew the two girls got on well.

What would that poor girl do if John had gone down with the plane? An icy shiver went through Pam, but she shut out her fears resolutely. She couldn't lose her John; it would be too cruel. Pam had always believed in God, though He worked in mysterious ways. Her Tommy – Tom's father – had been taken from her. Surely, she wouldn't lose John too?

Pam sent Artie back to work after he'd eaten and got on with some baking. It was nearly time for the others to come in for their tea when Tom woke up. He smiled at her and eased his shoulders.

'Sorry, Mum. I meant to take myself out of your way...'

'You could never be in my way,' she assured him. 'Shall I make a fresh pot of tea now? I've baked some rock buns and jam tarts – and there's a pie in the oven for our tea when everyone gets in. You and Lizzie will eat with us tonight.'

'How do you do it, Mum?' Tom asked. 'You just keep going, working all hours – and I know you're desperate for more news about John.'

'I keep thinking about his poor girlfriend...'

'His fiancée,' Tom corrected. 'He gave her a ring a week or so ago. I think he wanted to get married – even though he's only nineteen. Would you have said yes if he'd asked?'

'Of course, I would,' Pam said. 'They are young, but I wasn't much older when I had you. John has his future mapped out and he will make a success of it.'

'If...' Tom shook his head. 'I know you believe he is still alive, Mum, but the odds are against him. More than half that crew didn't get out...'

'I know.' Pam acknowledged his judgement. 'But I'm not ready to accept it. No one knows for sure yet. We'll wait before we give up hope of seeing your brother come through that door with a smile on his face. When you were lost and on that hospital ship, we worried you might be dead, but you weren't. Why shouldn't John be as lucky?'

'I hope he is, Mum,' Tom told her and got up to hug her. She hugged him back, fighting her tears. 'Even if he made it out of the plane, his chances of surviving in a prisoner of war camp are still not good.'

'Don't say that,' she said gruffly. 'John will survive if he can – he loves that girl, so he has something to live for…'

* * *

Lizzie saw the tiredness in her husband when she got home from work. He was trying to be cheerful and to do justice to his mother's food, but he was bone-weary. The long journey had been too much for him. He needed to rest and she was glad she'd moved all her appointments either to her assistant or another day.

'I'm staying home tomorrow to look after you,' she said as they walked the short distance home after supper. 'You need to rest, Tom.'

'Yes, I know,' he said. 'I suppose I should have let Artie go alone – but I couldn't. He isn't very sympathetic and… She was so brave, Lizzie. I could see how badly it hit her, but she refused home leave in favour of getting back to work.'

'Her mother would have cosseted her to death,' Lizzie said. 'I'm not surprised she didn't want to go home. I don't think her parents realised how much she loves John, and they might have said the wrong things.'

'I probably did anyway,' Tom acknowledged. 'I couldn't pretend – couldn't give her false hope and let her think it would be all right…' He saw the expression in Lizzie's eyes. 'I know you all thought I was dead, but I was lucky. If John survived the crash

– and that is a big *if* – he is alone in enemy territory and could be shot on sight.'

'Or he might be a prisoner of war,' Lizzie said. 'There is a chance for him, surely, Tom?'

'A small chance, yes,' he admitted and gave a strangled sob. 'God, that is an awful thought. I feel he might be better off dead. I can't imagine what it must be like for men who are taken prisoner...'

'It is better than being dead. John has too much to live for. He will come through if he has the chance.'

Tom nodded soberly. '*If* he has the chance. We don't even know that he survived the crash and we may never know.' They had, by now, arrived back home and Lizzie ushered Tom straight into their bedroom.

'You mustn't give up hope,' Lizzie said and put her arms around him as she saw tears on his face. 'I never gave up on you and nor did your mother. She won't give up on John.'

Tom held her close, burying his face in her hair. 'I know, Lizzie. You are right and I shall pray that my brother comes home one day, but it won't be easy for him. I feel so sorry for Faith – they've had such a short time together.'

'Maybe it will come right and they will marry one day,' Lizzie said. 'We have to keep on believing that, Tom.'

'Yes, I know,' he agreed. 'He is so young, Lizzie – they all are. Some of those pilots are barely finished with their education when they get their wings and then...' He shook his head. 'John isn't the only one; too many of them are dying all the time. There would have been five or six crew on board that plane when it was hit.'

'Yes, I know,' Lizzie said. 'And every one of them had a family who must be thinking the same as we are and hoping that their son or husband was one of the survivors.'

'Yes, of course.' Tom yawned and tried to hide it. 'Sorry, my darling, but I am really tired. I need to get to sleep.'

'It was too much for you going all that way and you hardly out of hospital...' Faith said as she propped some pillows up behind him as he lay on their bed.

'It was the least I could do,' Tom replied wearily. 'John would have done the same for me. He was closer to me than Artie. I think Dad is feeling it more than he lets on. They had one or two arguments when John refused to work on the land and Dad is blaming himself now, regretting every harsh word he ever said to John.'

'Isn't that how everyone always feels?' Lizzie said, snuggling into his warm body, but Tom had already fallen asleep. She kissed him softly and he murmured something but didn't wake.

Lizzie's heart was full. She loved him so much and was so grateful to have him restored to her, but she knew the news about John had hit him hard. He didn't have much hope that his brother would survive both a plane crash and almost certain imprisonment. His experience of war had been harsh, Lizzie understood that. Tom had seen death at close hand and couldn't quite believe in miracles, but Lizzie knew that they did happen. Because of a friend's tenacity, Tom was home with her. Shorty had got him away and perhaps someone would help John. They could only pray for his survival.

She felt her cheeks wet and knew she was crying, for what John must be suffering if he was still alive – and for Faith's grief. She would have to live with uncertainty and fear for a long time, because it might be years before they would know for certain whether John was alive or dead. Lizzie decided she would write to her, invite her to stay and tell her that they were all thinking of her and would help her if she should need them.

26

Jeanie watched as Pam served the Christmas dinner. She had worked hard making it nice with bread sauce and roast potatoes as well as three vegetables and the large cockerel they had killed for the occasion. Its skin was golden and crisp and the smell was delicious. Pam hadn't been able to make her usual amount of puddings, because she couldn't get enough dried fruit and many of the other ingredients, and they eaten a special pudding she'd made when John had come home, but she had managed to make a pear upside-down cake. The pears were from Arthur's little store of tinned foods he'd hidden up in the attic at the start of the war and were brought out one at a time for special occasions. However, despite the wonderful smells and the mouth-watering food, it was a largely silent meal. Everyone was conscious of the man missing from their home.

Artie had been out first thing and done the milking. Jeanie had joined him at the end and cleared out the cowsheds. She'd returned for breakfast and then washed and changed into a skirt and warm jumper. Grateful for the kindness shown to her and her family, Jeanie had managed to purchase small gifts for everyone, including her parents and Annie. Terry had taken those to London for her, choosing to visit his parents over the festive season and to take Tina with him. Annie wouldn't be there, but her present would be waiting for her when she eventually got home on leave.

Gift-giving took place after Christmas lunch for the Talbot family and Jeanie placed her gifts with others on the sideboard in the dining room. Arthur had lit a fire there first thing in the morning. The room was a long one with a table that extended to accommodate twelve people but was set for ten that day. A small gift had been placed by Jeanie's plate. She was a little surprised as she'd seen a parcel on the sideboard addressed to her from Pam and family.

Pam brought in the upside-down cake and placed it on the table. 'I only had enough dried fruit for one pudding, which we had soon after it was made. So, I made this today with some cream from the milk that Artie skimmed for me. I'm sorry it isn't more traditional…'

'It makes a nice change, love,' Arthur said. 'We get stuck with the old traditions. Doesn't hurt to change them a bit.'

'I used the pudding last time…' Pam faltered as her voice failed. She had been going to say when John was home. Jeanie remembered them having it when John had spent a couple of days with them after Faith went down to Portsmouth. Pam had made the excuse that he might not get home for Christmas.

'It tastes gorgeous,' Jeanie said to break the silence. 'I don't like Christmas pudding as much as this.'

Pam smiled at her but didn't answer.

Artie looked at her across the table. 'Aren't you going to open your present, Jeanie?'

His gaze was on the small parcel that she'd left untouched by her plate. 'Did you put this here?' she asked in surprise.

'Yes. I went to March and then to Ely to find the right thing…'

Jeanie picked up the parcel and undid the ribbon bow and then removed the tissue paper. She had thought it was nicely wrapped but hadn't dreamed it was from Artie. Opening the black satin box inside the tissue, she discovered a gold locket in an oval shape with an engraved front and a long chain. It was such a beautiful gift that for a few seconds she didn't know what to say.

'It is lovely, thank you, Artie,' she exclaimed and slipped it over her head. The locket nestled between her breasts. Her cheeks felt warm as she looked at him. Jeanie's gift to him was on the sideboard, but it was only a silk tie. 'I bought little gifts for all of you – on the sideboard…'

Artie got up and went to fetch some of the parcels. She saw that he had her gift and he handed her the bulky parcel from Pam and a smaller one from Lizzie and Tom. Jeanie hesitated, watching as Artie opened his gift. He looked pleased and grinned at her. 'I'll wear it next time we go to a dance,' he told her and then opened his gift from his parents, which was an envelope and contained money. Tom and Lizzie had given him cufflinks and there was a tiepin from Pam.

'Your father thought you would prefer money,' Pam told him as he put it away in his wallet. 'I wanted to get you a little something…'

'I like both,' Artie told her. 'The pin will go with Jeanie's tie – and the money is always useful. Thanks, Dad. I'll put it towards a car.'

'You can use mine until then,' Arthur said. 'If a suitable vehicle comes along, let me know and I'll buy it for your birthday, Artie. You're a good lad and I couldn't manage without you these days…'

Artie nodded his appreciation. His other gifts were all

opened, as were the rest of the family's, but Nancy's parcels remained on the sideboard. She had gone home, because, as she'd told Pam, it was her duty to see her mother was all right, but she would be back on Boxing Day and would open her presents then.

Nancy had given Pam and Arthur a box of chocolates. She'd bought Susan and Angela the same and to Lizzie she had given a box of handkerchiefs. Jeanie had a pair of silk stockings. Both Artie and Tom received a small box of tiny cigars. For Tina, there was a colouring book and pencils, but she would open them with her granny in London.

Jeanie had given her a pretty scarf before she'd left but regretted not keeping it for her return when Nancy said she would give it to her mother to go with her coat. Pam had kept Nancy's gifts back for that very reason.

'She would undoubtedly give them to her mother,' she'd remarked to Lizzie within Jeanie's hearing. 'Perhaps if she has them on her return, she'll keep them for herself...'

Jeanie hadn't liked Nancy too much when she first came to the farm. She was prickly and difficult to know, but now she felt a bit sorry for her.

'I hope Nancy will like the blouse we made for her,' Lizzie said as she and Jeanie got up to clear away the dishes and discarded paper. 'Did your gloves fit all right?'

'Yes, lovely,' Jeanie said. 'I haven't had leather gloves before – only woollen ones. I shall keep them for best, Lizzie. It was so kind of you to give them to me.'

'I was lucky to find them,' Lizzie replied with a smile. 'Thank you for my scarf, Jeanie. It is lovely and Tom likes his socks. Just what we needed.'

Jeanie shook her head. 'They were just small things but I'm glad you liked them...'

She was still a little in shock after opening her gift from Artie. Pam had bought her some good-quality material to make herself a nice dress for the summer and she had the leather gloves from Lizzie – but Artie's present was something she had not expected. A box of soap or something similar would have been more what she'd imagined he'd buy her – if she'd imagined it at all.

Why had he given her such an expensive gift? She hadn't even been sure he would give her a present – but that locket. It was the kind of thing a young man gave to his girlfriend. Did Artie think of her that way? Jeanie's stomach clenched at the idea. He must like her a bit to have given her such a nice gift – but did it mean anything?

Jeanie looked at Artie and saw that he was staring at her. He smiled and nodded as her hand went to the locket. She touched its smoothness and smiled. Artie grinned, clearly pleased with her reaction. Feeling shy and unsure, she picked up more dishes and followed Lizzie out to the kitchen with them.

'You go and sit down, Mum,' Lizzie told her. 'Jeanie, Susan and I will wash up and clear away.'

'I don't mind doing it...' Pam began, but she was shooed out of her own kitchen and went back to join the men in the sitting room.

'She works so hard all the time,' Lizzie said. 'We all tend to take her for granted, but she needs a bit of a rest after cooking all this lot.'

* * *

Jeanie was glad to be out of the way for a while. Artie's gift and his look had thrown her thoughts into confusion. She'd thought he just took her to the occasional dance because Pam told him to.

What did the expensive gift mean? Was he trying to say he thought she was special?

She knew he was very upset over John's fate and he'd been angry and morose by turns since the news. Jeanie had seen him crying in the barn. He'd thought he was alone, so she hadn't disturbed him, but she'd stood and watched him, her heart wrenching as he'd cried and then thrown something at the wall in sudden anger. His emotions were clearly muddled over John, but when he'd smiled at her across the table that lunchtime, Jeanie's heart had done a somersault, because, she could have sworn he cared for her... and yet, another day he would probably be careless and thoughtless and rile her up the wrong way. Jeanie didn't even know if she wanted more than casual friendship from him. Sometimes she thought she really liked him, but other times she wasn't sure of how she felt.

'You're thoughtful, Jeanie,' Lizzie said, breaking the silence that had fallen over them.

'I was just... wondering what it was like for the men out there at Christmas,' Jeanie improvised, because she didn't want to tell anyone her true thoughts. 'My sister has gone overseas to nurse the wounded in the field hospitals. Her letter said she wouldn't have a traditional Christmas and might be sunbathing instead... I suppose she is off to Africa or somewhere hot...'

'Lucky her,' Susan said. 'I hate the dreary weather we're having lately.' She sniffed. 'It hasn't been a good Christmas this year... Oh, I know we had a nice dinner and we all had gifts. Even Terry managed to get Tina a lovely doll; he showed it to me before he left, but you know what I mean...'

'Yes, of course, we know,' Lizzie said and put an arm about her shoulders. 'We all miss John.'

Susan rubbed at the tears in her eyes. 'I'm sorry. I am grateful for all the lovely things you all gave me – but it just hurts to know

John didn't get his presents. Mum has them all in her wardrobe, but she didn't put them out with the others.'

'I know. I asked her what I should do about a gift for John and she said if I bought something to keep, she would put it away for him. I bought him some socks,' Lizzie said.

'I wasn't sure what to buy for him either,' Jeanie said with a gulp. 'I gave him handkerchiefs in the end and Pam has them.'

Susan suddenly burst into tears and ran from the room.

'She'll go up to her bedroom and have a good cry and then come down when she's ready,' Lizzie said, looking at Jeanie. 'Everything is so hard just now. It must hurt you to see your brother using crutches?'

'Yes. He used to be so strong,' Jeanie said. 'At least we have him home, Lizzie, and I think he is getting better slowly. Being with Tina has been good for him. He said he would bring her back after Christmas and perhaps spend a bit more time with us. He seems to like it here and I'm sure the country air is good for him, though I know Dad wants him in London as soon as he can manage it.'

'Yes, he is getting better,' Lizzie agreed. She hung the tea towels up to dry. 'Shall we join the others – or should I perhaps go up to Susan?'

'I should let her cry for a while,' Jeanie said. 'I cried a lot when I heard the news about Terry, but it made me feel better. I knew that I had to be strong for his sake and so I've tried to be ever since.'

'And so must we for Pam and John's family's sake,' Lizzie said. 'The person I feel for is Faith – she is alone down there, no one to run to and hug. I tried to telephone her last night and this morning, but they said she was working.'

'She can't be working all the time,' Jeanie said. 'Perhaps she just doesn't want to talk yet.'

27

Faith stood staring out at the sea. She pulled her scarf tighter. Made of soft wool, it had been a Christmas gift from Lizzie. Pam had sent her gifts, too, though she hadn't sent them anything. She hadn't even sent cards that year, except one to her parents. She'd been too sunk in misery, and the festive season, like the whole of January, had gone by in a blur. She hadn't even replied to Lizzie's kind letter. Everything was too painful to think about, so she just shut it all out and worked every hour she could.

It was cold this February of 1941 and she shivered in the biting wind that blew inland, making her nose feel icy – as icy as her heart. In the months since she'd been told of John's disappearance, she had gone on working, giving little sign that she was breaking inside. Refusing all telephone calls and all the leave offered her, she just wanted to work until she was so tired that she couldn't feel anything any more.

She watched the waves rise and fall, white-crested and restless, as if they were trying to batter down the land defences. It was like watching the war of sea against land and in her mind, she saw the opposing forces of two armies – and knew the bitterness of loss all over again.

This wretched war just went on and on, not satisfied with the lives it had already cost, it took hundreds, thousands more all the time, and in Faith's heart, it was a wasteland of grief and regret.

Faith never read the newspaper reports of how the conflict was going – she didn't need to because the evidence was in the constant flow of wounded to their hospital and the deaths. Too many young lives gone. Why did John have to be one of the unlucky ones – and why hadn't she told him she would marry him whenever he liked?

Her regret tasted bitter in her mouth and she suddenly turned away and retched as the bile forced its way up her throat and out of her mouth. Faith leaned against a wall and wiped the spit from her lips. She felt awful. Probably had one of the winter vomiting viruses that went round the hospital and infected nurses, doctors and patients alike despite all they did to prevent it spreading. Disinfectant made the wards smell clean, but it didn't seem to stop the spread of colds and flu.

Still feeling a bit under the weather, Faith walked slowly towards a bench a little further along the seafront and sat down on a bit of broken wall, hugging her coat around her and fighting her misery. At this moment, she was almost tempted to throw herself off a high point and let the sea drag her under.

'Are you all right, nurse? You are a nurse, aren't you?'

The wind had torn her cap from her head so Faith had taken it off and pushed it deep into her coat pocket. She looked up and, as she did so, a feeling of recognition struck her, though for a moment she wasn't sure where she'd seen the young man before.

'Faith!' he said. 'I thought there was something familiar about you – but I was concerned when I saw you being sick just now whoever you were. Are you feeling ill?'

'Slash?' she faltered as the memory returned. 'We met at that pub in Cambridge – you and your friend... Rocky...'

He'd been smiling at her, but at the mention of his friend, a look of pain entered his eyes. 'I'm afraid he didn't make it back this time. I was lucky. I just caught a bit of shrapnel in my leg. They sent me home for treatment, but I'll be going back...'

She noticed he looked suntanned and wondered if he'd been fighting in North Africa with the Desert Rats, as the Seventh Division had been named by some newspapers.

'Oh don't,' Faith said and to her horror she burst into tears. 'I can't bear it. I can't bear any more deaths.' She bent her head, shoulders shaking. She sensed that Slash hesitated before sitting down and putting his arm about her shoulders, holding her to him as she wept into his chest. Her sobbing was loud and desperate and she felt him kiss her hair and stroke it as he did his best to comfort her. She gulped and looked up at him. 'I am so sorry. I didn't mean to cry all over you – but... my fiancé was killed – at least he's missing, presumed dead, and it hurts...'

'Yes, of course, it does,' he said softly.

'John wanted to get married, but I wanted to go on nursing and I was afraid they would send me home if I did and now his brother thinks he must be dead and—' She caught her breath. 'I just wish I was too...'

'That's foolish talk. John wouldn't want that...'

'But I let him think my nursing was more important...' Her grief was overwhelming her now. She'd shut it out, fighting all emotion, preferring to feel nothing, but now it was swamping her.

'I am sure he understood,' Slash told her and held her hands in his. 'I am sorry this happened to you, Faith, but don't let it make you bitter and don't lose all hope.'

'I... don't know if I can go on...' She stared at him, suddenly weak and hopeless. 'I can't bear it...'

'Yes, you can. It hurts, but you are stronger than this, Faith.' He looked at her for a moment, holding her gaze. 'It's cold out here. Why don't you let me take you for something to eat and a hot drink?'

Faith hesitated and then inclined her head. Since the news of John's death, Faith had shut herself away, refusing all offers of friendship. She hadn't wanted to go out with anyone – girlfriends and certainly not other men. It would have felt like a betrayal of John, but somehow Slash had got through the barrier and she'd let him in.

'Just friends,' she said, looking up at him uncertainly. 'I couldn't be anything else.'

'I wouldn't ask it,' he said and drew her up, tucking her arm through his. 'I am going to take you to my home. My parents are away at the moment, but I'm a pretty good cook when it comes to omelettes and I'll make you a nice meal and warm you up.'

* * *

The house was detached and rather nice inside. It had cream-flocked wallpaper, a rich Persian-style carpet in the living room and some nice dark mahogany cabinets filled with bits of silver and porcelain.

'Did you say your parents were away?' Faith asked.

'Yes, they've gone to a funeral up north,' Slash said. 'My mother's aunt died – I think she was in her nineties, but they used to visit when they could and she was a pleasant lady, so they went up for a few days to show their respect and help her daughter sort the house out.'

'You didn't go?'

'I couldn't. I just have another couple of days and then I have to report back,' Slash said. 'I've had three weeks rest, so now I'll be going wherever they need me, though I think I shall be taking another training course rather than going overseas immediately.'

Faith nodded and gave him a weak smile. 'I'm glad you won't be going back to the Front immediately.'

'We have to fight if we can, Faith,' Slash told her as he led the way into the big kitchen and began to prepare their meal. 'Put the kettle on and let's have some cocoa. I'll beat the eggs for the omelettes.'

Faith did as she was told. The kitchen was lovely and warm, with the shine of dark oak furniture set with copper pans and a mixture of bits and pieces. The crockery was all different kinds – a shelf of pretty teapots, two or three cups and saucers of one sort and then others and none of the plates matched.

Slash saw her looking and laughed. 'That's my mother for you, Faith. She never buys a set of anything. She likes variety and she just picks up the odd teapot or plate whenever she sees one she likes. She says that if nothing matches it doesn't matter if one gets broken because she can just buy another that she likes.'

'What a good idea,' Faith replied and laughed. 'My mother has her best tea and dinner service and when she gets it out – mostly when my uncle visits, because he gave it to her – she guards it like precious jewels and if something gets chipped it is a calamity...'

'Oh, Mum isn't bothered about a few breakages. Just as well when my brother and I were young...' His face clouded and he shook his head. 'Trevor is in the navy. I don't know where he is. We haven't heard anything for months... but he never was one for keeping in touch.'

Faith nodded and bit her lip. The kettle had boiled and Slash directed her how to make the cocoa. That made her smile a bit – as if she needed directions to make cocoa! However, it was lovely and creamy because he wanted a spoonful of condensed milk in his and she did the same for herself. Very sweet, hot and comforting. The omelettes and chips that Slash put in front of her were good, too, the eggs light and fluffy and the chips crisp but not burned.

'I can't make chips as good as these,' she said. 'Where did you learn?'

'Mum taught us to cook,' he said with a grin. 'She thought it might come in handy – and I must admit there have been times when it has been very useful...'

Faith found that she could eat. She'd hardly bothered to have more than a piece of toast or a sandwich for weeks, because everything had tasted like sawdust.

'Thank you for this,' she said. 'I think I may have been ill because I wasn't eating properly. At first, I thought a winter sickness, but I don't feel ill now – it was just an empty stomach.'

'Good.' Slash smiled at her. 'It can't mean much to you yet, Faith – but I really like you. I have right from the first time I saw you. I wished I'd asked you to write and you've been in my thoughts...'

Faith was about to shake her head, but something stopped her.

'I am not asking for anything, except to be counted a friend – but if you ever need anything, well, I want to help. You know where I live now and I'm going to make sure you have my contact details.'

'You're a nice man,' Faith said.

'I want you to stay in touch, Faith. Nothing more – just a postcard to say how you are and I'll do the same.'

'All right. I do need a friend,' Faith agreed. 'I've been feeling very alone.'

'I know. I watched you for a while before you sat on that wall. I was afraid for you. I thought... well, I've known what it is like to feel desperation and I don't want you to feel that way again....'

'Thank you...' Faith took a sobbing breath. 'I don't have to go to work until the morning. Would you take me to the cinema please?'

'Yes, of course,' he said. 'What time do you have to be back at the nurses' home?'

'About half-past ten, but... no one would know if I didn't sleep there. We're all working such long hours. It would be assumed I was on duty...'

'Would you like to stay here?' he asked.

'If you don't mind. I don't want to be alone for a while...'

'Then we'll bring some fish and chips back for supper,' he said. 'You can have my bed and I'll sleep in Trevor's room.'

'Thanks,' Faith said. 'I like it here. It reminds me of home – but if I went home, I'd have to answer a lot of questions.'

'I shan't ask,' Slash told her. 'But if you want to tell me something, I'll listen.'

'I don't know. I'm not sure yet,' she said and sighed as she pushed her plate away. 'That's the best food I've had for ages. I hope your mother doesn't mind us eating all her eggs.'

'Dad keeps a couple of hens in the back garden,' he said and laughed. 'If we're lucky, we get half a dozen or so eggs a week.'

Faith nodded. She got up and cleared the dishes into the sink and then started to wash them up. It was nice being here – a bit like the time she'd spent with John in the house they'd borrowed in Cambridge. The only difference was that she'd been in love with John. Yet it made her feel safe and warm for a while and she needed that – when she returned to work, the pain and the suffering on the wards would remind her of John's loss again.

* * *

Faith could see the man lying on the ground. Nearby, the flames from the crashed plane lit the sky and she could hear their roar, hear the explosion as it burst apart and then was consumed by fire. On the ground, the man was moaning, crying out in pain. He was calling for her. Faith tried to reach him, to take him in her arms and hold him, to stop the pain, but her feet felt as if they were glued to the ground. She struggled to reach him, crying out his name, over and over again.

'John... John... John...'

A hand touched her shoulder, shaking her gently, bringing her out of the nightmare. She blinked in the strong light and felt shocked as she gazed up into the eyes of a man. It wasn't John, but they were kind eyes, eyes that looked at her with love, and she suddenly found herself in his arms, weeping as he held her until the grief subsided.

She became aware that she was wearing just her silk petticoat and he was wearing a shirt and pants, his shirt opened at the front. He was aroused, but trying to hide it from her, lying awkwardly on his side but away from her.

Faith had no idea why she did it, but she pressed herself against him. Burrowing into his chest, she clung to him desperately, needing the solace of strong arms around her and the comfort that it brought just for a moment.

Slash held her close and stroked her hair and her back through the thin silk of her petticoat. He whispered soft, comforting words and eventually her sobs eased. She was aware that he was still aroused, but he simply held her and told her to sleep and after a while, she did.

* * *

When she woke again, Slash had gone. He'd left a note for her on the bed, giving her all the details of where she could contact him and telling her that he was her friend always.

Dressing hastily, Faith put the note away in her pocket and left the house, walking to her accommodation. She felt embarrassed at the memory of the way she'd pressed against him so needily. What must he think of her? It was just the way her grief had overcome her. Fortunately, Slash was a decent man and hadn't taken advantage of her vulnerability.

Her heart heavy, and feeling confused and uncertain, she washed and changed into a clean uniform before returning to her work on the wards. Life went on and she had to go on somehow, even though her heart was broken.

28

'I have to report for a medical,' Tom told Lizzie after reading his official letter. It was the end of March now and he was looking and walking better. Lizzie had noticed a slight restlessness in him these past few days and knew that he wasn't comfortable being at home while the war raged on. He and Arthur spent time together talking about the war and its consequences and they listened to all the news reports as well as reading the papers. 'It's in two weeks' time.'

Lizzie nodded. 'I need to go into the salon today,' she said. 'But I'm going to rearrange my appointments and take a few days off so we can spend more time together.'

'Do you think you could?' Tom asked. 'It's what I'd like, Lizzie – but you do have a business to run.'

'Ruth – she's the new girl I've taken on, because the salon is so busy – can do some of my appointments. I may have to go in for an hour or two some mornings – but I want to be with you as much as I can before you go back.'

'I'm not likely to return to active service just yet,' Tom said with a little frown. 'I think I may have a permanent limp – and if the doctors agree, I won't be serving in the army for long. At least, not in the way I did.'

'Will you mind if they put you on lighter duties?'

'Yes, in a way. I feel that I left my work unfinished,' Tom said. 'You know I can't tell you everything, darling, but... things didn't go quite as they ought last time, and I'd like to put that right.'

'Yes, I do understand,' Lizzie agreed. 'But if you're not really fit for active service, you couldn't do that – could you?'

'Probably not,' Tom replied. 'I think a lot may have changed. Shorty rang the other day. He told me some things that mean I shan't be going back to the same unit anyway.'

Lizzie nodded. She couldn't help being pleased inside but wouldn't let Tom see. He clearly wanted to go back and finish what he'd started, but after his severe injuries, that probably would not be possible. 'You were lucky,' she told him now. 'Your injuries have almost healed. Terry still has to have more treatment for his leg...'

'He has an appointment at Addenbrooke's Hospital in Cambridge. I am going in with him this afternoon. Perhaps they will be able to help him.' Tom said.

Terry had returned to them in January and was helping with light work on the farm, making himself useful and building his strength at the same time.

'I certainly hope so,' Lizzie said. 'Susan spends a fair amount of time with him, because of Tina. She says he still gets a lot of pain and soreness, even though he tries to hide it. You should be thankful your leg healed, Tom.'

'I know,' he agreed and smiled wryly. 'I'm a glutton for punishment, Lizzie. The best thing all round would be for them to discharge me, so I can return to work on the farm.'

'Yes, it would,' Lizzie smiled understandingly. 'Except that I know it isn't what you want, Tom. You still want to serve, don't you?'

'In some capacity, yes. I doubt it will be frontline stuff...'

Lizzie felt like cheering but knew she mustn't be pleased that Tom probably would be stuck in a boring clerical job that he'd hate. It would be better if they sent him home for good, but he might feel like a failure if he wasn't allowed to continue in some way – and she would rather he did what made him feel good than come home if it felt wrong for him.

'Well, we'll make the most of your home leave until your medical,' she said, 'and now I'd better leave or I'll miss my bus.'

'I could take you in the car,' Tom offered, but she shook her head.

'Save the petrol for when we need it. I catch the bus most days and I'll keep doing that until the war is over and we can afford a little car for me.'

Tom nodded and said, 'Your driving is improving.'

'Well, I've had lessons from good teachers,' Lizzie said and saw the flicker of pain in his eyes, because John had given her some of her first lessons and it made Tom remember. She squeezed his hand. 'Don't give up on him. He may still be alive...'

'It is more than three months since he went missing...' Tom's face tightened with controlled grief. 'We would surely have heard something by now if he was a prisoner.'

'You can't be sure. One of my customers heard recently that her husband was a prisoner of war and he'd been missing for months.'

'Yes, I know it happens,' Tom said. 'The only way we hear about it sometimes is if the Red Cross get in touch. They have their own methods of finding out these things.'

'Yes, I suppose it is because they are international and giving them limited access to prisoners by way of food parcels is a two-way thing – there must be thousands of German prisoners too.'

Tom murmured agreement, adding, 'You'd better run or you'll miss that bus.'

Lizzie laughed, snatched up her bag and left him sitting at their kitchen table. She knew that he would find jobs to do around the farm while she was gone. He was fine driving a tractor and he could manage light jobs in the yard – feeding and milking. Arthur wouldn't let him do much, but Tom preferred to help where he could. He hated sitting around. She thought he brooded over his last mission, which she gathered had gone wrong – and Tom being Tom blamed himself.

* * *

Lizzie caught her bus by the skin of her teeth, waving at the driver so that he waited at the stop for a moment to let her catch up.

'Late this morning,' the conductor remarked.

'Yes, I am. Thank you for waiting.'

She paid for her ticket and sat back, thinking of what Tom had been saying. He was very upset over John and perhaps that was one of his reasons for wanting to get back to the army. Artie muttered about the 'bloody enemy' a lot of the time and Lizzie thought he would have liked to join up, just to kill a few of the Germans in revenge for his brother's loss. Both Tom and Artie seemed to have given up hope of his survival, though Pam clung to it still and Arthur maintained a grim silence on the subject.

Was it possible that John might still be alive and in a prison hospital or a camp? She wondered if the Red Cross would make inquiries if she asked and decided it was worth a try. Arthur had written to John's commanding officer asking for more information, but so far, he'd received no answer – perhaps because the RAF had no more idea of the actual facts than they did.

Lizzie decided that she would make some phone calls from the salon. There was no point in doing it from the farm because it might arouse hope and expectation. It would be much better to do it quietly and see if anything came from her actions before she spoke of it to the family.

She would also ring Faith again, because so far no one had been able to reach her...

* * *

Faith hesitated when she was told that Lizzie Gilbert wanted to speak to her on the phone and then accepted the call.

'Lizzie,' she said uncertainly. 'I'm sorry I haven't been in touch. I just didn't know what to do or say.'

'We've all been worried about you, Faith,' Lizzie told her. 'You are like family to us. I know you weren't married – but John intended to marry you and that makes you one of us. I wanted you to know that we are here for you.'

Faith gulped, her voice not much more than a whisper as she fought her tears. 'I... I think I may need help, Lizzie. I'm not absolutely sure, but... I think I might be pregnant...'

For a moment, there was silence and then Lizzie's voice was in her ear, reassuring and warm, washing over her with concern and affection. 'If you are, Faith, you must come to me – to us. It would be the most wonderful thing if you are having John's child. We are still all hoping that John is alive and a prisoner of war – but, if he doesn't make it back, think how marvellous it would be for the family to have his child and the woman he loved amongst us.'

Faith gave a sob of relief. 'I think my mother would disown me; she has always been so strict about things like that – and Dad will be devastated, though he'll come round.' Tears were running down her cheeks. 'If I could come to you... we might tell them together. I think I could face it if you were with me, Lizzie.'

'Faith, dearest,' Lizzie said. 'If your mother is angry for a while, she will come round when the child is born... but you're not sure yet?'

'I've missed my periods,' Faith said, 'and I've been sick. It may be a bug, but I've been sick a lot of mornings and it sort of goes off later...'

'I have no experience of morning sickness, but that sounds about right,' Lizzie murmured. 'Have you seen a doctor yet?'

'No. I have been hoping it would go and I'd be all right...' Faith drew a deep breath. 'Do you think I'm dreadful?'

'No, of course, I don't,' Lizzie replied firmly. 'If there hadn't been a war, you would probably be married – or you'd have waited. A lot of girls have done what you did because the men they loved were being sent into danger. If Tom hadn't been able to get enough leave to marry me, we would probably have done the same. Just because you made love with the man you were going to marry isn't a crime and it isn't wicked. Besides, I am thrilled that you may be having John's child – and, if you are, Pam is going to be over the moon.'

'She won't think I'm cheap or wicked?'

'Of course not.'

Faith closed her eyes as Lizzie's warmth poured over her. 'I'll book an appointment and let you know – and if I am... Well, I'll stay on here until I can't, if you know what I mean?'

'Yes, of course, but don't try to hold on too long. I have a room for you and the baby – and we actually have beds now. The furniture finally arrived.'

'Thank you. I was so worried and... ashamed.'

'Nonsense! A baby is a wonderful event,' Lizzie said. 'We shall all be delighted.'

After Lizzie had finished chattering, Faith replaced the receiver and stood leaning against the wall, eyes closed and tears running down her cheeks. Lizzie had been so kind, making it easy for her. John's family would welcome her into their midst, even if her own parents were disgusted with her, and she knew they would be. Faith's mother had never made any secret of the way she felt about girls who had to get married in haste and she'd warned her against loose behaviour many times. She would never understand the desperation young girls felt who knew that if they didn't seize their chance, it might be too late, and they would never know the joy of physical love. At least Faith had had that little time with John when they'd been together in Cambridge. She would never forget how lovely it had been, despite the uncertainty of her situation now.

* * *

Faith left the doctor's surgery some days later feeling as if she'd been picked up on a whirlwind that had thrown her life out of control. She was pregnant... the doctor thought around three months. Happiness and then fear swept over her. She was glad she would have a child to love that was also John's, though nervous of the future as an unmarried mother and the stigma that accompanied it. She would wait until she was ready to go home and face the music and then live with Lizzie for a while – just until she found a home for herself. It would be hard bringing up a child as an unmarried mother, but perhaps John was still alive after all. Perhaps there was still hope that he would come home and marry her as he'd wanted...

29

Faith rang Lizzie at the salon the day Tom left for the military hospital in Portsmouth to have his medical. Lizzie had been on edge all morning, worried about the outcome, but when Faith told her the good news, she felt like jumping for joy.

'Everyone is going to love you for this,' she told Faith. 'Will you come down and tell them – or would you like me to tell Pam for you?'

'I can't get leave for a while,' Faith said. 'I am due for a week's leave next month. I'll come then and we can tell my parents – but if you could tell Pam in confidence. If she still wants to see me, I'll come and stay with you then, if I may?'

'Of course, she will,' Lizzie laughed. 'The only trouble will be that she will want to cosset you and keep you with us.'

'I shan't be able to work much longer anyway,' Faith told her. 'I am putting on weight and my back aches a bit. I don't think I should do too much heavy lifting for the baby's sake.'

'Then give in your notice and come to us as soon as you can,' Lizzie insisted. 'Don't worry about money or anything. I can give you a little job until you're on your feet again, Faith. The salon is busy and I need someone to answer the phone and make appointments, perhaps tidy up a bit.'

'You're inventing a job for me.' Faith accused but with a giggle in her voice.

'No, I'm not – but who cares if I am? You are just what we need to make us all feel better, Faith. We've been down, but this is wonderful news. I can't wait to see Pam's face.'

'Tell her I'll come when I can – if she wants me...'

'Of course, she will.' Lizzie repeated and smiled as she put down the phone as they both had work to do. She felt much better as she shampooed and set her next customer's hair and then the telephone rang again. This time it was Tom, and he sounded a bit odd.

'I've got some good news,' he said. 'You might not think so, Lizzie – but it went better than expected. I was passed as fit for duty and told to report to my base...'

Lizzie felt a shiver of apprehension. 'Are they sending you overseas again?'

'No, not yet,' he replied, 'but I can't tell you on the phone. I've got a few days' leave first anyway. I'll be home tomorrow and then we will celebrate.'

'I'm glad you're pleased, Tom. I can't wait to see you,' Lizzie said. 'I've got some news too—'

She heard the pips go. He'd rung from a phone box and his change had run out. Although he was having to return to duty, he was at least coming home for a few days first and it didn't sound as if he would be in danger, at least, not for a while.

* * *

Lizzie sat Pam down in her chair before she told her the news about Faith that evening. She was lucky enough to find her alone.

Arthur and Artie were still out in the yard and Jeanie and Nancy were upstairs getting washed and changed as they were going into Ely for the evening.

'It's news I think you will like,' Lizzie said. 'At least I hope you will – I think it is wonderful...'

'News of John?' Pam's face lit with hope.

'Not John himself – but... Faith is having his child...'

Pam's face went white and then red and then she burst into tears, but when she raised her head to look at Lizzie, she could see the joy there.

'John's baby?' she said in wonder. 'It is like a miracle...'

'Yes, that's how I felt,' Lizzie said. 'I still pray that John will come back – but now he hasn't gone completely. He will live on in his child...'

'Yes...' Pam gulped and wiped her face. 'So silly – I am happy, that's all...'

'I've told Faith she can come and live with me when she leaves nursing,' Lizzie said. 'We'll look after her until the baby is born and things are more settled. I can give her a little job if she wants it, just until she can manage for herself.' Lizzie left it there, because so much depended on whether John came back one day to marry his sweetheart. If he did, then Faith would remain close at hand as part of the family, but if he didn't... the future was hers to decide.

'You know you can rely on me,' Pam said and smiled warmly at her. 'I shall have to start knitting... Who would have thought it? Our John a father...'

'What will Arthur say?' Lizzie asked.

'If John had been here, he would've given him a ticking-off for not waiting until he was married. I might have had a couple of words myself – but now I am so glad he didn't.' She got up and hugged Lizzie. 'Bless you for telling me and for asking her to come here to Blackberry Farm. If you hadn't reached out to her, Lizzie, we might never have known. The poor lass must have been worried, because I know her mother will be shocked and angry, too; Sheila came from around here and was always straight-laced. When will Faith tell her parents?'

'She is coming to stay with me soon and we'll go to March and tell them together. At least, they can't turn her out in the snow.' She laughed, but Pam shook her head.

'It happened often enough in the past. I know of girls who got into trouble and were disowned by their family. Some of them were shut away in an asylum. Imagine that, Lizzie. Incarcerating a young girl just because she made love before marriage and got caught with a baby – what a punishment, to be shut away from life just for that.'

'I can't imagine it,' Lizzie said. 'I don't want to. It is too horrid. I just hope that Faith's parents won't be too shocked and say awful things they will regret.'

'Surely they won't?' Pam shook her head. 'She'll be punished enough with everyone staring at her. You know some spiteful tongues will have a go at her for having a child out of wedlock.' Pam's eyes reflected her own memories. 'I was lucky that Arthur married me when Tom was on the way. You know that he was a war baby, too. Tommy would have married me, but he didn't get the chance. My parents wouldn't have wanted to know me had they lived, but they were both killed in a train crash at around the same time as I lost my Tommy.'

'Oh, Pam,' Lizzie cried, shocked. 'I had no idea that you lost your parents too. I am so sorry.'

'As I said, I doubt they would have accepted me with my baby,' Pam said. 'I loved them, even though they were so strict and upright – but then I met Arthur and he fell in love with me just like that...' She smiled at the memory. 'Of course, I'd seen him before, knew him slightly, but he saw me struggling with a load of shopping and stopped his pony cart to give me a lift. He used to drive a high-stepping pony and what I'd call a governess cart in those days. I was a bit anxious because I thought my landlady might turn me out when she discovered I was pregnant.'

'It was much worse then than it is now,' Lizzie agreed. 'It must have been a relief when Arthur proposed.'

'I turned him down the first time. Oh, he knew about the baby. I'd told him when I asked if he had any cottages to rent. He came that day to tell me that he had found one I could rent but said he would like it better if I married him. I laughed and told him not to be daft, but he wouldn't take no for an answer. In the end, after he'd asked me a dozen times, I liked him so much that I said yes. He was so persistent and outspoken... but it wasn't love, not at first. That came after a few months of marriage when I realised how lucky I'd been. Arthur is kind and generous and he never criticised me or reproached me – not once in all the years of our marriage. And as far as he is concerned, Tom is his son. I think it was that – the unconditional love he gave us both – that made me love him.'

Lizzie nodded. She loved Pam like a mother and respected her. She'd known how she would react to the news of Faith's pregnancy. John was her youngest son and his loss was a hard blow for Pam and her family. In time, perhaps the ache in their hearts would fade a little and Faith's child would help to ease their grief.

'John will marry her when he comes home,' Pam said, bringing back her wandering thoughts. 'I know Tom thinks he's dead, but I don't. I believe he is alive, Lizzie. Perhaps in hospital, perhaps a prisoner – but I haven't given up hope...'

Lizzie nodded. As yet, her phone calls to the Red Cross headquarters had not given her any answers, but she had been told they would keep looking at their records.

'Sometimes, men get lost for a while before they are picked up,' the woman had said when Lizzie rang. 'He may have given a false name or he could be ill and unable to tell anyone who he is.'

She hadn't been very encouraging. Lizzie was glad she hadn't said anything to John's family. There was no point unless she got definite news that would make them smile.

30

Lizzie could see a little bump beneath Faith's dress when she took her coat off and smiled at her. It would be hard for her to hide it for much longer, though in the uniform and starched apron she wore for nursing, it wouldn't show as much as it did in the fine wool dress that clung to her hips and hugged her knees. Unlike the new dresses, which were being made shorter to save on material, Faith's dress ended mid-calf. It had a white collar and cuffs, a thin leather belt and was a pale blue colour, which set off her fair hair and matched her eyes – though they were deeper, more the colour of bluebells. Faith was a very pretty girl and Lizzie understood why John had fallen hard for her.

'Pam is so excited,' Lizzie told her. 'She has already started knitting for the baby. White coats and a beautiful lace pattern dress so far...'

Faith's cheeks turned a little pink. 'She won't think I am a dreadfully fast girl who set out to catch her son?'

Lizzie laughed and shook her head. 'It takes two to make a baby,' she said. 'We are all very excited, Faith. After all, you and John were engaged – it isn't like you picked up a stranger off the street.' Lizzie saw the flash of pain in Faith's eyes. 'Does it hurt too much when I speak of John?' she asked gently. 'I know it must. I am so sorry, Faith – but perhaps he will come home one day. Pam is sure of it.'

Faith closed her eyes as a tear trickled down her cheek. 'I know I shouldn't hope too much,' she said after a moment. 'I did love him very much, Lizzie.'

'Of course, you did, dearest,' Lizzie said and gave her a quick hug. 'We all know that and we understand – truly we do. No one thinks you a wicked girl.'

'My mother will, and she will say so. Dad will just look disappointed. I don't think I could have told them if you hadn't invited me to stay with you...' She looked around her. 'Does your husband mind?'

'Not in the least, but Tom isn't here right now, Faith. He had a medical, on the same day as you told me about the baby. When he got home, he explained that they had placed him with a training unit in this country. It means he will be able to come home some weekends – and he won't be going overseas, at least, for a while.'

'That's wonderful,' Faith said. 'I am so pleased for you, Lizzie. It was nice when I was in Cambridge and John sometimes came for a couple of nights when he had leave. He wasn't too happy when I was transferred.' She caught back a sob. 'I'd have said no if I'd realised...' She took the hanky Lizzie offered and wiped her eyes. 'It is so stupid of me. John wanted us to get married and I said we should wait so that I could nurse, but now...' She lifted her head. 'I thought nursing was so important to me, but it isn't. I've realised now that what I want more than anything is for John to come back so that I can be his wife...'

'We'll keep praying and hoping,' Lizzie said. Her heart ached for the young girl who had lost so much so soon. She was hardly nineteen, too young to have to face life without the man she loved. It wouldn't be easy for Faith to bring up a child alone, even with John's family to help her. 'Don't worry about the future too much. We'll help you all we can, I promise.'

'I just want to get it over – telling my parents...' Faith bit her lip. 'They are going to be so angry.'

* * *

Faith's fears were justified. Her parents were both at home that Sunday, as she'd requested in her telephone call. Her mother listened in silence and then got up and walked from the room, after giving Faith a look filled with reproach and disgust. Her father looked at her sadly.

Faith's eyes filled with tears. 'I'm sorry,' she whispered. 'We would have married as soon as John got leave if—'

'If I gave my permission,' he reminded her. 'John did telephone me to tell me he intended to ask you, but I told him you were still young to marry. After all, you have a whole lifetime in front of you. I'm not sure your mother would have been happy for you to marry for a while yet. I can't believe that you would let us down like this – let yourself down... and I am angry with him. He should have known better!'

'Faith hasn't done anything a lot of other girls have done since the war started,' Lizzie said. 'It's hard for them, not knowing if their loved ones will return. Please don't make her feel shamed, Mr Goodjohn. She has enough to bear as it is with John missing.'

He looked at Lizzie for a moment and she knew he was restraining himself from making a sharp reply. 'Faith is lucky to have a good friend,' he said and sighed heavily. 'I don't want to shame you or hurt you, Faith, and I'm sorry that John is still missing. It wouldn't have been quite as bad if he could have come home and married you. I can't pretend I'm not disappointed, but you are still my daughter and I do love you. However, your mother may not wish to see you. You know her views on unmarried mothers. It will take time to bring her round.'

'I know you're angry...' Faith began, but he shook his head.

'No, I am not angry with you, just saddened,' he told her and she gave a little sob. 'Don't cry, Faith. It's done and can't be undone.' He took his wallet from his jacket pocket and extracted some notes, holding them out to Faith. She shook her head. 'Take them and don't be foolish. I can't tell you to come home, because your mother would make both our lives a misery. However, I shall give you money so that you can live decently. I know Mrs Gilbert has offered you a home for the time being – so just take this, for the baby, if not yourself.'

Still Faith hesitated, but Lizzie stepped forward and took the five one-pound notes. 'You will need a lot of things for the baby, Faith, and when you stop work, it will be difficult enough. Accept your father's help,' she said and looked at her.

Faith nodded, her head down. 'Thank you,' she said in a small voice. 'I know you must hate this... me...'

'I dislike this situation,' her father said, 'but I couldn't hate you whatever you do, Faith. It has been a shock. I'll keep in touch and I shall want to see the baby when it is born – but I may have to come to Mepal. I doubt your mother will accept the child for a very long time, but I shall try to bring her round. She was so proud of you and she feels you've shamed her; you know what she is like...'

Faith nodded silently, because she'd always known her mother's views; nice girls didn't do what she had, in Sheila's opinion, so that made Faith a bad girl.

Lizzie took her arm and they left the house.

Artie was sitting in his father's car just down the road and they walked to it and got in the back. He glanced round at them but didn't say anything until he'd driven away. 'Does either of you want anything while we're in March?'

'No, not for me,' Lizzie replied. 'I can buy most of what I want in Chatteris and Ely.'

'No, I'm not ready to start buying baby things yet,' Faith said. She looked at Lizzie. 'I'll need to ask Pam what I shall want for a start.'

'Yes, do that,' Lizzie agreed. 'She may have some things put away – and we can go to Cambridge on a shopping trip when you're ready.'

Faith swiped her face with the back of her hand. 'I don't know how to thank you. I couldn't have got through that without you, Lizzie.'

'It wasn't pleasant for you,' Lizzie said, thinking that Faith's father was all right – but her mother... well, in Lizzie's opinion, she was a cold bitch!

Lizzie's own mother would have had a lot to say if she'd had to tell her similar news, but in the end, she would have let Lizzie stay in her own home, or she thought so. Just walking out like that without a word had been like a slap in the face for Faith.

'I feel so worthless,' Faith said. 'The way my mother looked at me before she went upstairs.'

'I shouldn't let the old battle-axe upset you,' Artie said suddenly from the front seat. 'For myself, I'm bloody glad you and John got it together before he was... well, at least, he knew what it was like and his child will make Ma smile again.'

'Artie,' Lizzie warned, but Faith had stopped crying.

'Thank you,' she said and her head came up. 'I'm not ashamed of what we did. I loved John and he loved me. I'm sorry my parents took it the way they did and I know I've let them down, but we were happy...'

'Good, then sod the rest of them,' Artie said with feeling and Faith laughed.

'Thanks,' she said. 'That makes me feel better.'

'It is your life. Yours and John's. I'll thrash the first man I hear say a bad thing about you, Faith. In my book, you're as good as married to him – and that's enough for me. What do you say, Lizzie?'

'I agree,' she said and nodded as she saw his outright speech had brightened Faith. Perhaps it was because the ordeal was over, but she seemed much better than she had when she arrived. It was as if she had faced up to the future and was ready to fight for what she wanted.

* * *

It was three weeks later, when Faith was back at work, that she discovered her uncle waiting for her outside the hospital when she left after a long shift on the wards. Faith was tired. Her back ached and so did her head and she'd made up her mind she was going to give notice the next day. It would be an unpleasant interview, because Matron would be annoyed that her training had been wasted. She was just beginning to be of real use and now she was leaving – it would not be a nice task, but it had to be done.

'Faith...' Uncle Ralph's voice startled her because she'd been lost in thought and hadn't seen him standing there. 'I had to come when your mother told me...'

Faith's heart sank as she saw the look on his face. He was plainly furious and her stomach caught with fright. 'If you've come to give me a lecture, I don't want to hear it.'

'It is not you I'm angry with, it's the bastard who did this to you,' he growled. 'If he were here, I would kill him. How dare he put you at risk like this? It is a good thing he's dead or I'd make him wish he'd never been born...'

Faith shivered as she looked at his face. It was so twisted with hate!

'Don't say that!' she cried. 'I loved John and he didn't force me – far from it. I wanted it to happen even before it did. I was the one that said we didn't have to wait. Besides, we don't know for sure that he is dead; he's missing.'

Her uncle's hand came up and slapped her face, making her recoil with the shock and hurt. 'You little slut,' he said, glaring at her. 'You've broken your mother's heart. She won't go out of the house because she is so ashamed of you.'

'How dare you hit me!' Faith said, blinking back her tears. 'That's not fair to call me that. I'm just having a baby, I haven't murdered anyone!'

Anger and hatred flared in her uncle's eyes and he looked at her so strangely that she took a step back, afraid of him. 'Why do you say that?' he asked and his hand reached out, taking hold of her wrist. He held it so tightly that she gasped with pain. 'What have you heard?'

'I don't know what you mean. You are hurting me,' Faith cried. 'I just meant having a baby isn't a crime. I'm not wicked. I haven't stolen anything. I haven't murdered or blackmailed anyone...' She drew a deep breath at the look in his eyes. Why did he look at her like that?

'Your mother gave me a letter for you,' he said abruptly. 'She wanted to make sure you got it – and your father wouldn't post it. They've had terrible rows over you. If their marriage breaks up, you can blame yourself.'

Faith stared at him. Once she'd loved him and she'd thought he loved her, but she hadn't known him. He was cruel and ruthless; she didn't know what had changed him, but something had.

She was certain he hadn't always been as cold and hard as he was now. She took the letter and put it in her pocket. 'I'll read it later.'

'Make sure that you do,' he said. 'Do you want a lift home?'

'No, thank you,' Faith replied. 'I think we've said all we need to say, Uncle Ralph – and I mean *ever*.'

Again, that terrifying look was in his eyes. 'I understand you intend to live with Lizzie Gilbert,' he said in an odd voice. 'Just watch yourself. I wouldn't trust any of that family...'

Faith refused to answer. She turned and walked away, praying that he wouldn't follow her. He had scared her. She didn't know him now. He wasn't the uncle who had indulged her with little treats when she was young. What had happened to him? What had he done that made him look at her as if he would kill her when she said that she wasn't a murderer?

Faith felt coldness at her nape. Her words had made him angry because he'd thought she was accusing him of murder... had he done something bad?

No, that was stupid, she reasoned with herself. Uncle Ralph wasn't a murderer. When he'd said he would kill John, that was just a figure of speech. People said things when they were angry. They didn't mean anything – and yet... Faith pushed the thought away.

She'd told him she didn't want to speak to him ever again and she hoped she wouldn't have to. Whatever he'd done or hadn't, he wasn't someone she could love or trust any more.

* * *

Faith read her mother's letter when she was in her room at the nurses' home. It was bitter and angry and told her that her mother never wanted to see her again. She didn't want to see the baby and she had disowned her. There was a lot more, but Faith couldn't read it to the end. She screwed it up in a ball and put it in the rubbish bin, fighting her tears.

She had known her mother would be angry, but she hadn't expected this bitterness. Faith shook her head. She would not cry. Why should she? It was her mother's loss if she didn't want to see her grandchild.

She sat down on the bed and picked up her notepad. She would write to Lizzie and Pam and tell them she would be there as soon as she could, unless she was dismissed immediately, in which case she would be at Blackberry Farm by the weekend.

31

Ralph drove furiously through the night. He'd been angry with Faith, that's why he'd delivered his sister's letter reprimanding Faith for what she'd done. How could she let herself get pregnant – and by a Talbot? She'd made him even angrier by some of her remarks; he'd watched his niece walk away and been tempted to go after her. When she'd flung that remark at him about not being a murderer, he'd thought for a moment that she knew – and it had made him want to kill her. He had almost taken that white neck in his hands and broken it. Only the thought of his sister's shock and horror had stayed his hand.

The little bitch! She was as bad as that Lizzie Gilbert. Anger and resentment burned inside Ralph. There was now only one person he cared for and that was his sister – and she was out of her mind with grief and shame.

It might have been better if he had killed Faith. His sister would grieve, but then she would be free of the shame of her daughter's wanton behaviour. Sheila had been brought up strictly. She'd had an aunt who had been put away in an institution because of her behaviour with a married man, and that had horrified and traumatised her as a child, making her more prudish and fearful of people's opinion. Her only daughter had let her down and upset her terribly, reminding her of her aunt's terrible punishment and making her angry and bitter.

The look in Faith's eyes when she'd spoken of blackmail and murder had unsettled Ralph for a moment. He'd thought she'd known – but she couldn't know anything. Even the London police inspector who was so suspicious had never been able to prove that Ralph had shot those gangsters. No one could know that he was planning blackmail, because so far it was only in his mind.

A little smile touched his mouth. Who would have thought that a senior officer would be so foolish as to blurt out the fact that he was sleeping with another officer's wife? He'd had too much whisky, of course, and he'd been careless, but he hadn't known Ralph was standing behind him when he used the phone to make an assignation with her.

At first, Ralph hadn't been certain of who the lady was, even though it was clear from the conversation that it was an illicit relationship. Arrangements to meet at a certain hotel at a certain time. Well, of course, Ralph had been there with his camera, positioned across the street, and he'd seen them arrive separately and greet each other. The photographs had turned out beautifully – so clear – of them embracing and looking at each other in excitement. The woman was beautiful. She had silvery blonde hair and she wore it in a glamorous pageboy style with a dark brown fur coat and a smart hat.

Ralph still hadn't known who she was. He'd put the pictures away safely in a drawer. They might come in useful. It was only when he'd seen the lady out with another man that he'd realised who she must be. A general's wife no less! Captain Whittaker was flying high in his affair with her and close to the sun. If his wings were made of wax like Icarus, he could fall.

Did he want to ruin the man who had taken him out of the stores and given him a decent and safe job? Ralph wasn't certain. Whittaker had money, but he wasn't that rich – and he was a stubborn devil. He might refuse to pay and arrange it so that Ralph found himself on the frontline if he discovered Ralph's identity. It needed careful thought and planning.

Perhaps the lady would be easier to blackmail? Ralph laughed out loud as he realised that he'd found the perfect answer. She would be frightened of her husband finding out, naturally. The general came from a landed family and was rich. His wife wouldn't want to risk being shamed and divorced. She would be sure to pay for the pictures – though she would tell her lover she was being blackmailed. Ralph frowned over that. Whittaker might be too stubborn to pay himself, but he would undoubtedly urge her to pay and she could find the money easily enough; she was rolling in the stuff by the look of the mink coat she'd worn.

Ralph decided he would ask for £5,000. It wasn't a fortune for a woman like that, but he would have to work out how to collect without giving himself away.

* * *

It was a day or two before Ralph found the solution. He'd been looking at the clandestine photos again, when he'd noticed the waste bin that had been erected just to the right of the hotel where the meeting had taken place. The general's wife would know where it was and he would give her a date and a time when she must deposit the package. It must be wrapped in brown paper and addressed to... Gilbert...

Ralph smiled. He enjoyed using the name of the man he hated more than any other. He didn't hate Whittaker. He merely despised him as a drunken fool. The woman was a slut and deserved what she got.

For two pins, he would send the photos to her husband. He didn't need the money that much, even though he no longer had the profits from the nightclub. Sometimes he regretted getting rid of that – but it had been safer. The London police were getting too close to discovering the truth about those gangland murders.

Ralph had hoped he might make friends at the officers' mess, be invited to their homes or given business tips, but it hadn't happened. Most of them didn't even see him. He was just the man who served drinks and said, 'Yes, sir,' and 'Thank you, sir,' like any lackey. So why not make what he could from them while he had the chance?

Selecting a photo that showed the general's wife looking up at Captain Whittaker in a way that no one could mistake, Ralph popped it in an envelope. He would just send this one for a start... give her a little time to fret before he made his demands.

Women were all filthy bitches anyway. There was only one he cared for because she loved him devotedly. Ralph smiled. When he got the money, he would treat his sister to a beautiful fur coat – just like the one the general's wife had been wearing when she met her lover...

32

Jeanie looked at Artie as he picked up her pail of milk and tipped it into the churn. He was frowning, clearly still angry or perhaps just upset over his brother's disappearance. John must surely be dead. It was May 1941 now and still no word had come of him being a prisoner of war; surely, they would have heard if that were the case? Jeanie sometimes thought it was worse for the family, not knowing one way or the other.

'You go up to the house and get your breakfast,' Artie said as she picked up a pitchfork. 'I'll do the mucking out today.'

'That's nice of you,' Jeanie said. She hesitated and then walked over to him, placing her hand on his arm. 'Is it John? Are you hurting very much?'

'It hurts like hell!' Artie said and she saw his eyes were bleak. 'The last time he was here, I was mocking him about his girl-friend. I thought... Well, never mind what I thought, but we parted not as brothers should but with bad words between us. I regret that so much—' There was a break in his voice. 'I know you think I'm a cold devil with no heart – but I loved him.'

'Of course, you do!' Jeanie said and, seeing him so distressed, broke her reserve. 'And I don't think you have no heart, Artie. I do like you...'

'Do you? Do you really?' Artie looked at her for a moment and then reached out for her and pulled her close, bending his head to kiss her.

Jeanie had never been kissed with such passion or such hunger and she melted into him, her heart thumping wildly and her head swirling. Without even thinking, she wound her arms around his neck and returned the kiss.

She stayed there looking up at him as the kiss ended. He was gazing down at her so oddly and then he smiled. 'I thought you didn't much like me,' he said softly. 'Or do you let all the boys kiss you like that?'

'Not quite like that,' she said, a hint of mischief in her eyes. 'I might have kissed one or two.'

'You're a minx,' he retorted, and she thought he wasn't sure whether to be disappointed or pleased. 'Are we friends then?'

'Of course, we are. I wouldn't have gone to that dance if I hadn't liked you,' Jeanie said. She gazed up into his eyes. 'But I won't be another notch on your bedpost, Artie Talbot. If you think I'll just drop my knickers without a ring on my finger, you can think again.'

Artie threw back his head and laughed. 'You little devil,' he said. 'I'm supposed to marry you, am I?'

'Who says it's you I want to put a ring on my finger?' Jeanie asked with a teasing look. 'I've got more than one who would if I let them...'

'Quite likely,' he said and chuckled. 'Well, maybe I'll be asking one of these days, but let's get this clear – I don't expect you to drop your knickers for me, as you so eloquently put it. After what happened to John's girl, I'm not having that for you...'

Jeanie's heart caught with fright. 'You're not going to join up, are you?'

'I would if I thought Dad could manage,' Artie admitted. 'When Tom offered me the chance to go, I wanted to stay – but since John was killed, I've been wanting to fight someone. If I could, I'd kill the bastards who ended his life.'

'But you won't go?' Jeanie said anxiously.

'I can't leave my father in the lurch,' he replied. 'If Tom had been invalided out, I would have gone, but as it is...' He shook his head. 'Thank God for you, Jeanie. I was going a little mad, I think, but you've brought me back from the edge – more often than you know.' He smiled at her. 'I'm glad you're here – and sorry if I took advantage just now. I just needed to hold someone, and you were there.'

'It was fine,' she told him. 'I understood why you kissed me.'

'You're a lovely girl,' he said. 'I'd like us to go out more often – really get to know each other, if you'd like that?'

'Yes, I think that would be nice,' Jeanie said, suddenly a little shy. 'Good, that's settled. Now let's get this mucking out done together and then have breakfast. Are you going to tell your parents we're courting now?'

'Let's keep it to ourselves for a while,' he said hesitantly. 'We work together, and we don't want to make things awkward. Shall we just see how we feel in a few months' time?'

'Fine,' Jeanie said with a shrug as she turned away to get on with the work. That kiss had made her think he might care for her, but now he seemed to have backed off a bit and she didn't want him to think she was chasing him. 'Otherwise, your mum will be buying a new hat.' She laughed, and he laughed and the slight tension was broken.

Jeanie smiled to herself as she picked up a pitchfork. She did like Artie a lot, but she wasn't going to let him know until he was ready to admit his own feelings – and she wasn't sure yet whether he truly felt anything warmer than friendship for her. The kiss had been more a reaction to grief and anguish over his brother than anything else. The uncertainty over John was distressing for all the family, not knowing whether he was alive or not was eating away at them – and the awful things was that they might never know the truth.

* * *

That night, Artie asked if Jeanie would like to go to the pub with him. She hesitated for a moment or two and then agreed. Jeanie wasn't sure how she would like visiting the local pub, but in the end, she discovered she enjoyed it.

They walked through the village and up past the small but pretty church to where the pub was situated, not far from the river. In the summer, it was a lovely walk along the washes and Arthur sometimes hired land there for the bullocks to fatten on the long lush grass that was soaked most winters by an overflow of the Ouse.

It was a cool evening, but inside the pub it was warm, though it smelled a little of smoke and beer. Sometimes these days, the pubs ran out of beer and spirits were already scarce and often kept under the counter for special customers.

Artie ordered a pint of bitter and asked Jeanie what she would like to drink. She considered for a moment, then, 'If I could choose, I'd have white wine, but I know they won't have any – so a weak lemonade shandy please.'

Artie nodded and turned to the barman. 'Do you have any white wine?'

A shake of the head confirmed what Jeanie had thought, so he ordered a lemonade shandy and took it over to the table they'd selected by a back window. It was too dark to see the view of the river but nice and cosy in a corner settle.

As they sat sipping their drinks, a group of young men entered and called a greeting to Artie. Two of them came over and looked at Jeanie with interest.

'Jeanie – meet George and Bill. They work on their family's land, same as me. Jeanie helps out for the duration.'

'We know who she is,' George said with a grin. 'We wondered where you'd been hiding her – keeping her for yourself. You always did like the best lookers.' His eyes gleamed with laughter and he looked at Jeanie. 'You don't want to bother with this loser, Miss Salmons. If you need an escort me and Bill would be pleased to take you dancing or to the flicks – wouldn't we, Bill?'

'Ignore him,' Bill said and offered his hand. He had a nice warm shake and an even nicer smile. 'Artie is all right – but if you get stuck, one of us is mostly around.'

'We were thinking of playing team darts,' George said, 'but there's only us two and you that play in tonight, Artie. We really need four of us.'

Jeanie looked at him innocently. 'I'll make up the four if you like. You'll have to tell me what to do, of course.'

George hesitated and then nodded. 'Who wants to partner Jeanie?'

'I will,' Bill said before Artie could claim her. 'I don't mind showing her how to play.'

Artie hesitated, looked at Jeanie and then nodded. 'All right – if Jeanie is happy?'

'Oh yes, I don't mind,' Jeanie said and smiled beguilingly at Bill. 'Thank you. It's kind of you to offer.'

'He's usually on the winning side,' George said half-grudging. 'Won't hurt him to lose for once.'

'Who says we'll lose?' Bill said and winked at Jeanie.

George went off to fetch the darts from the board and Bill explained that they started the game with a double, what that meant, which colour was a treble, and how they all had three darts each to throw at the board in turn. Jeanie nodded, her eyes wide and innocent as she listened and smiled.

Artie started the game rolling, getting a double twenty straight off, but then he only managed single twenties with his next two darts. Bill followed and got his double twenty, a treble and a single. George managed a double five with his third dart and cursed.

'Don't be nervous,' Artie advised as Jeanie was given the darts. 'Don't aim just look at what you need and throw.'

'Like this?' Jeanie asked. Her first dart was straight and true and landed plum in the double twenty, her second and third went in the trebles.

'Bloody hell!' George exclaimed and looked at Artie. 'Did you know she could play?'

'No idea.' Artie was grinning like the Cheshire cat. 'I just wish Tom was here to see you, Jeanie. He's the champion darts player round here – but I reckon you'd give him a run for his money. Who taught you?'

'I watched my dad a few times,' Jeanie said and laughed. 'Then I had a go and it just happened. Apparently, I'm a natural...'

George looked accusingly at Bill. 'You knew,' he challenged, slightly aggrieved.

'I had a feeling,' Bill admitted, 'but I didn't know she would be this good. You'll have to join the village team when we start playing local matches again, Jeanie. We've stopped them because most of the lads are away – but they will start once the war is over.'

'You'll have plenty of takers then,' Jeanie said, 'but if there are more ladies who would like to play, we might start our own team.'

'Yeah, much better idea,' George agreed and Jeanie had the feeling that he wouldn't like being beaten by a woman player.

'Come on,' Artie said, reminding them. 'Let's finish the game...'

* * *

Later, as they walked home, Artie was silent for a while and Jeanie wondered if he was upset because she and Bill had beaten him and George in all three games they'd played, but then he looked at her thoughtfully.

'You're a deep one, Jeanie Salmons,' he said. 'I didn't realise you had so many hidden talents.'

'That's because you don't know me,' Jeanie countered.

'We've been working together for a year or so now, but you've never mentioned you played darts.'

'Because there was no reason – and I seldom do. I can, but I don't often...' She smiled mysteriously. 'I might have other secrets,' she teased.

'I dare say you have,' Artie replied. 'You floored George, that's for certain. Bill likes you – but George isn't too sure. Mind you, he's always a sore loser. Brilliant with my motorbike when it needs a new part but not a good loser. He usually plays with Bill to make sure he wins.'

Jeanie nodded, but her chin jutted as she looked up at him. 'I won't miss on purpose just to please him,' she said, 'even if he is one of your best mates.'

'No, I don't expect you would,' Artie said and looked thoughtful. 'Got a mind of your own, haven't you, Jeanie?'

'Yes, I have,' she agreed. 'That's the way I am, Artie Talbot.'

There was defiance in her tone and he nodded, saying nothing as they went into the warmth of the farm kitchen.

Pam and Arthur were sitting in their chairs next to the range. Nancy sat at the kitchen table, drinking tea and eating a piece of toast and dripping. Everyone else had gone to bed.

'Had a good evening?' Pam asked, smiling at them.

'Yes – Jeanie showed us all how to play darts.'

'Ah yes, you told me once you could play a bit,' Pam agreed and nodded. She looked at Nancy. 'I played a bit when I was young. Do you play, Nancy?'

Nancy hadn't said anything until then but she looked up then. 'No, I've never tried. I played cricket a few times at my last farm placing, but not darts.'

'Pity, we could have got a ladies' team going,' Jeanie said. 'Is there any more tea, Pam? I'd like a cup before I go up – and then it's bed for me. It will soon be morning.'

'Yes, and I've got a big job for you two to start in the morning,' Arthur said. 'I want the milking shed whitewashed, so you'll need to fit it in with your normal work somehow, spread it over the next week or so.'

'I'm afraid that will be one of my last jobs for you, Mr Talbot,' Nancy said and everyone stared at her. 'I'll give you two weeks' notice and then I am leaving.'

'I shall be sorry to see you go,' Arthur said, looking surprised. 'I thought you were settled here?'

'I was – but a friend of mine has a posting in Sussex and I've applied to join her. I have to wait for two weeks and then I can go to her. Shelly is my... friend and we got separated when I took this job. She was in the ambulance service in London, but she has transferred to the Land Army to be with me.'

'Well, that will be nice for you,' Pam said to break the silence.

'You've been a good worker for us, Nancy, and as Arthur says, we'll be sorry to see you leave.'

'This is the best place I've had – but I need to be with Shelly. I'm going upstairs...' Nancy said abruptly and went quickly from the room.

Arthur grunted and went back behind his newspaper, rattling it before he settled again. 'Well, well,' Artie said softly and looked at Jeanie. 'It's like that, is it? Did you have any idea?'

'I thought she might be,' she whispered back. 'It was embarrassing, so I never said anything...'

'She didn't come on to you?' Artie frowned.

'A bit, not much after I made it clear I wasn't interested.'

'Good,' he muttered. 'I'm glad she's going. You just watch her, Jeanie.'

Jeanie laughed. 'She won't jump on me because I should punch her in the eye if she did.'

Artie exploded with laughter, drawing everyone's eyes to them. Jeanie blushed but he just grinned. 'That's my Jeanie,' he said. 'I might have known you could handle her.'

It was the next morning, when Jeanie entered the kitchen to fetch mugs of hot tea out to the milking shed, that Pam gave her an inquiring look. 'Are you courting Artie now, love – or is it still just friends?'

'We're getting to know each other better,' Jeanie told her. 'We've worked together for some months now, but I don't think he took much notice of me until recently.'

'You're probably right,' Pam said and laughed. 'You didn't mind my asking? Only he seems happier this morning than of late and I wondered.'

'Of course, I don't mind. You can ask me anything.'

'I've always been a bit anxious for Artie,' Pam told her, but shook her head when Jeanie's eyes questioned. 'Just a bit quiet and moody at times...'

'You know he was fretting? He thought he should join the army to get back at them...' Jeanie faltered and stopped.

'Because John is missing presumed dead?' Pam nodded. 'Yes, I knew it was eating at him. Well, I'm glad you two are friends now. You will keep his feet on the ground.'

'Yes, I will do that,' Jeanie agreed. 'Show him he can't always have his own way.'

'That's probably what he needs. I don't think many girls say no to our Artie.' Pam laughed. 'You'll bring him to heel, Jeanie – but don't break his heart, though I don't think that's your intention somehow.'

'You're a wise woman,' Jeanie murmured. 'I'm glad you're Artie's mum.'

'Tom calls me a wise old bird sometimes,' Pam said and laughed. 'Here's your tea, love. You'd best take it before it gets cold.'

* * *

Jeanie's mother rang her that evening. 'Oh, I'm glad you're there,' Vera Salmons said. 'I wondered if you'd had a letter or postcard from your sister?'

'No, I haven't heard from her since she was given that overseas posting, Mum.'

'Nor have I and I'm worried about her – we don't even know where she is...'

'I think she might be somewhere like Northern Africa in one of the field hospitals there.'

'That is so dangerous,' Vera said. 'It isn't just the war – there's fevers and snakes and goodness knows what...'

'Annie wanted to go, Mum.'

'I know. I don't think she is very happy, Jeanie. She loves her nursing, but she never seems to find a boyfriend, not one who makes her happy, anyway.' Vera hesitated, then, 'Are you happy, love?'

'Yes, I am, Mum. I played darts the other night and my partner and I won – that shocked a few folk.'

'Well, your dad was always a good player. I suppose you get it from him.' Vera sighed. 'You will let me know if Annie gets in touch?'

'Of course, I will. Perhaps she will write soon,' Jeanie comforted. 'I expect she is just too busy. Perfectly well and content but rushed off her feet, as most nurses are right now.'

'I hope that is it,' Vera said. 'I just wish she would write – but don't let my foolish anxiety spoil your day, Jeanie. I'll tell your father I've spoken to you when he comes home.'

'Where is he at this hour?'

'He volunteered for fire watching,' Vera replied with a sigh. 'He comes home and eats his supper and then he's off to do his war work – patrolling a factory. He won't tell me which factory, but I think it is the munitions...'

'I thought most of them had been moved to the country,' Jeanie said. 'I don't think it will be that, Mum, but it could be important machine parts.'

'Yes, perhaps you are right. These incendiary bombs are so dangerous. If they hit a gas main, it causes terrible fires. Well, they do wherever they fall really, but sometimes they are little fires to begin with and your father helps to put them out.'

'Yes, I can see why you're worried,' Jeanie told her. 'I suppose Dad feels he has to do his bit...'

'Yes – the daft man.' Vera sounded cross and then sighed. 'Oh, I understand why, Jeanie – but I feel this family has lost enough already.'

'Terry is doing really well now. I think you'll feel happier about him when you come down.'

'I am glad if he is,' Vera said, 'but he's lost a leg and his wife. That isn't going to change.'

'Now he is getting used to the false leg, he will be all right,' Jeanie said. 'Annie told him in a letter that Ellie was cheating on him. He was furious at first, but now I think he's healing. I saw him laughing with Susan the other day and he looked like the old Terry.'

'Susan? That's the one who is hoping to be a teacher, isn't it?'

'Yes. If she passes her exams this year, she will be off to university to train.'

'I might have some news concerning Tina when I do come to visit,' Vera said. 'I think I've found someone to look after her while I am at work. She is young – in her early twenties – and a war widow. Rebecca needs a permanent job, and she has a little girl of two, so it would be convenient for her to have Tina – they are of a similar age, so it might work well.'

'What if Terry wants her to stay with him? He seems settled on the farm, Mum. He gives us a hand with the milking and he's been out in the fields hoeing between the crop rows, lots of light work like hedge cutting round the farm, and I think he enjoys it. Pam says he's welcome to stay.'

'Your father wants him home. He can have his old room with us. He can't live with Mrs Talbot forever – and neither can Tina – and the worst of the bombing appears to be over. Unless they start again, but your father doesn't think they will. He says they've turned their attention somewhere else, though we still get plenty of air-raid warnings.'

'Well, you'll talk to Terry about it.' Jeanie decided to leave it there. It was for her mother and Terry to sort out, not her. 'We shall all look forward to seeing you soon, Mum...' She heard her mother say goodnight and then replaced the receiver.

Terry had settled well here and she thought it wouldn't help him to be rushed back to London, which was too full of memories. If it was up to her, she would let him stay here as long as he wished. Pam was happy for him to do so, and he'd started to help her as much as he could. In fact, Pam was teaching him to make bread and cakes. Jeanie thought her mother would be astonished when she tasted them, because it turned out that he was a decent baker.

Hearing the sound of voices in the kitchen, Jeanie went in and saw that Lizzie and Pam were looking at patterns for baby clothes and several balls of knitting wool.

'Faith will be here soon,' Lizzie said. 'I got this wool today in Chatteris and we're both going to make something for the baby.'

'Oh, I should like to help too,' Jeanie said. 'I could make bootees and bonnets – if you have any patterns?'

'I've got loads,' Pam said and smiled at Lizzie. 'It's nice to have a baby to knit for again.'

'Yes, we're lucky Faith is coming to us,' Lizzie told them. 'Her uncle took a letter from her mum – she said she didn't want to see Faith or the baby ever...'

'That is horrid!' Jeanie exclaimed. 'She must be so upset?'

'I think it is why she decided to leave the hospital. She just felt she'd had enough.'

'Well, it will be nice having her around,' Jeanie said.

'It's good that you're all friends,' Pam beamed at them. 'Now, how about a nice cup of cocoa...?'

33

'Well, I am shocked and sorry you are leaving us, Nurse Goodjohn,' Matron said in a tone of disapproval. 'I'd had good reports of you and I am disappointed. However, I am also a realist, so I understand these things happen. Therefore, I shall not lecture you on the morals of your situation. I dare say you have enough to worry you. I shall simply wish you good luck for the future.'

'Thank you, Matron,' Faith said and her throat was tight. 'I am sorry to have let you down.'

'We've all been young,' Matron said, 'and there is a war on. Will your young man marry you?'

'He would if he could, but he was reported missing and we haven't heard anything since...'

'Then I have every sympathy for you, Nurse Goodjohn. All this loss of life is heartbreaking – and in some cases we shall never know what happened to them.' Tears glistened in her eyes. 'My brother is missing, too, so I understand a little of your pain.'

'I hope he turns up,' Faith said, smiled gently and left as Matron nodded.

She walked slowly down the corridor, realising she was going to miss the activity of the wards, even the smell of antiseptic, but she'd decided it was time to leave. Her condition was beginning to show even under her apron and her back ached when she stood for a long time. Faith owed it to her child to take things easier until it was born.

She wasn't sure what she was going to do with the rest of her life. She'd considered she might continue nursing, just as a district nurse, but that wouldn't happen now. The stigma of being a single mother was too great for her to find a job like that. As an unmarried mother, her options were limited, but, because she had good friends, she would be much better off than many girls in her situation. Some girls in the past had found it too difficult and unwanted babies were left on the steps of orphanages or in a church porch, where they would be found and cared for, simply because the mother had no choice. Faith wanted to have her baby and keep it. Perhaps John would come home and the nightmare would end – or perhaps she could leave the child with his mother for a few hours each day and find a decent job. She was good with figures, so she might be able to work as an accountant's assistant or in an office. Perhaps she could learn to type...

Faith had always intended to return home after the war and marry. At the moment, she couldn't see how that would happen now. In the eyes of a lot of men, she would be tarnished; she had fallen for a child out of wedlock so she would be thought loose – and what man wanted a woman like that for his wife?

Faith brushed the tears from her cheeks as she left the hospital. Her situation could have been worse. She had to look to the future.

'Faith...' She didn't hear the voice immediately so lost was she in her thoughts, but then she felt the hand on her arm and turned. 'Faith, please, will you spare me a moment?'

'Slash...' She looked at him in surprise, because she thought he'd returned to his unit and, then in the next second, saw that he'd been wounded. He had a bandage round his head and a patch over his left eye. His left arm was in a sling. 'When did that happen?'

'Just after my last leave. We were sent... Well, it was pretty rough. I think a lot of the men were worse off than me, those who survived. They patched me up and sent me home for a rest.'

'Why didn't you let me know you'd been hurt? I would have visited you...'

'I wasn't sure you would want to see me like this.'

'Whyever not?' She was puzzled. 'I'm a nurse. I've seen a lot worse injuries.'

'Don't you see? I'm mad about you, Faith. I always have been. I really do care about you an awful lot...'

'Oh, Slash...' Faith made a choking sound. 'Please don't. I'm still in love with John. I can't just forget him even if... And I keep praying he will come back to me.'

'I know and I didn't intend to come and tell you, but seeing you looking so lovely and so sad I couldn't help myself.'

'You're such a lovely man and if...' She shook her head, because she couldn't give him hope when she didn't know whether she could ever love again even if John never came home. 'Let's go and have a cup of coffee,' Faith told him. 'You only just caught me. I am leaving Portsmouth soon.'

'Are you going home?' he asked as they crossed the street to the nearest café.

'Not to my home,' Faith said and placed a hand on his arm. 'There is something I have to tell you, Slash. I'm pregnant and the baby is John's...'

Slash hesitated, then, 'Faith, I want to look after you both. I'm asking you if you will marry me. I know you love John – but you can't go through this alone…'

He held the door of the café for her, allowing her to go inside to the steamy warmth and then followed. They found an empty table by the window and Slash ordered coffee and toasted teacakes from the waitress. As she went off with their order, he looked at Faith across the table.

'You will marry me, Faith, won't you?'

'I don't know…' she faltered. 'I like you, Slash. I always have – but I was – am – in love with John. It wouldn't be fair to you…'

'I just want to look after you – please let me do that…'

Faith hesitated, then, 'I will think about it,' she promised. 'I am going to live with Lizzie Gilbert in Mepal. She is John's sister-in-law. His family is excited about the baby, especially his mother. Give me a little time and then I'll let you know my decision.' She wrote the address down for him. 'You can visit me when you're feeling better. I doubt if they will expect you to report back for at least six months… if ever.' Faith touched his hand. 'Have you lost your left eye or do they think it will recover?'

'It is a permanent injury,' he replied with a wry twist of his mouth. 'I'll be getting a discharge soon – but it won't ruin my life, Faith. I'll go back to my job as a motor mechanic. I can see well enough to carry on and I'll make a good life for us.'

'I don't doubt it,' she said. 'I am not hesitating because of your injury. This is very new to me and I have to be sure for both our sakes. Otherwise, we would both be unhappy.'

'You are as sensible as you are lovely,' he said, his gaze going over her. 'Being pregnant suits you, Faith. 'You are glowing… more lovely than ever.'

'Thank you.' His words brought tears to her eyes and a lump to her throat. 'I appreciate the offer of marriage, Slash. I really do – but I need more time.'

'I love you, Faith, and I'll wait – for as long as it takes...'

'You are so kind,' Faith replied with a sad smile. 'But I'm not sure I'll ever be ready.'

34

Ralph enjoyed following the general's wife. She was still meeting Captain Whittaker, but she didn't look as happy as she had the first time he'd seen her. It hadn't taken him long to discover where she lived and he'd taken to shadowing her when he got the chance.

His last posting of two more photos resulted in a frantic call to her lover the next day, using the phone at the officers' mess. Ralph lingered behind a half-open door once he'd summoned the unfortunate man to answer the call. The look on Captain Whittaker's face had been most informative. She was upset and he was nervous. An arrangement to meet was made. Ralph moved away from the door seconds before the phone was replaced abruptly.

'Whisky,' the harassed Captain Whittaker demanded as he clicked his fingers.

Ralph took him a glass and his bottle on the silver salver. He smiled inwardly as the officer asked him to pour a double.

'Women are the very devil – what do you say, Harris?'

'I dare say you are right, sir,' Ralph replied. 'I don't have a wife

– the girl I wanted married someone else.' He sighed and got the response he wanted.

'Bad luck,' Captain Whittaker said and downed his whisky in one. 'Pour me another before you take the bottle, Harris. My wife lives in Scotland, thank God! She has her interests, I have mine. We have a daughter – lives with her mother.' He looked at Ralph keenly. 'Never found another girl to suit you then?'

'Not one I'd want to marry – but girls, yes,' Ralph smiled. 'There are obliging young women if you know where to find them. The kind who won't make a fuss if you don't always turn up...'

'Prostitutes?' Captain Whittaker started to shake his head. 'I don't care for that kind of thing...'

'Not girls from the street. I know a place where they are discreet and the girls are reserved for the right man. Very clean... if you felt the need, sir.'

'Perhaps... if...' Captain Whittaker shook his hand. 'I'll bear it in mind, Harris, but I'm fixed up at the moment.'

Ralph smiled to himself as he walked away. So, Captain Whittaker had a wife and daughter in Scotland... interesting. If the lady he'd targeted didn't pay up, perhaps that information might come in useful...

Two days after that conversation, he sent another picture and this time he gave instructions as to how much he wanted and where and when it was to be delivered.

* * *

Watching from a shop doorway across the street from the rubbish bin he'd selected for the drop, Ralph saw the woman in the fur coat approach five minutes before time. He smiled as she slipped a brown paper parcel through the open slit, leaving a piece of string dangling. After a quick and furtive glance round, she walked swiftly away without looking back – just as he'd instructed.

Ralph crossed the street after checking to see that no one was watching. He took hold of the string, pulled the parcel out and slipped it inside his coat pocket before walking unhurriedly away. It had been easy. Blackmail was simple if you knew how to carry it through and it was such an enjoyable crime. He'd picked on the most vulnerable party and he wouldn't be bothering Captain Whittaker. Safer that way. Smiling to himself, he patted his pocket. He would find other victims – it was an amusing way to coast through the war.

He was certain that a couple of the officers had heard about the girls he'd spoken of to Captain Whittaker, because of the looks they'd given him. With any luck, he might get some of them to visit the house in London. A few intimate pictures – particularly if the officer had a wife, but also if he was a prig who needed taking down a peg or two. However, wealthy, well-connected women were the best victims. Men might fight back, but women were such trusting fools...

* * *

Alone in his room at the base, Ralph stared at the open package. It contained nothing but a bundle of cut-up newspapers! He'd been cheated. The bitch had tricked him – but surely, she must know that he would now strike back. Her husband would get the remaining photos and they were the most revealing... that kiss and the look on her face. No husband would put up with that! Well, the bitch deserved all she got. If he wasn't trying to escape the notice of a certain police inspector, she might have had her white neck broken.

Ralph had an uneasy feeling that something had gone badly wrong. What had he neglected to do that had made his victim think she could get away with her little trick? The unease stayed with him throughout the evening shift at the officers' club. Why hadn't she given him the money? Surely, she couldn't want her husband to discover she was having an affair?

It was almost midnight when Ralph finally left the officers' mess room. Several of them had stayed drinking late. They hadn't taken any hints that the staff wanted to close up and because it was a private party, the military police wouldn't have broken it up even if anyone had dared to tell them that out-of-hours drinking was going on. Besides, they tended to turn a blind eye if it was officers these days.

The camp was in complete darkness when Ralph finally left the officers' club and began to walk to his billet. He had a torch which had been half-painted over so that he could shine a very weak light on the ground; it was barely bright enough to see his way, but it helped to prevent him tripping over obstacles in the blackout. He was fuming and fretting inside, planning his next move, when he heard a slight sound behind him.

Ralph half turned when he was grabbed and then a hand went over his mouth to stop him calling out.

'Bloody blackmailer,' a voice he knew hissed. 'Thought yourself so clever, didn't you, you bastard, but you made a mistake. When Helen delivered the package, you were seen and photographed – we turned the tables on you. Had a good laugh over it, too.'

Damned fool! He'd been so certain the woman would cave in, he hadn't considered that she might plot with her lover to set a trap for him. He should have waited until it was dark to collect the package.

Ralph struggled as the first fist went into his stomach and

then another and another. He reckoned there were about three of them, not including Captain Whittaker. He was punched in the face, beaten with some kind of cudgel and, as he lay on the ground, he was kicked. The final humiliation came as someone urinated onto his face.

All this, he bore in silence apart from a few grunts. They left him lying humiliated and beaten on the ground. He heard their laughter just before he passed out, but his last thought was that he would get even.

Whittaker had underestimated him. He had the upper hand, at the moment, but when the captain felt the bullets enter his flesh, he wouldn't be laughing then, nor would the soldiers who had given him a beating. Ralph would make them all pay once he knew who they were and it shouldn't be too hard to find out...

When he woke in the military hospital some hours later, Ralph refused to tell anyone what had happened other than that some soldiers – unidentified – had set on him on his way home from work. He was apologetic, but he had no idea who had done it and hadn't seen anyone's face because it was too dark.

'There are always a few bad types in any walk of life and the army is no exception,' the doctor told him. 'It's a wonder you weren't killed. As it is, you will be given your discharge papers once you're ready to leave hospital. I am afraid you are unfit for service after this. Your spleen was damaged and so was your shoulder. Apart from a lot of internal bruising, there was no further serious harm done, but had that kick to the head been harder, you might have sustained brain damage.'

'I feel as if I've been run over by a steamroller.'

'I dare say it does,' the doctor sympathised. 'Were they after money?'

'My wallet was taken,' Ralph improvised, though he knew nothing had been stolen. 'There wasn't much in it, though.'

'Well, you didn't deserve the beating you took,' the doctor said. 'In my opinion, with your lungs, you should probably never have been in the army anyway. I expect you will be glad to get home?'

'Oh, yes, I shall,' Ralph replied and closed his eyes.

At the moment, he didn't know what he wanted – but he would have his revenge. As soon as he was out of hospital, he would get a gun that couldn't be traced to him and Whittaker would pay the price.

Two weeks passed before Ralph was released from hospital. He went to his base to collect his things. As he was leaving, one of the officers he'd served at the club stopped him.

'I heard what happened to you, Harris,' he said. 'I am sorry for it – and that you are leaving the service. We've had our orders. Most of us are off this weekend.'

'I am sorry to hear that, sir,' Ralph said. 'You just keep your head down out there.'

'I'm looking forward to seeing some action,' the officer said and grinned. 'Some of them are in a blue funk over it. I think they imagined they would ride the war out enjoying an easy life at a training camp.'

'Well, you keep safe,' Ralph said, then, casually, 'Is Captain Whittaker being sent overseas, sir?'

'Ah yes, Harris. Got on well with him, didn't you?' the officer mused with a little nod. 'Yes – he has already gone, as it happens. Had some leave due, right after your accident.'

'Then I shan't see him before he goes,' Ralph smiled cheerfully. 'If you see him, sir, please wish him luck from me and tell him I shall be thinking of him...'

'Nice sentiment,' the officer said and moved on.

Ralph scowled after him. Whittaker had got away with it thus far, but if the enemy didn't do for him, Ralph would when the chance arose. A smile touched his mouth. He'd been cheated of his revenge for the moment, but a certain general would be getting a picture in the post that would cause his wife to regret the little trick she'd played on him. She was lucky he didn't do worse, but he couldn't be bothered. The beating had taken more out of him than he'd realised. All he wanted for now was to get home and have a rest. He would tell his sister about the beating and allow her to fuss over him. It would do her good and give him time to make plans...

Whittaker was a fool and a coward. He should have let his minions do the beating and stayed out of it, but he'd had to gloat. If he survived the war, he would pay for that, but now Ralph had other fish to fry. He hadn't forgotten about Tom Gilbert or his bitch of a wife.

Ralph scowled. It was a member of the Talbot family that had ruined his niece and distressed the only person in the world he actually cared for. He'd been told that John Talbot had gone missing. Ralph hoped he was dead – but if he wasn't, he would make sure that was rectified. As for John's half-brother, Tom Gilbert – well, he had plans for him. It was time he got taken down a peg or two. Now that Ralph had an honourable discharge from the army, he would have plenty of time to decide how to make both Tom and his wife suffer...

35

'It has been lovely having you home this weekend,' Lizzie said and kissed Tom lingeringly on the mouth, before letting him leave her to join the soldier who was driving him down to their base. 'Tell your friend to drive carefully.'

He looked back at her and smiled. 'Geoff always does,' he replied. 'It will be at least three weeks before I'm back. Take care of yourself, my love.'

'I shall,' she promised. 'Remember, Faith has worked her notice and is staying in Portsmouth for a bit longer, but then she'll come down to stay until she knows what she wants to do.'

'Good. It will be nice for you to have her company.' Tom got into the car. His friend waved from the driving seat and then they were off. It was sheer luck that Tom's new friend came from Ely. Apparently, they'd met before and knew each other, but they'd become friends at this new elite training camp, pooling petrol rations and arranging their free time when it was possible so that they could drive up together. If Tom had had to rely on trains, it would have meant often standing around on draughty stations waiting for the next one to arrive – time better spent actually getting home or back to base. 'Don't work too hard, Lizzie...'

His words drifted back to her, making her smile. Had Tom guessed? Perhaps she ought to have told him of her suspicion that she was pregnant, but she wasn't quite sure yet and she didn't want to raise his hopes for nothing. Lizzie thought she might have fallen on his last leave, some weeks earlier. Her monthlies hadn't come this time, but, although she was normally as regular as clockwork, she couldn't be certain until she got the results from the doctor. Lizzie had booked an appointment for the next week and had her fingers crossed.

She hadn't been in a hurry to start a family, but recently she'd been thinking of it more, perhaps because Faith was having John's baby. It would mean cutting down her hours at the salon, at least until the child went to school – and that could be a few years longer if they had more than one. Tom would like at least two and, in her heart, Lizzie felt the same.

Lizzie glanced at the paper Tom had left lying on the kitchen table. He'd been reading her an article about a German named Rupert Hess – one of Hitler's top men, according to the reporter. He'd parachuted into Scotland claiming he wanted to speak to the Duke of Hamilton and that he had an offer of peace, perhaps from Hitler. No one was sure whether to believe him. Even if they had, the terms would most likely be impossible to accept. Tom's opinion was that Hitler had to be beaten and beaten well if they were ever to have peace.

Sighing, she turned away and started to tidy up, her thoughts returning to her personal matters. She would have to look for an apprentice she could train and perhaps an improver – a girl who had some training and would be able to do more than just shampoo and tidy up. If she picked wisely, the new girl could probably take over the customers Lizzie normally looked after by the time she needed to cut down her hours. She would miss the work when she had to give up for a while, but having a family was more important. John's loss had brought that home to them all.

Lizzie smiled as she walked back to the house. Tom would be so pleased if she got the news they wanted about the baby. She and Faith would have their babies only a few months apart, which could be fun and something to share. If only John was coming home to share in the excitement and happiness...

It was just as well Lizzie had said nothing to anyone about her inquiries with the Red Cross. So far, she'd heard nothing back from them. Hope of doing so was fading. It looked as if Tom had been right all along and his brother had died in the crash...

* * *

'Keep up, Johnson,' Tom said to the new recruit who was lagging at the back of the exercise. The men were running around the parade ground with their rifles held about their heads and packs on their backs. He knew only too well how tiring the exercise was from his own early training. It was hard but necessary, because in war you had to be ready for anything – even crossing a river with your rifle held above your head and a pack on your shoulders. You might even have to raise the pack if the water was deep, so this training helped to prepare the men for the strain of such eventualities. It was Tom's job to make certain that they got fit enough to be selected for the more intense training for the elite group of men that was now being formed. 'If you fall behind the others, you could be shot.'

Johnson nodded grimly and tried to catch up to the others, but after a while he stopped and bent double, clearly unable to continue.

Tom frowned and walked to where he'd slumped down in a squat.

'Are you ill, private?' he asked, trying to keep his voice from showing too much sympathy.

'No, sir. Just not used to physical exercise. I worked in an office.'

'I see – then perhaps you shouldn't have volunteered for this training; it's going to be harder and more demanding than normal army training. The men who make the grade will live on the edge, always need to be alert and capable of anything.'

'I want to do it, sir. I'll try harder...'

'We're all going to take a break now,' Tom said. He hesitated, then, 'Unless you can keep up, you won't make the grade. This is an elite group – a special group that we're training to do difficult and dangerous work. If I report that you aren't up to it, they will send you back to the ranks and you may get an office job or something in the stores. I can do that it if you wish?'

'No, sir.' Private Johnson saluted smartly. 'I want to be a part of this special operations group.'

'Then I suggest you spend your spare time in the gymnasium getting fit,' Tom replied. 'Some instructors would have you straight off the course, but I know you're trying – I just needed to warn you that if you scrape through and you aren't fit, you could not only get yourself killed, you could let your team down and get them killed too.'

'I know, sir.' Johnson looked him in the eyes. 'You were one of the first – when it was just an experiment to see if a secret force could be used in advance of the army for important missions. You were sent into impossible situations and a lot of your friends were killed.'

'How do you know all that?' Tom asked.

'My father is related to Captain Morris,' Private Johnson said.

'He told us how he'd sent you in to do a job and you were betrayed and most of your group were killed. Only four survived.'

'Four?' Tom questioned. 'I thought it was just two...'

'No, four of you got away, but three were killed – and all the Norwegian partisans. They think it was collaborators and the partisans will know how to deal with them.'

'Do you happen to know the names of the men who survived?' Tom asked, but the young private shook his head.

'I wasn't supposed to hear any of it, but I did...'

Tom nodded. He'd believed that only he and Shorty got away. He would telephone his friend when he got the chance and see if he'd heard anything.

'Knowing all that, you still volunteered?' Tom raised his brows as Private Johnson nodded. 'Well, I can only say get to the gymnasium and put the extra hours in – and then we'll see...'

Tom blew his whistle and the other soldiers stopped and then sank onto the ground to rest weary limbs.

'Take a rest now,' he said. 'Have some food and this afternoon we'll organise a cross-country run.' He heard the groans and laughed. 'No, I shan't be coming with you. I'll be putting another batch of recruits through the training you've been doing this morning. Sergeant Ross will be taking you on the run. He will be the hare and you the hounds – so make sure you catch him or I'll find some interesting chores for you to do.'

A few murderous looks came his way, but Tom ignored them. He'd been through enough rigorous training to understand how they felt and he didn't hand punishments out for nothing, but if he suspected someone of shirking, he wouldn't hesitate.

* * *

At first, Tom had resented the new job he'd been given. He'd wanted to fight. The war dragged on relentlessly with little sign that the Allies were winning. There were victories like when the Bismarck had been sunk and the successful flight of a new jet-engined plane. Tom felt he ought to be doing more. If he couldn't fight or do the job he'd done previously, he would have preferred to be released to work on the farm, but it seemed he wasn't the failure he felt in the eyes of his superior officers and they wanted him to pass on his experience to new recruits.

'You know what it is like to go in behind enemy lines and get out again,' he'd been told by Lieutenant David Stirling, the man who was setting up this new secret force they called the SAS and he'd wanted Tom on his team. He'd come up with the idea to use these surprise tactics in the desert, but it could be adapted for land and sea. Different from Captain Morris' ideas in that it was more disciplined and streamlined. Whereas before it had been hit and miss, now the men were highly trained and likely to be more successful in their missions. 'Obviously, we can't ask you to go in again with that leg,' Tom had been told bluntly. 'You would slow the others down and could be a liability – but you have the experience. You know only too well what can go wrong and that is what I want you to pass on to these young men. We only want the best, Gilbert. We don't want too many failed missions...'

Tom had felt his words like a knife thrust but knew he wasn't being blamed or mocked. He'd done what he was asked and couldn't be accountable for the betrayal that had got so many killed. Tom would probably always feel a certain amount of guilt, but it hadn't been his fault. It would be *his* fault if he allowed unfit or unsuitable men to slip through the net, however. The force they were building had to be the best. The success or failure of future landings could be down to the men he was training now, because their ability to go in, find the enemy's weakness and report back on the strength of fortifications could make all the difference, and a little sabotage often unsettled things enough to make the enemy nervous. This was going to be a long war and quite likely one of attrition, like the dripping of water on stone; it would be the side that could endure the longest that would come out on top, though no one could truly win a war like this one.

Tom followed the men into the canteen. Even though it was now early summer, it could be pretty cold standing around the training ground sometimes when the wind whipped across the open landscape. At other times, it was scorching hot and sweat soaked his shirt beneath the thick uniform. If he could run like the men in shorts and shirt, it would be much better, but as yet, his leg seemed to show no sign of getting rid of the limp. He was afraid he was stuck with it.

'There is a telephone call for you, Lieutenant Gilbert...'

'For me?' Tom was shocked. His wife had a number for emergencies, but no one else. 'Thank you, private. I'll come at once...'

Tom's heart was racing as he made his way to the telephone in the officers' mess room. He picked up the receiver. 'Hello – is that Lizzie?'

'Not last time I looked,' Shorty's voice came over loud and clear and Tom's heart returned to its normal beat. 'I am being transferred to join you at the training centre, Tom – but I'm getting married first. It is this weekend in London. I wondered if you and your wife could manage to get here? It is in church, but the reception is small – just dinner at a hotel for a few of us.'

'That is great on two counts,' Tom said warmly. 'We'd love to come if I can get away.'

'I'm sure you can swing it – given they think of you as a hero,' Shorty joked. 'Tell them it is a matter of life and death...'

'I'll ask if I can get a pass,' Tom told him with a chuckle. 'So, Carole said yes then?'

'You told me she would and I finally got up the courage to ask. I've been given a promotion and her father has accepted me, so I can't get out of it now.' Shorty laughed. 'Can't believe it is happening. Or that I'm being transferred to join you training others. It seems they consider we've done enough, at least for now, and they think our experience is worth having.'

'I know,' Tom replied. 'It's great news, Shorty. Give me the details of the wedding. I'll ring Lizzie and ask her to meet me in London once I've got permission. I can probably get someone to swap duties if necessary.'

'I'm sure you can twist a few arms,' Shorty told him. 'They seem to think we're both heroes and were sent on impossible missions – so you should be able to wangle an extra pass if you ask...'

'I'll certainly do that, though I'm not sure about the hero bit,' Tom said but smiled. 'I know Lizzie is looking forward to meeting you. She has told me to invite you to stay – and that invitation is for you and your future wife, whenever you wish.'

'Thanks. I'll bear that in mind when I want a free holiday in the country,' Shorty jested. 'I'll see you this weekend. Don't let me down – you're my best man—'

Tom chuckled as the line went dead. It was just like Shorty to throw that in at the end. He would get the time off somehow and he'd ring Lizzie with the good news as soon as he could.

* * *

'That's lovely,' Lizzie said. 'I would really enjoy a wedding in London. It is a chance to see Vera and to have a little fun...'

'It is nice to have something good to look forward to,' Tom said and Lizzie hesitated, then, 'I might have some more news to tell you by then...'

'Oh, what?' he asked. 'Don't keep me in suspense, Lizzie – what have you heard? Is it about John?'

'No – it's about me, us...' She took a deep breath. 'I went to the doctor and he's done a test to be sure, but he thinks... we're having a baby. I was going to tell you when you came home.' The silence on the other end of the phone frightened her. 'Tom – are you there?'

'You took my breath away,' he said and she could hear the emotion in his voice. 'I just wish I could put my arms around you and kiss you – show you what this means to me.'

'Me too,' she said and tears were in her eyes. 'I should've waited until the weekend.'

'Oh no,' Tom said. 'This is the best news ever, darling Lizzie. Does Mum know?'

'I haven't told her yet,' Lizzie said, 'but she may have guessed.'

'Oh yes, she probably has, but tell her soon,' he said. 'She will be thrilled...'

'I wanted to tell you first, but I shall now,' Lizzie replied with a little laugh. 'It will be all babies now for a while.'

'Yes, of course. Faith is having a baby too...' She heard him sigh. 'I only wish John could be around to see it.'

'Yes, I know,' Lizzie agreed. 'We all wish that, Tom.'

'Sorry, I shouldn't have brought it up,' he apologised. 'It is a happy time. We mustn't spoil it or let what happened to John overshadow that...'

'No, we won't, but it is all right to be sad and worry for him, darling. I understand how you must feel.'

'Well, this is a day for surprises, Lizzie.' He was silent for a moment, then, 'Don't work too hard, my love. Take care of yourself for me, please.'

'I will,' she said. 'I shall look forward to seeing you this weekend and the wedding – and I'd better buy myself a new hat.'

* * *

Lizzie was thrilled to meet Tom's friend – the man who had saved his life – and she liked the girl Shorty had married in a very brief but happy ceremony. Tom and Lizzie were the only friends invited and the family party consisted of another five: the bride's parents and her younger brother, who had just joined the air force, and Shorty's brother and his wife. His parents had died when he was a child and his brother – older by some ten years – had brought him up.

The reception was in a small hotel. They'd done their best for the young couple, but the cake was just a cardboard one and the meal was cold chicken, mashed potatoes, greens and gravy, followed by a butter-cream and jam sponge – which Lizzie suspected was made with margarine. However, there was a large magnum of champagne and the toasts were made, accompanied by smiles and laughter at the telegrams Tom read out. His speech was funny and teased his friend, but at the end, he looked towards the bride and groom.

'I wish a brave man much happiness with his new wife and thank him with all my heart. If it wasn't for him, I wouldn't be here.'

'Just returning a favour,' Shorty said and grinned like a Cheshire cat, but he nodded at Tom and they exchanged a look that spoke of friendship and trust.

Afterwards, they walked to the station together – they were catching separate trains – Tom back to his base and Lizzie home to Ely and then the farm. She caught sight of some headlines concerning the war. German troops were moving towards Russia.

'Surely, they won't invade Russia?' she said as Tom stopped to buy an evening paper from a newsboy.

'If they do it might shorten the war,' Tom said. 'They can't fight on all fronts forever – but what we really need is for the Americans to join the war.

Lizzie nodded and sighed, hugging his arm. 'This has been lovely, Tom. I just wish you could come back with me for a few days...'

'Sorry, love, wish I could – but I was lucky to get a few hours. We're pretty busy at the moment.' He reached out for her, holding her close and sliding a hand gently over her tummy, which as yet showed little sign of the precious gift it carried. 'I love you so much, Lizzie. Promise me you will take care of yourself while I'm away.'

'I promise,' she said and kissed him. 'Do you know when you will be home again?'

'I'm not sure. There is quite a lot going on...'

'And you can't tell me anything more,' Lizzie said. 'No, I don't need you to say anything, Tom – just keep safe, my darling.'

'I'll do my best.' He stopped and kissed her. 'And you do the same...'

36

Lizzie was at work that warm summer Monday morning when Faith rang her to say she would be arriving that evening; she'd stayed a bit longer than intended in Portsmouth but had now done all she wanted and asked if it was all right to come. Lizzie told her she was looking forward to her visit. They spoke of train times and the merits of catching the bus or taking a taxi from Ely to Mepal, a distance of around eight miles or so.

'Oh, I'll take a taxi if there is one,' Faith told her. 'I've got a couple of cases to bring, so it will be easier. You are sure it is all right for me to come and stay? I shan't be in the way?'

'You know you won't,' Lizzie replied. 'It's all going to fit in nicely – you see, I've just found out that I'm having Tom's baby. I'll be a few months behind you, Faith, but we'll be able to share experiences and exchange knitting patterns. It should be fun, don't you think?'

Faith hesitated a moment and then agreed. 'Yes, I do, Lizzie. As long as I'm not making life harder for you…'

'We're all looking forward to it; Pam is over the moon that she has two grandchildren to knit for now.'

'Yes. She sent me such a lovely letter – told me that I would always be family and that you would all look after me.'

'That sounds like Pam,' Lizzie smiled. 'You must understand, Faith. You are carrying John's child and we all treasure you – not just because of the baby, but because you made him happy and we will always remember that.'

'You're all so kind. I'll see you this evening.'

Faith sounded on the verge of tears as she hurriedly replaced the receiver. Lizzie frowned. Clearly, Faith was very emotional. The uncertainty over John, and the fear that he was dead, must be awful for her, even worse than it was for the rest of the family, because she had also lost her home. Surely her mother would want to make it up with her one day. She was hurt and angry, but Faith was a lovely girl and her family would want to see her child in the future.

* * *

The tears were trickling down Faith's cheeks as she walked away from the phone box. She'd lingered in Portsmouth after being released from her work at the hospital, partly because she wasn't quite ready to become one of the Talbot family and partly because Slash had asked her to meet him again. He had renewed his offer to marry her, declaring his love all over again and promising to look after both her and her child.

Faith was torn by indecision. It would be good for her baby to have a father and she wasn't sure she could face being an unmarried mother, even though Lizzie and Pam had made her feel so welcome. Yet if she accepted Slash's offer, she would be respectable again. Perhaps her mother would welcome her once more if she had a husband and then her child would have its maternal grandparents.

It would mean disappointing John's family, though. They would think she hadn't cared for John if she just upped and married another man before it was even certain John was dead. Tears welled in her eyes and her throat was tight. She was so selfish and wicked thinking of herself when John was missing and probably dead. Faith wanted him to come home and things to be as they were – but she didn't believe it would happen.

She shook her head as she went to collect her suitcases. Her thoughts kept running round in circles, because she couldn't decide what to do for the best. Slash had promised to wait because she'd told him she needed time. Yet in her heart, she knew it wouldn't be fair, because although she liked him, she didn't love him – not the way she still loved John.

'I'd wait for you forever,' he'd told her and squeezed her hand. 'I don't think you realise how much you mean to me.'

Sometimes, it was all too much for Faith. It was only the thought of the child growing inside her that kept her going.

37

'I don't like to see you like this, Sheila,' Ralph said to his sister. 'Just because Faith has let you down, you shouldn't feel ashamed. You can't spend the rest of your life hiding away, as if you've done something terrible.'

Sheila Goodjohn looked at her brother. 'I feel as if I can never face my friends or hold up my head again,' she replied. 'I brought her up properly, Ralph – how could she do this to me?'

'I daresay it was his fault,' Ralph replied tersely. 'I don't like the family, Sheila. They think themselves so high and mighty – but Faith would not have done it if he hadn't persuaded her.'

Sheila dabbed at her eyes. She still had some of the beauty that had been hers as a young girl, but her mouth turned down at the corners and the sour expression made her look older than she really was.

Ralph touched her hand. 'Dry your tears, my dearest sister, and I'll take you out to tea.'

'Philip will be home shortly...'

'Leave him a note. From what you've told me, he doesn't deserve your consideration, Sheila.'

'He took her side, you know.' Anger flashed in her eyes. 'I couldn't believe it – his precious daughter let him down and he wants to forgive her and let her come home.'

'If he brings her here, you should leave and come to me,' Ralph suggested. 'You will always have a place in my home, Sheila.'

She raised her head. 'Sometimes I feel that I would prefer to leave him – but I should hate to live alone. Besides, he is my husband, and despite it all, I cannot simply leave him. It wouldn't be right.' She gave him a faint smile. 'You may wish to marry one day, Ralph.'

'I doubt it,' he said. 'I thought I wanted a young woman once, but she spurned me for another...' He sighed deeply. Let Sheila feel sorry for him. She had no need to know his private thoughts. 'I sometimes feel lonely. You are the only person who truly understands me.'

Sheila nodded, slightly wistful, as if she might wish to start a new life elsewhere if her sense of what was right allowed it. 'I've always been fond of you, Ralph. Those bruises on your face – tell me again how it happened...'

'I was just walking back to my quarters after working late and I was set on by rogues. My money was taken and I was beaten. I am lucky to be alive and I have internal injuries that may cause me problems in future. That's why I was given an honourable discharge and sent home – otherwise, I might have been overseas fighting for my country.'

'You feel it so, don't you,' she said, looking sympathetic. 'Here I am wittering on about my problems – and you've been through so much pain...'

'I'm all right – or I shall be.' Ralph put on his best brave face. 'And I feel for your troubles, Sheila. I was thinking I might buy a house in Cambridge. You would enjoy living there. I thought a nice large property where we could both have our own rooms.'

'Ralph! You really do mean it...' Sheila looked at him in surprise and he could tell she was tempted despite her scruples over breaking her marriage vows. 'I suppose it would be a new start. No one would know about Faith...'

'Not unless you told them,' he agreed. 'Well, you think about it, but I'm going to sell my property here and move. It is up to you – but if you feel the situation is intolerable, you only have to say...'

'I am so angry with Faith and with Philip,' she said. 'But I can't decide what to do for the best. I'm not sure I could leave my husband, even though he has taken her side. Besides, when the child is born, well, I may want to see it.' She looked up at him. 'I did so long for grandchildren to spoil, but now...' A sigh broke from her. 'How could she do it to me? My daughter – behaving like a slut.'

'If you do want to see the baby, I could arrange it,' he said. 'Let's face it, Sheila. You've never really been happy since you married...'

'He always took her side.' Sheila's face settled into a look of discontent. 'Give me some time to think about it, Ralph...'

'Very well, but I've decided I'm buying that house and I shall sell everything here, which means I shan't visit much...'

Ralph was annoyed with his sister. He had expected her to jump at the offer. After all, she never stopped complaining about her life and the way her husband treated her, preferring his daughter to her. She'd vowed she never wanted to see Faith again and now she was saying that she might want to see the child...

Women were so unpredictable. He scowled.

Faith was staying with Lizzie Gilbert now and that made it difficult for him to visit, but he would find a way, even though he'd been so angry with Faith the last time they'd met. If her mother wanted to see the baby, then he would make sure she got the chance. Ralph might be annoyed with Sheila for the moment, but she meant more to him than anyone else.

His anger against Faith had simmered for a while. When she'd told him she wasn't a murderer or a blackmailer in the heat of the moment, he'd thought she knew what he'd done, but of course she didn't. No one could, not even that interfering police officer, because he'd covered his crime too well.

His attempt at blackmail had backfired and that rankled. His bitterness over the beating was eating away inside him, but he'd suggested that Sheila live with him because there was still a tiny part of him that wanted the love she'd always shown him. Maybe it was time to let go of the past and build something better. He had little chance of revenge for the moment with the men he'd wanted to punish overseas – perhaps Hitler would do it for him. Ralph should concentrate his energies on making money, getting rich and powerful.

Ralph decided he would give his niece another chance for her mother's sake. Sheila's anger was beginning to cool and he suspected she would want to see her grandchild and for that she would need to build bridges to her daughter. Ralph had been fond of Faith once and, although he wouldn't forgive her, he could pretend to if it persuaded her to visit her mother.

Ralph nodded to himself. He had no need to fear anything from Faith so he would visit soon and talk to her – explain that her mother was upset but wanted to see her and the baby after it was born.

38

'Will you be all right, Faith?' Lizzie asked that morning in late July 1941 as she got ready to catch her bus to Chatteris. Faith had been living with her for nearly six weeks now and her bump was very noticeable whatever she wore, despite the flowing maternity dress Pam had helped her to make. 'I don't like leaving you alone, but I have customers booked and my assistant is busy...'

'Stop fussing and go,' Faith said and smiled at her. 'I'm perfectly all right, Lizzie. The baby isn't due for another few weeks – towards the end of August, the doctor said, and if I should go into labour, Pam is only a few minutes away.'

'That is perfectly true and she would probably be of more use to you until the doctor and midwife arrived than I should,' Lizzie said. She moved towards Faith and gave her a little hug. 'I've taken the next two weeks off to be here with you, Faith – but don't stay here all day alone. Walk up to Blackberry Farm and let Pam make you a cup of tea and some lunch.'

'I shall visit her,' Faith promised, 'but I want to finish the coat I'm knitting first. I only have a few rows to do and then I'll take it up to Pam and she will help me to stitch the arms in. I told her I wasn't sure of getting it right and she said she would help me.'

'Yes, Pam is good at stuff like that,' Lizzie agreed. 'She's had five of her own to knit for and she's made several cardigans for Tina too. I'm not sure where she finds the time...'

'Speaking of time...' Faith looked at the watch on her wrist. It was a gold one that her father had bought her and she wore it all the time now she wasn't nursing. Her father had been over to see her twice since she came to live with Lizzie and seemed to be very fond of her. He'd told her that he was working on her mother and hoped she would relent and want to see Faith again soon. 'You'd better go, Lizzie, or you will miss the bus...'

'Yes, I must dash.'

Lizzie knew she had to hurry as she picked up her bits and pieces and went out, but even as she got to the stop and the bus arrived, she couldn't help feeling anxious about Faith. She wasn't sure why, because the girl was sensible and if the baby started, she only had to walk a few yards and she would be safe with Pam.

Faith finished her knitting and put the pieces of white wool into a brown paper bag. It was gone eleven and Pam would have her pastries in the oven baking by now and they could sit down for a few minutes to enjoy a chat and a cup of tea while the mystery of fitting the sleeves was explained. Faith had done it before, but they'd looked bunched and she'd had to unpick it and do it again twice before she was satisfied that it looked right. Pam had told her she would show her an easier way to do it. The weeks she'd spent living with Lizzie and visiting Pam had been peaceful, happy ones for her. If she had realised how nice it would be, she would have given up nursing sooner and not lingered in

Portsmouth as long as she had. The freedom and camaraderie, and the loving relationship between all the family, was something new to her, because her parents had never shared the same kind of contentment as she'd found here. A sigh left her as she thought how happy she could be if she were John's wife and living close to his family.

Tears stung her eyes. Faith thought about John often, remembering his ready smile and laughter. He'd been kind and generous and she wondered, looking back, why she hadn't just said she would marry him the previous year. Why had she been so wrapped up in her nursing that she'd thought it was more important? She knew now that nothing was more important than love and she regretted her lost chances. If only he would come back to her...

Faith brushed away the sudden tears. It was foolish to cry when it didn't help.

The sun was shining outside and Faith didn't need a coat as she left Lizzie's house. It felt good to be out and her spirits lifted. Somehow when she was here near the farm, John seemed very close. Pam couldn't be convinced that he was dead and of late Faith had begun to believe that his mother was right. Nothing more had come after that first telegram and so they had no right or reason to hope that John was still alive, but they still did. She knew that the men of the family had given up hope, but Faith and Pam clung to it.

Pam was so thrilled about the baby and she was busy knitting and making things for Faith to use. John's cot and lots of other things he'd used as a baby had been fetched from the attic, ready for his own child.

Sometimes, Faith regretted that she couldn't share this time with her own mother, too, but she knew that wasn't possible. Her father had told her the last time he'd visited.

'Your mother still won't see you,' he had said regretfully. 'I've told her how much she is missing – and will miss if she refuses to forgive you. She'll never have the pleasure of seeing her grandchild grow up.' He'd looked at her sadly. 'You will let me continue to visit and see the baby, won't you?'

'Of course, I shall,' she'd told him and her eyes had filled with tears. 'I'm sorry I've let you down, Dad...'

'You haven't,' he'd told her and she'd seen the love in his eyes as he looked at her. 'I was a bit shocked at first, that's all mainly because of your mother. You could never disappoint me, not truly, Faith. I love you and I know John would have married you if he could – if it hadn't been for this war, it would never have happened.'

'John always wanted to wait,' Faith had told him, tears on her cheeks. 'But we were so much in love and we were afraid – afraid that we would never know...'

'Yes, I understand, Faith,' her father had said and leaned in to kiss her cheek. 'You wanted to be with him that way in case he didn't come back.' His voice had been choked with emotion. 'I am so sorry, Faith. So sorry that this should happen to you, that you should lose the man you loved so much and now your mother...'

'I still have you and I have my baby – and John's family are so kind and generous,' Faith had replied with a smile. 'Perhaps John is just missing... he might still come back. They thought his brother Tom was dead for a time...'

'I shouldn't get your hopes too high, love.' Her father had looked at her sadly.

Faith had known he didn't believe that John would come back, but Pam did and that gave her hope.

* * *

As Faith walked into the farm kitchen, the smell of jam tarts and Pam's almond buns met her and made her mouth water. Pam's buns were delicious straight from the oven. They were made a bit like a madeira cake but with a few drops of almond essence and tasted wonderful.

'I know you like these,' Pam said as she put the plate of fresh baking in front of her. 'Now you just tuck in, love. If I'm right, you've eaten nothing since Lizzie left for work.'

'I was busy finishing the coat,' Faith told her and placed the bag on the table as she took one of the buns and bit into it. 'Oh, this is lovely!'

'Before the war, I used to put a little butter-icing on top,' Pam said. 'Now, we're lucky to have anything nice. It's only because we have such a large family with the land girls as well that I can do as much baking as I do – it is easier when I can share the rations. Seems to go further, though we only get the same as everyone else...'

'You get the same fat and meat rations,' Faith agreed, 'but you have fresh eggs. Jeanie was telling me her mother would kill for half a dozen fresh eggs.'

'Vera does like a nice egg,' Pam agreed. 'I keep telling her to come down for a visit and when she does, I make sure I send a few eggs and a bit of whatever we've got home with her. She visited a while back but doesn't come enough because she is a busy midwife.' She hadn't been down since Faith's arrival, but Lizzie had told her all about Jeanie's family, and she'd met both Jeanie and her brother, Terry – and, of course, the little girl who everyone spoiled.

Faith nodded. 'Babies don't stop coming just because there is a war on...'

'That is what Vera says,' Pam laughed. 'Now, let me have a look at this baby coat... Oh, that's a lovely pattern, Faith. What I do is give the pieces a gentle iron first to straighten the edges, because the armholes tend to curl a bit otherwise, and then I pin them in place. That way, I can see if they are fitting properly before I sew them. I overstitch the edges like this....'

They bent over the delicate wool garment together so that Faith could see exactly how Pam managed to get her baby coats looking as good as shop-bought ones. Faith smiled and nodded as she saw how the flat stitches were better than the running ones she'd used.

'Yes, that looks lovely,' she cried as Pam finished. 'Thank you so much...'

'You're very welcome,' Pam said. 'I like helping, Faith. Thank you for letting me be involved in this happy time.'

'Yes, it is a happy time,' Faith said, smiling at her. 'It is happy because you've made it so, Pam – you and Lizzie and all your family. You've all been so kind to me...'

'You are very precious to us,' Pam told her. 'Not just because of the baby, though that is a wonderful gift – but because you loved John and he loved you so very much.'

Faith felt the tears come up and spill over. She wasn't crying out loud; they were silent tears. Wiping them away, Faith embraced John's mother and then they both gave a little cry as they felt the kick.

'Well, I never,' Pam said and laughed. 'I think you've got a footballer there, Faith – and I think he's nearly ready to make his first appearance.'

'Do you think so?' Faith asked. 'It should be another few weeks, I think.'

'Babies come in their own time,' Pam said, eyeing her thoughtfully. 'It will surprise me if you go that long...'

Faith gave a little giggle. She'd thought she'd fallen for the baby on John's last visit at Christmas, but they'd made love before she moved to Portsmouth and it might have happened then, even though she'd had her monthlies after that. She knew from reading her medical books that it could happen that way, though it didn't often. 'He can come as soon as he likes,' she said. 'I'm more than ready.'

'It does get wearisome towards the end,' Pam agreed and then glanced at the clock. 'I'd better start getting lunch ready – you will stay and eat with us?'

'Are you sure? I was going to make a cheese and salad sandwich...'

'I've got a nice chicken casserole with dumplings in the oven and a rice pudding for afters. Much more the thing for you, love – and there is enough for us all, because I've cooked lots of vegetables from the garden.'

* * *

It was nearly four o'clock when Faith left the farmhouse and walked the short distance to Lizzie's home. She'd had a few twinges in her back while helping Pam put the dishes back on the oak dresser but hadn't said anything. As yet, she didn't have any real pain and it might be days or weeks before she went into labour.

Faith frowned as she saw the back door was open. Surely, she hadn't left it that way? Lizzie wasn't due back until around six that evening. Had her husband come home unexpectedly?

Walking up to the door, Faith hesitated, a little prickle at the nape of her neck. 'Is that you, Lizzie?' she asked before entering.

No one spoke, but she sensed that someone was in the kitchen and a cry of dismay left her as she went in and saw the man standing by the table. He had his back to her, but she knew him at once and was angry that he'd walked into Lizzie's house without an invitation.

'What are you doing here? You had no right to come here – and I know that door was shut. You shouldn't have walked into Lizzie's house just like that...'

'The door wasn't locked,' her Uncle Ralph said as he turned to look at her. 'That was foolish of you, Faith. Had I wanted I could have stolen everything...'

'How long have you been here?' she demanded, still angry that he'd walked in the way he had. 'No one locks their door here. We don't expect thieves.' She felt emotional and upset, realising that she ought to have locked up when she left, though Lizzie never bothered.

'I didn't come here to steal,' Ralph told her and his eyes had gone cold with anger. 'Your mother is upset. She wants to see you... and to see the child when it is born.'

Faith looked at him hard. Something about him made her flesh creep and she didn't believe him. Faith didn't want him intruding into her peaceful life. 'Dad said she wasn't ready to see me yet,' she said, her gaze meeting his steadily. She saw something flash in his eyes. 'You're not telling me the truth – not the whole truth, are you?'

'So, I'm a liar now. I suppose that Lizzie Gilbert has been telling you things – turning you against me and your family...'

'No, Lizzie hasn't told me anything,' Faith replied coldly. 'Is there something to tell, Uncle Ralph? What have you done to Lizzie that you think she might have told me?'

'Nothing! Nothing she didn't deserve anyway.' He looked furious now and Faith felt shivers down her spine as he moved towards her. 'Her husband wants taking down a peg or two and one of these days that's what I'll do – but he isn't important. Let me take you home, Faith. Once your mother sees you, she will forgive you.'

'No!' Faith gave an involuntary shiver and jerked away from him. 'I don't trust you. When Mum is ready to see me, Dad will tell me... You...' She shook her head. 'It doesn't matter. Just go away and leave me alone. I don't like you now. You've changed...' She was frightened of him and just wanted him to go away.

'You little bitch!' Ralph's temper seemed to erupt and he reached out for her and grabbed her by the shoulders, shaking her back and forth in an explosion of anger – more anger than her small outburst warranted. Faith screamed in terror and went for his face with her nails. 'Damn you! I'll teach you to mock me...'

'Stop it! Leave me alone,' she cried, but he was no longer listening to her, caught up by whatever possessed him, he seemed lost in his rage.

Suddenly, he hit her several times around the head and then pushed her up against the wall and banged her against it, again and again, as if he'd lost all control. His spittle was in her face as he raged, her blood on the newly painted wall, dripping from a wound to the back of her head down her neck. Faith felt the pain and begged him to stop hitting her, but he just continued to vent his insane rage on her, yelling things she didn't understand in her dazed state. He gave her an almighty shove, thrusting her backwards so that she fell onto the kitchen table, a sudden pain shooting through her body at the violent impact. She cried out in agony and then slumped to the floor like a rag doll, barely conscious.

'My baby...' the thought was in her head though she wasn't sure if she had spoken the words aloud. 'My poor baby...'

And then her eyes closed, and she knew nothing more.

* * *

Faith was unaware that Ralph had kicked out at her before he left. She could not have known that he ran through the village to where he'd parked his car so it would not be seen, nor did she know that he drove away as if the Devil was on his tail. She was slipping into the abyss until the pain of labour brought her back and she screamed. Unable to get up from the floor, she screamed again as an unbearable pain ripped through her body.

It was coming too soon. Surely, it was too soon! Faith tried to hold back the urge to push, wanting to keep her baby safe until she was in the hospital as she'd planned, but there was nothing she could do to stop what was happening to her. Her head hurt so much and the pain racking her body was too much.

She crawled to the open door and screamed again, crying out for someone to help her, but the baby was coming, and she could do nothing. Faith could feel the urge to push and she felt tears of regret on her cheeks because her head hurt so much where her uncle had banged it against the wall and she could not think properly, could not focus. Her eyes were getting misty and she knew that she could not summon the strength to go in search of help. Her baby would be born, but she could not help it into the world, because her strength was ebbing, and she knew that she would not see her child's face. Summoning her remaining strength, she screamed one last time before slumping back as her baby entered the world and her blood drained sluggishly into a pool on the kitchen floor...

39

It was Jeanie who thought she heard a scream as she left the cowsheds. It was faint but it had a desperate ring to it. She stood listening for a moment and then heard it again, but faintly. Artie had followed her out from the shed and looked at her, one eyebrow cocked. Since Nancy's departure and until a new girl arrived, he'd taken to helping her with the milking.

'What's wrong – aren't you hungry?' he teased.

'I heard something... I think it was... Faith, the baby!' Jeanie started to run, then paused and looked back. 'Get your mum. I think Faith is in trouble.'

Artie nodded and strode off towards the kitchen.

Jeanie kept on running. She was close enough now to see that the back door was open and that made her heart race. There was definitely something wrong at Lizzie's house and she had an uneasy sensation at her nape that made her feel tense and afraid of what she was about to find.

As she paused and looked into the kitchen, Jeanie heard whimpering – the whimpering of someone in distress, but it didn't sound right. If Faith was giving birth, surely, she would be hollering for help at the top of her voice? Entering the kitchen, her heart hammering, Jeanie gave a cry of distress as she saw Faith on the floor. Her child had been born and was lying in a pool of its mother's blood, whimpering. The strange noise she'd heard was the baby, not Faith.

'Faith! No – Oh, no... Faith...' Jeanie gave a frightened sob.

What had happened here? Faith was lying very still – too still.

As Jeanie ran to her and knelt beside her, she could see the cuts on her lip and the marks on her cheek – there was a lot of blood in her hair from a bang to the head, sticky now, so it had happened a while back. Seeing a chair overturned and some broken crockery, Jeanie had the sickening feeling that Faith had been attacked shortly before she gave birth.

How long had she been lying here? Jeanie touched her skin. Faith was cool but not icy cold. She was still alive but close to death by the look of her. Jeanie gasped, fear for the girl she'd come to like these past weeks coursing through her as she understood the extent of her injuries. She'd been badly injured and yet somehow, she'd given birth all alone. Tears of pity and shock trickled down Jeanie's face as she bent over her, willing her to live and yet sensing that it might already be too late. *Oh please, don't let it be too late*, and yet she could now see the injury to her head was horrendous.

'Faith, can you hear me? Please blink or move your hand if you can...'

'What is it?' Jeanie heard Pam's voice behind her. She sounded out of breath and then she gave a little cry of distress. 'What happened to her? Did she fall?'

'I think she was attacked,' Jeanie said. 'Look at the injuries to her head and face, Pam. I think someone attacked her and left her injured and she gave birth to her baby somehow before becoming unconscious.'

'My God!' Artie's voice was loud and concerned. As Jeanie looked up, she saw he was staring at a patch of blood on the wall and a shudder went through her. 'What kind of a beast would attack a woman so far gone with child?'

'Go home and ring for an ambulance and the police,' Pam instructed. 'We'll stay here in case she comes round, but I think there is little chance of that... The trauma to her head and then this...' She indicated how much Faith had bled during the forced premature birth.

'Don't touch anything if you can help it,' Artie said and was gone.

Pam joined Jeanie and they both knelt by Faith, looking at her and then each other. 'Artie is right. Whoever did this is a beast – a madman. Faith never hurt anyone, and she was so happy earlier. I can't imagine why anyone would want to harm her.'

The tears were running down Jeanie's face. 'I heard a scream as I left the sheds. It wasn't loud and, at first, I thought it was just a bird...' A tiny forlorn whimper behind them made them remember the child. For a few moments, their concern for Faith had overwhelmed them both, but now it was for the child.

'We have to look after the baby... poor little mite.' Pam had suddenly come out of her shock. She got up and went to Lizzie's dresser, looking for the things she needed – something to tie the cord so that she could cut it without causing harm to mother or baby and a sharp knife.

She knelt by Faith and did what had to be done, neatly and efficiently, and then scooped the child up. It started to cry as she carried it to the sink, ran a little warm water while holding the baby to her chest and then gently washed it. She used the clean towel she found hanging from a rail near the sink to dry and wrap the baby while she went in search of something more suitable. Faith's basket containing baby clothes and a knitted shawl was on a chest near the larder. Pam wrapped the baby in the shawl and then, crooning as it screamed and cried for its mother, she rocked it in her arms.

'It's a miracle,' Pam said. 'John's son – he's fine. He's beautiful... I can't understand how he survived this, but I thank God for it...' She sounded choked with emotion, tears trickling down her cheeks.

Jeanie didn't turn her head or answer. She was still kneeling beside Faith, trying to rouse her. 'I feel I want to hold her and warm her,' she said, 'but Artie said not to touch anything...'

'It's because the police will want to see the way things are – but you can put that rug over her.' Pam pointed to a plaid rug. 'I think Lizzie uses it for picnics but she will understand.'

'She will be devastated,' Jeanie said. 'What a terrible thing to happen in her lovely new house,' she shivered and looked around nervously. 'What do you think happened?'

'I can't think straight,' Pam said. 'It is horrible. Has she moved at all?'

'Not since I arrived. I think she must have screamed when the baby was born and then passed out...'

'She gave birth to John's son alone,' Pam said. 'What must she have suffered, Jeanie? And what will John say if she dies?' She was crying too now, silent tears trickling down her cheeks. 'How long until the ambulance gets here?'

'I don't know.' Jeanie knew Pam didn't expect her to know the answers; she was just talking to keep the horror of what had happened here at bay. Jeanie wanted to scream and cry herself, to run away to the safety of her own room and weep until she couldn't see the blood and the cuts on Faith's lovely face. It hurt. It hurt so much and she didn't know how to bear it.

She started in fear as she heard a noise behind her, but it was Artie returning.

'The ambulance is coming, but the doctor from Sutton is on his way. He said he would be quicker. The police are coming too. They want you to stay here, Jeanie. You haven't touched anything?'

'I put a rug over her to try to keep her warm,' Jeanie said, 'and Pam rescued the baby. She had to cut the cord and...'

Artie had gone white. He rushed back outside and the sound of him being sick could be heard. He reappeared a few minutes later, looking sheepish.

'Sorry. I don't know how you can bear it...' Jeanie got up and went to him. 'Should you leave her?'

'I don't think she knows I am here,' Jeanie said and gave a sob. 'I think... I think she is dead...'

'Oh God, no!' Artie groaned. 'First John and now...' He stopped as his mother shot a fierce look at him and then, before he could say more, the doctor arrived at the back door. He was clearly shocked and out of breath.

'I jumped in my car and came immediately,' he explained. 'I can't understand what happened to bring on the birth...' He glanced around the kitchen. 'Good grief! Was she attacked?'

'Yes, we believe so. I've sent for the police,' Artie told him grimly. 'What kind of a beast would do this?'

Doctor Morton had gone to his knees beside Faith's motionless body. He felt for a pulse and then used his stethoscope before looking up at them, a terrible look in his eyes. 'I am so sorry, but it's too late... too much loss of blood, but it was probably the head injury that killed her. We'll need a postmortem to confirm it, but I'd say that was it. Whoever beat her, murdered her.'

'No, oh, no,' Jeanie looked at him in distress. 'She was alive when I got here. I am sure she was...'

'I cut the cord – did I do something wrong?' Pam asked, looking pale and shaken.

He shook his head. 'You didn't do anything wrong, Mrs Talbot. You probably saved the baby's life – but she gave her life, giving birth in the most terrible way, and the head injury was possibly terminal anyway. The shock and trauma of what happened to her must have brought the birth on very suddenly; it was a miracle the child survived.' He looked at Jeanie. 'You found her here when?'

'About twenty minutes ago, I suppose,' Jeanie said and glanced at her watch. 'We had just finished milking...'

'It was twenty minutes ago,' Artie confirmed.

'She may have been lying here for some time.' Doctor Morton looked at his watch. 'It is nearly six...'

'And she left my house just before four this afternoon,' Pam said and looked at him in distress. 'It could have happened soon after she left me... Oh God! If only I'd popped down to see if she was all right or walked back with her...'

'You couldn't know a monster was waiting for her,' Artie said and then turned in relief as the local police officer arrived, swiftly giving him the story as they knew it. 'Jeanie found her like this twenty minutes ago. I came and rang the ambulance and the doctor and then you... We think she was attacked.'

'Have you touched anything?' Sergeant Thorne asked, glancing round. 'Looks a bit of a mess...'

'I put the rug over her,' Jeanie said. It had been removed by the doctor and was lying on the floor by Faith's body. 'Pam cut the cord and looked after the baby...'

A wail from the newborn made them all look at Pam. 'I arrived when Artie came to fetch me,' she explained. 'Is it all right if I take the child up to my kitchen? I have some powdered milk there and I can make a bottle up – this child needs a feed...'

'Yes, take the baby, Mrs Talbot,' Sergeant Thorne said. 'I'll come up and get your statement later.' He looked around him again. 'This is a bad business. Who could have done such a wicked thing?'

'We've been asking ourselves the same thing,' Artie said. He hesitated then, 'One of us should give Lizzie a ring. Best if she stops with you tonight, Mum. I'll clear this lot up when Sergeant Thorne says it is all right, wash that wall and maybe paint it too... Can't let Lizzie walk in on this...'

Pam walked quickly up to the farm. Arthur was there with Susan and the children looking anxious. She saw the children's scared faces and told them there had been an accident.

'Take Angela and Tina upstairs and then make them a warm drink,' she told Susan, who obeyed after one look at her mother's tear-stained face.

Pam related as much as she knew to her husband and then placed the newborn baby on an armchair while she made up a bottle. Arthur was staring at her in silence, struck dumb by the awful events.

'We've never had anything like that round here before,' he said at last. 'It must have been a madman – someone escaped from a lunatic asylum...'

'I can't think of anyone who would want to hurt her like that – to murder her,' Pam said. She had made up the bottle and she sat down on the chair with the baby in her arms and touched the teat to his mouth. It was a moment or two before he latched on, but then he sucked lustily. 'Poor little mite. You should have your mother's milk – but she's gone and this is the best we can do...'

'Did the doctor look at him?'

'Just a brief glance. He was too shocked. I can take him in to the surgery if need be.'

'Poor little devil,' Arthur mumbled. 'It is a rotten shame, Pam. What are we going to do with him?'

'Keep him of course,' Pam replied. 'He is John's child and that's all there is to it.'

'Haven't you got enough to do?'

'I'll have help,' Pam told him. 'Jeanie and Susan will help – until Susan goes to college.'

'It is you the burden will fall on,' Arthur warned. 'You already have a full day, love.'

'Then I'll have a fuller one,' Pam replied firmly. 'He is my grandson, and I shall look after him and that's that...'

'Of course, it is,' Arthur said. 'Didn't expect anything else. I'll see if I can find someone to come in and help you in the mornings.'

Pam looked up at him and smiled. 'You old softie. You would never have let John's son go. I know you.'

'It's all we've got of him,' Arthur said and then looked up as Lizzie walked in the door.

'What's wrong, Mum?' Lizzie said breathlessly. 'I saw the doctor's car... Oh, has Faith had the baby? That's marvellous because I have wonderful news for all of you. The Red Cross think they may have found John... If it is him, he is alive, but he was badly wounded and he doesn't know who he is...'

Pam stared at her and then started to cry. Loud noisy sobs that started the baby off and his wails were even louder. Lizzie moved quickly to take the baby from its grandmother's arms and soothe it. Arthur was crying too, sobbing, his head in his hands.

Lizzie looked from one to the other in dismay. 'I thought you would all be so pleased...' As she saw their faces, the light of pleasure died from her eyes. 'What is it? Has something happened... to Faith?' She glanced down at the child in her arms. 'Have they taken her to hospital? I knew I shouldn't have left her today, but she was so...'

'Sit down, Lizzie,' Arthur said, his head coming up. His face was grey with grief but determined. 'Give the baby back to Pam.' He looked round as Susan entered the kitchen. 'You'd better sit down, too, love. We have some bad news and it's important that you both listen carefully. For the moment, we all have to be very careful...'

Lizzie sat down, looking shaken. Pam had stopped crying and took the child from her. She went out of the room and her footsteps could be heard going upstairs.

'Pam is grateful for the news about John and you can tell us how you came to know later,' Arthur told Lizzie. 'Now I have to tell you both that Faith is no longer with us. She was attacked this afternoon. We don't know who did it and that is why you two have to be careful. Lizzie, it happened in your kitchen. Faith was attacked and she must have given birth, but then... well, she died before the doctor got there. We don't know all the details. There will be an inquest and a postmortem, I expect... leave all that to the doctor and the police. All we need to know is that she died after giving birth to John's son...'

'No! It's horrible,' Lizzie cried and Susan gave her a frightened look but said nothing. 'If only I'd stayed with her and cancelled my appointments...'

'If you had, we should probably have lost you too,' Arthur said. 'Don't blame yourself, Lizzie. Faith was with Pam most of the day. She walked home alone, but it was broad daylight. Who could have suspected a madman was lurking?'

'If it was a madman...' Lizzie said and Arthur stared at her. 'It's just that she mentioned a quarrel with her uncle... Ralph Harris. He is a nasty bit of work and I wouldn't put anything past him...'

'That remark stays in this kitchen,' Arthur told her. 'I'm not saying you're wrong, Lizzie, but you have no proof. Unless someone saw him... or whoever it was, we don't know what happened.'

'Surely her uncle wouldn't...' Susan looked as if she might faint, but before any more could be said, there was a knock at the door and then Doctor Morton and Sergeant Thorne entered, followed by Jeanie.

'I need to get changed,' Jeanie said and went straight to the door leading to the stairs. Her face told its own story as she glanced briefly at Lizzie and then disappeared.

'What happened?' Lizzie asked the police officer.

'I should say she was violently attacked by someone who was either in the house or she opened the door to...' He frowned. 'Do you lock your back door, Mrs Gilbert?'

'Only when we go to bed – we don't need to, or we thought we didn't need to in the daytime...'

'Your brother-in-law is clearing up for you,' Sergeant Thorne said. 'I would advise you not to sleep there alone tonight – or any night until we've caught this monster. That's what he is.' His face twisted with emotion. 'My wife is expecting her baby soon, if it happened to her... I know how you're all feeling, so I'll make this as brief as possible. Where is Mrs Talbot?'

'Upstairs dressing and feeding the baby, I imagine – our grandson,' Arthur said and he nodded.

'I'll go up and take a look at the child and ask her to come down,' Doctor Morton said. 'This is a bad business and no mistake – but we won't make it worse by neglecting that baby. I'll just make sure everything is as it ought to be.'

Arthur nodded and the doctor went out.

Lizzie looked at the police officer. 'I wasn't here, because I've been at work all day – so I'll go up to Pam if I may...'

She got up and left hurriedly. Susan followed as soon as she was allowed, leaving Jeanie and Arthur with Sergeant Thorne. He finished writing in his notebook and then looked at Jeanie.

'You didn't see anyone running or walking away?'

'No. I just heard the scream... I think when the baby was born...' She hesitated, then. 'I did see someone in the lane near Lizzie's house just before we started the milking, but he had his back to me and I couldn't tell you who it was or even make a guess.'

'Did you notice what he was wearing?'

Jeanie thought for a moment and then nodded. 'Yes, he was wearing grey slacks and a blue shirt. He didn't have a jacket, but it was a warm afternoon. I think that is why I noticed him, because he was smartly dressed and most people round here wear working clothes, unless they are going somewhere.'

'You saw the back of his head – so what colour was his hair?'

'Brown... dark brown,' Jeanie said, 'and it was short, as they have it in the army.'

'Army haircut,' Sergeant Thorne nodded. 'You see – you knew more than you thought, Miss...?'

'Jeanie Salmons,' she said and smiled. 'I hope you'll be able to catch him, Sergeant. I hate to think a man who could do such a thing would get away with it.'

'We don't know the man you saw had anything to do with it,' he reminded her. 'Might be quite innocent, but it all helps. We'll ask around the village and see if anyone noticed a stranger getting off the bus or a car parked for a while or just someone they saw walking about that made them curious.'

Jeanie nodded. 'If he is some kind of a monster, other people might be in danger...'

'I think this person may have known his victim,' Sergeant Thorne said, but before Jeanie could ask his reason for suspecting Faith had known her attacker, the back door opened and Artie entered. He looked at his father, who beckoned him and then whispered in his ear. Artie looked startled and then nodded at whatever he'd been told.

'Fingers crossed she is right,' he said and then, as the police officer looked at him, 'Lizzie thinks John may still be alive; she's heard something from the Red Cross... Oh my God! What will we tell him?' He ran his fingers through his hair, his feelings plain for all to see. It had been a hard and emotional day for them all.

'We'll face that when we come to it,' Arthur grunted. 'They aren't sure it is him yet. I pray to God it is because your mother has been through enough.'

'You could do with some good news,' Sergeant Thorne said and stood up, tucking his notebook into his top pocket. 'If you think of anything else, please let me know, Miss Salmons.'

He nodded to the two men and left.

Artie looked at Jeanie in concern. 'Are you all right, Jeanie? You were the one that found her.'

'It was awful,' Jeanie said and tears welled in her eyes.

Artie moved quickly to her side and held her as a deep sob shook her and she wept into his shoulder for a minute before rousing herself to ask for more details about John.

'Lizzie hasn't told us everything yet,' Arthur said. 'Just that a man has been discovered, wounded and with amnesia, who just might be our John. Pam is convinced it is, of course. She has never given up hope.'

'I pray she is right,' Jeanie said and Artie nodded and was about to say something when the door to the stairs opened and Lizzie, Pam and the doctor entered the kitchen. Pam was smiling and thanking Doctor Morton as she showed him to the door and waved him off.

'Well, I think we all need a cup of tea and something to eat,' she said when she returned to the table. 'John's son is fine, which is wonderful. I think that is down to you, Jeanie. If you hadn't heard that scream and investigated, he could easily have died before Lizzie got home.'

'It's horrible,' Lizzie said and went to fill the kettle. 'I thought I had such wonderful news about John and now...' She gave a little gasp and sat down, tears welling over again. 'Poor, poor Faith. I can't believe it happened – and in my house.'

'It won't be easy for you to go back there,' Pam said. 'Stay here with us until we hear that monster has been caught.'

'That might be forever,' Lizzie objected. She looked at Artie. 'You cleaned everything up?'

'Yes. You wouldn't know anything had happened... but Mum is right. Perhaps Tom can get leave and come home for a while to help you get over it...'

'I am going home after I've had a cup of tea with you,' Lizzie said firmly. 'I have to, Pam. If I don't, I might become too scared to live there at all. I have to face it...'

'I'll stay with you for a while,' Jeanie offered at once. 'It won't seem so bad if there are two of us...'

'Are you sure?' Artie looked at her hard. 'You were the one who found her...'

'And I stayed with her while you fetched Pam,' Jeanie reminded him. 'I'll be all right – and Lizzie can't be there alone. Not until he has been caught or she feels safe.'

'I could come too,' Susan offered from the hall doorway. 'There's safety in numbers.'

'Thank you, Susan dearest,' Lizzie said, 'but it will be enough if Jeanie stays for a couple of nights. I'm not frightened to be there alone – it's just the thought of what Faith must have suffered...'

Her words were met with nods of agreement and then silence. No one wanted to think about that lovely young woman lying there helpless and alone as she gave birth.

40

After they stopped talking about the tragedy of Faith's terrible death, Pam insisted Lizzie stay for supper so that she could explain how she'd heard about the man who might be John.

'I got in touch with the Red Cross, because they have some contact with prisoners in the camps,' she said. 'I thought if he was captured in Germany after his plane crashed, they might have him on a list – and they did have someone who resembles John. However, he wasn't in a camp – he was in a Belgian convent...'

'A convent?' Arthur looked at her in surprise. Pam nodded, because Lizzie had already told her some of it while they were upstairs.

'Yes. Don't ask me how or why, because all they told me was that he'd been found injured and taken in by the nuns. He has been very ill and he was dazed when they took him in, unable to tell them who he was. A head injury that seems to have given him amnesia, but his other wounds are not life-threatening and are healing.'

'We can't know for certain if it is John,' Arthur said, frowning.

'No, but it sounds as if it might be. They know he is an airman and English and the build, hair and eyes sound right...' Lizzie hesitated, then, 'Would I be right in thinking that John had an operation for appendicitis when he was a boy?'

'Yes, he did,' Arthur said and his knuckles turned white as he gripped his armchair. 'He had a grumbling appendix and they took it out just in case. He missed sports at school for a whole term and we didn't hear the last of it...'

'The man the nuns cared for has an old scar, probably for appendicitis,' Lizzie said. 'He is currently in Switzerland. Some group or other managed to get him away after the convent was searched by a German patrol. The nuns said it was no longer safe to keep him. They hid him but were afraid of a return visit.'

'Sounds as if they are brave women,' Arthur grunted.

'Yes.' Lizzie was thoughtful. 'I suspect that he may not have been their first British fugitive, but, of course, I'm reading between the lines. The Red Cross only told me the basics.'

'They are supposed to be neutral, that's why they are allowed to send parcels to prisoners,' Arthur nodded to himself. 'You didn't tell us you were trying to find out, Lizzie?'

'I couldn't until I had something to tell you. Even now, it might not be John – but it sounded so much like a description of him...'

'Will they send him back home?' Pam said and looked anxiously at her husband and then at Lizzie.

'They are neutral,' Arthur said. 'That means they can't take sides, Pam – and that means they can't help John to get home, but there may be those that will?'

'He is resourceful,' Lizzie said. 'If there is a way, he will get home – and if not, I am certain he will write, once he remembers who he is...'

'Will that happen?' Pam's eyes were anxious, searching.

'I asked them that, and I was told no one knows. Amnesia is

often caused by damage to the head – a kind of brain trauma – so she said on the phone, temporarily in some cases, but sometimes it can last much longer or be permanent.'

'If he were here in England, we could visit and then we'd know if it is John,' Pam said. 'Could we go out to where he is – would they let us?'

'I don't think they would let us,' Arthur said. 'Did she tell you where – which hospital, Lizzie?'

'No – and I didn't think to ask, but she did say that they are hoping he will be given permission to travel home when he is well enough.'

Pam closed her eyes for a moment. 'Thank God,' she whispered. 'I know it is John. I was sure he was alive and now I've been proved right.'

Arthur looked as if he wanted to say more but clamped his teeth on his pipe and kept his thoughts to himself.

'If it is John someone will find out for us,' Lizzie said. 'I asked the Red Cross lady and she told me that they have people who can discover these things. She wouldn't say more, but I think we can hope now...'

'If it is John – what are we going to tell him?' Artie asked, the second time he'd raised the question, and silence fell as they all looked at him. 'I don't think we should tell him that Faith was attacked – not at first anyway. It will be bad enough that she died having his child...'

'If he remembers her, it will devastate him to know that she's dead,' Lizzie said. 'You can't tell him until he's well or he might never recover...'

Pam gave a little sob. 'It's not fair,' she said in a choked voice. 'We may have John back, but we've lost Faith – why did it have to happen?'

'Nothing is fair in love or war,' Arthur grunted. 'When he is ready, the boy will be a comfort to him.'

'What about Faith's family?' Susan asked doubtfully. 'Won't they claim the child? John and Faith weren't married so—'

'Over my dead body,' Pam said so fiercely that everyone looked at her. 'I mean it. That baby is John's and while I'll admit Faith's family have visiting rights – he doesn't leave this house, except with his father when John gets home.'

* * *

It was past eight when Lizzie and Jeanie left the farm. Artie walked them home, warning them to lock the door after him.

'Don't open it to anyone you don't know...' He hesitated, looking at them uncertainly. 'If you like, I could sleep in a chair tonight? Stay with you?'

'Thanks, Artie, but we're all right,' Lizzie said. 'We'll be careful, don't worry.'

After he'd gone, Lizzie looked round her kitchen, feeling slightly uneasy, but Artie had made a good job of clearing up and there was nothing to see – nothing to show that a young woman had died there. She drew a sigh of relief and glanced at Jeanie.

'We'll have to change the sheets in F—' she caught her breath on a sob as she stopped herself saying Faith's name, '—In my spare room. I was going to do it tomorrow. I'd booked two weeks off to be with her.'

'It was to have been such a happy time,' Jeanie replied, looking sad. 'I know we have the baby and that is wonderful and we may get John back – but...' She drew a sobbing breath. 'Why? Why would anyone want to harm her, Lizzie?'

'I'm not sure, unless...' Lizzie frowned.

'I think Faith knew her attacker,' Jeanie said. 'She put up a struggle and he hurt her, but I'm not sure whether he meant to kill her. The doctor said the injury to her head killed her, but having the child the way she did and lying there with no one to help her must have hastened it. If only I'd heard her sooner... if I'd popped down for a chat before I started the milking, I might have scared him off...' Jeanie sat down heavily on a kitchen chair. 'She must have suffered so much...' A little sob escaped her. 'I read a story once about a young woman who gave birth to her child alone in a wood and then died, but for it to happen to someone we all knew and cared for...' She shook her head.

'I know – it's frightening...'

Jeanie looked at her sharply. 'It won't happen to you, dearest Lizzie,' she said. 'I'll make sure I'm with you all the time, unless you're with Pam or Tom...'

'Bless you,' Lizzie said and sat down next to her. They clasped hands. 'I'm not really frightened of giving birth, but...' She shook her head. 'Someone hurt Faith badly and I think I know who it was...'

'You believe it was Ralph Harris, don't you?'

Lizzie nodded thoughtfully. 'I know she quarrelled with him the last time she saw him when he visited her in Portsmouth. She told me he had changed and seemed sinister. He frightened her then by the way he looked at her and he hit her.' Lizzie hesitated, then: 'She thought he looked a bit mad... or evil. She wasn't sure which, but I know she didn't like him. She told me she used to love him but not any more ...'

'Yes, that does sound a bit sinister,' Jeanie said. 'I can't help thinking that if I'd only visited her earlier...'

'You can't blame yourself,' Lizzie said quickly. 'I wanted to stay with her today. I had an uneasy feeling. If I had, she might still be alive.'

'We'll always wonder,' Jeanie said and sighed. 'Shall we change the beds and then have a cup of cocoa?'

'Good idea,' Lizzie agreed. 'I'm going to write to Tom this evening, tell him the news about John – and Faith, of course. Oh, why couldn't it have been just good news?'

'I know what you mean,' Jeanie agreed and swiped away a tear. 'I didn't know Faith well, but I liked her – and she didn't deserve to die like that.'

'No one does,' Lizzie said and leaned towards her, taking her hand to squeeze it. 'We have to remember her as she was – the good things – and try to forget the rest. I'll just make certain all the doors and windows are locked and then I'll come and help you – though if I'm right, her uncle isn't likely to return. Whatever happened here, I don't think he intended to murder her...'

41

After Jeanie and Lizzie had left, Arthur telephoned Faith's father to break the news of his daughter's unfortunate death.

'I can't make it easy for you,' he said. 'I am very sorry to tell you, Mr Goodjohn, but Faith died giving birth this afternoon.'

'No! I don't believe it...' Faith's father sounded stunned, shocked and devastated. 'She wasn't due yet... What happened? Oh my God! How?' He gave a sob of anguish.

'We believe she was attacked,' Arthur replied. 'Someone hurt her and she gave birth early and alone. Jeanie found her just after the baby was born, but she had lost a lot of blood, and before the doctor could get there, she had passed... I am so very sorry. She was with my wife until nearly four in the afternoon, happy and talking about the baby, but at six, Jeanie heard screaming as she left the cowshed and she went straight to the house. She sent for my wife and the doctor and the police, but it was all too late... though I am happy to say the baby survived it all and is fine, a beautiful boy.'

'Oh my God, who could have hurt her like that? Why? She never hurt anyone in her life.' Faith's father gave a strangled sob.

'This is terrible news. She was so young, her life hardly started. I can hardly credit what you're telling me, but I know it must be true.'

'I wish I could tell you that she is in hospital recovering, but I'm afraid there was nothing they could do.'

'And the child is all right, you say? I'm sorry, I can't take this in...'

Arthur patiently repeated the news, 'She and John had a son; my wife is looking after him and we'll keep him here at the farm until John comes home. We've reason to believe he may now – but, of course, you and your wife are welcome to see the boy whenever you wish...'

'Your wife is willing to care for him?' Faith's father sounded bewildered, clearly still too shocked to take in the news.

'She will love him as her grandchild whatever happens and we'll bring him up if my son doesn't make it home.'

There was silence for a moment, then, 'Yes, I think that may be for the best. I'm not sure what my wife will say – but Faith chose to come to you when her mother turned from her. John is the boy's father and he belongs with your family – but I shall want to see him. I'll call in if I may and we'll discuss the funeral arrangements. Faith is my daughter and I'll be paying for it, of course.'

'That is up to you; if it's what you want, of course. My wife and I will take care of things this end and we want you to know that you will always be welcome in our home, Mr Goodjohn. We loved Faith and her parents are family.'

'Thank you. I shall certainly visit regularly to see the child, but I am not sure about her mother.'

'She may wish to see the boy when she is ready. My wife says that Faith wanted to call her baby Paul if she were to have a boy. I think that's what we'll call him, at least until John can have his say.' Arthur paused. 'If your wife changes her mind, that's fine with us. Everyone is entitled to change their mind – and she was hurt that Faith had behaved in a way she thought wrong.'

'I was disappointed, but my wife... she was very badly affected, Mr Talbot. Her aunt had a child by a married man when she was young and the disgrace was thought so bad that the child was given up for adoption and she was sent to an institution for the insane – they did that back then and it affected Sheila, more than I ever knew.' Faith's father sighed. 'Sometimes I struggle to see the woman I married in her... but she is my wife and I shall support her as best I can...'

The receiver went down abruptly, as if Faith's father couldn't take any more. Arthur shook his head over it as he related their conversation to Pam.

'We'll have no trouble over the boy with Philip Goodjohn, but his wife may object when she has time to think about it. She was angry with Faith for letting her down, but now the girl has gone, she may decide she wants the baby...'

'I won't give the boy up to her,' Pam said firmly. 'He stays with us where I know he will be loved and cared for whatever happens. A mother who could turn against her daughter just because she got pregnant – well, she isn't right to have the child, Arthur. Besides, Faith wouldn't want it. She told me she loved being here with us and she would want her son to be brought up here, too – or with John.'

'You're certain he's coming home, aren't you?'

'Yes, I feel it inside,' Pam agreed. 'I've always believed that he would come back one day, even when it seemed stupid to hope.'

'Supposing he never recovers his memory?'

'Once we get him home, he will,' Pam said confidently. 'I know my John. When he has his family around him, he'll get well again...'

'We don't know what he has suffered,' Arthur warned her. 'You mustn't expect too much, love.'

'I'm not a child, Arthur,' Pam said and smiled to take the sting from her words. 'I know he could be scarred or crippled – or changed mentally – but he is my son and when he feels himself loved and cared for, he will come back to us. It may take time but he will... Look at Terry. Vera thought she'd lost him when he wouldn't go home and he couldn't bear to see Tina for a long time, but then he did, and now he loves his daughter and seems to be getting on well.'

'You'll miss Tina when she goes,' Arthur said, looking at her. Terry had decided to return to London at his father's request. He'd said they had enough to do, coping with Faith's terrible death, which was true.

'Yes, she is a sweet little thing, but I'm glad she has her father back and I know Vera missed her. She couldn't manage her because of her work, but now she has found help and, besides, Terry said he would like to visit with Tina sometimes. She was happy here. It wouldn't surprise me if he moves back this way one day. His father needs him, at the moment, but when the war ends – if it ever does – there will be men looking for jobs and he'll be free to make his own mind up about where he lives.'

Arthur nodded. 'Now that Terry will be working, he can pay for the child's keep and his own, so Vera may well feel she can give up her job and look after her family.' He frowned. 'She had an older girl serving as a nurse overseas too – maybe she'll come home soon and help out?'

'Vera says Annie is doing a worthwhile job out there and she wouldn't ask her to come home. I think she has heard from her recently, though she doesn't say anything about coming home yet. I know Vera worries for her...'

'This war has ruined a lot of lives,' Arthur said with a frown.

'We got Tom back, thank God, and, if our prayers are answered, we'll get our John home – but a lot of folk won't get their sons back, Pam. I heard of another local lad's death today...'

'That is sad,' Pam said. 'I am sorry for his family and for a young life cut short.' She closed her eyes for a moment and then looked at him. 'What do you think happened to Faith – you haven't seen any strangers about recently? Anyone lurking?'

'No, I haven't seen anyone hanging around but...' Arthur leaned forward and knocked his pipe out over the fire. 'I did see a car I recognised parked in Brangehill Lane when I passed on my way home from seeing to the pigs.'

'There's not many folk live down that way who have cars,' Pam said with a frown. It was only a few minutes' walk from the lane to Blackberry Farm. 'You said you knew it?'

'It belongs to Ralph Harris,' Arthur replied, looking at her grimly. 'I didn't say when Lizzie was here – but I think she may be right. It could have been him that hurt Faith. I'm not saying he intended to kill her – but I know he has a temper. Tom doesn't trust him. He asked me to keep an eye out, to make sure Ralph Harris didn't do anything to upset Lizzie while he was away.'

'Do you think he came looking for Lizzie? He must know she doesn't want to see him after what happened before...' Lizzie had been hurt by the man and disliked him very much. She'd told Pam that she'd refused a lift from him one night and that he'd been nasty to her over it. 'Surely, he wouldn't?'

'Come looking for Lizzie to make trouble *or* harm his niece?' Arthur looked grim. 'I think that man is capable of either, Pam. From what Tom told me... well, I only know one thing for sure and that's that I saw his car at around three-thirty...'

'He could have been waiting for Faith when she got home...' Pam shuddered. 'Do you think you should tell Sergeant Thorne?'

'Not sure,' Arthur said and frowned. 'It's one thing to suspect something, Pam – but another to go to the police and get someone in trouble. He might have been in Mepal for a good reason...'

'And he might not,' she retorted. 'I think you should go down there tomorrow and tell Sergeant Thorne what you saw and why it might be relevant. After all, if this Ralph Harris was somewhere else, he can prove it, can't he?'

'I suppose so,' Arthur said reluctantly. 'I'll have a word, but I'm not easy in my mind. I'd rather not cast aspersions on an innocent man...'

'Better that than leave a guilty one free to kill again,' Pam insisted and Arthur sighed. What a terrible thing he was suggesting if he was right – that Ralph Harris should kill his own sister's daughter, whether by accident or design, was beyond belief.

* * *

'Ralph Harris, you say?' Sergeant Thorne looked at Arthur. 'I know of the man... Actually, he had an altercation with Tom after that darts match. Now I come to think of it, he was a bit strange when I went after him for damaging the truck as he drove off...' His gaze narrowed. 'This isn't a bit of revenge because of what happened by any chance?'

'I would have thought you knew me better than that,' Arthur said. 'I saw the car parked down the road. I know for a fact that Faith told our Lizzie that she didn't trust him and didn't want to see him... the rest is up to you to discover.'

'Well, it won't be, because I've called in the Yard,' Sergeant Thorne told him with a frown. 'I thought we had a madman in our area, but I'll put this information in my report and we'll see what happens. It's the best I can do. I expect someone to come this afternoon. He may want to look Mrs Gilbert's house over and to talk to Jeanie and your son since they were the ones who found Miss Goodjohn.'

'I am sure that can be arranged,' Arthur agreed. 'I telephoned Faith's father last night. I thought the news should come from me... though I suppose you've been in touch?'

'I sent a local man to see them. Must have been just after you rang. He said her mother was in a terrible state, crying and screaming... Apparently, they had to get the doctor to come and give her a sedative.'

'Well, news like that is enough to send any mother mad,' Arthur agreed gruffly. 'Can't imagine what I'd do if it was one of mine. Bad enough that it was John's fiancée and we're just so thankful the baby survived...'

Sergeant Thorne nodded grimly in agreement. 'My colleague said the doctor told him Mrs Goodjohn was on the brink of a nervous breakdown, poor woman.'

'Well, I'm sorry for her loss,' Arthur said. 'It may help if you catch whoever was responsible – but it won't bring that poor girl back.'

'That's the pity of it,' Sergeant Thorne replied grimly. 'Even if we get him and he hangs, we can't give Miss Goodjohn back her life.' He shook his head sorrowfully. 'As if there wasn't enough trouble with this war...'

'You lost a cousin recently I understand?'

'My wife's cousin,' Sergeant Thorne confirmed, 'but I liked young Phil. He was a good lad.'

'Always that way.' Arthur shook his head over it. 'Well, I'm sorry for your loss, Bill.'

'And I for yours, Arthur.' They smiled as the friends they were. 'I'll make sure to give the man from the Met all the info and I pray we'll get the bugger – whoever he may be...'

Arthur grunted and went off to tell Pam.

Pam made Arthur a cup of tea, looking satisfied that he'd done as he ought, and sighed. 'I feel sorry for Faith's mother – but she has only herself to blame. If she'd welcomed her daughter with open arms, perhaps this wouldn't have happened.'

'Don't judge her, Pam, love. We don't know that,' Arthur observed and retired behind his paper. In a few minutes, he would have to walk round the yard, see what needed doing, but just for now he wanted to relax and forget the horror that had come into his peaceful world.

42

'Ralph, I have to see you,' Philip Goodjohn was relieved when his wife's brother picked up the phone. He'd been trying to reach him ever since she'd collapsed into her bed, but this was the first time he'd answered. 'Have you heard what happened to Faith?'

'No. What do you mean?' Philip thought his brother-in-law sounded odd. 'What has she been saying?'

'Faith can't say anything. She died yesterday evening after giving birth.' He heard the gasp at the other end and then silence. 'She gave birth too soon, alone, and she'd been attacked—' His voice broke. '—My little girl was attacked by a monster who ran off and left her to suffer agony and die in a pool of her own blood.'

Silence for a long moment, then, 'I am very sorry, Philip. I can't believe it. I thought she was staying with friends... I mean, I was told she'd gone off somewhere. I don't know where...'

'She was staying with Lizzie Gilbert in Mepal,' Philip replied, choked by his own tears. 'Her mother wouldn't have her here, so she was staying near the farm owned by John's family – you know they were engaged...'

'Heard something,' Ralph said in a strangled voice. 'Look I'll visit later this evening. I have to go now, sorry...'

Philip heard the receiver go down sharply and looked at it in disgust. He'd always thought Ralph a selfish bastard and now he knew he was right. Hadn't even given him time to tell him how ill his sister was – and she thought the sun shone out of his backside! Well, served him right for even ringing. It was against his better judgement, but he'd thought a visit from her beloved brother might calm his wife. She couldn't stop crying over Faith and nothing Philp said would comfort her. Blaming herself she was, saying over and over that it was her fault.

'You might have been a bit kinder to the girl,' Philip had told her. 'But I can't see as it was your fault. Faith was just in the wrong place at the wrong time.'

'You know nothing,' his wife had screamed at him. 'Get Ralph! I have to speak to him. I need him!'

Philip walked slowly upstairs to the spare bedroom, where his wife had taken herself off when she woke, saying she wanted to be alone. His head was bent with the weight of his sorrow, but when he opened the door, the look from his wife was one of anger rather than shared grief.

'I rang Ralph. He says he'll come this evening. He sounded very strange... think he must be upset...'

'Go away,' she said. 'Leave me alone. I don't want to see anyone – not you and not my brother...'

Changed her mind then! She was in such a state he didn't know what to do to help her.

'You'll make yourself ill if you go on like this,' Philip told her. 'Will you let me bring you some toast and a cup of tea before I go to work?'

'You're going to work?' she spat the words at him, laden with disgust. 'Our daughter has been murdered and you're going to work?'

'I shan't be long – just got to make sure that the men know what to do,' he said. 'I'll come back later. Besides, you don't need me. It's better if you rest now, love.'

'Just leave me alone,' she replied and flopped back on the bed, turning her face into the pillow to weep.

Philip left her. He couldn't do right whatever he said or did. He'd taken Faith's side when she told them she was pregnant and argued she should come home, and now he was paying the price of his wife's anger. If Ralph had come round, perhaps she would have cheered up a bit. They had to face the truth, however awful it was – and Philip knew he needed to get out of the house, to talk to the men he worked with, to retain some normality. Otherwise, this nightmare was going to overwhelm him. If his wife had turned to him, let him comfort her, it might be different, but as it was, he couldn't stand being in the house another moment.

* * *

Ralph stared at himself in the mirror and felt sick. He'd been angry with Faith when she'd stood up to him and told him to leave and he'd hit her – too hard and too much. A memory of him banging her head against the wall over and over flickered into his mind and sickened him. At the time, his anger had possessed him, but he hadn't meant to kill her... The realisation of what must have happened after he'd stormed off in a fury hit him like a body blow and he doubled over and vomited.

What kind of a man was he? He'd always had a temper and he'd always looked out for number one – but when had he become the monster he now was? Ralph couldn't stand the sight of himself. What had he done? Memories of Faith as a sweet and loving child swamped him in remorse.

After the shock of Faith's father's news, he'd been stunned, hardly knowing what he was saying or doing. Then had come the terror. He was known in Mepal. It was a small village and his car would have been noticed. Had he left any clues? Had Faith given any details about her attacker before she died? He was shaking so much that for several minutes he couldn't think straight. He had told Philip that he would visit that evening, but he couldn't – if he saw his sister, she would know. She might even have guessed already.

Ralph tried to recall what he'd said to her about his visiting Faith. He'd bragged about making her see sense – about making sure that his sister got to see her grandchild whenever she liked. Would she work it out that they'd argued and that Ralph had hit her...?

His fevered mind went back over the scene in that kitchen. He'd hit her head against the wall and then he'd slapped her about the face, knocking her into the pine table and then, as she lay on the ground, he'd kicked her in the stomach. It must have been that kick that made her give birth early and... killed her.

Ralph hadn't blinked an eye when he shot and killed those gangsters in London, but they were scum and deserved it; he'd blackmailed and paid the price and he'd do it again if he saw an easier mark – but he hadn't meant to murder his niece. The memory of her sweet face when she was a little girl was there in his head, haunting him, and he felt tears on his face. He hadn't meant to kill her! He'd just lost his temper – and his temper had become uncontrollable at times.

Ralph shuddered. He couldn't visit his sister and her husband. Philip would kill him if he guessed what he'd done, and he would, because Ralph couldn't hide his guilt from his sister.

She knew him too well and would see that he'd done something bad. His thoughts went round and round in a maelstrom of regret, fear and guilt. How had he come to this? What had happened to him?

He had to get away – somewhere he wasn't known. His mind in a daze, Ralph left his house. The door locked itself behind him, but upstairs the bedroom window was wide open. He took nothing with him but the keys to his car. No thought of the future, where he would go or what he would do, was in his mind. His only desire was for escape, though whether from the law, his sister's recriminations if she learned of his crime or his own tortured thoughts, he did not know.

Getting into his car, he drove, leaving the busy market town behind and heading down a lonely country road. It was the kind of road that a driver should be wary on, because of the twisty bends and bumps in the poorly repaired surface, but Ralph pressed his foot to the floor, pushing his car faster and faster.

As he drove, he was beginning to find excuses for himself. It wasn't his fault. He'd only pushed Faith about a bit. Women often died in childbirth. Besides, she was a wanton little bitch and deserved all she got. Yet even as he made his excuses, Ralph's foot pressed ever harder on the pedal, his speed increasing as he approached the blind bend. Then, when he was about to take it, a tractor and trailer came round the corner and Ralph threw up his arms to protect his face as he went into it head on with a resounding crash that shattered his windscreen and tore apart the metal of his car.

* * *

Philip Goodjohn took the call late that evening. He listened to the message from the local police officer and felt sick. Ralph had been found in his car; his injuries so severe that he wasn't expected to live.

'Normally, we'd send someone round to see you and your wife, sir,' the voice on the other end told him. 'We were advised that your wife was ill – the shock of your daughter's death, we understand. So, we thought it might be best to telephone rather than knock at the door.'

'Yes, thank you,' Philip replied, feeling as if all the breath had been sucked out of him. As he replaced the receiver, his only thought was how to tell his wife that the brother she'd always adored was badly injured and unlikely to survive? He wasn't sure that she could take the news, at the moment. Perhaps it might be best not to tell her just yet. After all, there was little point in her rushing to be at Ralph's bedside from what the police officer had told him. She was still grieving for Faith, still shocked and guilty, too, because of the way she'd refused to see Faith.

Philip felt the weight of grief and sorrow for the loss of his daughter as much as his wife, but he had to struggle on somehow. His wife needed help if she was ever to recover and he had a grandson to love and cherish, as he had his beloved daughter. The boy had a home, but Philip would visit and one day that child would inherit whatever he had to leave...

Lifting his head, he went into the kitchen of a house that seemed curiously empty despite his wife lying upstairs. He had the feeling that he was alone and would be for the rest of his life, married and yet not married in the true sense, because the rift between them was too wide and there was no way he could see of healing it.

43

Arthur glanced up from his copy of *The Times* as Pam brought Sergeant Thorne into the kitchen. She looked pale and concerned and he put down his paper instinctively.

'I wanted to let you know as soon as I could,' Sergeant Thorne said. 'I had a phone call from the station in March this morning – Ralph Harris was killed in a collision on the Manea Road two nights ago. His car collided with a tractor and, although he was taken to hospital, he died the next day of his injuries. The tractor driver was also injured, but, thankfully, he is recovering in hospital. His statement has been taken and he claims that Mr Harris was driving like a madman. The local police are inclined to believe him...'

'Dead?' Pam sat down on the nearest chair, her face white. 'Had anyone spoken to him of our suspicions?'

'No.' Sergeant Thorne shook his head. 'I rang the station and asked a few questions but was told he was a respectable businessman. I also got in touch with the Metropolitan Police, and asked them to send an Inspector down to look into what happened to Miss Goodjohn. He arrived this morning and is going to make some inquiries – but, given the theory I put to him about Mr Harris being the one who attacked her, he thinks we may never know the truth.'

Pam drew a ragged breath and then met Arthur's eyes. 'I still think it was him – and Lizzie does too. We're both convinced. It's the only thing that makes sense. If it was the random act of a madman, why has no one else been attacked?'

'I agree,' Sergeant Thorne said, surprising them. 'If it had been a frenzied attack by a lunatic, there would surely have been far more wanton damage done. There was very little broken or disturbed, so it wasn't a rampage – just an attack on a defenceless young woman. An act of anger or hatred rather... something a man might do in a sudden rage.'

'No decent man would do such a thing,' Arthur protested, 'but from what Tom told me, Harris wasn't worth his spit.'

'Remain vigilant for a time,' Sergeant Thorne said, nodding his agreement. 'But I think we'd have heard if any further attacks on women had occurred, so it does look as if your suspicions may be right.'

Pam nodded and asked if he would stay for a cup of tea, but he refused, saying he needed to get back to assist the officer from London in his inquiries and took his leave. Pam made the tea and they sat in silence over it for a while.

'Perhaps he was driving like that because he realised what he'd done?' Pam suggested. 'He might just have learned that she was dead – he might not have intended to kill her.'

'It was the baby coming like that when she was injured and all alone,' Arthur said. 'If she hadn't been so close to her time, she would probably have survived what he did to her... poor girl.'

'She was a dear, sweet girl and she would have married our John when he is home and well enough.' Pam gave a strangled sob.

'If the man the Red Cross have discovered is John,' Arthur reminded her.

'I know you're trying to save me more grief if it isn't,' Pam told him and smiled. 'Thank you, dearest Arthur, for always being here for me and giving me such a good life. I love you and honour you – but I know I am right. I've never believed John was dead, not truly. Something inside kept telling me he was still alive.' She sighed deeply. 'Troubles never come alone. I don't know what John will do when he knows what happened to the girl he loved. It was our job to make sure she was safe for him...'

'And we did, as far as we could,' Arthur said, a sharper note in his voice. 'Whatever happened after she left you, wasn't your fault or Lizzie's. We'll never know for sure what happened or why, but we can't blame ourselves and we won't. Do you hear me, Pam? I'm not having what that man did ruin all our lives. We'll grieve for Faith as we would a daughter, but we won't carry the burden of guilt.'

Pam nodded and wiped a tear from her cheek. 'You're right, Arthur, but then, you usually are. I'd best get on and start the midday meal. Jeanie and Artie will be in for theirs soon.' She smiled at her husband. 'I think those two rather like each other and we might have another wedding one day...'

Arthur raised his brows at her. 'I can't say I'd noticed anything, but I leave that sort of thing to you. I wouldn't mind if they made a go of it – would you?'

'I should be happy. I am very fond of Jeanie.'

'Yes, nice girl,' Arthur nodded, looking pleased. 'Gets on well with our Lizzie.'

'Yes, they are good friends. I think Lizzie will come for lunch, too. She was going to write to Tom but managed to get hold of him by ringing a number he gave her for emergencies, and he has been given compassionate leave and should be home this afternoon. I'd best do some baking...'

On the radio, the song, 'All Over the Place', from the popular comedy film, *Sailors Three*, sung by Tommy Trinder, was playing softly in the background, reminding them that life could also be good as well as sad.

'Yes, my love, you do that,' Arthur said and his voice was tender with love and concern as he watched her move about the long room, bringing the ingredients she needed from the pantry. 'I'll just have a wander, but I'll be back in an hour or so,' he said and got up. Pam would right herself as she worked and he could do with a breath of fresh air. They'd had enough heartache at Blackberry Farm with one thing and another. He just hoped things would get better before too long.

As he walked slowly towards the bottom field where a crop of potatoes was growing nicely, he heard the noise of an aeroplane overhead. It was flying low, obviously heading for the base up on the drome, as the locals called it. His gaze followed it, watching as it got lower and disappeared from his view as it landed. He gave a little sigh of relief – another pilot back safely from wherever he'd been sent. There were so many young men risking their lives just now and they had come from Australia, New Zealand and Canada, as well as the Americas.

It was no longer strange to hear a different accent in the pubs in Sutton and Mepal or to see them cycling to and from the drome. Some of the villagers went to lie in the diches near the airfield at night, watching the planes fly out on whatever mission they undertook and then counting them back in again. Arthur hadn't done it himself, but he knew that Artie and Jeanie went, and they weren't the only ones. These gallant young men were welcome here and visited many of the local homes; people were grateful to them and gave them food, even though they often had little enough to feed themselves or their children. His family did better than most, because the hens gave them eggs and they always had potatoes and vegetables they grew themselves – and the odd pig went astray now and then. Arthur made sure that a few deserving folk got a bit of extra pork; none of them questioned where it came from. It was against the rules and carried a risk, but he did it anyway.

Arthur thought they should invite some of the airmen to the farm for a meal and he made up his mind to talk to Pam about it. If he suggested it, she would be all for it and it would take her mind off other things...

Seeing Artie and Jeanie walk to the kitchen door together, laughing and teasing each other, he smiled. It looked as if Pam might be right about those two, though Artie would take his time. He wasn't like his father in that way; one look at Pam and Arthur had known she was the one for him and he hadn't cared a jot that she had another man's child. Tom was his son in every way but one... A sigh broke from him as he thought of John. Pray God he would be home soon; if not, it would put too much strain on his beloved wife.

A new land girl was due to arrive in the next week or so, but how long she'd stay was another matter. It was a man's job really, Arthur thought, out in all weather and sometimes working in sucking mud, heavy dirty work that only the toughest of the girls could tolerate. He hadn't thought Jeanie would stick it, but she had and Arthur was glad if Artie had found himself a decent girl at last. He smiled at the thought of them married and living in Sutton, which was where they'd likely settle. Artie would be on hand for his beloved fen land and once Tom was back to stay, he would take care of the heavy land again. Once all this was over – the suffering and hardship they were all having to endure. This damned war had something to answer for! Arthur had nearly lost

Tom and he still wasn't sure about John being the mystery man the Red Cross had discovered, though he prayed his wife was right.

He suddenly saw Lizzie waving to him urgently. She had something in her hand and Arthur's heart thudded with fear as he recognised it as being a telegram, but then Lizzie was running to greet him and he could see she was laughing. He took quick strides to meet her.

'What is it?' he asked and his breath almost stopped as he saw the triumph in her face. 'Is it our John?'

'Yes, he is alive,' Lizzie said, sounding as if she would burst with the news. 'He has recovered his memory and knows who he is – and he is being sent home in a few days... Well, to hospital in Cambridge...'

Lizzie laughed as Arthur suddenly hugged her. 'Bless you,' he said gruffly. 'Thank you for finding him for us.'

'I just made inquiries,' she said, but she was hugging him back. 'Isn't it wonderful?'

'A miracle is what I'd call it,' Arthur said. 'Come on up to the house. We have to tell Pam – and Artie will be so relieved; he took it bad when he thought John was dead. This calls for a celebration! I'll get out that bottle of sherry I've been saving – we'll all have a drink.'

* * *

Pam was at the kitchen door, John's baby in her arms, watching them as they walked arm in arm through the yard. From the smile on her face, she knew, even though it was Lizzie who had received the telegram.

'John is coming back,' she said as Lizzie ran the last few yards to her and they hugged and kissed in shared joy, holding John's beloved child tenderly between them. 'It's funny – I had a feeling that he was thinking about us just now. I told Paul his daddy is coming home to him...'

'He'll be in Addenbrooke's for a while,' Lizzie told her. 'The telegram says John Talbot alive and being sent to Addenbrooke's imminently. That's the trouble with telegrams, they don't give enough detail.'

'It's all we need to know for now,' Pam said and, of course, it was.

Her eyes met Arthur's and they nodded in shared pleasure. Their son was being sent back to them. They would be able to see him in hospital and bring him home as soon as he was well enough. The shadow of Faith's tragedy hadn't gone away – it never would – but the problem of how to tell John about his son and the death of the girl he loved was for the moment put aside in the joy they all felt.

Tragedy had touched them all at Blackberry Farm, but their family was strong and the bonds of love held them together. Tom would be home for a while, Lizzie was having a baby – two babies in the family! – and Artie was courting a girl he obviously loved, even if he didn't quite realise it himself yet, and John would be coming home. For the moment, it was more than enough – it was marvellous!

MORE FROM ROSIE CLARKE

We hope you enjoyed reading *Heartache at Blackberry Farm*. If you did, please leave a review.

If you'd like to gift a copy, this book is also available as an ebook, digital audio download and audiobook CD.

Sign up to Rosie Clarke's mailing list for news, competitions and updates on future books.

http://bit.ly/RosieClarkeNewsletter

Why not explore the *Welcome to Harpers Emporium* series, another bestselling series from Rosie Clarke!

ABOUT THE AUTHOR

Rosie Clarke is a #1 bestselling saga writer whose most recent books include *The Shop Girls of Harpers* and *The Mulberry Lane* series. She has written over 100 novels under different pseudonyms and is a RNA Award winner. She lives in Cambridgeshire.

Visit Rosie Clarke's website: http://www.rosieclarke.co.uk

Follow Rosie on social media:

twitter.com/AnneHerries
bookbub.com/authors/rosie-clarke
facebook.com/Rosie-clarke-119457351778432

Sixpence Stories

Introducing Sixpence Stories!

Discover page-turning historical novels from your favourite authors, meet new friends and be transported back in time.

Join our book club Facebook group

https://bit.ly/SixpenceGroup

Sign up to our newsletter

https://bit.ly/SixpenceNews

ABOUT BOLDWOOD BOOKS

Boldwood Books is a fiction publishing company seeking out the best stories from around the world.

Find out more at www.boldwoodbooks.com

Sign up to the Book and Tonic newsletter for news, offers and competitions from Boldwood Books!

http://www.bit.ly/bookandtonic

We'd love to hear from you, follow us on social media:

facebook.com/BookandTonic

twitter.com/BoldwoodBooks

instagram.com/BookandTonic